29²

NANCY PENNICK

Allison-Hayes Publishing

Copyright © 2016 by Nancy Pennick

All rights reserved.
Printed in the United States of America

First Printing, 2016

This is a work of fiction. Names, characters, businesses, places, events and incidents are either the products of the author's imagination or used in a fictitious manner. Any resemblance to actual persons, living or dead, or actual events is purely coincidental.

ISBN-10: 0-9968106-2-5
ISBN-13: 978-0-9968106-2-3

To my friend, Rosanne,
and in memory of her son, Nathan.

Prologue

Good versus evil. Is life that black and white? There should be shades of gray which make us pause and say, "It's not that bad. I can do this. There's hope." Am I being too optimistic?

I once believed in happy endings, but not anymore. Not since the day my brother Doug stared me down with his cold, calculating eyes and said, "First there has to be war before there is peace."

He's evil. He haunts my dreams. He is the reoccurring nightmare—always chasing me, interrogating me, harassing me. He physically beats me, and I'm never sure what he wants. Whatever it is, something inside tells me I'll protect it at any cost. My mind scrambles to figure it out, but there's never an answer. As hard as I try, I don't have a clue.

I continue to have the dream, night after night. Maybe the dream will go away … once he finally gets what he wants.

Chapter One

Choices. Mistakes. Weren't they called learning experiences? I never had the chance to finish my life as a normal teen, giggling with friends over things which didn't matter to the adults in our lives but were important to us. I'd been thrust into a world I had no idea existed, needed to think quickly and make life or death decisions in an instant.

First major bad choice? Breaking up with Lucas Montgomery. Too late now to change the outcome. When I recalled my high school days, I longed to return until reality set in. I remembered the truth, a four-letter word—Doug, who ruined those days. My brother took away the happiness and innocence of my last two years of high school.

Now, I had a chance to start over, make choices and mistakes I should have done years before and hope I didn't mess up. I stared in the mirror as I got dressed for class and wondered if I'd done the right things. On my own for over a year, I confided in no one except my two best friends. Surrounded by a huge campus of strangers, it was a lonely existence but one I chose.

I drove to school, parked the car in its usual spot and walked toward campus. *Spring quarter.* I shook my head at how fast the time had gone. I'd been at UCLA since last summer, heading straight to California after my brother Dean's wedding, determined to graduate in less than three years.

I walked from the parking structure to Westwood Plaza, past the Bruin bear statue, to meet my friend before the first day of class. The mascot's overwhelming presence, mouth open with sharp fangs exposed, reminded me how far I'd come. I drew strength and toughness from that bronze sculpture every time I passed it.

As I gazed at the bear, which seemed ready to strike in an instant, I felt empowered. I, too, would be ready at a moment's notice if anyone tried to attack me. Back home I'd started karate lessons and continued them once I'd settled in LA. I found a shooting range, too, and signed up for classes. Soon, I'd apply for a handgun license. Dramatic as that may sound, I had my reasons. Truth was, I was afraid of my oldest brother and feared the precautions I took were not enough to protect myself.

I took a deep breath of courage as I walked by the bear and headed for my destination. Nathan Kalas, one of my best friends from back home in Virginia, had started at UCLA the year before me. He waited on a bench under the shade of a huge sycamore tree. I waved when he spotted me and jogged to where he sat. He had two iced lattes in a container, handing me one as I joined him.

"Hey, Allie, good to see you!" He nodded as I took the caramel latte. "Did you give up one of your jobs this quarter as promised?" Nate had been like a big brother for as long as I could remember and said what was on his mind.

"Yes, I'm keeping the one at the library and quitting the late nights at the burger shop."

"Yay," Nate said in a deadpan voice.

"I need to support myself, Nate, you know that. I have the off-campus apartment, tuition, books, spending money—"

"Like you spend money. All you do is work and study. I'm surprised you haven't graduated already. What are you, a junior?"

"Almost … and don't forget I take karate classes."

"So that's your social life?"

4

My life wasn't exactly newsworthy since Lucas Montgomery had disappeared from it. I dedicated my existence to protecting his and spent my time keeping a low profile. My social life the last year of high school was non-existent. I studied, worked at the bookstore, volunteered on school committees, went to the karate studio and fell into bed exhausted every night.

Nate had come home from California to take Ashley Donovan, my other best friend and his girlfriend, to our senior prom. They begged me to go, but my response was, "Three's a crowd."

No matter how much they begged, I wouldn't give in. It was Ash's night, not mine. She deserved to shine and have Nate to herself. Ashley had been my rock that year. I wouldn't have made it to graduation without her. Nate and Ashley were still together, but long distance made it tough. Ashley had enrolled at the hometown community college for a year then she'd come out to California to room with me.

"Hey? You in there?" Nate placed his arm across my shoulder. I winced.

"Sorry." He removed his arm and closed one eye, studying me. "Did you get that tattoo?"

I stared at the ground. "Yep. I told you I was going to."

"Just don't become a walking painting."

"It means something, Nate. I didn't randomly decide to do it."

"I know. It's just that …"

"What?" I faced him and looked straight in his eyes.

"All these things are reminders of Lucas. I thought you were trying to forget him."

"It helps. What can I say?" I shrugged. "It's not about him. It's about me. Anyway, the tattoo's not that big."

"Let me be the judge." Nate turned my body so my right shoulder faced him. He slid the strap of my top to one side and examined it. "Okay, it's about two inches high, maybe four across. The Phoenix rising?"

I swallowed hard. The Phoenix symbolized my new life. The one I had to create after Lucas left town. "The Phoenix may burn down, but it always rises from the ashes."

And I had burned down, trust me.

"You artist types." He shook his head as he rubbed my lower back.

"And what are you, Mr. Filmmaker?" I swung around and lightly punched his arm.

"Ow! My tattoo!" He scrunched up his face.

"Very funny. You don't have tattoos."

Nate laughed. "You shouldn't have that one on your foot either. Lucas told me they're not letting Niners do that anymore. It used to be a symbol they shared in the past, a way to identify each other. If he knew you had that, he'd freak. Now that Doug is on the lookout for ..." Nate shook his head. "You should get it removed."

"No," I said, and crossed my arms.

Even though I'd never see Lucas again, I had to keep him near me in some way. The XXIX on my right arch was that reminder. He had been born on February twenty-ninth, making him quite special, part of the Twenty-Niners or Niners for short. I stared into Nate's eyes. "And when did you talk to Lucas about tattoos? It sounds like you're still in contact."

Nate shifted on the bench. "No, we're not. It was back in the day, high school."

A part of me had hoped he'd say he'd spoken to Lucas recently. "Right. You two became best friends, didn't you?"

"Yeah, and I miss the old guy. I hoped to celebrate his eighty-fourth birthday next year."

"Yeah, when he finally turns twenty-one on Leap Day." I covered my face and sighed. "I can't discuss it."

"Really? You can get tattoos but not discuss our Niner friend, the guy who ages every four years?" Nate's voice grew louder.

"Shhh, keep your voice down." I hissed. "And don't mention my brother, Doug, either."

"I'll change the subject. But can I point out that Doug hasn't bothered you since you moved here?"

"Nate!"

"Okay." He held up his hands.

"Sometimes that life seems like a dream, like Lucas and I never happened." My mind drifted to the recurring nightmare I kept having. In that dream I had no idea what Doug wanted. In the real world, I knew exactly what he wanted. Lucas.

"I know what you mean. Being out here in LA makes it easy to forget."

"No, that's not what I meant." I shook my head. "It's hard to explain. Wherever you are, life goes on as if Doug's special army doesn't exist. No one, except a few of us, knows the Niners exist. That's what makes it so surreal. We know, but the rest of the world doesn't."

Nate patted my hand. "For now, let's pretend it doesn't exist. You told me you weren't all work and no play. Convince me."

"I started dating last November. You know that."

"Yeah, what was the guy's name again? Jerry? Does he have a roommate named Ben? I know you picked that name when I asked you about the date in the supermarket. We were in the frozen food section, if I remember correctly."

"Very funny. I'll have you know I'm seeing someone this weekend."

"Really, Allie?" Sarcasm filled his voice, reminding me of our discussions throughout the years. Nate could call my bluff. Maybe Jerry was imaginary, but this guy wasn't.

"Yes, really. His name's Will. I met him in class last quarter."

"Okay, little one, I believe you," Nate said, calling me the name he gave me long ago.

"Nothing serious though."

"Already decided that?" Nate chuckled. "You really need to try harder to get over Lucas. I don't think he'd want you to be celibate for the rest of your life. He'd want you to be happy."

"Nate! Just because I confided in you, doesn't mean you have to throw that in my face!" I'd never slept with Lucas or anyone else for that matter. I knew he and Ashley had been intimate but didn't want details. If Ash talked about her sex life, she kept it general.

"Okay, calm down, just saying. You turned nineteen in November, and I thought—"

"Well, don't," I said too sharply and immediately regretted it. I took Nate's hand. "I'm sorry I snapped."

"I'm sorry I bugged you. Forgive me?"

"Always," I smiled. "But I really do need to get going. See you later?" We hugged and parted ways.

Nate went to his photography workshop, and I headed to class. When I graduated I'd have a degree in Art History. I eventually planned to live in a big city, like New York or Chicago, just as I'd planned back in high school.

I'd get a job in one of their museums. But, wherever I ended up, the city had to be big enough that I could get lost in the crowd.

As I entered my classroom building I heard a familiar voice. "Allie, wait up!"

Will. I was glad to see him. It had been so long since I kissed a boy or was held in someone's arms. I'd never tell Nate, but he was right, I made up Jerry so he'd leave me alone. Will was a real flesh and blood person. He had the California good looks—dark blonde hair, blue eyes, chiseled jaw, and a light tan. His muscles rippled under his light blue shirt as he came closer.

"Will, hi. I'm on my way to class, *Art and Politics in Contemporary Americas: Post World War II.* Should be interesting." I laughed.

"Sounds like an upper division class. Me? I'll never get out of lower division classes." He pretended to pout.

"Don't be so hard on yourself. I took extra classes." A lot of my advanced placement classes from high school were taken at the community college and qualified as intro classes for college. Officially, I started my junior year this quarter.

"We still on for this weekend?"

"Yes. Do you know where my apartment is?"

"Yeah. See you after class?"

I hesitated. I didn't want to take things too fast. We met for lunch or walks on campus but hadn't seen each other daily.

"If you want." A warm flush crept up my neck. *Am I blushing? God, I hope he can't tell.*

"What? Are you kidding? I'm happy I got you to go on a real date." Will leaned over and kissed my cheek. "I'll wait for you out front."

He disappeared down the hall as I lifted my hand to my face. A sweet kiss, but no tingling, no excitement like the first time Lucas touched my hand. *Stop comparing him to Lucas.* I needed to give this relationship time to grow and not expect so much. Maybe I could find true love again, just in a different way.

I doodled on my notebook during class while the professor discussed what would be covered during the quarter. I perked up as he talked about how the media and art world protested or condoned U.S. capitalism and imperialism after the war. My interest piqued with the word imperialism—*the extension of power or authority over others in the interests of domination.* I shivered as I read the definition on my phone, checking again to make sure I understood the meaning. It reminded me of my brother, Doug. The psychopath.

Doug was the head of a special military operation called the STF 329. This special task force was responsible for everything that happened to Lucas and me two years ago. I should say Doug was responsible for most of the damage. As commander, he wanted to assemble an army of men and boys born on February twenty-ninth.

These men, the Niners, aged once every four years on their real birthday, making them quite desirable to the STF. Besides the age factor, they had multiple super abilities. They could see in the dark, hear conversations from far away and their intelligence exceeded us mere mortals by light years. They invented things we could only dream about, sharing what they could with the world at the appropriate time.

Why this syndrome didn't affect girls born on that day, I'll never know. Maybe we don't need superpowers to get things done.

As I sat in class, thinking about Niners, it reminded me of how Lucas could track me. When we first met, he scanned me without my knowledge. His phone always showed my whereabouts. I prayed nightly that he had stopped, for his sake as well as mine. If I thought he looked for me, I might give in when I saw him.

Class ended, and curiosity took over. Would Will be waiting for me? As I exited the building, I saw him standing in the sunlight, aviators on, looking like a model for GQ. Three years older, I wondered what he saw in me. Me, who must look like a pathetic teenage girl who placed studying above everything else.

"Will!" I raised my hand to wave and block the sunlight from my eyes. He saw me and jogged over.

"Done for a while?" He took my hand. "How about a walk in the park?"

"Sure."

The botanical gardens on campus were lush and beautiful. We strolled along, chatting about nothing. As we reached the path, Will guided me to a cement bench under the shade of a ginkgo tree.

"Now Ms. Sanders, I have something important to ask you." He leaned back and placed the aviators on top of his head. With a twinkle in his eye, he said, "Will you be my girl?"

His smile, cute and boyish, differed from another boy's that could make me melt and say yes to anything. I tried to stay in the moment and put it out of my mind.

"We've been seeing each other most of winter quarter," Will said. "I thought you felt the same way I did—"

I realized I hadn't answered. "Yes, Will, I'll be your girl," I whispered.

Those words sounded so familiar, I froze. The last time I saw Lucas I wanted to tell him if we could live another life I'd be his girl, but he'd stopped me before I could finish. The unsaid words had hung in the air between us, unspoken yet understood. If multiple lives existed, I yearned for the next one to be with him.

Will leaned over and kissed me. I felt my body pulled closer as his arms wrapped around my waist. He hugged me to his chest, so close, so gentle I could feel the steady beat of his heart. He looked into my eyes and kissed me again. The kiss felt warm and sweet with just a touch of begging, as if he knew he was asking for more than I could give.

I hadn't been this close to anyone in a long time. I didn't want the kiss to stop and reached around his neck, relaxing my body as I melted into his. I inhaled his manly scent of summer and citrus. I slid my hand onto his shoulder, feeling strength radiate from him. Something told me I'd be safe.

"So, I don't have to wait until Saturday to see you again?" Will pulled back and looked at me.

"No, you don't."

"No more keeping me at arm's length?"

"Is that what you thought I did?" My head spun, trying to remember the past few months. We had a class together and started meeting at the library to study before my shift at work. We had coffee or grabbed a quick lunch a few times a week. "I worked a lot, Will. You know I quit my second job."

"Yeah, you told me. I'm happy you did."

"But I picked up a few more hours at the library."

"Allie!" Will's eyes widened then he smiled. "You're quite driven. I admire that."

"Thanks." I gazed down at my hands, playing with my fingers. If I threw myself into this, I might as well go full steam ahead. He had no clue that I'd never slept with Lucas or anyone else. He'd be my first. Not the time or place to introduce *that* topic. I didn't want to ruin the moment with "Oh, by the way, I never slept with anyone in my life and decided right here and now you'll be the one" speech. I tabled it for later.

I stood and pulled him up with me. Will wrapped his arms around me, and I dissolved into his chest. Looking up into his crystal blue eyes I couldn't resist. I kissed him, finding his mouth more than willing. "I've got a short shift at the library. I'll see you later," I said between kisses.

"Let me walk you there." Will searched for my hand as we strolled through the gardens and out to the campus.

The sun shone a little brighter. The sky appeared a little bluer or maybe I just hadn't noticed for the past year. Most days, even the sunny ones, had a fine gray film over them. If today was an indication of my future, then I'd hold onto it for as long as I could.

* * * *

Saturday turned into a hectic day. I worked overtime at the library and rushed to my faithful red Jeep to get home for my date. My car symbolized home, driven all the way across country from Virginia. As I put the key in the ignition, I remembered I'd left something important at Nate's apartment when I visited last night. I needed to get home, showered and changed for my date but really wanted the laptop I'd left at his place. I didn't want it getting lost in his mess.

I dug for my phone and called from the parking lot. "Nate, I'm stopping over to grab my laptop. I hope it's not buried alive."

"Sure, little one, no problem. Give me a minute to straighten up. I'll have your laptop ready and waiting."

"Oh, and Nate, I think I'm ready."

"Ready for what?"

"A real relationship with Will. I didn't tell you last night. He asked me to be his girl."

"You're ready for everything that goes with a serious relationship?"

"If you mean am I going to sleep with him? The answer is … eventually."

Nate didn't respond to my revelation. Instead he said, "Gosh, this place is a mess. I've got cleaning to do before you get here."

Surprised at his sudden concern for the condition of the apartment, I shrugged it off. I started the Jeep and slowly descended the ramp of the parking garage and out to the street. Nate didn't live far from campus. I'd arrive at his house in less than ten minutes.

After parking the car, I let myself in at the end of the building. We had keys to each other's places. I ran up the side stairs to the second floor. As I walked down the hall, something caught my eye. A dark-haired man dashed around the corner to start down the main staircase. He had the same build and walk as Lucas. I rushed past Nate's door to the top of the steps. Peering down the flight of stairs, I saw no one but heard the front door slam. I wanted to follow, but something stopped me. I had a real date with a real man who was kind and sweet and had even asked my permission if I'd be his girl. I turned away from the landing and walked back to Nate's. I called out his name as I opened the door.

"I'm here." Nate popped up from behind the opened refrigerator door. His brown eyes twinkled like he just heard a good joke. His reddish-blonde hair stuck out in all directions. Tall and slender, but muscular, that was my Nate. My laptop sat on the kitchen counter. He started wiping something off the cover.

"What'd you get on it?" I cross-examined him.

"Nothing." He winked.

I glanced around the apartment and noticed the clutter. "Good cleaning job." I pointed to all the shirts piled on his sofa.

"Hey, that's my laundry. I still have to put it away."

I shoved the pile to the side and sat down. "This may sound strange, but I think I saw Lucas leaving your apartment."

Nate looked up from the computer and frowned. "Why would he be here?"

"You tell me."

"Nothing to tell. You probably saw someone who looked like him. Lots of students live in this building. Did you see his face?"

"I only saw him from the back. He went down the main stairs. By the time I got there, he was gone."

"So, you chased after him."

"I guess so."

"And if you caught him, and it wasn't Lucas, then what?" Nate raised his eyebrows and stared at me.

"I'd apologize."

"I thought you're over him."

"Never."

"Are you planning on telling Will, your first lover, that?"

"No, and don't call him that."

Nate handed me my computer. "There. All shiny and new. Have a good time on your date with Bill."

"Will, his name is Will." I poked him.

"Fine, I knew his name was Will, just testing to see if he's a real guy."

"Would you like me to take a picture for proof?"

"That would seal the deal."

I gave him a little shove then a hug. "Gotta go. I need to get ready. I'll see you on Monday at our bench."

"You're not going to call me tomorrow with details of the date?"

"What are you, my girlfriend?" I chuckled. Nate could always make me laugh, even in the darkest moments. "I'll call Ash first then maybe you."

"Have fun." Nate gave me a peck on the cheek and opened the apartment door. "Be careful out there."

I jumped back in the Jeep and headed for home. Although I had a small one-bedroom apartment, it felt like home. I'd brought items from Virginia to make the place cozy and comfortable, shipping most of it during my visit home for the holidays. I invested in copies of my favorite works of art and bought furniture from local second-hand stores. After living in the dorm my first two quarters, I couldn't wait to live alone, too many prying eyes, too many questions. Everyone wanted to know my high school history or a list of past boyfriends

Before I went home for Christmas, I had my apartment picked out and made a deposit. When I returned I was ready to move in. My mom would have a broken heart if she knew I considered this more my home than Virginia.

Hands on hips, I stood staring into my closet, I had no idea what to wear. The closet contained tons of casual clothing, but a dress seemed appropriate. Luckily, I'd been playing at the computer one day when I'd had nothing better to do. That resulted in picking out and buying a few random dresses. I settled on a pale blue jersey pull-on dress with cap sleeves and scoop neck, I slipped it on, and it hugged my body in all the right places.

I lifted the lid to my jewelry box. Lucas' heart-shaped necklace stared up at me. Scooping the heart into my hand, I held it close and started to cry. I didn't see that coming. *No crying!* I had worn the necklace until New Year's Eve, and on that night, I made a promise to take it off for good. I should have put it away, out of sight.

I grabbed a simple silver round pendant and ran to the bathroom. There, I did my make-up and stepped back to check myself out in the full-length mirror on the door. I studied the girl I saw.

Brunette hair, cut to the shoulder, shorter than high school. Blue-green eyes, that I liked to call aqua, actually had liner and mascara on them. A touch of blush and pink lip gloss finished the look. I had a relatively good figure, and the dress accentuated the curves. *Not bad, Allie, you clean up well.* I heard the buzzer and walked barefoot to the living room to let Will in.

As I waited by the open door, I heard him come up the steps. My heart beat a little faster, excited for the date. "Will!" I waved to help him find the apartment. "I just need shoes. Come in."

"Nice place." Will looked around and stood in front of one of my reproductions. "Monet?"

"Yes." I stood on my tiptoes and kissed his cheek. "I'll be right back."

I took a few deep breaths in my bedroom, smoothed my dress and grabbed a pair of open-toed wedgies. "Ready!" I said as I slipped on the shoes.

"I have dinner reservations then we'll hit a late movie. How does that sound?" Will seemed nervous.

"Anything we do is fine."

When we reached the parking lot, Will helped me in his car and hurried to the other side. If the date went well, it would be a sign I could move on, something I thought I would never be able to do.

We dined at an upscale French restaurant. Will tried his best to impress the Art History major girl by ordering for us. After we finished, he gave me a choice of foreign films, and I finally had to stop him. "You don't have to try so hard. I don't think foreign films are on your top ten list. Nate told me about a limited release he recommends. How about that?"

We agreed to give it a try then return to my apartment for a glass of wine. I had a few unopened bottles waiting on the shelf. Nate indulged me with a bottle every now and then. He felt sorry for me sitting alone in my apartment every night and said he wanted to picture me with a glass of wine in hand. I hadn't felt the need to use them until now.

As I unlocked the door to my apartment, a realization hit me. I enjoyed the night and didn't want it to end. Kicking off my shoes, I strolled to the kitchen and grabbed two wine glasses, the bottle opener and the wine. Will took the bottle, deftly opening it.

"A very nice wine from Napa Valley, I see. Bella's a good winery." Will held the bottle out studying the drawing of a beautiful woman on the label. "Your friend, Nate, is good at picking wines and movies. When do I meet him?"

"You will soon." I got out my phone and snapped a picture of us holding up our glasses. "I'll send this to him right now, with our thanks."

After I sent the message, I lit some candles, turned on music and settled in on the sofa next to Will. He removed the glass from my hand and placed it on the table next to his. Suddenly I found myself in his arms, with things going way too fast and my head spinning, but not because of a glass of wine. I got lost in the moment and let it take me away, somewhere far away where I couldn't think of anything or anyone else.

Chapter Two

I paced the floor, contemplating if I should call Ashley. I'd been up since eight, even though it had been a late night. California time was three hours behind, but Ash liked to sleep late.

"Hey, Allie." Ashley answered on the second ring. "I got your text and picture. How was your date? He's adorable!"

"Wonderful! I think it could turn into something serious."

"Wow, it's about time."

"Ash? I have to talk to you about something."

"Start talking."

"Last night I went a little farther than I intended on our first date." I cringed.

"It's not really a first date, Allie. You've been seeing him since January. It's the end of March. And define too far. Did you—"

"No, no, not that! I didn't sleep with him, but it came really close."

"How close?"

"I'd rather not say, but here's my problem. If that was our first date, what's going to happen on the second?"

"Allie, you've been living in your sheltered world for too long. Just trust yourself, and if it's right, you'll know. You better have the sex talk with Will before anything happens."

"Make the big announcement? I'm a virgin?"

"Well, yeah, you two have to talk."

"Okay, but I need your help with what to say. I don't plan on seeing him alone until next weekend, so I've got time." We ended the conversation talking about Nate, as usual.

I was running late for my shift at the library. I didn't consider working at the Arts Library a job. I loved being there and would have done it for free. Throwing on proper work clothes, I dashed out the door and jumped in the Jeep, heading for campus.

As I stepped into the library, my breath hitched. I swore I saw Lucas walking down a corridor. His dark hair and chocolate brown eyes flashed through my mind. *Stop it!* I couldn't have Lucas sightings everywhere I went. What was wrong with me?

"Hey." I felt arms wrap around me, and for a second, envisioned Lucas behind me. I leaned into his chest, absorbing the warmth then turned to face him.

"Will!" I acted more shocked than I should.

"Sorry, didn't mean to startle you. I know you have to work but wanted to stop by and see you." He kissed the tip of my nose.

"Are you going to be around later?" I reached for his hand. "I have a break at three. We can do lunch."

"You probably haven't eaten. Can you wait till then?"

I pulled a breakfast bar from my bag. "I'll be fine."

Will ran his hand through my hair. "I want you to take care of yourself, Allie. Sometimes I feel like you're going through the motions just to get through life."

That was profound. I needed to start seeing Will for who he was, not as a distraction. He leaned in to kiss me. I backed away, the Lucas sighting still fresh in my mind. "I've got to get going."

Guilt spread through me when I saw the expression on his face. I cleared my throat and shifted my bag to the other shoulder. "I'll see you at lunch," I said as I continued on to the library's main desk. "Three o'clock, our usual place."

I shelved books and helped people find the section or book they needed during my shift, but my mind kept drifting elsewhere. I saw a place of hope and love and even a future. I wanted to slam the door shut on it and get back to the robotic existence I lived for almost two years. Life would be much easier. I hurt no one, and no one hurt me. But Will had managed to push through that door.

Suddenly, a feeling of nausea swept over me. My legs trembled as I steadied myself against a bookshelf. I didn't know if I could do this. I wanted to put the brakes on this new relationship, all because of Lucas—the man I could never have or see again. *Darn!* Why did I think I saw him at Nate's, then here? Did I want him to secretly follow me? Was I feeling guilty about trying to move on with Will?

I heard Ashley's voice telling me it was time. She never knew the truth about Lucas and his family. She thought they left town because his dad got a new job. Ash thought Lucas and I agreed a long-distance relationship would never work. Nate and I made a pact that she should be kept in the dark, never to enter the Niner world. We felt it was too dangerous, so she'd never understand my pain, not fully.

I pushed the book cart toward the back of the library. As I walked along, my brother Doug crept into my mind. He always did whenever I thought about the Niners. His sly smile, his steely gray-blue eyes, close cropped brown hair and crisp uniform appeared before my eyes. He had interrogated me, kidnapped and threatened me in the name of loyalty and country. But what he'd really wanted was information about Lucas and the Niners. He only cared about making a name for himself. He once told me about a plan to find an antidote to the nuclear bomb. He was sure the Niners had the answer. Lucas assured me they didn't. Although Doug had some Niners on his task force, he felt he needed more to find the answer.

I shook my head and returned a book to the shelf. The repetition of finding a book's place among the others calmed me. I promised I would put Lucas out of my mind, and here I was thinking about Lucas *and* Doug. Well, no more.

I glanced at my watch. *Three o'clock.* I headed for the break room and pulled my bag from the locker. Maybe some food would help my mood. As I walked to the restaurant, I decided it was confession time. Embarrassing? Yes. But, at least it would be out in the open. I was a virgin. No sense prolonging the agony.

Will waited outside the restaurant and opened the door when he spotted me. I met his smile, and he placed his arm around me as we went to a table. The pain of the tattoo had faded, so no wincing. I didn't want to discuss tattoos when other topics were more important. My heart pounded as I tried to think of an opening line.

After we were seated and had our food in front of us, I decided to dive right in. "Will, I have something to tell you. And I want you to know it's okay if you want to break up after you hear what I have to say." His brows pulled together, and he tilted his head with a questioning gaze. I continued, "I never slept with anyone before … ever."

The puzzlement on his face turned to amusement as he reached for my hand. "Is that why you've been so standoffish lately? I wouldn't break up with you, Allie, because of that. I want to see where this relationship goes. If you're not ready for something, just tell me. When you are, let me know. I can respect that."

"Oh, Will, I thought you'd—"

"What? Not want to see you anymore because you won't sleep with me? That would be pretty shallow. I plan on sticking around for a long time, if you'll have me."

"Why?" I whispered. I didn't get it. The stories I heard in the dorm made my head spin. I knew girls who'd love to date a guy like Will or sleep with him once to brag they did.

"Have you looked in a mirror lately? Not only are you beautiful, there's something about you, something special. It makes men fall in love with you. You can't tell me guys haven't been after you since you were ten." Will smiled his cute grin, and I relaxed.

"No, not really." I felt the warmth creep up my neck and into my cheeks as I thought back over the years. I'd had one high school boyfriend, Josh Reed, before Lucas. After that, I stopped paying attention to boys in high school. "You're okay with everything?"

"Absolutely, no worries. Anyway, you're worth the wait." He reached across the table and squeezed my hand.

I finished my lunch and grabbed my things. "Got to get back. I'll see you tomorrow before class." I left the tip because Will never let me pay my part of the bill. I kissed him on the cheek as I slipped past him.

He grabbed my arm before I got away, pulling me to his level. "I think I'm falling in love with you, Allison Sanders," he whispered.

Speechless, I nodded and broke away like I was in a hurry. Confusion took over as I rushed to the door and outside into the fresh air, gasping for breath. Pacing back and forth in front of the restaurant, I tried to clear my mind. I was sick of going over the pros and cons of this relationship. *Make a decision and stick with it!*

I ran back into the restaurant. Will was paying the bill at the counter. As he turned to leave, he saw me. I tugged on his arm when he reached me and led him outside. "Me, too, Will. I think I'm falling in love, too."

I threw my arms around his neck. He spun in place, lifting me off the ground as he planted kisses all over my neck and face. I had done it. I was going to let myself love again. I could finally be free of the past and ready for a new beginning.

* * * *

Will and I had been together almost two months, and we spent most of our free time together. If and when I was ready for sex, I'd let him know. Will was almost too good to be true, as Ashley kept reminding me.

We had long talks as we strolled through the gardens on campus. He told me about his family—a younger brother in high school who played on the varsity baseball team, and two loving parents. He understood my contempt for Doug without asking too many questions and my love for my other brother, Dean.

"Dean and Autumn have been married almost a year." I described the wedding in detail. Will listened, pretending not to be bored, making me love him all the more.

"They have a home in Duck, North Carolina. Do you know where that is? Right on the Atlantic coast. It's beautiful. One day we'll go there."

"And I'll return the favor," he replied. "I'm going to show you around this state." Will had been a California boy his whole life.

"I'd love to go to San Francisco and see the Golden Gate Bridge." I sighed as I pictured the two of us strolling through the city.

"I'll put it on the list. But first, we have to go to Napa."

"Wine country?" I thought of the Bella wine Nate always brought me.

"A weekend in Napa Valley would be romantic." Will nibbled my ear, and I giggled.

I let out a happy sigh as I thought back on those moments. But today I needed to catch up on long distance phone calls. I missed Ashley, but mostly my mom. She had become an innocent victim in the whole sordid affair. Dean and Autumn visited LA twice a year for his art shows, so I got to see them. I had mixed feelings about my dad. I felt bad, but he had let Doug kidnap me after all.

A wave of panic rose up whenever I recalled the night I came home to find an ambulance parked in the driveway. I thought something had happened to my parents. But no, Doug had convinced Dad he needed to question me in a place where I couldn't escape, for my own good. He mentioned cults, and Dad had panicked. He pictured his little girl running off with those terrible people, never to be seen again.

Doug had thrown me over his shoulder and into the back of an ambulance as Mom screamed in the background. He then took me to an old, desolate motel outside of town, wanting to interrogate me and see what I knew about Lucas. He suspected something but never got me to break down. I never said anything incriminating so I considered it a draw. Except maybe in Doug's mind, he had won after all. He got to throw me around a bit. Let me correct that—a lot. He even smacked me in the face. God, he scared me that day. His cold eyes held no love for me, his little sister. Luckily, Lucas and his family had been able to rescue me from that hellhole.

Doug and I had always had a rocky relationship, even though we were sixteen years apart. I learned something about him cooped up in that motel for days. I found out why he hated me. He had let me fall from a chair when I was a toddler and never tried to catch me. I hit my head, cutting it open. I still bear the scar today. Is Doug sorry? No, quite the opposite. He blamed me for losing his girlfriend, the love of his life, over that. She witnessed the whole thing, and it made her sick.

I always wondered why no one ever talked about the scar on my head. Then I finally realized my parents wanted to sweep the incident under the rug and protect Doug. They wanted us to be one big, happy family.

I shook my head as if to rid the memories. "I'll call Mom first." I could picture her in the kitchen, hair falling in her face as she started dinner.

"Allie, I'm so glad you called. It seems like ages since I've talked to you."

"It hasn't been that long, Mom."

"Two weeks is long to your old mother."

"You're not old, Mom." Not entirely true. My parents were in their early forties when I was born.

"Are you still coming home on the first?"

"July first? Yes, like I planned."

"And staying till the end of the month?"

"Yep."

"We have to make some plans, things you want to do while you're here. We'll have the family barbecue like always. Doug never gets to see you."

"Whatever." Mom knew Doug was a sore subject.

"I wish you'd let me give him your phone number, Allie. He wants to talk to you. I know he's sorry."

I bit down hard on my lip to keep from screaming. Mom was told to never to give him my number. I had to change it a few times over the years when she'd given in to his demands.

"Oh, I better let you talk now, I know you're busy. How's that new beau, Will? Dad wants to know if he's treating you right."

"He's fine. Tell Dad he treats me very well. Actually, I want to talk to you about Will. Is it okay if he comes to Virginia for a visit? Meet the family? It won't be until the last week of July."

"Oh, sweetie, is it serious? I'm so happy for you."

"Maybe. I think so." When I thought of Will, my heart fluttered. "Mom, I could see myself married to him one day." I decided to prepare her for the big disclosure. "It means I'd probably live out here."

Silence hung between us, and finally she said, "I just want you to be happy. If living in California is what you want, we'll support you."

"Thanks, I'm sorry to cut this short, but I have a few more calls to make."

"Sure, that's fine. I love you."

"I love you, too, Mom." I flopped back on the sofa hoping I had done a good enough job preparing Mom for the worst. I pictured her running around the house, trying to find Dad and strategize how they could convince Will and me to move there instead.

I flipped through my contacts for the next call. "Ash! How are you?"

"Allie! I don't know how I am! Don't tell Nate, but I went on a date. Well, not really a date. I just hung out with this guy."

I gasped. I always pictured my two best friends together forever, but in a way, I didn't blame her. "Are you going to tell Nate?"

"Yeah, I'll be truthful. He'll be home in a few weeks, but it's been so hard. I get lonely."

"I understand."

"Thanks. It was only one time. When I got home from the date, I knew I'd made a *big* mistake. It made me miss Nate all the more. It's hard to commute to college and live at home. I wanted some excitement in my life."

"Ash, quit being so hard on yourself. It sounds harmless to me."

"We made out a little."

The hair on my arms stood on end. "And …?"

"Maybe more than a little. That's all. Now let's talk about you. How's Will?"

I decided to let her change the subject. "He's going to come for a visit when I'm home. Everyone will get to meet him."

"Great! Sounds more serious than you let on. Am I going to be a bridesmaid soon?"

"You never know." I teased. "No, not really! I have two more years of school, and the way Will's going, it may take him three. But I'm not going to wait that long to—"

"Oh, you're finally going to do it!"

"Will's going home this weekend, and when he gets back … surprise!"

"Are you going to tell him?'

"Didn't I just say 'surprise'?"

"Well, I'll try very hard to keep it to myself. But you better call me the minute it happens." Ashley started to laugh. "You know what I mean."

"You'll be my first call. Gotta run. Karate class. Love you."

After returning from class, I hopped in the shower. Will and I had scheduled a quick dinner date before he left for the Memorial Day weekend. His brother was in a baseball tournament, and Will had promised to be there. He begged me to go but I couldn't call off work. Anyway, it gave me time to plan the seduction.

The apartment door buzzer rang. I pushed the button to let Will into the apartment, propped the door open and hurried to the bedroom to finish getting ready. Grabbing a pale yellow sundress, I threw it over my head. As the dress started to slide down my arms, I felt strong, warm hands wrap around my bare waist. The dress went up in the air and fell to the floor. Turning, I gazed into beautiful blue eyes filled with longing. "Will," I whispered. He pulled me close, kissing my hair, my neck, my shoulders, lingering on the tattoo. "Will, dinner—"

"Can wait."

I came close to giving in but didn't want to ruin the surprise. Candles, champagne and a sexy black dress were involved. "I love you, but you do have to get on the road soon." I slipped from his hold, picked up my dress and tossed it on.

"You win, this time." Will put his arm around me as we walked to the door.

"I may have a little surprise for you when you get back." I teased. "Something *very* special. Dinner? My place?"

"I won't be back until Tuesday, but it's a date as long as you're the dessert." I saw his eyes sparkle as he got the hint.

"You'll have to wait and see." The corners of my mouth slightly turned up as I tried not to give away too much information. "I'm going to miss you while you're gone." I reached for his hand. "I told my mom you're coming to visit."

"She's okay with it?"

"She's already planning the wedding."

"Might not be a bad idea." We both laughed.

After dinner, Will dropped me off in front of my apartment. I took his face in my hands, studying every curve, every line. His lips, full and soft. A straight nose and chiseled jaw any model would kill for. His short, dark blonde hair combed to one side. He smelled of summer and citrus. *My Will. He wants me.*

I placed my lips against his. I felt the want in his kiss, his hands unable to keep off my body. He rubbed my shoulders and slipped his hands up and down my arms. "Have a safe trip," I murmured between kisses. I slipped from the car, holding onto his hand for as long as I could. He waited until I made it inside, and I watched him drive away as I stared out the window.

When I got to my apartment, I called Nate. Thank goodness he had turned twenty-one in January. I'd go over and start sweet-talking him into buying me a bottle of champagne for the big day. If he gave the excuse he didn't have time, I'd drive him to the store myself. "Nate, I'm coming over to hang out," I announced as soon as he picked up.

"Will left, I take it."

"Yeah, but you know I love you. You're not second best."

"Okay, come on over. But I have work to do."

"Then you're up for buying me a bottle of champagne?"

"To drink tonight?" His voice held a touch of concern.

"No, silly, I want it for when Will comes home. I'm planning a special dinner for him."

"How special?"

"None of your business! I'll be there in a few." I grabbed my keys and ran down to the Jeep. Driving through West LA felt comfortable. It had been home for almost a year. I hoped it would turn into forever.

I found a parking spot close to the apartment's side door and jumped from the car. Out of the corner of my eye, I spotted something shiny and bent down to pick it up. I gasped as my heart skipped a beat. An ID bracelet engraved with the initials, LA, lay on the concrete next to my car. It was just like the one I'd given Lucas for his birthday our junior year in high school. LA—Lucas, Allie.

I dashed toward the building, let myself in and flew up the stairs. "Nate!" I screamed as I opened the door. "Look what I found!" I placed the bracelet in his hand, mine noticeably shaking.

Nate examined it. "So?"

"It's the gift I gave Lucas for his birthday. It's proof he's here. You even bought it for me, remember?"

"Of course, I do." Nate nodded. "Take a deep breath and think for a minute. Where do we live?"

"Los Angeles."

"LA for short. I'm sure there are lots of these floating around. Probably some fraternity wears them."

My heart sank. "I just thought—"

Nate put his arm around me. "I know."

He guided me to the couch and pulled up pictures on his computer pad, ones he he'd taken of me the day I'd posed for him. He showed what he'd submitted for class and the professor's comments.

"Beautiful subject?" I crinkled my nose as I read. "Very natural. Use her again."

"I think you earned my grade, little one, but I have more to do. Hope you don't mind if I work while you talk." Nate drank from his beer then offered me a sip.

Declining the offer, I said, "So you're going home right after finals week, right?"

"Yeah, I'd like to stay a few more days, but my girl won't stand for it."

"So you and Ashley are exclusive and still a couple?"

"Of course, unless you know something I don't."

"No, just wondering. It helps every once in a while to talk about your relationship with your partner."

"I'm picking up on something here." He closed one eye as he studied me. "She feels neglected?"

"A little."

"Don't worry. I'll call her after you leave."

"Then I'm leaving." I kissed his cheek and rose from the sofa.

"That was a short visit. What about the champagne?"

"You've got all weekend."

"I think I'll keep this." Nate held up the bracelet. "You don't need a constant reminder of—"

"Thanks, you're always so good to me." I didn't want him to say the name. "If I could trade Doug for you as a brother, I'd do it in a minute." I pointed at him. "Don't forget. Buy champagne."

I headed for the door and home. Calling Ash trumped champagne. I knew he'd get it to me by the end of the weekend. Anyway, it had been a long day, and I needed some rest. I tried to keep Will front and center in my mind as I made the drive to my apartment, but somehow Lucas kept getting in the way.

Back home, glass of wine in hand, I pulled out my little black dress and decided to try it on one last time. Will called right in the middle of the fitting. We'd seen each other just a few hours ago, but it felt like forever. I sat on the bed and listened to his excited voice.

"My brother won the first game in the tournament, Allie. Scouts for the major leagues came to watch him."

"Was he excited?"

"That and more! He's torn between college or going with a major league team."

"You'll help him make the best choice, Will. That's what big brothers are for. I'll see you Tuesday night?"

"Can't wait. Love you."

"I love you, too."

I got back to my trial run for the night of seduction. I brushed out my hair, flipping it forward and back to my shoulders for more volume. Spinning around in front of the full-length mirror, I studied my reflection. "Jewelry."

Silver dangle earrings would look great. I rummaged through my jewelry drawer looking for just the right pair and set a few on the dresser as the apartment buzzer rang. I thought it a little strange for someone to come over this late, close to 11 p.m. Or did Nate forget his key again? He'd be surprised to see me dressed liked this. I padded through the living room in bare feet and pushed the intercom. "Nate?"

"Yeah."

"Use your key."

"Forgot."

He probably had the bottle of champagne I wanted, feeling guilty for not going with me earlier. Impressed by his promptness, I buzzed him in. I decided to surprise him and answer the door in my vampy four-inch black heels. I slipped them on, buckled the crisscross upper straps and maneuvered carefully to the door. I threw it open, waiting to see his reaction, but it was mine I needed to control.

Chapter Three

"Lucas!"

The man I'd loved forever and could never get out of my heart stood in front of me. He leaned against the doorframe, single red rose in hand. His dark hair was shorter, not long and shaggy anymore. Cropped short around the back and sides, it gave him a neat appearance. The top was longer and cut in jagged, spiky layers. He looked like a typical California guy, wearing a white shirt with rolled-up sleeves, a pair of designer blue wash torn jeans and sandals. I immediately got lost in those dark, brooding brown eyes.

We said nothing. Lucas swept me into his arms and carried me to the bedroom, never taking his eyes off me. I felt my body placed gently across the bed. He grasped my one leg and rested it on his knee. His fingers ran down my shin to the buckle of my shoe. He undid it, letting the stiletto fall to the floor. He placed my leg back on the bed with care and cupped the heel of my other foot in his hand. He brought it to his lips caressing the toes with his lips. His hand worked the buckle, and I felt the shoe slip from my foot.

I closed my eyes, breathing as if I couldn't get enough air into my lungs. My heart beat against my chest, and the sound drummed in my ears. I'd had too much wine and convinced myself my mind was playing tricks on me. If I could conjure up Lucas like this, I prayed I could do it again.

His mouth brushed my lips, startling me. My eyes flew open as he pulled me to my feet. Lucas slipped the straps of my dress from my shoulders. He kissed one shoulder and traveled up my neck. My hands found the buttons of his shirt, fumbling down the row until I could slide it from his shoulders. I spun around so the zipper of my dress could be pulled down. It floated to the carpet as I drifted into another world.

Lowered to the bed, Lucas slid in next to me. My Lucas. I couldn't get enough of him, kissing him over and over, never wanting to stop. This moment could change everything. I wanted Lucas to make love to me, be my first and only, even if it was a dream.

* * * *

The next morning, I woke groggy and disoriented. My hand flew to the other side of the bed. No one lay next to me. *Did I dream that? Did I fall asleep on my bed after trying on my dress?*

I pulled myself up from the mattress and looked down. I wore a white shirt with the sleeves rolled up. My stomach did a flip. *Not a dream.*

A shirtless Lucas stood in the doorway, coffee mug in hand. He smiled that dangerous smile, and that was all it took. He slipped back into bed, and we made love again. Afterward, as I lay there holding him, I realized we'd never spoken a word. I concentrated hard to make sure it wasn't a dream. My fingers traveled up my arm and gave a quick pinch. *Ow! Okay, I'm awake. So, if I'm awake ...*

Suddenly, the independent girl in me took over, the one who protected him for almost two years, the girl who gave him up, so her brother would never find him. *Why now?* Indignation welled inside me. I deserved an explanation. I slipped out of bed and headed for the bathroom to shower and dress. Then I would confront my long lost boyfriend.

When I emerged from the bathroom, Lucas slipped by me, shutting the door behind him. I gave the door a quick punch and stomped back to the bedroom. Next to my bed, I noticed his bracelet lying on the table and saw a tiny piece of dirt embedded in one of the links. Alarm bells went off in my head. Lucas planted it in Nate's parking lot, hoping I'd find it. Not able to wait any longer, I pounded on the bathroom door. "Lucas, you need to come out! Now!"

Wet and smiling, he opened the door. "Want to join me?" I glared at him. "Hand me my clothes." He pointed to a chair in my bedroom. I couldn't resist and kissed him through the opening. I went into the bedroom, tossed him the pants, and he slipped them over his boxers. "Shirt?"

"I kind of like wearing it."

"You can wear it again tonight." He winked.

I pulled him out to the living room, shirtless, grabbed a bottle of water from the fridge and poured Lucas another cup of coffee. "Start talking." I handed him the mug and sat next to him.

"Still don't eat breakfast?" His eyes darted to the water bottle. "There's a lot to tell. Where do you want me to start?"

"Anywhere."

"Okay, I'll give you an overview since I last saw you. After the breech in Virginia, the family moved back to the Niner compound in Montana. My nephew Sam and his son Joe lived with Gene and me until the school year started."

"I don't like the overview. Boring." I folded my arms and stared at him.

"Then ask me anything you want."

"Sam and Joe lived with you? They didn't go back to their house in Bozeman?"

I pictured Lucas' nephew Sam in my mind—early forties, dark-haired and eyes like Lucas', a little shorter than him, just over six feet. He could be quiet, and when I'd first met him it felt like he was judging me. He was introduced as Lucas' father. Sam's son Joe stood in as Lucas' little brother.

"Yeah, just for a few weeks, but eventually they went home. Sam knew Gene wasn't well. They hid it from me … like always."

My eyes widened. "Gene?" I swallowed hard. "Is ill?"

"My brother's no longer with us, Allie."

My anger subsided as I remembered how kind Gene could be under his gruff exterior. Like father, like son. Gene and Sam—I loved them both. Tears filled my eyes, and I didn't fight them back. Lucas gave me time to grieve the patriarch of the Montgomery family.

"I'm sorry about your brother," I whispered.

He got up and found my tissue box.

"Thanks," I said as he sat back down. I took a few sips of water to gain my composure. "I know you hated how they treated you at times. They did it because they love you."

"Gene and I were brothers, Allie. Just because I look like a teenager doesn't mean they should treat me like one. And Sam's his son, my nephew. The kid's half my age." He glanced at me out of the corner of his eye. "You know what I mean."

"I do, but they view you differently. Even though you watched Sam grow up, he's older than you now. He became your father figure. Your family's very protective."

"You can say that again." Lucas ran his hands through his hair. "Even Joe thinks he'll be my father one day."

"We talked about that before. You said you wouldn't let that happen."

"It doesn't *need* to happen. In the world's eyes, I'm twenty, soon to be twenty-one next year—leap year."

"When school started did Sam move back to town so Joe could attend public school?"

"My great-nephew didn't like the idea, but there were circumstances. He would've stayed in the village with me and gone to school there."

"Circumstances?"

"I'll tell you later. I want you to understand I never would've left you. You made that decision for both of us. It was hard on me. I suffered."

I placed my hand over my mouth, eyes wide with sympathy and understanding. "I suffered, too," I whispered.

Lucas placed his hand on my leg. "After we left Virginia, I needed a distraction. I finished my high school classes that fall. During that time, Gene became ill and couldn't hide it anymore."

"What was wrong?"

Lucas took a deep breath. "His heart. The Niners did everything they could to help him. You'd think we would have been able to save him with all our technology. Just when we thought we had him on the right track, Gene had a heart attack and died."

"Lucas, I'm so sorry!" Tears filled my eyes again as I thought of Gene and his dancing brown eyes, looking so like Lucas.

"As he said, he lived a good life and never expected to make it well into his eighties. He always pictured himself crashing and burning on his motorbike."

"I'm glad that never happened."

"Me, too. He was a good brother and a better friend."

"So, while I toiled away senior year, you were done and taking care of Gene. Then he passed. I never knew."

"Yeah, sorry. I wanted to contact you when I found out he was sick but decided to honor your wish. Instead I began to research colleges. I didn't want to be far from home, and I gave up on Harvard or Yale. I started taking on-line college classes that winter. But Gene insisted I go wherever I wanted. He didn't want me to stay home and take care of him."

"When did you leave?"

"I came here at Nate's suggestion. I started spring quarter of your senior year."

"Wait! Let's back up here. Nate suggested you come to LA? You've been talking to him this whole time?"

"I never agreed I'd stop talking to him, Allie. He's my best friend."

I could almost forgive both of them for their deceit. Lucas finally had a best friend outside the Niner community.

"I moved into the apartment complex where Nate lives."

"So that *was* you I saw—"

"I was in Nate's apartment when you called about your date with Will, and I admit, I wanted you to notice me. I waited until I heard you come up the side stairs and headed for the main ones."

"To torture me?"

"I was jealous. You said you wanted a real relationship with this Will guy. I couldn't stand it. I could've stayed away if—"

"I remained single and a virgin." I threw my head back on the sofa. "I was doing a pretty good job until you took care of that last night." I smiled at him.

He took my hand and lifted it to his mouth. His eyes connected with mine. "I will always love you and watch over you, whether you want me in your life or not."

"That makes you sound stalker-ish." I giggled. "But I know what you mean. You were always in my thoughts, too. No matter how hard I tried to fight it. You were there."

Lucas had kept tabs on me all this time, making sure I was safe. *And* he was jealous. How could I stay mad? He was right. I called the shots and broke things off.

"And what about the ID bracelet? How did you know I'd find it?"

"I could only hope. I wanted to remind you of our love. I tried to break you down. I wanted you to tell Nate to help find me. I never wanted us to end. *You* did."

"So you tracked me during those years, after I told you not to."

"Yes, I had to protect you. Thankfully, Doug's become less of an issue. I think you're off his radar, especially since you moved out here. But you never can be too sure."

"Ugh! Don't even say his name. I don't want to think about him. Ever." I looked away. "But we have to talk about him, don't we?" I paused, trying to stay composed. "He's the reason we had to separate. Don't you remember the night at the diner?"

"How could I forget?" Lucas' voice shook. "If we could live another life, you would be my girl?"

I swung my head back to look at him. "Yes," I whispered. "The day I will never forget. My heart had been ripped from my chest and stomped on. I became a shell of myself after you left. All because of Doug." I burst out crying.

Lucas placed an arm around me. I leaned into him as he rubbed my back. "We're trying to monitor him. We have new intel."

I sat up with renewed interest. "Tell me."

"Not yet. You still need to ask your questions about the past two years."

"Fine." I searched my mind, thinking of what I wanted to know. "Did you play a part in getting me to LA?"

"Nate and I thought it would make it easier to watch over you. I couldn't believe you weren't dating and were so focused on work and school when you got here."

"You know why I couldn't be with anyone else." I bit my bottom lip. "And when I'm finally able to make a clean break, you decide to show up in my life again. Why?"

"You put in the order for champagne. That did it. I told Nate, no more games. I took my chance and came over here. You could've sent me away."

"And now what? Do you think anything has changed? I still want to protect you. If Doug finds out we're back together, he'll make our lives miserable again."

"We're back together?" Lucas smiled the smile that made me melt.

I leaned over and kissed him. "Yes, we are."

"It will be different this time. I had time to plan. I still want you to decide where we live, how we live, that hasn't changed. I can protect us better. Our technology has grown even more since we parted." A determined look spread across his face.

"I need to finish this quarter and stick to my schedule. No need to make anyone suspicious. I have plans to fly home July first for a month. Although now I don't want to be away from you for a minute! But I have to. You understand, don't you?" Lucas solemnly nodded his head. "Then I'll be back for fall quarter with Ashley. We're planning to room together, get a new place." I glanced around. "I hate to give this up."

"I have a two-bedroom that I'm sure Nate would love. He'd have room for his equipment. I'll suggest it to him. He and Ash can move in together. Problem solved."

"And where would you live?"

"Here with you, if that's okay."

"More than okay." My stomach growled. "Come on, let's finish dressing. We're going out for lunch, like a real couple. You can tell me more then."

My phone rang as we were ready to head out. Will's name flashed on the screen, and it brought me back to reality. My heart pounded as I realized I had to break someone's heart. "Hey, Will. How's everything going?"

"Allie, I have some good news ... and bad." Will sounded pretty happy for having bad news. "Tyler's going to revisit some colleges that recruited him. He wants me to tag along."

"That's wonderful news. I take it he's been offered some scholarships."

"Yeah, he's got a lot of decisions to make."

"You definitely need to go with him. You'll be a great help."

"Now, the bad news. I won't be able to come home this week. I'll probably stay through next weekend, do my studying here and see you a week from Monday. Don't know if I can wait that long, especially since you have that surprise waiting for me." His voice grew low, filled with passion.

My heart skipped a beat. I didn't have the heart to tell him on the phone it was over. "I'll see you before class, like always. We'll talk then."

I saw a flash of disappointment cross Lucas' face. With his super power hearing, he heard both ends of the conversation. I managed to hang up without saying "I love you" as Will continued to say it over and over again.

I flopped back on the sofa and hoped Lucas would forgive me. "I couldn't do it over the phone," I wailed.

Lucas pulled me up and into his arms. "No, you couldn't. You like to do things the right way. I'll let you handle it and stay in the background."

"Thanks. Will's a great guy."

"I know."

"You checked him out?"

"Forgive me?" Lucas stuck out his lower lip. "I thought you were starving. Show me the way to the restaurant you like. Although," he said as he tapped his chin, "I might have an idea where we're going."

We walked a few blocks to one of my favorite organic restaurants. Seated in a back corner, we settled in and continued our conversation.

"Do Joe and Sam live alone in town?" I didn't have the heart to ask about Sam's wife, Stacy. The memory of our last meeting still burned in my mind. She had caused our heartbreak when we found out she'd become an informant for Doug, anonymously, of course.

"As I said, they moved back to town a few weeks after we returned. I live alone in the village now."

"Sam and Joe got a new place? Stacy's in the house with Hannah?" There, I finally said her name aloud. Hannah, on the other hand, was an innocent victim. In grade school when I met her, she really thought Lucas was her brother instead of her great-uncle.

Lucas hesitated, took a sip of his drink. "They moved back with Stacy."

"What?" I clenched my fists until my nails dug into the skin. Stacy was the leak they never could find. She knew her way around Niner technology. The Montgomerys had gone on the run because of her.

"Remember I said there were circumstances?" He gazed into my eyes, searching for understanding. "She was pregnant."

My eyes opened so wide they began to water. Finally I found my voice. "Isn't she a little old—?"

"Yeah, I know, she was forty at the time. Serena says that hormones could've played a part in her breakdown."

"Serena?"

"Remember Julian? The head of our Niner compound? His wife is our head physician and chief of staff."

"Wow, give me a minute." I moved the food around on my plate, barely wanting to eat now. Should I forgive Stacy just because she had a baby? "Stacy wasn't pregnant the whole time she was informing Doug of your whereabouts, Lucas."

"I know. But Sam loves her, Allie. If he can forgive her, I guess we all can. I have another great-nephew who just turned one. They named him Gene."

"I guess that helps … a little. Still, I don't trust her."

"None of us do, the Niners that is. She's not allowed at the compound ever again. If I want to see the baby, I go to their house. Sam and Joe are still welcome at the village." Lucas chuckled. "Joe still thinks he's in training to be my father one day."

"I love Joe so much!" I thought back to the sullen fifteen-year-old who'd probably graduated high school by now.

"Yeah, he's a great kid. So that's about it. What else do you want to know?"

"Where do you spend your summers?"

"I go back to Montana. It will be harder this year because Gene won't be there. I came straight here after the funeral and only went back for a few days over the holidays. I promised Julian I'd stay the summer, but now that you're back in my life, I'll cut the visit short."

"And what should I tell Ashley?"

"Nate will tell her he ran into me on campus and renewed our friendship. He's going to say he stayed out of our relationship drama. If we got back together, it was meant to be."

"But she can't tell anyone."

"He's got that covered. She knows Doug didn't approve of you dating me. The less anyone in Virginia knows the better."

"You two thought of everything. And now my last question. In all your eighty years, Lucas Montgomery, have you ever slept with anyone else?"

Lucas let out a hearty laugh and shook his head. "Where did that come from?" He reached for my hands. "You're the only one for me."

"That didn't answer my question." I gave him a hard stare.

"No, Allie, I've never slept with anyone but you." He left a large dollar amount on the table, more than enough to cover the bill and tip. "Come on. Let's go."

We headed outside and started for the apartment. I could walk in the bright sunlight, holding hands with Lucas and never tire of it. "Let's drive to the pier and spend the rest of the day at the ocean," I said.

"You love the water, don't you?" Lucas put his arm around me and pulled me close. "Dean might get jealous if you find a new favorite beach."

"He's got nothing to worry about. I love his home in the Outer Banks. It's just that his house is so far away."

"Maybe you should try and make an effort to get there on your visit home." Lucas kissed the side of my head. We raced for the Jeep as we approached the apartment.

In less than fifteen minutes, we arrived at the Santa Monica Pier. We spent the rest of the afternoon riding the historic carousel, playing in the arcade, and eating funnel cake with powdered sugar. I wanted to stay until the sun set and ride the Ferris wheel one more time. We were two big kids making up for lost time.

We strolled back to the car hand in hand as it grew dark. I hadn't felt like this in a long time. A huge weight had been lifted from me, and I was happy. I almost forgot the meaning of the word. Did I have those kinds of days with Will? I loved him in my own way. He was safe and comfortable. But I wasn't *in* love with him.

"Hey, why the sad face? Is it because I didn't win that giant panda bear you wanted?" Lucas teased. He knew the opposite to be true. I begged him not to win the bear. It would've taken up half my bedroom. "You know I could've won it." He poked me in the side.

Lucas brought me back to reality as I jumped away from him, squealing. "Yeah, blah, blah, blah, you're so strong. Stronger than any man on the pier." I laughed and ran as he chased me, not wanting to spoil the wonderful day. I couldn't wait to get back and be alone with him in our apartment. I smiled as I pictured us there. I already had him moved in.

Chapter Four

Lucas and I spent every waking moment together. I cut back my hours at work, and we met after every class. He insisted on taking me to the beach for a daily walk, whether it was at dusk or early morning. He was an old soul, as our English teacher had called him, and believed romance should be an important part of our relationship.

The week went by too quickly. My mind became a jumbled mess, trying to sort through everything that had happened in such a short period of time. Not long ago, I planned a seduction dinner for Will. Instead I slept with Lucas. I cheated on Will and needed to end things with him soon.

Will called daily. I'd cut the conversation short, blaming work or running late. If he was suspicious, he didn't act it. He told me he had a surprise for me when he returned home. I hoped he bought a t-shirt or had an autographed baseball from his brother, not anything too serious. In less than twelve hours he'd be home, and I had to be ready.

I invited Nate over for Sunday dinner. I hadn't seen him since Lucas showed up at my door. We'd sent a few texts back and forth but there had been no face to face. Voices came from the living room signaling his arrival. Nate held up his hands for protection as I walked out of the bedroom.

"Don't hit me!" He pantomimed ducking from a pretend punch. "He made me do it." Nate pointed at Lucas.

Instead I grabbed him and hugged him with all my might. "I was mad at first. Shocked you knew all this time, but I've had time to think. It makes sense. You didn't need to be in the middle of this."

"Whew!" He wiped his forehead. "So we're good?"

Lucas patted Nate on the back. I saw the camaraderie they'd developed. "It's all on me, Nate. You did the right thing. I had to wait until Allie was ready to accept me back into her life."

"And now?" Nate raised his eyebrows at me.

"We're back together forever. We're not going to let anything or anyone tear us apart. If I don't finish classes, I don't care. We're going to live in Montana at Victorian Village."

"That place is awesome." Nate high-fived Lucas.

"You've been there?"

"Yeah, I went up to stay with Lucas during Spring Break last year. We had a really sweet time riding bikes in the mountains, hanging out in nature. But I love your car, Allie. What'd you name her? Beetle?"

A twinge of jealousy ran through me. "Oh, you met Beetle?" I always felt she could be a real person.

"A mind of her own." Nate laughed.

"What?"

"A lot of improvements since your last visit," Lucas said. "Since she's assigned to me, Beetle has sensors that trigger when you need her, and she comes to get you. We're connected telepathically through a small chip I carry in my phone. I think her name and the place where I am. She leaves the main facility and picks me up. She's a hovercraft, too."

"She can fly above ground and even take you up and over the mountains," Nate added.

"Oh." I pouted, suddenly feeling left out.

"You'll see soon enough." Lucas rubbed my back, trying to make me feel better. "Come on, let's eat."

As we sat at the table, I thought about Nate getting involved with the Niners and didn't like it. I knew I had to say something. "Nate, just be careful. You never know if Doug's still watching you."

"I'll probably be on his radar forever, but that's not going to stop me from living my life, Allie. Besides, I'm an honorary Niner. Right, Lucas?"

Lucas smiled and nodded, but I could only cringe. Nate held up a phone that looked quite familiar.

"Is that—?" My mouth dropped open.

"The latest Niner phone? Yep." Nate held it like a prized possession.

"Allie won't let me give her one," Lucas told him.

"Why? This is all you need. It connects me to all things Niner. They're so beyond what we can ever imagine—"

I felt like I'd lost my appetite. "I don't really need one." I'd given up the phone once before and wasn't quite ready to accept a new one.

"Whenever you're ready, let me know," Lucas said.

"If I take the phone, it's like I'm asking for trouble. Do you know what I mean?" I glanced back and forth at the guys.

"Doug. I get it, little one. But hasn't he left you alone?" Nate guided me to the couch after we finished eating.

Tears pricked the corners of my eyes. "Every time I think of Doug …" I made fists and shook them. *Psychopath!* "He kidnapped me! How could he do that to his own sister?"

"Traumatic, I know." Nate shook his head and looked at me intently, "You're not over it yet, are you? Did you ever talk to someone?"

"What?" I snapped my head in his direction, making eye contact. "You think I'm crazy?"

"Not at all. Being kidnapped isn't a common experience. You might feel better if you talked about it."

"I don't want to talk about it. All I want to say is … I. Hate. Doug."

Lucas sat on the other side of me. "Nate's right, Allie. If you ever need to talk—"

"I'll let you know," I interrupted.

"And remember, you also found out he abused you as a baby," Lucas said. "That was a big revelation."

"One-time abuse. But according to him, it was my fault." I reached up and rubbed the back of my head. The scar was a souvenir of that time in my life. "I was trying to get away from him and accidentally fell, hitting my head."

"After he pinched you," Lucas reminded me, "and *let* you fall. And he still blames you for losing his girlfriend. That's so twisted."

I'd never told them about the new abuse that happened at the motel and decided it might have to stay that way forever. "Guys, I have an early class tomorrow and need to meet Will, so I'm going to bed. Nate, you can stay and visit with Mr. Night Owl if you want." I kissed Nate's cheek, gave Lucas a quick kiss and went into the bedroom.

Lucas normally slept a few short hours but had been coming to bed with me until I fell asleep. Now I was alone in the bedroom, and it felt quite foreign, even though he'd only been back a week. I liked his arms around me and wanted him with me. I flipped around in the bed, unable to sleep, while my mind swirled with thoughts of Doug. I wished we hadn't talked about him right before bedtime. Sitting up, I decided to join the boys again and maybe have one more glass of wine. I headed for the door that was slightly ajar and stopped before opening it wider. The guys' conversation had turned serious.

"Are you going to tell her?" Nate's voice was barely a whisper.

"No. She'd never agree to come back to me if she knew."

"So you'll get married, have kids and when she dies, you will, too, by taking your own life. Allie will never know that's your plan?"

I suppressed a gasp and grabbed my stomach. A sick feeling grew inside me.

"That's far into the future, Nate. I'll have lived a full life by then. How can I go on for hundreds of years without her? You promised to go to your grave with this secret. I'm going to have to hold you to it."

"We got pretty drunk that night, didn't we? I think you've wanted to tell me all along. The liquor just gave you the courage."

"Yeah, I suppose. Hey, you know what? Let's call it a night. We're getting pretty morbid."

"Totally … but I'm glad you two are back together, man. Allie hasn't been the same since you left. I see a light in her eyes that's been missing for years."

I heard the door shut and jumped back in bed, trying to fight back tears. Did I just hear Lucas say he wanted to end his own life when mine did? Tragically romantic, but not what I'd expected or ever wanted. I closed my eyes and tears squeezed out of the corners onto my pillow. Did I have to end this relationship again? Deciding to wait until morning to think more clearly, I dozed off and slept fitfully for the rest of the night.

* * * *

Waking the next morning, the conversation from last night immediately sprung to my mind. Lucas would eventually come to his senses and realize it was the wrong thing to do when the time came, wouldn't he? As much as it was killing me, I decided not to bring it up. I had decades to convince him how foolish his plan was. For now, I had to break up with Will and that was turning my stomach inside out. I could smell Lucas' breakfast and the thought of food made me want to throw up. I texted Lucas from the bedroom asking him to come in.

"What's wrong?"

"Not feeling the greatest."

"Nervous about Will? It will be over soon. And you're not doing this alone. I'm coming with you."

"No!"

"You won't even know I'm there. I promise."

I knew better than to argue and had no way of stopping him. "Fine, but do *not* interfere."

Lucas sat on the edge of the bed and held me until I was calm. I leaned back and gazed into his chocolate brown eyes. "I really need to get out of here and get some fresh air."

I threw on jeans and a tank, ran past his plate of food, holding my breath, and out into the cool morning air. Slowly breathing in and out, I headed for the Jeep.

I pictured Will waiting in front of the building where we each had our first class. He'd look like a model for a summer catalog shoot without being pretentious. I, on the other hand, was a nervous wreck. As I hurried down the sidewalk from the parking garage, I saw Will coming to greet me. He smiled and waved, looking happy to see me. My heart wrenched. I left my sunglasses on so he couldn't see the guilt in my eyes. As he bent to kiss me, I turned my head and his lips landed on my cheek.

"Gosh, I missed you! You look great." He didn't seem to notice the head turn and continued to fill me in on his week. "I haven't let you say a word, Allie. How was your week?"

"Can I tell you after class? Running late," I mumbled. I knew I was going to hurt him and would have to apologize over and over, but it would have to wait.

"Can I take my girl to the park?" He called after me.

"The park will be fine." My heart raced, but I felt relieved to have a momentary reprieve.

As I entered the lecture hall, I felt someone following me. "Can I take my girl to the park?"

"Lucas." I spun around and bumped into him. "You promised!"

"I can't help it. You know I have good hearing!"

I couldn't be mad at him, but I had to fix this and soon. I'd hurt Lucas, as well. "It will all be over soon, I promise. But let me do it alone and my way, please. I'll text you when it's over."

"Nope, I'm going with you." He sat down next to me.

I shouldn't have come to class. I couldn't concentrate on the lecture. Grabbing Lucas' hand, I gripped so hard I thought he'd pull away, but he didn't move or say a word. At least he didn't follow me after class as I headed outside to look for Will.

Will stood in his usual spot, arms crossed, leaning casually against the wall. Tears welled in my eyes as he raised his hand in recognition. We strolled along the sidewalk to the gardens, hand in hand. I made small talk about work. We found a bench in the shade. I took off my sunglasses and put them in my lap. We locked eyes, and I let him kiss me, a sweet, gentle kiss that would be our last.

"You're breaking up with me, aren't you?" Will's voice sounded calm and steady.

"How did you know?"

"That tortured soul look isn't in your eyes." He glanced away. "I have a feeling whoever put it there is back."

"Will—"

"You don't have to say anything, Allie. I loved you … love you. I was going to ask you to marry me today. Pretty stupid, huh?"

My heart sank. *So that was the surprise.* "No, it wasn't stupid at all."

"And if things were still the same between us, what would you have said?"

"Yes. I would've said yes," I whispered, unable to look at him. I told the truth. He deserved at least that. What I didn't tell him was that I'd marry him for all the wrong reasons, to escape the past and dull the pain.

Will put his head in his hands and silently wept, making it all the more agonizing. "Could you go now, Allie?"

"I don't want to leave you like this."

"I'm not your responsibility anymore." He wiped his eyes on his shirtsleeve. "Please?"

As I rose to leave, I searched for the right words, but they never came. "I'm sorry, Will. So sorry." I placed my hand on his shoulder and walked away.

My body was wracked with guilt and pain even though I knew it was the right thing to do. I walked and finally ran to the parking lot, found the Jeep and drove home.

As I stepped into the apartment, Lucas sat at the kitchen table, reading a book. "I didn't expect you back so soon, thought you needed some space," he said.

"Thanks, I'll be fine. I do need a little time." I threw my stuff in the bedroom and came back to sit with him.

"I didn't expect him to cry, Lucas. I didn't expect it at all." I put my head down on my folded arms and felt him rub the top of my head. *Good-bye, Will, if only you knew how much you helped me. I'll be forever grateful.*

* * * *

We closed the apartment today. July first arrived too quickly, and it was time to go home. Lucas would soon leave for the airport, and my flight departed later in the day. When fall quarter started, we'd live here together. I promised he could add his own touches to make the apartment less girly as we'd boxed up some things to be safely stored at his Montana home.

"The Niners will get the boxes, right?" I swept a piece of hair back that kept dangling in my eyes. "We're sending them to a safe house in town like we're some secret operation." I smiled and clarified. "But not like Doug."

"Noted." Lucas didn't look up from sealing the last box. "We have more than one house. I don't want all the packages going to the same place. I'd send these to Sam, but I still don't trust Stacy." He stacked the boxes on top of each other. "I'll drop them off at the post office on the way to the airport." When he finished, he walked over and took my hand. "Can we sit for a minute?"

Lucas led me to the sofa. We sat facing each other, one at each end of the couch. I started to curl my feet under me, but he reached for the right one. "I want to talk about this." He stroked the XXIX tattoo in the arch, making me giggle.

"What about it?" I lifted my shoulders.

"You never should've gotten it." His voice was stern.

I shook my head. "Why not?"

"It's not a Niner symbol anymore, Allie, that's why. It's become more than that. It identifies us to the enemy. Does Doug know you have that?"

"No."

"If he did, he'd keep a closer watch on you." Lucas ran his hand through his hair and sighed. "Don't you get it? It's not some right of passage. It's serious. Maybe deadly. You're getting it removed as soon as I can get you to the compound."

"No!"

"Please don't argue."

I pulled my foot from his hand. "The last time I looked, you still had yours."

"That's different."

"Now you sound like my parents. My dad used to say, 'do as I say, not as I do'. I'm not a child, Lucas. I can make my own decisions."

"Fine! But please just think about it," he whispered.

"Let me know when yours is removed, and we'll talk." I gave him a smile, showing all my teeth.

"Since you're up for challenges, I guess it's time I tell you about Doug."

My eyebrows shot up. "What now?"

"We found some interesting news. A private company is set to take over the STF, but Doug's still in charge. The government gave him special permission to work for them. The military doesn't have the money to fund the operation, and they want it to succeed. He doesn't have to answer to them anymore, just send monthly reports."

"What the hell?" I covered my mouth. "Now he can do whatever he wants. He reports to no one?"

"I wanted you to know." He pulled me into his lap. I rested my head on his shoulder. "How are you feeling?"

I hadn't been feeling well this past week. We decided the stress of breaking up with Will and finals week was the culprit. I'd only had a few days to relax, but now I was stressed again. "I'm better, now that everything's done. I just need to sleep for a day then I'll be back to normal."

"Rest up when you get home. Don't do too much." He kissed the top of my head. "I hate to say this, but I have to be on my way. While I'm in the air, we won't have contact. I can't track you but will after I land." He winked at me.

I laughed because Lucas had an addiction to tracking. "You don't need your tracker for my flight. There's a website that does it for all the airlines. Use that. Let's make a deal. No real tracking until I call you from Virginia."

"Really?"

"Can you quit cold turkey?" I teased.

"Is that a challenge?"

"Yes, it is. Can you do it?"

"Absolutely."

I snuggled against him. "You know you can track me anytime, anywhere. I'm teasing you."

"No, you're right. There's no need. I have to stop being so obsessive about your safety."

"Look at the time. You've got to get going." I kissed him and held on for the longest time. "I'll miss you." I wanted to feel his arms around me a moment longer, but knew he had to get to the airport. I slid off his lap and strolled over to the boxes. "These are ready to go."

Lucas joined me and slipped something into my back pocket.

"Hey, what's this?" I pulled it out to see a Niner phone like Nate's.

"It's time, Allie. You need it. You never know." He shrugged.

"Okay, I'll take it."

We kissed one last time. Lucas kept telling me over and over how much he loved me as he backed out the door with an armload of packages. July was going to be a long month. I sat on the sofa, feeling a little nauseated. I racked my brain as to why I had been feeling so queasy. My eyes flew wide open when I realized I hadn't paid much attention to what my body was telling me.

"No!" I breathed as I jumped off the couch.

Grabbing my purse, I dashed across the street and down the road to the drugstore. I returned home with two pregnancy tests. As I headed for the bathroom, I couldn't believe I had been so clueless. As I paced through the rooms of the apartment, waiting for the time to be up, I knew the answer before I even saw it.

Chapter Five

I was pregnant.

My plans drastically changed in the minutes I waited for the test. Lucas needed to know, and it had to be done in person. I couldn't go home and prayed I could change my flight. I somehow managed to call a taxi and get to the airport. After being dropped off at the entrance, I rushed inside to scan the airline list for a flight to Montana.

Finally, my turn came at the counter, and I transferred my flight from Richmond, Virginia to Billings, Montana. Luckily, there were still seats available on a flight that left in an hour. My heart hadn't stopped pounding since I left the apartment.

I drew in deep breaths, trying to get my heart rate back to a steady pace. I had no time to process the fact I had a tiny person inside me. My emotions changed from excited to scared and back again. All I could think about was Lucas as I walked to the gate. "Mom!" I had to call her.

"Allie?" She answered on the first ring.

"Hi, Mom. I can't get out of LA today."

"Why not? What happened?"

"When I got here they told me I was bumped." I lied. "I'll get another flight. Don't worry. You know I fly stand-by to save money."

"Oh, sweetie, we'll send you money so you can fly home now."

"No, Mom."

"Why are you so stubborn? You never let us help you."

"I know, but really, I'll be fine."

"Will you call when you get your flight?"

"Of course! I just wanted you to know so you didn't worry. I love you."

"I love you, too."

My hand trembled as I hung up. *Poor Mom.* I hated lying to her. She didn't deserve that treatment, but I had to keep her in the dark. Next to Lucas, she was the only person I wanted to protect. She had no clue Doug blamed her for not being a Niner. Born during a Leap Year, he missed February twenty-ninth by a mere minute. Mom waited on him hand and foot, but it was never good enough, and she never knew why.

I looked up rental cars in Billings and found an agency that offered valet service. All I had to do was call when I got to baggage claim, and the car would be parked outside ready and waiting.

When boarding finally began, I made sure to be first in line. Lucas insisted I have a first-class ticket even though I fought it. Now, I was grateful for the comfortable leather seat that helped soothe my nerves while waiting for take-off. Soon we taxied down the runway and lifted into the air. I mapped out the drive in my head, hoping I could find the same dirt road Lucas used when we went to the compound the first time.

My mind drifted to the summer of junior year. Lucas had invited me to visit his home in Montana. At first my dad objected, but Lucas' "mom", Stacy, would be going, too. How could he say no?

We'd dropped Stacy at her home in Bozeman and continued on. Far from any town or city, we'd swung off onto a dirt road, driving through a sea of pines. The Niners skillfully hid their compounds, and Lucas had me find the entrance when we reached a dead-end filled with overgrown brush and huge trees. At the time, I thought it odd but now I was glad he'd prodded me to find it.

My biggest fear was running late. The Niners could see in the dark, but I needed some daylight to study the trees and shrubs. By my calculations I should arrive by 7:30 p.m., plenty of time.

A million questions spun in my head, but most importantly, I needed to know if this baby would inherit his father's unique Niner abilities. I longed to get to Montana as quickly as possible to find out the answers.

I couldn't get off the plane quickly enough after the flight attendants opened the door. I called the rental car valet and jogged all the way to baggage claim. I breathed a silent thank you as my suitcases appeared and headed out to the waiting car. I tipped the driver as he put my bags in the back and jumped in. Taking a few deep breaths, I started for the highway, not looking forward to the two-hour drive ahead of me. I turned up the volume on the radio and rolled down the windows for fresh air. I tried not to watch the clock but couldn't help it. The hour inched closer to five, and I had miles to drive. My mind raced, but my nerves calmed when I spotted the first sign for Bozeman.

When I arrived in town, I pulled into a gas station to get my bearings. As I got out of the car to stretch my legs, I saw the mountain range straight ahead. The rental had GPS so I double-checked my position to make sure I was on track. Getting back in the car, I headed for the road that would take me to Lucas.

As I drove, I watched for dirt roads along the main highway. The mountains were growing closer, and I knew it had to be soon. The first time I came with Lucas, he made a sudden turn into a sea of pine trees. Now it seemed that pines and shrubs grew everywhere. I glanced at the dashboard. The clock said seven-forty.

For just a moment, my mind cleared, and a familiar picture came to mind, so clear it almost looked real. I struggled to keep it in focus. The memory of driving straight into the mountain flashed to the forefront of my brain. I remembered wanting to scream, but Lucas had swerved to the left just when I thought it was too late. I knew the road continued on and around the mountain, but at the time, it looked like it ended with nowhere to go except straight. I trusted my instincts and decided to recreate the same scene. As I grew closer to the massive mountain, I spotted a cleared dirt area on my left and made the turn.

The forest seemed darker than I remembered. The road swerved to the right and left, around trees and boulders. It started to feel familiar until I came to a fork in the road and had to slam on the brakes. *This wasn't here before! The road didn't have choices last time.* I wanted to cry but instead decided to trust my judgment. I picked the road to the left and continued driving. As I came across more twists and turns, every swear word I knew came out of my mouth.

Lucas' voice popped into my head. "We need to add diversions and more off-shoots to that road. Too many people have off-road vehicles these days". He had told Julian, the compound commander, those exact words. Obviously, changes were made.

Glancing at the clock again, I panicked. I wasn't sure where I was or how long I'd been driving. *Please let me find the dead end!*

I turned on the bright lights to illuminate the forest. The car could only take so much of this off-road driving, and I should have thought of that when I ordered a rental. My stomach twisted in a knot. I blasted the air conditioning to keep from heaving. Then suddenly, I ran out of road. I slammed on the brakes and stared at the wall of trees and shrubs.

Although it had been two years, it seemed like yesterday. I saw myself pointing to a spot where there were no tall trees. "There," I said aloud and punched the car through the bushes. Branches hit the windshield and scraped the side of the car. The noise it made sounded like animals clawing at the metal. The car crashed through to the other side and ended up on a paved road. "I made it!" I screamed. "Yes!"

Speeding along the smooth surface, I drove through another forest until I arrived at the next safeguard to the compound, a large concrete wall running through the countryside with a sign that said, "Private test facility. No trespassing." A steel door embedded in the wall sat across the road. I recalled Lucas tapping numbers into his phone as he said them aloud, and the door had opened. Had that changed, too? *My Niner phone!* I'd forgotten all about it.

"Why did I tell him not to track me?" I slapped my forehead as I fired up the phone. "Stupid Allie!"

I sat staring at the steel door and knew command center had me on their radar. They had to wonder what this strange car would do next. It could be a test, either for them or me, the gatecrasher. I studied the phone and decided to tell it Lucas' code.

"Five-oh-eight." Success! The doors slid back, and I drove in.

Out of nowhere, a half dozen over-sized motorcycles sped up to the car. Their riders looked like they wore outer space riot gear, sleek not bulky in design. One of them rode up to the side of the car as I rolled down the window and shouted, "This is private property." He reached up and removed his headgear. "Allie?"

"Sean!" I opened the car door as he slipped off his bike.

My legs felt wobbly and gave out when my feet hit the pavement. Sean caught me in one swift movement and lifted me into his arms. I clung to him, knowing I could trust him. He had moved to Virginia with the Montgomerys after the security breach at the Montana compound, devoting his life to making sure Niners stayed safe. Sean was in his early thirties, making him one hundred and twenty-eight in my world.

Niner men had an air about them—handsome, strong, and intelligent. Sean had dark hair, cropped close to his head, with a day or two worth of stubble on his face. His green eyes had a look of concern and confusion as I stared into them now.

I let him carry me back to the car. He said something to the man behind him, motioning for the rest of the riders to leave. At his command, they disappeared into the darkness. He placed me in the backseat and stood outside the car. A few moments later, I heard another motorbike. Sean talked quietly with the new rider then Lucas slid in the car.

"Allie, what are you doing here?" I threw my arms around his neck, clinging to him, not able to speak. He turned from me and yelled, "Sean, get us back *now*."

I heard Sean talking over his communicator as he got in the car. We sped toward the main building of the Montana compound—command central. Sean parked the rental on the first level as Lucas carried me to the elevator, and, we zipped up to the fourth floor. He took me to the lounge area, placing me on a large white leather sectional. No one seemed to be around.

Lucas sat next to me and handed me a glass of water. "I know I only left this morning, but it seems like forever since I've seen you." He kissed my cheek, the side of my head, my hand, anywhere he could as he waited for me to catch my breath.

I set the glass down on the round table in front of me, took his hand and leveled a steady gaze into his eyes. "I'm pregnant."

His eyebrows shot up as his eyes widened.

"How?"

I stared at him as if I couldn't believe he'd asked.

"Well, I know how. I just mean I thought you planned to sleep with Will and went on the pill or something." Lucas shrugged. "You never said anything."

"And you never asked," I answered.

Lucas broke into the widest smile I'd ever seen. "I'm going to be a dad?"

He kissed me for the longest time, and I began to feel the tension drain away. It was going to be okay. We were going to be a family, and no one could come between us.

"Let's get her to the hospital. Let Serena take a look at her, just to be sure." Julian's voice startled me, and I jumped.

"Julian!" I placed my hand over my heart. Suddenly my eyelids felt heavy. I could barely keep my eyes open as I yawned.

"Tomorrow, Julian. Right now, I'm taking her home."

I didn't protest when Lucas picked me up and headed for the elevator. Beetle waited on the second floor to whisk us home. I wanted to hug the little car. It felt so good to see her. Instead I gave her crimson side a pat and whispered a hello.

"You're back on the grid, Allie. All you have to do is ask her to come to you." Lucas took my hand as we road along. "I'll get the newest chip embedded in your phone. The one that's in there is already outdated."

As we approached Victorian Village, street lamps lined the avenues—quaint, old-fashion gaslight types. "Why the lights? You can all see no matter what time it is."

"You forget, not everyone's a Niner."

"Oh, right. That's so nice. I saw the lights before. Must have forgotten. Don't know why I'm asking." Babbling and not making sense, I finally dozed off on Lucas' shoulder.

I woke on the sofa in front of the fireplace. Lucas sat at the end of the couch, watching me. "Hey," I murmured as I pushed myself up and brushed my hair back.

"You're one determined girl." Lucas smiled. "We thought we had an intruder until you punched my code in the phone. I knew it was you, but we had to be sure."

"I forgot I had the phone. I'd been using my old one. Thank goodness you gave it to me. I was so afraid I wouldn't find this place before it got dark."

"I would have found you, trust me. I planned to start tracking you within the hour."

I curled up next to him. "Lucas?"

"Yes?"

"Are you happy about the baby? Really?"

"How can you even ask that, Allie? Of course, I am."

"Is there anything I should know?" I lifted my head to look at him.

"What do you mean?"

"About our child ... will he ... or she ... be different or ..."

Lucas chuckled. "Oh, you mean because of me. Well, let's see, he—or she—will be a little smarter, a little stronger and a lot healthier than the ordinary kid."

"I can live with that." I smiled as I fell asleep, dreaming of our life as a family in quaint Victorian Village.

* * * *

Serena, Julian's wife and chief of staff at the hospital, had me sit in a chair resembling one in a dentist's office.

"I'm glad I finally got to meet you. I've heard so much about you." Her eyes, a lovely liquid brown, met mine as she smiled. She was a beautiful African-American woman with sleek, chin length hair parted to one side and perfect make-up.

"The last time I was here, I wanted to be with Lucas. I was much younger then." Immature, I wanted to say.

"Understandable." She nodded as the chair tilted me back.

Still fully clothed, Serena placed a screen over my abdomen, punched some buttons and entered something on a small hand-held computer.

"Done!" She brought the chair upright and sat down next to me. "Any questions?"

"That's it?" I wrinkled my brow.

"Yep." She held out her hands. "Easy, wasn't it?"

Behind her I saw a photo of two smiling little girls, dressed alike, and gestured toward it. "Are those your girls?"

"The twins! Yes, they are." She reached for the picture frame. "This is Sophie, named after Julian's mother, and the other is Kristina."

"Beautiful names! The girls are darling. How old are they?"

"Seven. They're at day camp now, but I'm hoping you'll get to meet them. Julian's so fond of Lucas. They're like brothers."

I thought back to the day Julian had told me his story. The Niners had rescued him from a Southern plantation in the 1800s. His mother, a slave, had known something was wrong when her baby didn't grow like other children and hid him away, claiming he had died. Niner babies grew very slowly and at a year old appear to be about three months old. Fearing for her child's life, she gladly handed him over to the men who promised to raise him when they showed up at her door. The Niners eventually came back for the rest of his family.

Julian had been brought up in the Pennsylvania compound, Patriot Village. He'd met his first wife there and she'd helped design Victorian Village when Julian became leader of the new Montana compound. Now he had a second life with a new wife and children.

Serena leaned back in her chair. "Do you want to hear about your baby?" She smiled like we were old friends.

"Yes, of course. I'm just a little scared."

"That's very natural, but, you know if you have your baby here there will be less to worry about."

"Really?"

"Yes, I had the girls here. It was still a long process, but little pain." She put out her hand.

"Let me have your phone. I'll put everything you need to know on it. Your due date is March fourth, give or take a few days. I already sent the date and the information to Lucas. We like the fathers to be informed, too."

"Great." I nodded. "Serena, before I go, would you mind telling me how you and Julian met? What's life like as a Niner's wife?"

"Sure, I'd be happy to, but there's not much to tell." She shrugged. "I interned at a hospital in Pennsylvania when Julian's son was brought into the emergency room after a car accident." She paused when I gave her a questioning look. "Atticus still lives in P.A. Julian visits him often, and after the breach here, we lived with him for three years."

I remembered that the Montgomerys had traveled to Pennsylvania back in high school due to a security issue at the safe house in Virginia. Lucas never told me they had to leave, and I nearly lost my mind when I discovered he was gone. I thought I'd lost Lucas forever, but I'd been wrong. He'd come back to me. From then on, I made Lucas promise to keep me informed of any and all decisions. I never wanted to be in that much pain again …until I sent him away for good.

Serena continued, "When Julian arrived at the hospital to see Atticus, I thought *he* was the son, not the other way around. He asked me out while we were wheeling Atticus to the car after treatment, and we've been together ever since."

"When did he tell you he was a Niner?"

"The day he asked me to marry him. I had no idea until then! Funny how they have to look in the real world for a mate. There's no Niner women. Maybe there's a reason for that." She giggled. "Julian knew I had to make a decision whether I could live this kind of life, but I have no regrets. I know he'll be with me till the end and be there for the girls. I take it one day at a time. I don't think about the future. I just live in the present, as I suggest you do, too."

"Thank you." I put my out hand. She took it and pulled me to my feet. "Now go find Lucas and celebrate! Oh! By the way, it's a boy! Congratulations!"

"You know already?"

Serena nodded. "Sorry, did you want to know? I guess I was excited for you."

"I think I wanted to know." I smiled. "Don't be sorry." I gave her a hug and headed for the exit where Beetle patiently waited.

"It's a boy," I whispered to the car. A slight shudder of the engine made me think she approved. *Take me to Headquarters.*

Beetle zipped along the streets, sometimes elevating over the roofs of houses. I think she was excited. We flew into the building, and she stopped in front of the elevator.

"Thanks." I patted her side expecting her to take off and park. "You don't have to wait. I'm fine." She hesitated for a moment and seemed to let out a sigh.

"Go on." I laughed.

As I stepped out of the elevator, I spotted Sean, Julian and Lucas in the lounge area. "Surprise!" I held up my hands. "It's a boy," I said, expecting applause or congratulations, anything but the somber faces staring back at me.

"Allie, sit down." Julian gestured to a place next to Lucas. "We need to talk."

"You're scaring me, Julian."

"It's not as bad as he's making it sound." Lucas pulled me close at I sat. "Right, Julian?"

"Allie, I want to be honest with you." Julian folded his hands and leaned forward. "Your due date is March fourth of next year. You could be early or late. Do you know what next year is?"

"Um … a new decade?" I had no idea what he meant.

"Leap Year." My stomach did a flip, and my heart beat faster. "There's a possibility your baby could be born on February twenty-ninth, Allie."

"Is there something we can do to stop it from happening?" I instinctively placed my hand on my stomach.

"We don't interfere with Mother Nature." Lucas hugged me. "There's something more we need to tell you." He nodded at Julian to continue.

"A Niner father rarely has a son born on the same day, but when it does happen the child has even more powers than the father. All of our qualities are heightened times two or as we call it—twenty-nine squared. Niner-squared."

"What about Doug?" It was the only thing that came to mind when Julian said my son would be twenty-nine squared.

Doug longed to get his hands on Lucas and other Niners so he'd never stop until he had his nephew in his possession once he found out. The nightmares I'd had for the last two years could possibly come true. Doug wanted something I had, and now I finally knew what it was. Not Lucas as I first thought, but my unborn child, one I didn't know existed at the time. I'd never shared those dreams and didn't intend to now. All I knew is that I had to keep my baby safe.

I turned to Lucas with tears in my eyes. "I hate him." He understood the meaning as I'd said it a million times over the year we were together.

"We'll do everything we can to protect the baby and you." Lucas kissed the side of my head. "And remember it's just hypothetical. The baby may be born March fourth, and we won't have to worry about any of this."

I knew what I needed to say next, in front of witnesses. "And you promise to be here for him, no matter what, whether he's an ordinary child or Niner-squared? He'll need you after I'm gone more than ever. Do you promise?"

"Of course, I promise." Lucas looked at me and frowned.

"We have to protect our son from now on." I announced. I had this overwhelming sense of protection and knew I would do anything to guard this baby from harm.

"Allie," Julian said gently, "There's one more thing. When we say the child will do everything times two, we mean aging, too. He will age every two years, not four."

"I don't understand." I shook my head. "I finally learned the ways of the Niners and now you're changing the rules on me?"

But the more I thought about it, the more I liked that idea. My baby would be two years old on his next leap year birthday instead of one. I wouldn't be an old woman still waiting for my child to grow up.

"I want you to meet someone, Allie. It may help you feel better." Lucas got up and walked through the maze of technology stations. He returned with a tall, blonde, muscular man with chiseled features. Good looking, like all Niner men.

"Allie, this is Rik. He used to be on Doug's Special Team."

My stomach flipped, my heart slammed against my chest and I froze. Hearing "Special Team" brought back memories of my kidnapping. Doug held me prisoner in an old motel outside of our hometown. I'd overheard my captors talk about the Niners who worked for the STF, calling them the Special Team. The guards didn't know their real identity. They just thought they were smart. I'd passed the information along to Lucas after I was rescued.

One of them must have defected—Rik—and he now stood before me.

"Julian was able to contact Rik and met with him," Lucas said. "Rik decided the STF wasn't for him, after hearing our story, and left. He had no idea Doug had been hunting down Niners to join the ranks. He's a wanted man now, and we're doing everything we can to protect him."

"You knew my brother, I take it," I asked out of curiosity.

"Yes, he's a dedicated soldier, believes in the cause." Rik had an accent which I tried to place.

Lucas noticed and said, "He's Dutch. Do you remember me telling you about Abraham? Abe, as we called him? Born in the Netherlands, he was the founder of the Niner compounds in America. He brought Rik to the states after one of his trips back home."

"Yes, I remember Abe. He was like a grandfather to you." I took Lucas' hand. "I'm sorry he passed away, but he lived a long time, right?"

Rik laughed, but it had a sarcastic tone. "Long time? You're well-schooled in Niner history, Allison. Yes, Abe lived to the ripe old age of one hundred and twelve in Niner years. My father would say he lived a long and productive life."

Father? He considered Abe his dad? I did a quick calculation in my head. Abe died at the age of four hundred and forty-eight real years, somewhat young for a Niner.

"He was a father to many, not just you, Rik." Julian stood and faced him. "Abe would be pleased you found your way back to us."

"I had nothing left in Montana after he died."

"You had us. Your brothers." Julian crossed his arms. "Will you ever accept that we are your family?"

Rik sighed and dropped his shoulders. "I'm sorry, Julian. You're right. I always had to fend for myself until Abe found me. When I lost him, I felt alone in the world again. Joining the army and working my way up the ranks gave me purpose. When I qualified for the secret ops program, I found myself again. I felt I belonged."

I'd been sitting quietly listening, but now had questions. "Rik? How did Doug know you were a Niner?"

"Army intel has grown in the new century, Allison. Niners in any branch of the armed services were tagged and brought in for testing."

Tagged and tested? Sounds so scientific. I shivered as I thought of what could happen to Lucas. "How did that happen?"

"Records going back to World War Two showed that certain men were stronger, faster and needed little or no sleep. All of their birthdays were February twenty-eighth or March first, the dates we Niners use. The records were computerized in the 21st century and new technology found the similarities in the group. Doug Sanders volunteered to head the committee to find out more about us."

I just bet he did. "Does he know Lucas is a Niner?"

"Not really. Lucas was on Cap's list though. You should know that. I believe you were kidnapped because of it."

I hoped my fear didn't show. Rik called me Allison twice, like Doug would have. Now he referred to Doug as Cap, a friendly term. If he didn't trust him, why would he still speak of Doug that way?

"I'm afraid Cap hasn't given up looking for Lucas." Rik's words jarred me from my thoughts.

"What? Does he know about this place?" I asked.

"No, he doesn't. The STF Niners will never reveal the compound locations. It's part of the deal."

Mistrust grew inside me. "Why did you *really* leave the STF, Rik?"

Rik threw his head back and laughed. "You are a persistent one. I became disillusioned and wondered why more Niners didn't sign on. The other four and I had sent word that we were treated well, and there were no negative undertones to the secret force. We were working on something big and it could change the world, but we needed more help."

I held back a shiver. *I know what it is, Rik, and so does Lucas. Doug's looking for an antidote to the nuclear bomb. It would make him the most powerful man in the world.*

Doug had worked hard to get me on his side when I was in high school. He preached loyalty and country, but I didn't buy it. I had a strange feeling it went beyond patriotism. Doug's words always stayed with me. "Sometimes there has to be war before there is peace, Allison." My stomach lurched as I recalled his frightening motto. I snapped back to attention as I realized Rik was still talking, fighting the bile rising in my throat.

"I guess I was brainwashed and thought I was helping the country. But when I heard Doug used his own sister to flush out Lucas? That was the final blow. We weren't humans to him, just robots. I left, and Julian welcomed me back with open arms. End of story."

I turned to Lucas, suddenly wanting to leave. "Would you mind taking me home? I've had quite a day. Thanks for everything." I stood and hugged Sean and Julian then shook hands with Rik.

Lucas took my hand as we headed for the elevator. "Are you okay?" he asked. "Our exit seemed so abrupt."

"We'll talk in the car." I was aware of Niner hearing. Beetle pulled up and soon we zoomed toward the village.

"She's faster than I remember." I looked over at Lucas and saw him laughing.

"Upgrades, Allie, always working on upgrades."

"Lucas, do you trust Rik?"

"Yeah, why?"

"Well maybe your 'born a Niner, die a Niner' club is too close to see it, but I don't trust him. How do you know he's not a plant?"

"Julian would never had let him back in. I'm sure he did an extensive interview and evaluated him carefully."

"Hmm."

"Tell me why you don't trust him."

"He left the STF too easily. Think! Four Niners stayed. If there are only five of them, wouldn't they have been a tight knit group and confided in each other? Leave together? If Rik had doubts, why didn't they all have them?"

"You bring up a good point. I'll talk to Julian."

"I don't want to go against the Niner code or anything." I teased. "Just be careful. He's been on the outside for a long time. His loyalties are split. Did you notice he called my brother Cap? That's a nickname. Something you use when you're fond of someone."

"I never thought of that. See, we need you in our lives. We're too sequestered and need some fresh thinking."

Beetle pulled into the drive, and I was happy to see the barn-red Victorian house again. It had been dark when we arrived last night. I'd felt too tired this morning to look around so now I took everything in—the wide front porch that wrapped around the side of the house, the white swing in the corner, the gingerbread in the peaks of the house. Lucas rushed around to my side of the car, lifted me out and carried me up the porch stairs. I tried to protest but didn't really have the strength. He crossed into the house and up the flight of stairs to his bedroom.

"You need to rest."

"Stay." I reached out, and he slid onto the bed, snuggling close. We couldn't resist each other. I felt his lips on mine, soft and gentle. My head spun with happiness as I tugged at his shirt. I wanted to feel his skin against mine, not wanting to wait any longer to make love.

Afterward, as we lay in each other's arms, I asked, "What are we going to name the baby?"

"If you don't mind, I'd like to name him after my father. Zakary."

"Zak, I like it. And his middle name can be my father's. James."

"Zakary James," Lucas kissed me. "I like it, too."

We slept entwined in each other's arms, exhausted from the last twenty-four hours. When I woke, sunshine poured through the window. At least I hadn't slept the day away but knew it must be close to dinnertime. Lucas was gone so I slipped out of bed and over to my suitcases, opening the one on top. A little blue teddy bear was nestled in my clothes with a heart around its neck that said, "I love you."

"How did Lucas get you in my luggage so quickly?" I laughed. "Never mind. I already know the answer. He barely sleeps and has hours to do things." Apparently, he hadn't slept as much as I'd thought. I smiled to myself.

I needed fresh clothes, pulling some from the open suitcase. After changing, I headed for the stairs and heard a woman's laugh float up them. I stopped in my tracks. "No, it can't be." I flew down the stairs to see if it was true.

Chapter Six

"Ashley?" I ran to her.

Her hazel eyes shone with excitement. "Yep! It's me." She tossed her silky dark brown hair over her shoulder. "Surprise!"

I grabbed her into a huge bear hug. Nate joined in, and we hugged and talked at the same time. "Wait!" I held up my hand. "Everyone, sit down. I can't understand a thing you're saying."

"Let me start." Ashley pleaded, looking at Nate and Lucas. "Nate got a call from Lucas yesterday asking if he'd come to Montana. He told him about the baby. I'm so excited for you! Congrats! Have you picked a name? Do you know your due date? Are you going back to school?"

Old habits died hard for Ash. She always asked multiple questions without waiting for the answers, as I fondly recalled from high school. I used to drive her crazy by giving yes and no answers, but now I gave her the answers she wanted. "We already know the sex of the baby and picked the name. We're going to use both our fathers' names—Zakary James. I'm due March fourth and yes, I'm going back to school."

"Well, maybe not." Lucas said. I drew my brows together as I looked his way. "You may have to take some on-line classes here until the baby's born, then we'll go back."

Ash touched my arm. "When Nate heard about the baby, he knew you needed me, Allie. He asked Lucas if he could tell me about the Niners. He knew I could be trusted."

"Or I kill you." Nate grabbed her around the waist.

"That, too." Ashley giggled as she leaned against him then her expression changed. "I always felt vaguely left out, and now I know why. I wish I'd known sooner, maybe I'd done things differently." She hung her head.

"Aww, I don't want you to feel bad." I patted her arm. "I had to keep it a secret. You can see why."

"Well, I know everything, and I hate Doug, too," Ashley said. "When we're back home, I'll do everything I can to help you."

"Thanks." I fought back tears. "And sorry we can't room together fall quarter."

"Nate and I will be fine. Lucas is leaving everything in his apartment for us."

"Dinner's ready," Lucas announced and led us to the kitchen. He opened the transporter which looked like a microwave.

"You microwaved dinner? How sweet." Ashley teased as she settled in at the high-top table.

"Nope." I shook my head. "That's the food transporter. Lucas placed his order on the phone. It's sent through that." I pointed at the transporter with my fork. "Don't worry, Ash, I thought the same thing when I first saw it. A microwave."

She wrinkled her nose and nodded at the black box. "You're telling me that someone made food and shot it through space to that thing?"

'Something like that." Lucas opened the door to the small appliance. "Fresh and hot." He placed plates of steaming pasta and cold, crisp salads in front of us.

"Enjoy."

During dinner Lucas explained the inner workings of the house. "I think it might be easier to show you," he said as we finished. "Follow me."

"Wait! Shouldn't we clean up?" Ashley glanced around the room. "Or is there some type of robot for that?"

"I'll show her. You and Nate go ahead." I opened the dishwasher and pulled out its numerous drawers. "Just put everything in here."

"That's it?" Ashley's eyes widened. "I could get used to this."

After cleaning up, we headed to the great room on the other side of the kitchen. Lucas demonstrated how the picture above the fireplace dissolved into a flat screen TV. I started to tell them about the giant white wall located on the opposite side of the room, but Lucas stopped me.

"There have been improvements since you've been here."

"You just have to think commands as long as you have your phone with the chip inside." Nate patted his pocket. "Everything's done telepathically, just like Beetle."

I raised my eyebrows but said nothing. "Can you still go anywhere in the world?"

Lucas put his arm around me. "Of course. Anywhere you want to go."

I wrapped my arms around his waist and gazed up at his smiling face. "Let's take them to Paris then I'd like some girl time. Maybe you and Nate can find something to do?"

Lucas pressed his lips together. "I guess so."

"Not for long." I kissed him on the cheek. When I pulled back, I hoped he'd see it in my eyes. I needed to talk to Ashley alone. "It's wonderful having them here."

"Motorbikes," Nate called out. "I'm in."

Lucas walked up to the wall and swept his hand across the wide screen. "Paris?"

"Wait!" I was confused. "I thought you said no more verbal commands or punching codes into your phone? You think the command in your head."

"You still can punch in codes or say commands if you're old school." Lucas winked. "The old Niners protested so we haven't completed the upgrades. They had problems switching to the new technology." He pointed to his phone. "The chip picks up our brainwaves just like Nate said. Think your command, and it happens. Everything works like that now."

I grabbed a blanket and spread it on the floor. Lucas strolled to his refrigerated wine cabinet. He deftly grabbed four long stem glasses from the shelf above, a bottle from the fridge and handed them to Nate. "I had to place an order for sparkling juice."

He returned to the cooler and took out another bottle. "This one's for you, Allie. I didn't have any in stock." He patted the top of the cooler. "My wine transporter."

As he settled back on the blanket, I took the juice bottle from his outstretched hand. The label had the familiar sketch of a beautiful woman with *Bella* written in script across the top and *Napa Valley, California* scrawled across the bottom edge.

"Lucas, this label has an old-world flavor to it."

"Listen to my art history major." Lucas nodded in approval. "You're right. It's a drawing of Levi's mother. He sketched her from memory." Lucas took the bottle from my hand and opened it. "The winery's named after her."

"Levi?" Ashley looked at me.

"Oh, sorry. Levi's in charge of the whole western region of the United States and lives in the California compound. I've never met him. He's two hundred years old, our time." I held up two fingers and giggled.

Ashley shook her head. "Still hard for me to process."

"I know. These Niners live a long time. I used to tease Lucas he was a vampire without the teeth."

"Hey!" Lucas gently poked me in the side.

I faced him. "Tell me, my vampire lover, Levi makes wine?"

He opened his mouth as wide as he could and came straight for my neck.

"Lucas!" I held up my hands, holding back a laugh. "I'm sorry. I won't call you a vampire again."

He gave my neck a feather kiss and said, "The California compound is outside of Napa. Their vineyard is a cover but also the family business. His wife owns and operates the winery. I must admit they make great wine. Their dry red is my favorite."

I turned to Nate. "The wine you gave me at school had this same label. I was always mesmerized by the woman."

Nate nodded. "Lucas brought me cases of the stuff. I thought it only fair to share with you."

'Fifty! He's fifty!" Ashley shouted, quite off topic. "Oh, sorry, I figured out how old Levi was in Niner years." She reached for the bottle and studied the label. "Levi didn't have a photo of his mother?"

"You have to remember he was born long ago, Ash, and may never have had one." I answered. My friend sat opposite me, comfortable in this new world, being her old Ashley self, asking questions. I loved her so much at that moment.

"Yeah, I'm having a hard time getting used to it." Ash rubbed her forehead. "So, Levi's really fifty even though he's lived two hundred years?"

"Yep, you'll do a lot of multiplying and dividing by four," I said.

"So next year, Leap Year, he'll be fifty-one or two hundred and four. Lucas," Ashley said as she pointed at him. "You'll be eighty-four!"

"Twenty-one actually. He'll stay that age for another four *long* years." I joked. Then it dawned on me in a few years, I'd be older than Lucas.

"Age doesn't matter." Lucas held up his glass.

"Easy for you to say!" Nate touched his glass to Lucas' as we all laughed.

"Lucas? Is that your phone?" I thought I heard a chime. "Seems like old school." I nudged him with my elbow.

"I programmed it that way. You can also set it so you're the only one who hears it." He glanced down at the screen. "Excuse me for a minute." On his return, I noticed he didn't look as relaxed.

"Allie, can I talk to you?" He motioned for me to come into the other room.

I shook my head. "Lucas, I think we better get used to being a team of four. If it's something we all need to know, tell me here."

He sat back down on the blanket, looking serious. "Julian's talked to Levi. They decided to transfer Rik to Napa."

"Rik?" Nate looked at us for an explanation.

"Erik Van Aken," Lucas said. "A Niner who used to be part of Doug's special task force and defected last year. Julian had been trying to contact the STF Niners ever since Allie gave us that information."

"Now I'm confused." Ashley held up her hand.

Nate scooted closer to her and wrapped his arm around her shoulders. "I never got to that part of the story." He looked at me. "I tried to fill her in on as much as I could on the plane." He faced Ash. "Remember I told you that Doug kidnapped Allie?"

"You mean the made-for-TV movie you told me?"

"Yeah, that one." Nate nodded. "When Allie was inside the motel she overheard her two guards talking outside the room. They mentioned the Niners, but not by name, and she realized Doug didn't tell them everything. They had no idea that Doug had taken Allie because he was looking for Lucas and other Niners."

"So," Lucas said. "We wanted to pass along the information to Doug's Niners. We thought they deserved to know. Rik was the only one who left the task force. Allie pointed out that it seemed strange he was the only one who left. The Niners should be a close-knit group, make decisions together. Rik also called her brother, Cap, instead of Captain Sanders or even Doug. Levi thinks it best if he's not around Allie. Rik already knows she's pregnant and could be gathering information. Levi will put him to work stomping grapes or something in Napa. He'll keep an eye on him." Lucas smiled as he tried to lighten the mood.

"If they think he's a spy, why not let him fend for himself? Make him leave." Ashley crossed her arms and frowned.

"Well, it doesn't work that way," Lucas answered. "We always take care of our own, good or bad. We're not perfect. Rik was born in the Netherlands and put in an orphanage. He never knew his real parents or where he came from. No one really paid attention to him or his growth rate. Eventually he was turned out on the street at the age of seven, in Niner years, to fend for himself. They felt he must be done growing and had to be a man by then. Funny thing is, even though we're smart, our emotional growth matches our real age. We need guidance like any kid. He lived on the streets until he was twelve. That's when Abe found him."

"Abe?" Nate and Ashley said at the same time.

"He's passed on. He only got four hundred plus years on earth." Lucas hung his head. "Not fair for someone as compassionate as he was."

"Fair?" Ashley tried to hide the surprise in her voice.

"Ash," I said. "Most Niners live longer than that, over six hundred years."

"Oh." Her face went blank.

"Abe established the American compounds in the late 1700s. He became like a grandfather to this one." I pointed at Lucas.

"Abe liked to make trips back home to Europe," Lucas continued. "The Netherlands was a favorite since he was born there. His family had a portrait done by Rembrandt."

"Rembrandt!" Ashley gasped and covered her mouth.

"I'll take you to the archive museum where we house lots of Niner memorabilia, and you can see it." Lucas took a sip of wine, seeming very pleased.

I poked him in the arm. "Are you holding out on me? There's a museum full of art?"

"I told you there was a lot you missed on your first visit. There are still secrets to reveal."

"Very cryptic, my man." Nate leaned over the blanket and slapped hands with Lucas.

"Levi has doubts about Rik?" Inwardly, I rejoiced.

"Yes, he does. He knows Rik's background. The only person he had strong ties to was Abe. The only other bond he made was with his new country. He was always very patriotic and defensive about his new home. After nine-eleven he joined the military. He's been away from the Niners for over thirty years, left right after Abe's funeral. We heard he was contacted by the STF and asked to become part of the special force about ten years ago."

"Ten years ago? Doug returned home from overseas," I said. "I was told I'd see him more often, but he probably came home to take command of the STF. I remember waiting for him to show up for my birthdays, but he never did." I shook my head.

"Allie, that's so sad, but remember—" Ashley held up her glass, and everyone joined her. "We hate Doug."

"With that," Lucas announced. "Nate and I will let you have your girl time. I want him to get some riding in before dark. Although I could keep riding, it might be a little dangerous for him." Lucas winked as he got up, and Nate followed him out the door.

"Have fun you two," Ashley called after them.

I waited until the front door shut, and Beetle had whisked them away. "Ash, I'm so glad you're here. I know the Niners don't want too many people on the outside knowing about them. I don't know how they keep everyone from telling the world about them."

"It's a big family, Allie. That could be the reason. I feel honored to be a part of this and would never tell. I'll always protect you, Lucas and my soon-to-be little nephew." She reached out and patted my stomach.

"You and Nate will be the godparents." Suddenly I wanted to talk about the baby but didn't know if Ashley felt the same.

"Nate says there are stores here in the village. Let's baby shop tomorrow."

"And we can do some shopping on the wall." We grabbed each other's hands in the excitement of the moment. Then Ashley's expression changed.

"What? What is it?" I screamed.

"Calm down. I need to tell you something. Swear you won't tell Nate."

"I swear."

"Remember our conversation about me seeing someone?"

"I think you told me you went out with a guy once, and it felt wrong."

"Well, I lied. Back then I felt like Nate was seeing other girls behind my back. Now I know he hung out with Lucas and couldn't tell me. He never was specific about what he was doing in LA or who his friends were. I was alone and thought I should just get on with my life. I started seeing this guy. It was casual at first, just hanging out but we got a little serious."

"How serious?"

"I slept with him one time. When you called I wanted to tell you but lost my nerve. I was afraid you might tell Nate, and I'd lose him forever. My life would be over." Ashley began to cry.

My heart broke for her. "I'd never tell him. I completely understand."

"You do?"

"Yes, I felt like I cheated on Lucas when I dated Will."

"Did you sleep—?"

"No! But I was going to until Lucas showed up at my door."

"You have to tell me all the details."

Ashley and I talked for over an hour about my time with Lucas in LA, and how I drove through the pine forest to get here.

"Props to you for driving alone. It was confusing enough with two of us in the car." Ashley sounded better after her confession. "Allie, to change the subject, I do have a serious question. What are you going to tell your parents?"

"When I go home this month?" I rubbed my cheek. "Nothing. I'm not showing, and no one needs to know I'm pregnant. Lucas and I haven't discussed what I should say or do."

"I have an idea for when the time comes. Tell your family it's Will's baby, the two of you broke up then you discovered you were pregnant. Happens *all* the time." She rolled her eyes.

I had to laugh. "Does it?" I mulled over what she'd said. "I don't think I told my parents Will's last name. No one could track him down to make him do the right thing."

"Well, he'd be a little shocked to hear he's a father when you never slept with him." Ashley giggled. "But from what you told me, he'd step up and marry you."

My heart sank when I thought of Will. "Yes, he would," I whispered.

"You still care about him, don't you?"

"Not in the madly in love kind of way, but yes, I do. I wish him the best and hope he finds happiness."

"You'd do just about anything to protect this baby, right?"

"If I have to, yes, but let's not go there. This could turn out to be a perfectly normal baby born in March." I hung my head. Now it was my turn to cry.

"I didn't mean to upset you." Ashley crawled over and sat closer to me. "Come on, let's sit on the couch. You can tell me what's bothering you."

As we climbed up on the sofa, I didn't know if I could explain in words what swirled through my brain. "I know this will sound dumb." I hesitated. "Imperialism."

"That's what's bothering you?" Ashley suppressed a smile.

"Yes, it means to have power over others in the interest of domination."

"Wow, that's deep. You're worried about that?"

"Think about it, Ash. *Doug*, the *STF*, what do they want?"

"Oh, I see what you mean. They want to take over the Niners and rule them."

"Exactly. Now I have one more fear."

Ashley looked like she was afraid to ask.

"You know how people act when they discover gold or oil or any precious metal? Something that's rare? They celebrate and know they'll become rich and maybe even famous. More people come and want in on those riches and will do anything to get their hands on even a little piece of it. Doesn't money and power rule the world?"

"Yeah, I never thought of it that way."

"If this baby is born on Leap Day, he becomes that precious commodity, something people want. If word got out, he won't be viewed as human, but something that can be used to achieve those goals."

"Do you think that's how Doug sees the Niners?" Ashley sat quietly for a moment. "That's scary. Make that, *Doug's* scary." She shivered. "If he finds out about the baby, he'll become all the more vigilante. The baby would be a star among the diamonds."

"Exactly, you get my point. The baby will age every two years, not four, and if Doug found out, he'd want to raise my baby himself."

"All the more reason to say it's Will's."

"Not while I live and breathe." Lucas' voice shot through the room. "Doug will die first."

Chapter Seven

Alone in the bedroom, I tried to explain the conversation to Lucas.

"You didn't hear how we ended up at that conclusion. Well, her conclusion." I told Lucas my thoughts and fears from the evening, and his face softened.

He sat on the edge of the bed and pulled me down next to him. "You're the best thing that's ever happened to me, Allie. I never thought of our struggle as imperialism. It's a good way to describe the Niner situation with the STF. I can see why you want to protect Zakary, but let's wait and see if we need to. Deal?"

"Aww, you called him Zakary. That's so cute." I patted his cheek.

"How about if we focus on him for a while and not try to conquer the world just yet?" Lucas kissed me. "You need some sleep, and I need to go to Headquarters."

"No. Stay." I grabbed his arm. Suddenly I was afraid again. "I only feel safe when you're nearby."

"Allie, you are safe, but I'll stay until you fall asleep. Remember, Nate and Ashley are here."

"Let's discuss what we'll do next. Ashley's right, Lucas. We need a plan. I can't go home after this visit. I can have the baby here. My parents won't know about him."

"That would be a big secret to keep. Let me discuss it with Julian. We'll talk in the morning."

"You'll be here when I wake up?"

"Promise. And we'll shop for the baby."

"Now you sound like Ashley." I teased. Lucas lifted me up and placed me on my side of the bed, covering me with a blanket. "I love you, Lucas Montgomery."

"I love you, too." He kissed my cheek and flicked off the light. We spooned in the darkness, my body fitting perfectly against his. My head swam with frightening scenes of which I had no control. Lucas must be in the same mindset. He squirmed around as if he couldn't get comfortable.

"Go to Headquarters. I'll be up all night at this rate." I laughed and gave him a nudge.

"A promise is a promise. I'll try harder to keep still."

He became so still I had trouble telling if he was breathing, but I drifted off to sleep and never knew he left. I woke with a start the next morning and ran for the bathroom. My stomach rolled over. Nausea consumed me. "Somebody!" I managed to call before I retched in the toilet.

Ashley burst into the bathroom. "I'll get someone. Hang in there." I glanced up just in time to see her roll her eyes. "Teenage pregnancy!"

I didn't know how long I sat on the bathroom floor until Serena appeared, crouching next to me. She placed a small rubber ball in my hand. "Squeeze this." She put her hand on top of mine and helped me pump the orb. My stomach calmed. The nausea subsided.

I took a breath, finding my voice. "What is this?" I held out my hand. The tiny blue ball sat in my palm.

"It's our morning sickness ball. Keep it on you at all times. When you feel a wave come over you, start squeezing. It works miracles."

I stood up, feeling better. Serena handed me a glass of water. "Drink." She guided me back to the bedroom and sat me on the bed.

"Thanks, Serena."

"Call anytime, that's what I'm here for." She brushed my hair back from my face. "You're holding up well after hearing you could have a Niner baby. And, by the way, Lucas apologizes for leaving. He was here but didn't think you saw him."

I could only nod as I recovered from hurling in the toilet. Thank goodness I wouldn't have to go through that again.

"Ashley told me you're going shopping today. Stop by the park and meet the girls if you have time. We're having lunch and playtime between my shifts at the hospital." She headed for the door and turned back. "Really, Allie, it's going to be okay." Her eyes held a look of compassion, and I knew I could trust her.

After I dressed, I hurried downstairs to find Ashley eating breakfast alone.

"Hey, thanks for the help." I squeezed the ball as the smell of her food reached my nose. I settled in on the couch, waiting for her to finish.

"Serena says you have to start eating breakfast, Allie." Ashley appeared with a bowl of oatmeal loaded with fruit.

I picked around the oatmeal and begin to eat the fruit. "Where's Nate?" I asked.

"Never came home. He called to say he'd get some sleep at Headquarters." I pictured him curled up on the white leather couch, and Lucas putting a blanket over him. "He said we should do what we want today. They'll see us at dinner."

"Let's have some fun then." Excitement took over the feeling of dread. "Ash? First, I have a question. What day is it?"

Ashley let out something between a snort and a giggle. "July third. We're flying home on the fifth."

"I need to call my mom."

"It's done. I called your mom before Nate and I left Virginia. I said we were flying out to California to keep you company and bring you home. She knows all the flight details and will probably be at the airport to greet you. So be ready."

"As long as Doug isn't with her." I shuddered as I set the bowl on the table. "Come on. I want you to love this place like I do."

"I'm ready to pick out a house!" Ash pumped her fists.

"Really?" I studied my friend. She'd embraced this life as quickly as I had. I believed we could do anything as long as we stuck together.

"Julian said Nate and I could pick out a house if we wanted. Blue flags mean they're available."

"We have to be neighbors. Let's look on the way."

We started out the door, arm in arm, across the brick street made of recycled tires. A side street perpendicular to our house would take us to Main. Ashley couldn't make up her mind which house she liked better as we walked. A pale yellow home with a white wrap-around porch with gingerbread trim caught her eye. Then she changed her mind when she came to one painted in earth tones—hunter green with sienna red trim. A plain blue flag flew at both homes. It would be great to have Ashley and Nate live down the street.

"You'd really consider living here?"

"Heck, yeah!"

"And what if you have children?"

"We don't have to go there yet. I'd consider being an adoptive Niner parent first."

"What?" Ashley seemed to know more than I did. "Did you read a handbook or something?"

Ashley laughed. "No, but that would be a good idea. I'll have to suggest it."

"So how did you find out about adoption?"

"You know me. I ask a lot of questions."

"No kidding. I guess it comes in handy sometimes. So what did you find out?"

"Sometimes parents don't want to live here, especially if they have other children. But they want their Niner baby protected. Families in the village volunteer to raise the child. The boys still see their birth parents but live here. Those boys are more like foster children."

I was surprised to hear that, but on the other hand, it made sense. I'd do anything to protect my son, too.

"Abe established the program after returning from Europe with Rik. He saw the need and began recruiting families instead of just having Niner men raise the Niner children left in their care. And if they have no parents like Rik? Adoption is the answer."

"Wow! I'm impressed!" I stopped when we reached Main Street. "When did you have the time to find all this out? You just got here."

"I went to Headquarters with Nate while Lucas was putting you to bed for the night."

"Putting me to bed? I'm not a baby!" I laughed hysterically with my best friend. "I missed you, Ash." I linked arms with her again. "There's a great coffee shop in the square. We can get lunch there."

"Serena said the baby store's across from the playground. Let's go there first." She tugged me in that direction.

We picked out lots of blue clothes at the shop, but I was drawn to the natural colors of cream and green and brown. The sales clerk didn't ask questions, just helped as needed. She packaged everything to be sent to the house.

I dragged Ash to the coffee shop, suddenly craving a fruit smoothie. We ordered salads and headed over to the park to eat at one of the wrought iron bistro tables spread throughout the area. As we were finishing, two adorable little girls ran up to the table. Although they looked identical, they were dressed completely different.

"I bet you're Kristina, and you're Sophie," I said, hoping I'd chosen the right name for the right girl. They giggled and pointed to each other. "Darn! I got it wrong!" I gestured toward Ash. "This is my best friend, Ashley."

The girls giggled again.

"Mind if we join you?" Serena pulled a chair over from another table. "Girls, you can play for ten more minutes then we'll get lunch."

They ran for the swings and Serena arranged her seat so she could see them. "How are you feeling, Allie?"

"Much better, thanks to the ball. It's a lifesaver."

"Did you two shop yet?"

"Yeah, I think Allie bought the store out." Ashley began to clean up our lunch.

"Hey, I'm perfectly capable of cleaning up after myself." I placed my hand over hers.

"I don't mind. Just don't get used to it." She winked.

It was a typical girls' day out. After all I'd been through it felt good to have a normal day. I got to know Serena better as she shared what life was like living at the village. "Pretty normal overall but remember as much as we get to enjoy the technology, they need us. Without us, there'd be no Niners. Women rule." she said with a smile as she finished.

We reached the red Victorian just before dinner. Ashley and I decided to order an upscale meal for the guys and have a cozy dinner. I lit candles and used the good china that I'd ordered from a village shop. The box sat waiting on the porch when we arrived. As I set the table, I saw Beetle fly into the driveway from the front window. "They're here, Ash!"

We both wore sundresses, make-up and had our hair pulled up in high ponytails. It felt summery and fun. Ashley greeted them at the door. She took one look at Nate and ordered him upstairs. "Shower and shave!" His reddish blonde hair, matted to his head, didn't stand up in its usual peaks.

Lucas appeared in better shape, but I pushed him toward the stairs. In less than a half hour they came downstairs, and we led them into the dining room. Nate poured wine and sparkling juice and made a toast.

"To the four of us, a team for life."

After dinner, Lucas ordered dessert, turned on background music and had the fireplace set to no heat. The house was always at a comfortable temperature, no matter what it was like outside.

"Everyone relaxed now?" Lucas sat next to me on the sofa. I glanced over, knowing he was about to change the mood.

"We came up with a plan but will only put the parts we need into motion and only when the time comes." He turned to me. "Allie, you'll leave with Nate and Ashley for Virginia on July fifth. Sean will be on the plane as your bodyguard. I'll be on a private jet at the same time."

"You're coming, too?" I let out a sigh of relief.

"You didn't think I'd let you go without me, did you?" Lucas kissed my shoulder. "I'll live at the old safe house. Sean will open the diner and run it while we're there. It's been closed, supposedly for repairs."

"That's a long time to be closed," Ashley said. "Almost two years. You probably lost all your customers." She paused. "Oh, never mind. You don't really care. It's just a front." She smacked her forehead.

The diner held special memories for me. The Montgomerys had run the restaurant while in Virginia. I loved going there to sit in an out-of-the-way booth and watch Lucas work. After he'd left, the urge to drive to the diner had become overwhelming. I'd sit in the empty parking lot and cry for hours. I knew I should have stayed away but couldn't. Now I could visit again without a heavy heart. Lucas would be in Virginia. When I needed a breather, I could go to one of my favorite places, the Montgomery safe house.

"Ashley, you're going to play the most important part while we're home." Nate said. "You may have to drive Allie around since her Jeep's in California."

"We're in the process of bringing it here and storing it in the parking garage at Headquarters." Lucas informed me.

"I'm sure my parents will let me use one of their cars. I know you have a lot going on at home, Ash," I told her.

"No, this month, you come first. Whatever you need, I'm there."

"Okay, as long as I can give you gas money."

"If that makes you feel better, I accept."

"So that's settled," I said. "Sean and Lucas are coming to Virginia. Ashley and I will be together." I smiled. "That was good news. Dessert?"

Lucas jumped up before I could and placed a platter of baked goods in front of us. Tiny cheesecakes, brownies, cream puffs and chocolate chip cookies sat on the tray.

Nate finished first and set his plate on the table. "Good idea, Lucas. A little sweet before you add the sour."

I looked at both of them. "There's more?"

Lucas pressed his lips together then said, "When we get back from Virginia, Levi wants us to visit the Napa Valley compound. If Rik's a spy he may show his hand, try to contact Doug and let him know you're there. We'll protect you the whole time. We won't stay long. We just need to find out the truth."

"I'm going to be used as bait?" I bit my lower lip and hoped Lucas could see the fear in my eyes.

"If you don't want to—"

"No, we have to do it." I sighed. "It's just that we were having so much fun. It had to be ruined by the reality of Doug. I—"

Everyone joined in, breaking the tension in the room, and yelled "Hate Doug."

"I'm sorry, Allie." Lucas wrapped his arm around me. "It's a necessary evil. But do you know what tomorrow is?"

"Of course, Fourth of July."

"And you'll be my guests for the best party and greatest fireworks show there is. I hope that makes up for what lies ahead."

* * * *

I woke to find Lucas dressed but lying on the bed. I rolled toward him and placed my hand on his chest. "Remember the promise?"

"There's been a lot, refresh my memory."

"To take care of our baby, even after I'm gone."

"Yes."

"I mean it, Lucas. No offing yourself when I die or anything like that. I can't live with knowing you won't be here for Zak."

Lucas sat up, taking me with him. "Whatever makes you think I'd do that?"

"I heard you and Nate discussing it."

"Oh."

"Well?"

"That's a long way off and Zak will be—"

"Stop it! If I thought for one minute you'd leave our son on his own to deal with being a Niner-squared, I'd never forgive you."

"Allie, calm down. I did have those thoughts before the baby. If anything happened to you, I couldn't go on living. But now we have someone else to think about. I can't be selfish anymore. I'll be here for him whether he's a Niner or not."

"That's what I needed to hear." I patted his face then fell into his arms. This could be one of the last times we'd be alone for a while. I wasn't going to waste any more time talking. I got up on my knees and stripped my tank over my head. "Well?"

Lucas' face wore a look of surprise. "Well, what?"

"Do I look pregnant?"

His eyes shone with desire. "You look ... beautiful." He swept me into his arms. I wrapped my legs around his waist as he lowered me onto the mattress.

I took his head in both hands and studied his face, his dark, smoldering brown eyes and the slight smile on his face. I ran my hands down his back and pulled his t-shirt over his head. He sank carefully down onto me, covering me with kisses. "Let's stay like this forever," he whispered in my ear.

I fell asleep after we made love but woke with a start. The bed felt empty. Hopping into the shower, a wave of nausea hit me. I grabbed my little ball and began to squeeze. After drying off, I headed to my luggage. I'd packed a red t-shirt and white shorts to wear on this special day.

When I arrived downstairs, Ashley was working in the kitchen. Lucas and Nate had taken their coffee to the great room. She handed me a bowl of fruit as she came out to join us.

"Have you guys given any thought to getting married and setting a wedding date?" Ashley plopped next to Nate, smiling at me.

"No, it hasn't even crossed my mind." I gave her a wide-eyed stare. *Marriage! Why did she bring that up?*

"Then someone needs to do something about that." Ashley made eye contact with Lucas.

"Ash!" I glared at her. "All in good time. Lucas and I haven't discussed it. Everything happened so fast. And besides maybe he doesn't want to—"

Lucas put up his hand. "Quit talking about me like I'm not here. Ashley, you know we were overwhelmed this past month. We just got back together then Allie shows up here a few days ago telling me she's pregnant. We had a lot of important things to sort out. Of course, I want to marry her, the sooner the better. As a matter of fact, I was going to ask her during the fireworks show."

"And I ruined it!" Ashley smacked herself in the head. "Me and my big mouth!"

"You didn't ruin anything," I assured her. "It will still be romantic. We'll have lots of time to plan because I'm not getting married while I'm pregnant. I want to be able to toast the day with a glass of champagne."

Lucas' eyes widened. "Really? I thought we could marry here when we got back from Virginia." I stared at him not saying a word, and his face fell. "Fine, name the day."

"Well, you said I could go back to school spring quarter, so after that. A June wedding would be perfect." I looked at Ashley. "And I already have my maid of honor."

"And I have the best man." Lucas nodded at Nate. "Then plan to be surprised tonight, Allison Sanders!"

* * * *

We joined Sean, Julian and Serena for a picnic in town square to watch the children parade in patriotic costumes. Old-fashioned games for children and adults were planned afterward. Lucas and I teamed up for the water balloon toss but lost to reigning champions, Julian and Serena. A band played in the gazebo as children danced to the music in the soft grass.

I met a lot of people and hoped I could remember them all. A wonderful elderly couple, the Gilchrists, and their fourteen-year-old son, Ryan, stood out. He was their only child and a Niner. They were so devoted to him, living their lives here so he could be safe.

As we spread the blanket for the fireworks I asked, "Lucas, are the fireworks shot up in the air?"

"Yep. The mountain ranges do a great job of shielding them, but we have a force field on all four sides that blocks sound and the view besides our shield."

"Well then, I'll just enjoy the show."

I found myself surrounded by Kristina and Sophie, one little girl on each side. They leaned their little heads on me and patted my arm like we were the best of friends. As it grew darker, anticipation rose in the crowd. I heard the whoosh of a firecracker as it climbed in the air and burst into an array of colors that were richer and more vibrant than any I'd ever seen. Sparkling stars and rainbows shot across the sky. Flower shapes erupted from the ground, in twinkling rows of splendor. The show lasted over an hour, and I didn't want it to end. The grand finale contained shimmering colors that turned into gold as they fell to earth. As the last boom was heard, I looked over at Lucas, and he was on one knee.

"Allison Sanders, will you marry me?" He opened a black velvet box with an antique engagement ring inside as golden sparkles fell behind him.

I threw my arms around his neck. "Yes! Yes, I'll marry you." Everyone around us clapped. The twins danced around us like fairy creatures celebrating our good fortune. "The ring." I breathed. "It's beautiful."

"It belonged to my mother." He looked at me lovingly. "She hoped one day I would marry and encouraged me to find true love." Lucas slipped the ring on my finger. It fit perfectly.

I turned to Serena as the lights slowly came on around the square, showing her the ring. "I hope you'll allow these two little ones to be my flower girls."

Serena jumped up from her blanket and hugged me. "Of course! They'd love it! Welcome to the family, Allie."

Ashley reached out, and I pulled her into a hug. I wanted to soak up all the love and happiness that I could because I knew what was coming. I had to go home and lie and sneak around, but no one could know about this life, this other world I didn't know existed until a few years ago.

We strolled back to the house, Lucas and I, hand in hand. I enjoyed the gentle night breeze as we walked down Main Street. Nate and Ashley followed after us, and I heard her pointing out the houses she liked. Sean tagged along to take part in the meeting Lucas had called.

"I'll let Julian know you're interested in those two," Lucas gestured toward the houses as he nodded at Nate and Ash.

We made our way up the porch stairs as the lights automatically flicked on, and the door opened. Suppressing a yawn, I longed to head up the stairs to bed but knew final plans had to be made.

"Be prepared for anything," Lucas informed us as we gathered in the great room. "I'm just a call away." He handed Ashley a phone. "This is yours. Nate will help you. There will be time for lessons on the plane."

"I'm sure my mom will ask about Will," I said. "I'll tell her we broke up before I came home. Now that I have the morning sickness ball, no one will suspect I'm pregnant. Not showing at all." I pointed to my stomach waiting for confirmation.

Lucas pulled me close and laughed. "You look fine, beautiful as ever."

"I'll be right next door, so I can come over whenever you need me, little one." Nate had become so serious about Niner business. I hoped he hadn't forgotten his plans to be a famous director. He needed to get back to school and focus on his life.

"Thanks, Nate." I nodded at him. "All of you have been great. I have no doubt you'll help me. My only concern is Doug. I know Mom plans the family barbeque for the end of July. If I can get through that, everything will be fine." I looked at Lucas with half-closed eyes, and as if he read my mind, he announced it was time for bed.

Lucas stood and looked at his Niner friend. "Sean, you will take Allie to the airport. I'll see you in the morning." He glanced around at the rest of us. "He's our support system and security while we're out in the field."

"You make it sound like we're an army or something." Ashley shuddered.

"We have to think like Doug from now on, I'm sorry to say." Lucas shook his head. "Let's hope we don't have to resort to war."

I shivered. "Can we not go there, please?" What I really wanted to say was, "What if the STF won the war?" I had such blind faith in Lucas and the other Niners' ability to protect us, I never considered the alternative. Only I knew the depths Doug would go to get what he wanted. He'd use his family and abuse them, if needed, to accomplish his own goals.

* * * *

Sean arrived bright and early to take me to the airport. As I gazed around the bedroom, silently saying my goodbyes, I looked across the hall at the master bedroom. It took up almost half the upstairs, overlooking the backyard. Lucas' bedroom was in the front of the house and the guest bedroom sat at the end of the hall. I walked over to the master and planted myself in the middle of the floor. "Jack and Jill."

"Allie, what are you talking about?" Lucas stood in the doorway, brows crossed.

"Have you heard of Jack and Jill rooms?"

"No, I have no idea what you're talking about. We're packing and suddenly you're talking about nursery rhymes?"

"Give me a minute. Come in here. You, too, Sean," I said, knowing he could hear me downstairs. He had become a part of our family whether he realized it or not. Sean may be a loner and like to travel the country helping Niners, but I wanted him to feel he had a home with us, too.

I heard his feet on the steps then Sean poked his head in the room. "What's up?"

"I want Zakary right across the hall from us, not down the hall. This room's huge and way too big for a nursery. Is it possible to turn this into two rooms? One for a boy and one for a girl? With a connecting bath in between?"

Sean walked around the area and knocked on a few walls. "I could have this done in a few days."

Lucas gawked at me, mouth opened. "You want more children?"

"Yes, a girl, if possible. Now do you see why they call them Jack and Jill rooms?"

"Yes, and I think it's a great idea. Sean and I will work up some plans while we're in Virginia."

I kissed Lucas, hating to leave, even though I'd see him tonight. "Then I'm ready to go."

"Take care of her, Sean." Lucas called as we headed down the stairs.

Beetle and another car waited in the driveway. Nate and Ashley stowed their things in the new car. Sean and I jumped in Beetle for the drive to Headquarters, then on to the airport in one of the Niner black vans.

When we arrived in Virginia, my parents waited in the baggage claim area. Mom ran toward me with tears in her eyes. "Allie, you look so grown up! You're not my baby anymore." She grabbed me and hugged me tight.

Dad took my bags after we embraced, and we all headed for the parking garage. I hoped I didn't have to discuss anything too serious on the ride home, but Mom peppered me with questions.

"Now what kind of food does Will like? I know I have time to shop before he gets here, so maybe you can share a favorite recipe. I have the guestroom ready. I'm sure he'll be comfortable there. What do you think, Allie?"

Ashley shot me a sympathetic look.

"Mom, I'm so sorry you went to all that trouble. He's not coming."

"Why? Did something happen? We were so looking forward to meeting him."

"We broke up."

"Oh, I'm sorry to hear that. We were so happy for you and you seemed like you were getting back to your old self—"

"Clair." My dad interrupted. "We agreed not to overwhelm Allie and let her live her own life."

"Yes, we did. Sorry, Allie. I was just so excited."

"That's okay, Mom."

We pulled into Nate's driveway first. Ashley and Nate got out, and Nate's parents flew out of the house, arms opened, embracing both. I glanced over at my house and had, somewhat surprisingly, no feelings at all. It was just a house. I didn't miss it, my bedroom or anything about it.

Mom turned in her seat as we pulled out of the Kalas drive and over to ours. "Oh, Allie, I forgot to tell you. Doug's in California and won't get back until the last week of July. I'm glad I planned the family picnic then."

I smiled and nodded, but my stomach churned. It could only mean one thing. Doug knew I was pregnant. Rik must have contacted him, and he went to California to set a plan in motion. I'd just made it easier by coming home. Here I was, a sitting duck, waiting for him to scoop me up. He could kidnap me again and wait for the baby to be born. If Zak was born on February twenty-ninth, Doug would be a witness. If not, we became bait for the Niners, a win-win for Doug and the STF. Bile gurgled in the back my throat. I was going to be sick in the backseat of the car.

When we pulled in, Dad said he'd get the luggage. I headed for the door acting like I couldn't wait to see my bedroom again. I dashed for the stairs, but instead of enjoying the room, I slipped into the bathroom. Falling to my knees in front of the toilet, I threw up, over and over again, and the little ball could do nothing to stop it.

Chapter Eight

"Rik's a traitor," I said as I sipped lemonade on the Montgomery deck, staring out over a lush gorge filled with pines and summer trees. "I knew it all along."

"You've said that for three weeks now, Allie. You need to let it go. We'll take care of him when the time comes."

"How *do* you punish your own?"

"It used to be banishment, but now we quarantine the person."

"How?"

"He's not given access to Headquarters, any technology or permitted to leave the compound. A small chip is placed in the brain, right through the nose, to keep him on the straight and narrow. If he tries to leave or enters Headquarters, an alarm goes off. We go on lockdown until he's found."

"Well, I can't see anyone trying to remove a chip from their brain to escape so I guess it's a smart idea." I shivered.

"We try to be as humane as possible. The Niner can live out his life in whatever village he chooses, but if he tries to remove the chip, he dies."

"Are there any of those Niners around now?"

"Rik would be the first in a long time. We have one living in the Pennsylvania compound, but his crime was much different. He sold a few of our secrets to foreign countries and made quite a bit of money before we caught him. That happened back in the eighties. See? It's been a long time, more than a half century."

"Can we arrange for *Doug* to have a chip shoved up his nose?" We laughed then got back to our lunch. "I love the drawings you and Sean came up with for the baby's room."

"You can start picking furniture and colors. We'll do the rest." Lucas took my hand. "Thank you."

"For what?"

"For all of this—the baby, marrying me, coming back to me." He kissed my hand, ring-less for now.

"Stop, you're going to make me cry. And we're not married yet." I squeezed his hand. "But thanks for distracting me. I don't want to think about the family barbeque tomorrow."

"Remember, you have nothing to worry about. Sean and I will be stationed close to the house. They'll never know we're there. If Doug pulls anything ..." Lucas' face grew red with anger.

"Let's both take deep breaths." I curled my fingers through his. "I admit I'm a little scared."

Lucas lifted my chin, and his lips touched mine. I ran my hands up into his hair and pulled him closer with the kiss ending too soon.

"Instead of going home, why don't we find your bedroom?" I outlined his lips with my finger.

"As wonderful as that sounds, remember we're on a mission. But when we get home, all bets are off." Lucas ran his hands down my arms. "I'll walk you to the car."

I took a deep breath. "Okay." I had to force myself to leave this sanctuary. Anxiety filled me as I thought of what was coming, the dreaded barbeque and Doug.

* * * *

Mom had invited Ashley to the barbeque. She wanted to give her a big send-off like she did when I left for UCLA, bless her heart. She had no idea that Ash and Nate would be at school, and I wouldn't.

I sat on the deck with Dean and Autumn enjoying the sun when Doug arrived. "There she is! The little princess."

A flashback to another time swept through my mind. Doug had carried me, kicking and screaming, to a waiting ambulance and driven away. My heart drummed faster, and I fought to keep my composure. He sauntered toward me, bent down and kissed my cheek.

"Nice to see you again, sister. You're looking quite well, glowing in fact."

Glowing? Is that his way of saying he knows I'm pregnant? "It's probably sunburn. I sat out too long yesterday."

"So, Doug," Mom said. "Tell us about California. Did you get to see any sights? Or was it all business?" She covered her mouth. "Oh, we can't discuss that, can we?"

"It's okay, Mom." Doug kissed her forehead. "No harm done."

I glared at him suspiciously.

Dean offered Doug a beer, and the two headed to the grill to talk with Dad.

"You're still not fond of him, are you?" Autumn whispered to me and gave me a knowing smile.

I returned the smile. The less said the better. I spotted Ashley and Nate cutting across the backyards to join us. Instantly relieved, I bounced down the deck steps to join them. "Don't leave my side. Doug knows. He said I was glowing," I whispered to them.

Ashley nodded, but Nate looked confused. "I'll explain it to you later," she told him as she patted his face.

Mom slid open the back door and stepped out of the kitchen. She carried a huge cake, set it in place and waved for us to come and see. When we reached the table, I stared down at the words written in blue and gold, school colors. "Good Luck at UCLA Allie and Ashley".

"Wow, Mrs. Sanders, thank you!" Ashley hugged her. "It looks so good. Can we eat it now?" Everyone laughed as Dad called out that dinner was ready.

He proudly handed us giant plates filled with steaks and ribs along with corn on the cob. Mom placed a huge bowl of salad on the table along with a basket of wheat rolls. The setting looked so innocent, so picture perfect, just a typical day with the family.

As dinner came to an end, I noticed Nate acted a little strange, fidgeting in his seat, playing with his leftovers. "Nate, I'd love to walk out and see the motorbike trail you're working on."

"Sure, it's not quite done, so I could use your input." He hopped out of his chair. "You, too, Ash."

"What's up?" she asked when we reached the trail. "I'm getting this strange beeping on my phone and can't figure out what I'm supposed to do."

Nate took her cell and showed us the message. Luckily, we were far enough away that no one heard me gasp. Julian had sent an alert. *STF caravan headed south, arrival time, twenty-one hundred hours.*

"Does he ever give up?" I hissed.

"No," Nate said as he nodded toward his yard. "I'm going to slip into my house, discuss this with Lucas and get back to you. Try to enjoy some family time."

Ashley and I strolled back to the deck. My head hurt so badly, I didn't hear a word she said.

"Allie? Did you hear me?"

"I'm sorry. What?"

"We've got to get you out of here. Are you packed?" Ashley gave everyone a huge grin as we climbed the deck stairs. "We're going up to Allie's room for girl time," she said.

"Oh, we have to cut the cake first." Mom jumped up and grabbed the cake knife. She placed large pieces on plates and encouraged everyone to take one. I felt Doug's eyes burning through me as I waited.

"We'll take ours up, Mom." I kissed her cheek, knowing how hard she tried to make us happy.

As soon as we got to my room, my phone rang. Lucas' face appeared on the screen. I couldn't hold back the tears any longer. "I can't be kidnapped again, Lucas. Please tell me you have a plan."

"I do, Allie, but try to calm down. Sean's waiting at the end of the driveway. Have Ashley take your luggage out the front door to the van. You're leaving in an hour on a private plane. Tell the family your flight has been changed. Ashley will back you. She'll say she has to leave to get ready. You announce you're going with her and will leave for the airport from her house. In reality, Sean will be waiting at the end of the street. You'll transfer to the van and drive with him to the airport."

"I get to act as the decoy? This is fun, real espionage." Ashley rubbed her hands together as her eyes widened. "Show's on."

She grabbed my luggage, tiptoed down the stairs and out the front door as I watched from the top of the stairs and held my breath the whole time she was gone. As she reentered the house, Ashley waved for me to join her. I stole down the steps, looking right and left as I went.

"Don't worry, Allie. I'll do the lying for both of us." She reached out and squeezed my hand when I reached her. "Now make a sad face." We put on dejected-looking faces and headed out to the deck.

"Thanks for dinner, Mr. and Mrs. Sanders, but I need to get going. Allie and I just got updates on our phones.

Our flight's been changed to tonight. I have to get home and pack." Ashley gave my mom a hug.

"I'm already packed so I'm going with her and leave from there. I'll say my goodbyes now." I gave Autumn and Dean a collective hug. Over their shoulders I saw the disappointment in my mother's face. She ran towards me, arms opened, to hug and kiss me.

"Oh, those airlines! I wanted you here a few more hours!" Mom wiped a tear from her eye. Dad stood behind her, waiting to say goodbye. As I turned to leave, I bumped right into Doug.

"Escaping so soon?" He engulfed me inside his arms, pulling me close so I got a huge whiff of his cologne. His head dropped so he could whisper in my ear. "We'll meet again very soon, sister dear."

Ashley grabbed my hand as we walked around the house and down the drive to her car. "That confirms it, Allie, he knows. Can you believe he said, 'escaping so soon?'"

"That's not all he said." I confided the rest.

"Is there any love in that man's heart?" Ashley hopped in the car and started the engine. "Look around, see anything or anyone unusual?"

"No, let's get out of here."

A black van was parked on the side of the road close to the end of the street. I called Lucas to make sure it was Sean. Sean jumped from the driver's side and ran to the passenger side of Ashley's car.

"Good thinking, Allie. I'm glad you checked to see if it was me. You're going to be a Niner yet." He gave me a big smile as he opened the door.

I clasped hands with Ashley one last time. "Be careful. Doug may show up at your house."

"Don't worry, I won't be there. Nate's picking me up. We're staying at the Montgomery house tonight."

I slipped from my seat, refusing to look back. Sean helped me into the van, and we drove away ... away from the house and this life forever.

* * * *

Sean and I flew in a private jet to Billings and drove in a Niner black van to the Montana compound. The Niners had jets at their disposal all over the world. The one we flew in had been fueled up and ready to go within an hour of the call.

The cover story had a nugget of truth. Our flight to California really did have a time change so I didn't have to worry if Doug checked out my story.

While I'd been at home, I'd poured over old scrapbooks and photos, trying to get a better sense of my brother, Doug. He'd played in Little League and had been on the high school football team. He'd had birthday parties and Christmas stockings. My parents had taken my brothers on vacations, to amusement parks, zoos and water parks. I could find no indication of a deprived childhood or anything else to have made him so cold-hearted. He'd been loved and nurtured. I'd been looking for clues that would have explained his strange behavior but found none. Could a person be born a psychopath? Was it in his DNA?

Doug had the typical cheerleader girlfriend during his high school years. I'd come came across pictures of Doug and a beautiful dark-haired girl. She had deep blue eyes, long dark silky hair and a soft, round face. Mom said Kimmie didn't want a boyfriend in the service and had broken up with Doug before he reported for duty. But I knew better. He blamed *me* for the break-up. Kimmie saw me fall off the chair when I was a toddler, and that Doug had done nothing to stop it.

When we reached the house in Victorian Village, Sean settled me in and headed for the door.

"Sean, please don't go. Let's talk about Zak's room and the plans you've drawn up. I need a distraction and don't really want to be alone."

"I'll stay as long as you like, little one." He had picked up on Nate's nickname for me, and it touched my heart. "I'll show you our preliminary sketches, and if you like the drawings I can start work tomorrow."

He pulled out his phone and projected the plans on the wall. We passed the time discussing a few changes and placing virtual furniture in the rooms. I ordered dinner, and we continued to work while we ate.

We found a common bond, me and this big, burly man who scared the wits out of me the first time I met him. He now felt like a brother and a friend.

"I'll stay down here tonight if you'd like," Sean said after I'd yawned more than a few times.

"Would you?" I grasped his hand in thanks. "I'd feel much better if you were here." I rose from the couch, and he pulled me into a bear hug.

"You're family, Sean," I whispered. "Don't ever forget that."

* * * *

The next evening the front door swung open and Lucas called out, "Anyone home?"

I flew into his arms, ecstatic he'd made it home safely. "You saved me once again." Sean rose to leave. "Sean, don't go. Let's show Lucas the work we did."

"Yeah, stay, we can talk after this one goes to bed." Lucas pointed to me. I grabbed his finger, making Sean laugh. "Will you be traveling to California with us, Sean?"

"Of course," he answered.

"We're still going?" I pulled my brows together.

"Now more than ever." Lucas led me to the sofa. "Rik has to see that the Virginia plan didn't work. We're hoping he confesses and sees the error of his ways. I'm sure he'll come around."

If this group had one flaw, trust would be it. They saw only the good in their fellow Niners and blindly accepted their word. They may have the super powers, but I have the instinct. If they thought Rik had redeeming qualities, well so be it, but I would never trust him. I said my goodnights, biting my tongue … for now.

* * * *

I woke early and heard voices downstairs, so I rushed for the steps.

"I'm awake!" I called down. As I reached the bottom, I spotted a large truck, lumber piled high on its flatbed, through the front window.

"I'm so excited!" I hugged Sean as he passed by.

"Won't take us long." He pointed to a crew coming up the street. "Two or three days, tops."

"I'm impressed." I called to him and joined Lucas in the great room.

Baby rooms were displayed on the wall. Lucas flipped through the pages we'd marked the night before. I couldn't decide between a navy and white theme or shades of beige and green with an elephant design. Either way a dark wooden sleigh-bed crib would be the focal point of the room.

"I love them both, but I've made my decision." I pointed at the blue and white. "Maybe we can buy the elephant print for my California apartment." I looked at Lucas. "I don't like that Doug's there now. I wish it was us instead."

"The STF is building a base somewhere in the mountains." Lucas shook his head. "I'm afraid Doug might take you there if he finds you. Do you see why I want you here and not at school?"

"Yes, I'll stay here until the baby's born, but if he's born on the twenty-ninth, can Rik be told the twenty-eight? Then I can go back to school in the spring."

"I think that can be arranged." Lucas smiled. "Hopefully, Doug will have his sights set on someone else once he finds out the baby's just a regular guy." Lucas laughed, and I leaned into his chest, giggling.

I looked up into his eyes and that was all it took. I was thrown against the pillows. Lucas' mouth was on mine. My hands ran up his back and into his hair. He rolled to his back bringing me with him while I was still kissing him with all of my being.

Hammers began to pound, and power saws buzzed, startling us back to reality.

"The work has begun," I said between kisses.

"Yes, and that's just the beginning." Lucas slid out from beneath me and sat on the edge of the sofa.

"Lucas, I don't have to renovate the whole house." The noise reminded me we wouldn't be alone if we kept changing the house. "I want some privacy before the baby comes. I wouldn't mind doing the bedrooms, change the décor in the guest room, and we can decorate our room together."

"Deal. Let's get started. That should take us a few weeks then it's off to Napa. Think of the trip as a mini vacation. I really want you to meet Levi."

Mini vacation? Is that how you view the trip, Lucas? I doubt it. You're just trying to distract me from the real reason we're going.

Lucas wanted me to meet Levi, but there were other reasons he wanted to make the trip. The Napa compound was closer to UCLA, and we may need it in the future. I was convinced Lucas would ask me what house I liked best and make me find my way to a hidden entrance, calling it a game, like the first time I'd come to Montana. But I'd know why he was doing those things. We'd never be free of Doug and had to stay one step ahead of him. We had to be prepared. In some ways, Rik had become a bigger threat to me than Doug. He'd gone rogue once before, and I believed he'd do it again.

Chapter Nine

We landed in San Francisco on a sunny September morning. Lucas promised we'd drive to the Golden Gate Bridge before heading to Napa. My sightseeing list also included Fisherman's Wharf, ride a cable car and tea in Chinatown.

Finally, we set off for our destination, following the signs to Napa Valley. The beauty of the area took my breath away. Rows and rows of grapevines greeted us, and when we reached the town, a sign welcomed us to wine country. Everywhere I looked, nature surprised me. The mountains loomed in the background making a magnificent backdrop to the scene. Many of the wineries, built with large stone, gave off an old-world feel.

I finally had to ask, "Are we there yet?"

Lucas smiled and nodded. "See that sign?"

The small wooden block had Bella's Winery engraved on it. The sign stuck out of the dirt in front of a gravel road. We turned and drove for another half mile before a wonderful old gray stone building appeared. The winery seemed like an out-of-the-way place, but the parking lot had plenty of cars.

"Wow, this is a popular place." I gazed past the sleek, one story building and noticed a huge outdoor deck overlooking a sweeping vista of grapevines and mountains. Flowers grew everywhere. Hanging baskets and large containers accented the landscape.

"I always stock up on a few cases when I'm here." Lucas slowed the car but continued to drive right through the parking lot.

"Don't they magically appear in your wine cabinet?" I teased.

"It's more fun to come here." He smiled. "The winery grew in popularity by word of mouth. Levi never advertises."

"If this is just a front, wouldn't he want fewer customers?"

"No, it's not a front to him. He's always dreamed of operating a winery with his family. So, in a way, it's both."

"It's gorgeous property. It would be hard to leave this place." I couldn't believe I said that after protesting the trip.

We drove to the end of the parking lot where rows of grapevines stretched before us. Two dirt tire tracks ran along the side of the field as if a tractor had traveled up and down there. Lucas drove right onto the grass and over to the tracks.

"Hey? Are you allowed to do that?" I wrinkled my nose as we bumped along.

"What do you think. Allie?" Lucas looked at me from the corner of his eye. I could see a smile forming on his lips.

"We're probably on some secret mission now. We're headed for the Niner compound. Right?"

As we reached the last row of vines, he crashed the car through them.

"Oh my gosh, Lucas! The grapes!" I covered my mouth with my hand as a bunch of purple orbs hit the windshield.

"Just making my own wine." He winked.

I put one hand on my stomach, hoping I could make it through the rolling and smashing.

"You okay?" Lucas seemed alarmed.

"Yes. Keep driving." I was past my first trimester and the queasiness had subsided.

We emerged from the foliage and a huge barn loomed before us. I assumed we were at the back of the property. The doors opened on Lucas' telepathic command. He drove into the building, waited for the doors to shut behind us and stared straight ahead. I watched in awe. The back wall of the barn receded into the ground, revealing a concrete wall. That solid wall slid into the barn structure, and Lucas guided the car through the opening then stopped on the other side. More commands sent the wall back in place making it look like an ordinary barn again.

A huge concrete wall the color of sand extended for miles in both directions on either side of the barn, standing over ten feet high. Although it was built as a deterrent to trespassers, the wall was beautiful. We traveled on a road along the barrier that curved toward the mountain. After driving a few miles, giant doors embedded in the concrete wall appeared. They blocked anyone from entering the California compound just like Montana. Similar signs were posted. *Private Property* and *Trespassers will be Prosecuted* glared at me.

The doors slowly swung back on Lucas' mental command. An exact duplicate of our headquarters back home lay straight ahead, and I realized the Niners had modeled their communities on one architectural plan. Immediately I felt at ease.

"Could you find your way in here?" Lucas broke the silence.

"Yes, but I don't know the commands. How did you get all those doors to open?"

"Well, you just tell them to open once you're programmed into the mainframe. We'll take care of that while we're here."

My hunch became a reality. Lucas wanted me to learn how to get into the compound. We'd be house hunting soon.

Headquarters consisted of four floors, same as Victorian Village. Lower level was reserved for visitors' cars. Second floor had the Niner cars to use while on the property and the fourth was command central.

"What's on the third floor, Lucas? I've never been on it."

"Our weapons station, battle gear and the black vans you've seen Sean drive."

"The black vans? That's your battle tank of choice?"

"They're much more than that, Allie. They can be converted to many types of transportation. We can use them on land, sea and in air." Lucas parked the rental, and we headed for the elevator. When the doors opened on the fourth floor, a tall, muscular man with friendly hazel eyes, a clean-shaven head and neatly trimmed salt and pepper beard waited to greet us.

"Levi!" The two embraced, and Lucas turned to me. "Allie, I want you meet Levi Zimmer."

We shook hands, and I noticed the usual Niners traits—strong and handsome. Each Niner man, no matter the look, had an aura about him. Levi guided us to the lounge area filled with black leather sofas and love seats, teak tables and chairs. I was happy to see it decorated differently.

"Jared! Joseph! John!" Levi called out, and three dark-haired muscular young men appeared from the maze of stations. "Lucas is here. He wants you to meet his fiancée, Allie." That was the first time I'd been called Lucas' fiancée and happiness bubbled up inside me.

"My sons." Levi swept his hand in front of them.

"Hi, I'm Allie." I shook their hands. They all appeared to be around my age.

"J-men!" Lucas greeted them as if they were old, dear friends, and they probably were. He watched them grow up, and now they were the same age. Lucas turned back to Levi. "We'll be looking at homes today, if that's alright with you, Levi."

"Do we need a home here, too?" I asked innocently.

"Wouldn't hurt," Levi answered for Lucas. "Most of us have multiple homes across the country."

"Doesn't that make it hard to keep track of things?" I lifted my shoulders.

"If you forget something, all you have to do is have it sent—"

"Through the teleporter. I know." I smiled.

"Or buy new," Lucas added. He grabbed my hand and led me to the elevator. "You need to pick a new car while we're here. It won't compare to Beetle but maybe you'll find something you like."

I didn't want to act childish, but I stuck out my lower lip. "I want Beetle. She better have a twin sister," I said, hoping he got my joke.

As the elevator doors parted, an exact replica to my Future Beetle waited on the second floor. Instead of being red, her colors were a shiny blue and silver.

"Beetle sends her regards." Lucas chuckled as he opened the door. "Now you just have to name her."

"We already have a Beetle. How about Bee?" I asked. Bee took us out of the main facility and down the road to the village. "What's the name of this compound?"

"Spanish Village." Lucas pointed ahead. "And you'll see why in a minute."

As we approached the village, I saw the first row of homes, all Mediterranean design. The stucco houses were breath-taking with their low-pitched roofs of tile or terra cotta. Wrought iron accents and balconies adorned the houses painted in warm and neutral colors of mossy gold, taupe, sandy beige, and pale peach.

"Watch for the blue flags and let me know when you see one you like."

I knew from Montana the flag meant the house was available. Deciding not to protest, I'd pick a house and think of it as a vacation home. My real home was a barn red Victorian house in Montana.

"This one." I gestured out the window at a small ranch. "Pull in here."

All the driveways were made of natural flagstone, adding to the beauty of the area. Native plants sat amid red mulch in the front yard. As I stepped out of the car, I felt pleased with my choice. The one-story design was simple, less ornate than some. Hopefully the inside would be as charming as the outside.

A small front porch led to an embellished wooden front door. Carvings of floral designs decorated each panel. I ran my hand over the dark wood, feeling the love put into it. Instantly, I fell in love with the door, and the person who carved it. They must have had a lot of patience if they could create something as beautiful as that. "Is this hand carved?"

"Yes, one of our old Niners did every door in the community."

I raised my eyebrows, shocked by the news. *Every door?* "He's very talented."

Lucas unlocked the door after reporting the address to command central. We walked into a foyer that went straight back to a massive living space. A living room sat directly in front of me with an open kitchen and breakfast nook to one side. On the other side of the living area a hall led to two bedrooms, one being the master. One more bedroom was at the front of the house, opposite the kitchen.

I walked through the kitchen. It led to a huge family room overlooking a patio and the backyard. "This is perfect! I'm done house-hunting." I leaned against the countertop in the kitchen.

"You don't want to look at anymore?" Lucas tilted his head as he looked at me.

"Not really, do you?"

"No, I like this one, too. I'll let Levi know we've made our choice, and we'll take the flag down." Lucas disappeared, and I wandered around the house.

"Allie, we're going to have dinner with Levi and his family tonight. If you want, we can shop first and meet them at the restaurant later," Lucas said as he appeared in the kitchen where I stood examining the appliances. "Ready?"

"The town is laid out in the same grid-like fashion?"

"Yes, exactly the same. It helps when we visit other compounds."

"You Niners think of everything," I teased as I gave him a poke in the side.

I took his arm as we strolled down our street, making our way to Main and turned toward the square. The shopping area appeared larger and more modern. I missed the quaintness of Victorian Village. No playground in the middle of the square, only a large fountain.

We headed for the furniture store. I decided to embrace the style of the house and picked out Mediterranean furnishings and décor. Lucas chose a bedroom set made of rich dark wood while I found a burnt orange silk comforter and red, brown, orange and gold tapestry toss pillows. A pale gold sectional caught our eye. We both thought it'd look great in the family room. I chose a dark gold leather sofa for the living room. No other furniture was needed for now. I hoped Lucas got the hint that I didn't plan to live there.

"That was easy." Lucas pointed to a few bar stools that would go great with our kitchen countertop, and some end tables and lamps for the living areas. "We'll take these, too." He took my hand after placing the order and gave instructions on where to set everything up in the house. "Dinner with the Zimmer family is next."

We walked out into the evening air and made our way to a small Italian eatery. Levi waved from the back of the room. His three boys sat at the table along with a lovely petite, raven-haired woman I assumed was Levi's wife.

"Allie, this is Suzanne, my wife." Levi gestured toward her.

"Nice to meet you." I shook her hand and sat down next to her. "And these handsome men are your sons?"

"Yes," Suzanne nodded. "They're two years apart with John being the youngest at twenty-one." She beamed like a proud mother.

"Suzanne runs my winery." Levi leaned over her to speak to me. "She picked all the wine tonight."

"But I brought some grape juice for you." Suzanne took my hand. "I didn't want you to feel left out."

"Don't worry, I'm fine. I've had some of your sparkling juice. It's wonderful."

Levi popped the bottle open and poured me a glass. "To great friends!" He lifted his glass.

An amazing night transpired, with so many stories being told, I struggled to remember them all. The boys told about adventures they'd shared with Lucas. Levi relived rescuing Julian from the small cabin on the plantation and bringing him to Pennsylvania. Suzanne and Levi told how they met while their sons rolled their eyes. Everyone asked questions about my family and friends except for Doug. I found that odd and a little unsettling.

"We can't wait to meet Nate." Jared told me as we said goodnight. "We heard he's quite the computer genius. Even without Niner help!" We laughed, and I assured him Lucas and I would bring him to visit in the spring.

As we walked home, questions whirled in my head. "If John's twenty-one that makes Joseph twenty-three, and Jared, twenty-five? They all live here? Did they go to college?"

"Jared, the oldest, went to the University of California at Davis where he studied the wine business. He works with his mother at the winery and hopes to start his own one day. Joseph just graduated and is job searching. John is undecided at this point. He took a year off and is helping at the winery."

"They have a ready-made business where they can work and live if they wish."

"Yeah, I think Suzanne would love them to stick around. She likes having the boys close."

"One more question." I paused. "Why didn't anyone mention Doug?"

"I asked them not to. You've been through enough. I want the next few months to be stress-free."

"There is no stress-free in the real world, Lucas."

He put his arm around my waist. "But you're in the Niner world." He kissed the side of my head.

When we arrived at the house, I couldn't wait to see the new décor. I rushed to the bedroom and found everything in place.

"It's beautiful! I can't wait to test it out." I called to Lucas, hoping he got the meaning. "How's the sectional?" He didn't hear me, which was totally odd, so I navigated through the rooms and found him in the family room. Lucas stared out at the night sky but turned when he heard me come in.

"Did you hear me?" He gave me a look like I should already know the answer. "Of course, you did. Why didn't you answer?"

"I was enjoying the view but now that you're here—" Lucas pulled me close to his body, wrapping his hands around my waist. "What did you say about the bed?" His lips found mine, and he kissed me as if it might be our last. I returned the kiss with more intensity. I ran my hands up his strong back and felt his hands slid up my sides, pulling me closer. I loved that he made me feel I could slip away at any moment, and we had to savor every moment together.

"Lucas," I pulled back and looked up at him, "I never saw Rik. Is he still in Spanish Village?"

"Yes, he thought you might not want to see him after what he did ... passing along that information to Doug."

"He confessed?" I exclaimed.

"Yes, and he's sorry. He didn't know what came over him. He was overjoyed that Doug would be an uncle. It just slipped out during a conversation he had with one of the STF Niners. He stays in contact with them." He stared into my eyes which I hoped were on fire. "Don't look at me like that, Allie. He's still beating himself up about it. And as I said, he's truly sorry."

Sorry he got caught, I bet. Red flag, anyone? Rik talks to the STF Niners, and it's okay? I didn't believe Rik was sorry. The Niners could be so naïve sometimes. If they wouldn't be suspicious of him, I would have to do it for all of us.

Chapter Ten

The fall days gave way to winter. As I did my daily walk to the village square, I didn't mind the cold. Montana's icy temperatures never penetrated Victorian Village. The town had its own climate control, set at thirty-two degrees.

When the first snow fell, it reminded me of the first time I'd seen Victorian Village at the Montgomery home in Virginia. I was a junior in high school and madly, naively in love with Lucas. I said it looked like the North Pole as Lucas showed me the village. Now, I got to experience it in person.

January had been a boring month. I couldn't find enough to keep me busy while Lucas went to Headquarters, but February came too soon. If I could just get through the month and into March, my baby would be safe. Zak and I could even visit my parents. He'd be a normal boy, growing each year as he should. That would hopefully keep Doug off our trail. I planned to use Ashley's idea—tell the family Zak was Will's baby. *Oh, Will, I'm sorry to do this to you, but I'm eternally grateful.*

I marked off the February days on a calendar each night before I went to bed.

"Well, that takes care of the twenty-eighth," Lucas said. "I know you're nervous, Allie. That's why I took the week off."

"Only one more day to get through." I squeezed his hand as he helped me into bed.

"Would it be so bad?" I saw the hurt in his eyes. I treated his condition like it was a disease.

"No, of course not." I touched his cheek. "I would love to have a Niner baby. I'm scared for different reasons."

"Doug."

That was all he had to say, and I burst out crying. Lucas held me close until I sniffed and wiped my eyes. "Lucas, we have to protect Zak. If wishing he won't be born tomorrow is terrible, then call me any name you want."

* * * *

I tossed and turned, unable to get comfortable. I rolled over to look at the time. The clock said ten in the morning. February twenty-ninth had come. Lucas sat in a chair in the corner, doing work from his phone. I dozed on and off for another hour. Finally, I decided to get up and start my day. As soon as I moved, Lucas rushed to help me. "I'm fine," I said as I walked to the bathroom.

Staring at my reflection in the mirror, I studied my face. My eyes had dark circles under them, the blue-green color faded to a dull aqua. Brown strands of hair stuck to my forehead. A bead of sweat lined my top lip. Then I felt something run down my legs.

"Lucas!" *What day is it?* I suddenly couldn't remember.

Lucas popped his head in the bathroom and took one look at the floor. "I guess it's time?" He glanced at his phone. "Serena said to take our time even though your water broke. It may still be awhile, but we should come as soon as we can." Lucas brought the clothes I'd picked out for this day into the bathroom.

I grabbed his arm as he was about to leave. "You didn't answer me. What day is it? The date?"

"It's the twenty-ninth."

"It's going to happen, isn't it? Zak will be a Niner-squared."

"Not necessarily, you could be in labor for hours." I flashed him a look that said he needed to stop talking. "Sorry, I was only trying to help." He shrugged.

After I dressed, Lucas helped me down the stairs and opened the door to expose Sean on the other side. "The cavalry has arrived," he announced.

I tried to smile. "Lucas, where's my bag?" He left me in Sean's capable hands and ran back upstairs.

"Your carriage awaits," Sean said as he guided me to his black van.

"Sean, you're staying the whole time, right?"

"If you want me to."

"Lucas will need a distraction."

Sean laughed. "I can take care of that." He helped me into the back of the van and climbed into the driver's seat. Lucas hopped in the back with me, and we flew to the hospital in record time. A sharp pain hit me, and I screamed.

Sean rotated in his seat. "Lucas, go inside. Let them know we're here." He slipped out of the driver's side. "I'm coming, little one."

Time went by in a blur. People rushed past me as Sean placed me in a wheelchair. Serena came toward me, mouth moving, but I never heard what she was saying. Someone pushed me to a room, and the door shut. Finally able to take a breath, Serena helped me into a gown and settled me into a chair similar to the one I'd sat in for examinations. I glanced around to see the room was empty except for her.

"Whenever you feel a contraction, push this button, and the chair will help absorb the pain. Trust me, I know it sounds weird, but it works. Otherwise, I want you walking around until I say to stay in the chair. The chair will turn into the delivery bed. You won't even have to move. Lucas will be the only one allowed in, besides me and my nurse, unless you say otherwise. I'll be back to check on you throughout the day."

"Serena?"

She turned at the door. "Yes, Allie?"

"You haven't said a word about what day it is."

"My job is to bring a healthy baby into this world. If Zakary decides it's today, then it's meant to be. Today I'm your doctor. Tomorrow, I'm your friend." She walked back to my chair and squeezed my hand. "If anyone can handle this, it's you and Lucas. You two are strong and have a great love."

I stared at her. No one had ever said anything like that to me before. I always felt we were meant for each other, whether together or not, but to hear someone else say it made it all the more real.

"I'll send Lucas in now." She stroked my hair back from my eyes. "He's pacing outside the door and probably worn out the tile!"

Lucas slipped past Serena as soon as she cracked open the door. "I have Ashley on the phone. I figured you'd want to see her."

"Ash." I saw her concerned face on his screen. "I'm fine, don't look so worried."

"I know you're in great hands, Allie. Are you okay that today's—"

"Yes, I know it's Leap Day. I'm fine with it. I'm so excited to see Zak I don't care what day it is anymore. We'll deal with it." I took Lucas' hand. Relief spread through me. I *was* fine. No more worrying what Zak would become.

"Well, I'm not going anywhere. I'll be in the apartment all day. Hang in there."

And we did hang in there. We made it past dinnertime and I had to insist Lucas eat. Sean took Lucas' place while he was gone, keeping me entertained. Lucas ate in record time and returned in twenty minutes.

"How was dinner?" I smiled, trying to distract him. "We only have five hours to go."

"I don't even remember what I ate." Lucas grasped my hand. "What if I told you I don't care when Zak is born. I just want you to be okay."

"Is that why you look so sad? Don't worry. I'll be fine, and I don't care when Zak is born either!"

The light came back to Lucas' eyes. "You can handle anything, you know that." He kissed my hand.

"Lucas, get Serena." I had an overwhelming feeling Zak was coming. He probably heard us talking, giving him permission to be born when he wanted. I sat down, and the chair slowly tilted back.

"Allie, look at me and listen." I saw Serena's face as she burst into the room. "When I say push, push hard, but not until I tell you." My body told me Zak wanted to come into the world, but I waited and finally heard, "Push."

Silence filled the room then I heard a cry, a baby's cry. Lucas wiped tears from his eyes as the nurse took Zakary to a table to clean him and wrap him in a blanket. I held out my arms, aching for my baby, and she placed him in them when she finished. His eyes were wide open, big brown eyes like his father's and tiny wisps of dark hair. He looked so much like Lucas, it astonished me for being a tiny baby. I took his little hand and kissed it. Gazing up at Lucas, I remembered something that had slipped my mind all day. "Happy birthday, Lucas," I said as I handed him his son. "Happy birthday."

Chapter Eleven

Now that Zak had joined the family, it took a few extra days to get ready to move back to LA. Just a month old, he was quite strong for a baby his age. He could hold up his head and was very alert. He laughed and cooed, even doubled his birth weight. When awake, he demanded our attention.

On the flight to California, Zak slept the entire way. Everyone commented on what a beautiful baby he was, probably because he had been on his best behavior.

"I've done some research on Niner babies and the regular kind," Lucas whispered as he held up a baby book.

"The regular kind?" I closed one eye and stared at him.

"You know what I mean." He hit his forehead with his fingers and laughed.

"What did you find out?"

"That we're in uncharted territory. Not much has been written in our world on Niner-squared children. There haven't been too many. We may have to learn as we go."

"Don't you think he's growing unusually fast?" I whispered.

Lucas nodded his head. "Thus the research."

"Thus?" I giggled as I remembered Lucas had been around for eighty-four years. But in reality, my fiancée had finally become old enough to drink on his birthday.

"Here's what I do know." He looked me in the eye, so serious I stopped giggling. "Niners are three months old on their first birthday. They look like helpless infants, but their minds develop in leaps and bounds."

"Babies with super minds," I said.

"Yeah, but by the second year, the physical takes over. They are walking and talking by year's end. Amazing, if you compare that to six-month-old babies. Probably happens for self-preservation."

"Makes sense. The first year the brain develops, and during the second the body."

Lucas pointed at Zak. "He's doing both. This baby book says a one month old can barely lift his head and is getting used to his environment. He's more like a four-month-old according to this." He held up the book.

"Shhh." I grew nervous someone could hear although Sean sat in the seat behind us. Being a Niner, he could hear every word.

"I plan to keep track of his growth for the Niner biology department," Lucas said in a loud whisper. "We've been told this kid will do everything twice as fast as a normal Niner baby. We have no data so it could be quite different. We don't really know."

"Oh." I looked at my sleeping child as the plane landed. I wanted him to stay a baby for as long as possible. I assumed he would, but he might have other plans.

Sean hopped up when the plane landed. "I'll get the gear," he informed us. "You go ahead. He held back the departing passengers until we were safely off the plane.

My trusty red Jeep had been driven to LA by a volunteer Niner, part of the Montana security team and also Sean's friend. They embraced at the luggage pick-up, and the other man headed back into the airport.

Sean threw the keys in the air. "We've got wheels." He glanced at Lucas. "We've got to get you a ride while I'm still here."

"The three guys can go car shopping while Allie's at school." Lucas slapped Sean on the back as he held up the baby seat.

We piled into the Jeep, car seat already installed, ready to make the trek to my apartment. My heart fluttered with excitement. I felt like I hadn't been in LA for a long time. Life had been so different then—a nineteen-year-old girl living alone and attending UCLA trying to get through her days. Now she returned as a twenty-year-old mother engaged to the love of her life.

Lucas unlocked the door to the apartment and an overwhelming feeling of missing the place and this life swept over me. Now the three of us would get back to that life, maybe find a bigger place to live after I'd finished the quarter. Lucas and I discussed living in LA and were confident we could do it. I wanted to get a job in an art museum for the summer, even if I had to be the cashier behind the snack bar.

Nate and Ashley came over as soon as they heard we arrived.

"Oh, Allie, he's adorable," Ashley said as she rushed to Zak to pick him up. "Zakkie, how's my little guy?" She pulled him close as he coocd and smiled.

"Sean?" Nate patted him on the back. "I heard you're staying with us. Happy to have you. We're not staying long, Allie. Just came to say hi, meet Zak and pick up the big guy." He gave me a hug. "Ashley? Sean? Ready?"

Sean nodded, but didn't seem eager to leave. He glanced over at me.

"We'll be fine, Sean. Don't worry. Enjoy your time in LA." I smiled to reassure him, but the hairs on my arms stood on end. Sean appeared stressed, as if he anticipated an unforeseen event. I shook my head to wipe the thought from my mind.

* * * *

I had no idea what to expect on the first day of the quarter, but it fell into place. My routine hadn't changed. I knew where to park and the correct buildings for classes. I met Nate and Ashley for coffee, did a little studying in the library then headed home.

"Lucas!" I called out as I unlocked the apartment door. He laid on the couch, baby on his chest. A new diaper box had been torn open, and a half-full bottle lay on the floor. Breakfast dishes were still on the table.

"Can't do it all alone, Mr. Mom?" I giggled as he held his finger to his mouth.

"Just got him down," he whispered.

I took Zak and placed him in his bassinet in the corner of the living area. I returned to Lucas and ran my hands over his chest. He took me into his arms. I put my finger to my lips and gestured toward the bedroom as I pulled my t-shirt over my head. What a perfect ending to the day.

* * * *

"Allie," Lucas shook my shoulder. "Wake up. You're late for class."

"This is my day off," I grumbled.

"No, you have one class on Tuesdays and Thursdays, remember? Today's Tuesday. Do you think you can take Zak with you?"

"So much for Mr. Mom?" I teased as I rubbed my eyes and got out of bed.

"No, I have a conference call with Napa and Montana today. I'll do some grocery shopping, too. If you take Zak, it will make things easier. It won't happen again."

"I'll take the carrier. We'll be fine." I placed it at the door as we talked. "I won't be gone that long."

"Great, love you!" Lucas went out the door as I brushed my hair and put on a little make-up. "Well, Zak, you're coming to school with mommy today."

"Mum-mum."

I couldn't believe my ears. "Did you just say my name?" Lucas had left, and I couldn't ask him. "You're too young to talk!" Should I write it down for Lucas' journal? I didn't have time. I'd be late for class. I grabbed my backpack, the baby and dashed for the car. After strapping Zak in his car seat, I headed for campus.

I found a convenient spot in the parking garage and popped the trunk. I opened the back door and took Zak from his car seat and placed him in the carrier. He snuggled close to my chest as I slung the baby bag over one shoulder. My book bag would slip onto my back once I managed to pick it up from the garage floor. It stared up at me as if to say, "Good luck." I slammed the trunk shut and backed into someone walking by. "Oh! Sorry, I didn't see you. I'm not very organized today."

"I always thought you were quite organized," a familiar voice answered back.

I looked straight into Will's eyes. "Will! Hi!" He looked like a wounded puppy as he glanced at the baby in the pouch attached to the front of me.

"You look wonderful, Allie." He picked up my book bag and carried it as we exited the parking garage. "I can see why you broke off our—"

"Will, no, I wasn't cheating on you." I stopped. In a way, I had cheated on him. I looked for the right words to describe what had happened. "I wasn't pregnant when I broke up with you." That wasn't exactly true, so I finally gave up and admitted defeat. "I'm sorry how things turned out."

"Looks like things turned out well for you." Will pointed to Zak.

"Oh, yes, we're very happy." I wanted to smack myself. "Keep putting my foot in it, don't I?"

Will smiled. "No, I just wished it worked out differently, that's all."

We stopped in front of my classroom building. "It was nice seeing you again." I started to put out my hand and changed my mind. I stood on my tiptoes and kissed his cheek.

As I headed up the stairs, I felt overwhelmed. *That was totally unexpected.* I never thought I'd run into Will in the parking garage. Now that could happen every Tuesday for the rest of the quarter.

After class, I decided to grab some coffee and think of a good way to explain what happened to Lucas. When it came to Will, Lucas had a jealous streak. I strolled through campus and arrived at the coffee shop. Lucas walked into the café just as we did and joined us at the table.

"Tracking me?" I asked coyly.

"When you didn't come home, I got worried, that's all. Then I thought I'd take Zak off your hands in case you were busy."

"Aww, that's sweet." I dug for a bottle in the baby bag. "Zak met Will." I said, keeping my eyes lowered, still rummaging through my bag.

"And you told him about us?"

"Not exactly, the less said the better. He knows I'm happy."

"Good, then you'll have to work on avoiding him from now on. I don't want him getting too curious."

"I'm a big girl, Lucas. I think I can handle Will if I run into him again, not that I plan to." I gave him my best smile. The ringtone on my phone distracted us.

"It's my mom," I whispered. Lucas knew I hated to ignore her calls. I held a finger to my lips and answered. "Hi, Mom." Zak wiggled in my arms, and I flashed Lucas an "Oh my gosh" look.

"Allie, sweetie, how are you doing?"

Zak squirmed harder. He wanted to eat, and I hadn't found his bottle in the bag. I pantomimed to Lucas to find it. He gave me a quizzical look. I gestured to Zak, and he reached out to take him. I shook my head no. Just at that moment, Zak let out his "I'm hungry" wail. Lucas got the message and desperately searched the baby bag.

"Is that a baby crying, Allie?"

"No, Mom, no baby."

"I swear I hear a baby. It's very close by."

"I'm in a coffee shop." I thought I had her convinced until Zak cried harder. Lucas held up the bottle in triumph.

"Allie, I know a baby's cry when I hear one. That one sounds like it's right on top of you, like you're holding … oh, my goodness … you had a baby, didn't you?"

"Mom." I tried to interrupt, but she was on a roll.

"That's why you didn't come home at Christmas. You were pregnant. It's Will's baby, isn't it? He broke up with you in the summer, and you didn't tell him. You had it all on your own, you poor thing. Didn't you think I'd help out? We wouldn't have judged you. I'm booking a flight and coming out right now. How are you managing?"

I knew Lucas had heard every word. I muted the phone and whispered, "Should I let her think it's Will's?"

"I hate the idea." He pressed his lips together. "But, yes, let her think that. She really put the facts together quickly, didn't she?"

I nodded sadly.

"But don't let her come out here. Try hard to convince her to stay in Virginia."

I returned to the conversation. "Mom, you're right. That's why I didn't come home. I had Zak over a month ago." I cringed realizing I'd given too much information.

"You had the baby in February, and I'm just finding out? His name is Zak?"

"Yes, Zakary James, James for Dad. Please don't tell Dad or Doug, especially Doug."

"Oh, honey, I have to. Your father will be heartbroken as it is."

"That I had a baby or he didn't know about it?"

"Well, both, but he'll get over it. Now when do you want me?"

"Mom, I don't want you flying out here. I have everything under control. I'll send a picture to your phone."

"Fine, but I'm going to see my grandson soon." Mom sounded stubborn.

After we said our goodbyes, I threw my phone in my bag, upset by the latest developments.

"You know we couldn't keep this from her forever." Lucas rubbed my arm. "If we stay here how could you keep your parents from visiting? You'd have to eventually go home, too."

"I could go alone, and you'd stay here with Zak."

"I'd never let you go there alone."

"I know." I sighed. "It's all so confusing. We don't really have a plan, do we?"

"No, and I guess we better make one. Ready to go? This guy's nodding off."

Lucas walked me to the parking garage and put Zak in his seat. "I'll see you at home." He smoothed my hair back to give me a kiss.

Out of the corner of my eye, I swore I saw Will slowly drive by. Could I torture the poor guy any more than I already had? Then again, he may have moved on, I didn't ask. He could have a beautiful, loving girlfriend or two or three. That was how I'd think of him from now on—with a gorgeous blonde, brunette or redhead on his arm. He'd never know how truly sorry I was.

* * * *

"I can't believe you've held your mother off this long," Ashley said as she picked up Zak. "Say Auntie, come on, Zakkie, you can do it."

"Everyone's jealous that he's said mum-mum for two months now and nothing else." I laughed. "I can't believe he's sitting up and almost crawling. We've given up consulting baby books."

"I can't get a Da-da out of him for the life of me." Lucas came out of the bedroom with a small packed bag. "I hid all the guy stuff. Your mom shouldn't find a thing." Lucas would stay with Nate and Ashley during Mom's three-day visit during finals week.

"We'll come over for dinner and try to be here as much as we can." Nate patted my shoulder. "The time will fly."

Dejected, I hugged them goodbye one last time and got Zak ready for the trip to the airport to pick up his Grandma. I made my mother swear she'd come alone and not tell Doug. Dad couldn't get away from work, so it worked out perfectly. Dean and Autumn were the only family members who knew Lucas and I were back together and that Zak was our baby. The kidnapping had opened their eyes, and they were on my side.

I needed to hear Lucas' voice as I approached the airport and called him. "Lucas, I'm almost there."

"Be careful, Allie. Drive slowly, especially around the terminal."

"Okay, Dad." I teased. "I'll keep you on speaker until the last possible second."

I pulled into LAX and searched airline names to get in the correct pick-up lane.

"You're doing great." Lucas told me. I almost forgot he was there.

"I think I see her." Mom stood on the sidewalk, not waiting in the terminal like I asked. "I have to hang up, Lucas. I love you. Wish me luck."

"I love you, too. I wish it could be different. I wish we could both pick her up."

"I know, I'm sorry this hurts you."

"It's for the best and the safety of Zak."

I turned off my phone and rolled down the passenger-side window. "Mom!" I waved and hoped she saw me. I put the Jeep in park and ran to the back, lifting the hatch.

"Allie, get in the car with your baby. I can do this." Mom suddenly was next to me, startling me.

She lifted her bag, placed it inside and hopped into the backseat right next to Zak. "I'm so happy to finally meet this little guy!" she said.

Mom talked and played with Zak the whole way home. Tears filled my eyes as I thought of how I had deprived her of her grandson. She began to sing, and I heard him laugh. When he said, "mum-mum", she was delighted.

"He's talking already, Allie? He's only three and half months! That's really something! And he's so beautiful—those dark eyes and hair. I thought Will was blonde. Oh, what does it matter, he takes after our side." She grew quiet for a moment then said, "But no one has those dark eyes. We all have shades of blue."

"Mom, you're rambling. I don't know what to answer first."

"I can't wait to hold him!"

"Well, you've got your chance now." I pulled into the apartment and parked the car, relieved she would be distracted. I didn't want to explain Zak's dark eyes.

Mom insisted on carrying her luggage all the way to the apartment. I got her settled in my bedroom. She gave Zak his bottle, praising what a good baby he was. She told me not to worry about a thing while she visited, just take my tests and do well. In a way, I was glad she'd come.

Lucas met me every day after class during her visit, and I gave him Zak updates for his journal. "I look forward to these moments." He kissed my cheek as we headed for the parking garage.

"I've missed you so much, Lucas! I'm glad this is the last day of our lie. I want you home." I stuck out my lower lip then smiled. "Mom's impressed Zak can sit up and almost crawls. She thinks he's very smart and handsome."

"Well, of course, he's all that and more. I can't wait to come home. I miss you two so much." Lucas took my backpack from my shoulder and slung it over his as we walked.

"I told Mom to check her flight. We've arranged for a car to pick her up this afternoon."

"Here's my car." Lucas gestured to the new car he purchased when we first arrived. "Remember I'm just a phone call away." We kissed a little longer than one should in a parking garage, but I hated to let him go.

Lucas watched until I reached my car, then pulled out and drove down the ramp. I popped the trunk, threw my bag in, and jumped into the Jeep. I turned the key in the ignition. *Dead?* I kept up with maintenance, and the Niners always checked it over so I tried again. The jeep still wouldn't start. My heart began to pound, and panic rolled through me. Trembling, I called out Lucas' name, and the phone connected us.

"Lucas! The car won't start."

"I'm turning around. Stay calm. I'll be there in a minute."

I counted the seconds until he returned while I paced by the side of the car. Lucas zoomed into an open spot across from mine and hopped out.

"Strange, your car's in top shape," Lucas said as he lifted the hood. "A loose wire?" He gave me a look that chilled me to the bone. "Allie, get in my car. Let's go."

Lucas raced to the driver's side of his car. I hopped in the passenger side, and we sped toward the apartment. I didn't care if he broke every traffic rule I wanted to get home. The car jerked to a stop in the closest parking space to the building. My head spun, thinking of every possible scenario. I bit my bottom lip so hard, I drew blood. We ran up the stairs, burst into the living room and found my mom writing a note at the kitchen table.

"Oh, Allie!" She placed her hand on her chest. "Lucas!" She appeared shocked at the sight of him. "I was just leaving you a note. Since you were running late, I let Doug take Zak for a walk in his stroller. They should be back soon. He said I should just leave when the car gets here and not worry. He'd watch the baby until you got back."

I swallowed, but the lump in my throat didn't budge. "Doug?" I croaked.

"Yes, he called this morning after you left and said he was in California. I said I was, too. What a coincidence! He asked why I was here. I told him I was visiting you and the baby. He's not too happy that Will fellow left you alone with a baby. He said he'd stop by and have a talk with you. I had no idea he meant today but was grateful to see him when you didn't come home. I didn't want to miss my flight."

Tears welled in my eyes. I dug my nails into my palms to keep sane. "Mom, Lucas is Zak's father. We didn't want Doug to know because of what happened in high school. He's out to get Lucas for some reason. We'll never talk to Doug or have anything to do with him again."

"It all makes sense now." Mom studied Lucas' face. "The eyes. Zak has Lucas' eyes." She turned to me. "I'm so sorry, sweetie. I know you asked me not to tell him about the baby, but Doug's so stressed out about his job, I thought it would do him good to hear a little positive news. He was thrilled to hear he had a nephew."

"Stressed out? How?"

"Oh, you know Doug. He can't talk about his job. He said something about needing a new America. It has to do with the economy. It's not great, you know. Maybe he's afraid they'll cut funding to his program. Then the next thing I know he's talking about the nuclear bomb. That boy …" She shrugged one shoulder as she laughed. Her phone rang, interrupting the rest of her story.

"The car's here. I don't want to leave like this. Did I do something wrong?"

"No, Mrs. Sanders, you didn't do anything wrong. Have a safe trip home." Lucas escorted her to the door.

He grabbed her bag, and I gave her a quick hug. They walked out the door together, and I stood staring at the empty room.

Finally alone, I began to scream, a long, loud, piercing yell. The sound bounced off the walls, coming back at me like a punch to the stomach. A thousand knives stabbed through my heart as I sank to the ground and pounded the floor over and over. Sobs came from my body, so sorrowful I couldn't believe they came from me. Doug had my baby. He wasn't coming back. He didn't take Zak for a walk. He didn't want *me* and Zak. He only wanted my child, and now he had him. Doug had kidnapped my baby.

Chapter Twelve

"Did you get any sleep, honey?" Ashley pulled my hair back from my face and wrapped a band around it. "Lucas said you didn't eat. At least have some water."

"I'll throw up if I do," I whispered. I'd reached zombie state, felt no emotions and wore a blank stare. I clutched Zak's baby blanket, inhaling his baby scent.

"You have dark circles under your eyes, Allie. They look sunken into your face. That isn't a good sign. Dehydration could set in." Ashley led me into the living room. "She's as ready as she'll ever be," she told Lucas.

Lucas opened the door to the transporter that Sean had installed while he was here. "Serena sent me a sleep patch. They only use them in the hospital. You'll sleep for eight hours. It will help for the drive." He reached for my arm.

"No!" I yanked away from Ashley's grip. "I need to be awake. I might hear from Doug."

"Do you think he'll call with a ransom?" Nate asked.

"Nate," I whispered as I reached out for him.

"Allie." Lucas kept his voice low and soft. "I can remove the patch at any time, and you'll wake up."

"No."

"The girl said no," Ashley said. "We need to get going instead of arguing. How long will it take to get to Spanish Village?"

"About seven hours." Lucas grabbed the keys to the Jeep. "Let's head out." I moaned and cried on the way to the car. "Ash, she better ride with you. I can't drive and comfort her at the same time."

Ashley opened the back door of Nate's car, and I climbed in. She slid in next to me. My world had crumbled around me with no way to stop it. I sat in a trance during the trip, waiting to be told it was just a dream.

Nate's voice broke into my dreamlike state. "We need to break the law this time, Lucas. Put up the shields and get us there."

I wrapped Zak's blanket tighter around my arm, bringing it to my nose. *My baby, my precious baby. Is he scared?*

We passed a police car, but he didn't seem to notice that we were well above the speed limit. The scenery went by in a blur until Nate pulled in Bella's parking lot. We got out and joined Lucas in the Jeep. He followed the same route to the barn. I watched Ashley's face as we drove along the grapevines and could tell she loved the place as much as I did. But the beauty of the area was marred by the reason we'd come—Zak's kidnapping.

I zoned in and out until we reached Headquarters. Then I began to shake as Ashley helped me from the car. I could barely stand. The parked cars began to spin around me. I tried to focus on walking, taking one step at a time, but the last thing I remembered my legs collapsed, and I fell to the ground.

* * * *

I woke in a hospital, IV in my arm. I struggled to remember if I had some type of surgery or maybe I just had the baby. I glanced over to see a dark-haired woman sitting next to my bed. "Serena?"

She lifted her head. "No, Allie, it's me. Suzanne, Levi's wife? You're in California."

"Did I have the baby?"

"Yes, you did, over three months ago."

"Zak." As soon as I said his name it came back to me. "He's kidnapped," I whispered.

"I'll let everyone know you're awake," Suzanne said.

Ashley immediately came through the door.

"Thanks, Suzanne," she said as she took her place. "Hey, how you doing?" Ashley asked gently as she patted my arm.

"What happened to me?"

"Doctor said you're dehydrated. The IV should fix you up."

"Well, get this off me." I pulled at the oxygen tube in my nose and pointed at my hand. "I have to know what's going on. How are they going to rescue Zak?"

"You just rest and don't worry. Everything's under control. Sean and Julian are on their way from Montana."

"I don't want to rest, Ash. I feel better. Help me get out of here. Where are my clothes?" I looked down at the hospital gown. Suddenly, I realized how weak I looked to everyone. I was a grieving mother, but now I had to go into warrior mode. Wasn't that why I took karate classes and visited the shooting range? Kick-ass Mom needed to be in full force. I had to bring Zak home safe.

Ashley glanced around as if someone would see her. "Your IV's almost done. I guess it's okay if you leave." She undid the connection from my hand and slipped the needle out. I pulled the tube from my face and grabbed my clothes, pulling them on.

"Where are they?" I asked as we headed for the door.

"Headquarters," Ashley answered. Bee waited outside the hospital, and we climbed in. "Love Beetle's twin, she's been a big help to me. I've been to your house in Spanish Village and ordered a bed for tonight. There was nothing in the guest room. You weren't into decorating the place, were you?"

Ashley knew I didn't want to make that house a home. "There's no crib for Zak ..." I didn't cry, knowing I had to remain strong. "Don't say it. We don't really need one yet."

"We'll order one when we get back to the house, okay?" Ashley took my hand. When we reached Headquarters, Bee dropped us off by the elevator and self-parked. "Still have a hard time getting used to that." Ashley shook her head.

We rushed inside. The fourth floor seemed miles away. Slow motion took over until I reached the conference room then everything came into focus. Lucas jumped from his seat when he saw me, eyebrows high on his forehead.

"You're not doing this without me." I held my hand up to resist being sent away. I looked around the table. Levi and his three sons, Nate, Julian, Sean and Rik had been called to the meeting. "What's he doing here?" I screamed as I lunged at Rik.

Lucas got between us. "He knows the STF best. He'll get us into their base. We're going to use as few people as possible to gain entrance. Once inside, we'll find Zak and return to the compound. We leave early morning."

"Fine, what time?"

"You're not going, Allie."

I decided not to argue with Lucas in front of all these people. I grabbed a chair at the table and plopped down, crossing my arms.

Lucas turned back to the group. "Four vans will go to the STF outpost. Rik has given us the location in the mountains. It's about an eight-hour drive from here, but for us? Ten minutes max. We'll shift the vans to whatever form is needed."

I learned that the tires of the vans pulled up and out to create a jet for flight or sealed together to speed across water while the rest of the van shifted accordingly. They could also turn into helicopters or hovercrafts for special landings.

"Nate will ride with Julian. Joseph, you're with me. Sean and Rik will team up and Levi and Jared will be in the fourth van."

A well-thought plan but Lucas had missed one thing. "What about me?" I demanded.

"You can head up the command center with John." Levi patted his youngest on the shoulder. "We'll be in constant contact."

Again I remained silent and let the men finish their meeting. On the way out, Rik called to me. "Allison, may I have a moment?"

No, Rik, you may not. I nodded and followed him over to the lounge area with Lucas right behind me.

"I'd like to explain myself. We got off on the wrong foot, and I want to clarify my position."

I didn't answer but gave him a steely gaze.

"Your brother, Doug, is a respected and valued member of the military. They released him so he could head this private venture. He's admired by his men. Many left the military to follow him. He's the first to go in and the last to come out of any situation. He'd give his life for the cause and this country. That's the part I don't think you understand or are aware of … the cause."

"Oh, I've been well-schooled in the cause," I said sarcastically.

"Then you should know your brother dedicated his life to putting together a top-notch team to come up with a way to counteract the nuclear bomb. Besides the destruction of life, it makes places uninhabitable for decades, gets in the water, and contaminates the food. People who survive an attack may die years later because of its effects. Picture a world where no country can ever threaten the United States with nuclear weapons. They'll have no power over us. We'd have a safe, controlled antidote to any bomb sent our way. The world could be at peace. No more war or threats of destruction."

"So you condone taking an innocent baby to achieve this goal?" Even though he explained it better than Doug had, I fumed inside.

"No, that's why I agreed to share my STF knowledge with the Niners. You have to remember the Task Force has Niner technology, too. The other Niners and I have developed weapons and other devices with our advanced technology for the STF."

"Why isn't Doug happy with the Niners he has?"

"They aren't enough. He needs more brain power. Niners of different ages may help us."

"But Zak's just a baby! He can't even talk." I paused and studied Rik. "Does Doug know what a Niner-squared is?"

"I'm sorry to say he does. We told him about it, in theory only, but when Zak was born he figured it out on his own."

"With your help."

"I only let him know you were pregnant, and Lucas was the father."

"So, he's not sure when Zak was born."

"I can't say positively. I've had no contact with anyone for months."

"Well, thanks for clearing that up." I stood to leave, and saw Ashley and Nate leaning against the wall. I approached them and asked, "What do you think?"

"I think he's full of bullshit," Nate said.

"At least you know why Doug's so driven," Ashley whispered.

"Choosing nuclear weapons over family always gives me a warm, fuzzy feeling." I slammed my hand against the wall. "See you back at home."

Bee waited patiently outside the elevator and popped her doors when she saw Lucas and me. As we climbed in, I said, "I don't believe him."

"Well, I have to if I want my son back." Lucas grabbed my hand. "How are you feeling? And why did you leave the hospital?"

"I'm fine. I needed to hear the plan for rescuing *my* son."

"Okay," Lucas gave me a sad smile. "Let's stop fighting. He's *our* son."

Bee pulled into the drive, hovering above the flagstone. "Bee," I said. "It's safe to let us out."

I felt a kinship to the car, as if Bee and Beetle had a sister connection. Bee gave a shudder and opened her doors. "Thanks." I petted her side as I slid from the seat.

The Mediterranean house wasn't home, but it looked inviting. A soft glow shone through the windows, and the outdoor landscaping lights were on. As I walked through the front door, I noticed Lucas had finished decorating the house with pieces we'd admired on-line which seemed like a lifetime ago. I didn't care what the house looked like. I just wanted my baby back.

I headed to the guest bedroom to see what Ashley had ordered. "So-o Ashley." I murmured when I saw the decor. I admired how quickly she had made it her own. Her favorite color, blue, was incorporated into the room. A rich, dark oak four poster bed had a cream and dark blue patterned spread with a dark blue quilt folded across the foot of the bed.

Wandering through the rooms of the house, I tried to focus on anything but Zak. I fought hard to stay in control. I headed to the master bedroom and could hardly look across the hall at the baby's room. When I forced myself to look in, I saw a crib with the elephant comforter and the rest of the décor I loved. The neutral colors went well with the house and the large, playful elephant on the blanket and rug were just as I'd remembered. The obvious absence of my baby in the room overwhelmed me, and I couldn't hold back any longer. I took a few steps into the room, dropped to the rug and wept.

Strong arms wrapped around me and carried me to our room. I wanted to fight, resist sleep for as long as possible. "No. No sleep." I protested.

"I'll wake you for dinner." Lucas' voice sounded so reassuring; I drifted off to sleep.

* * * *

"Allie, wake up." Ashley's voice seemed far away. "Dinner's ready."

I rolled over to find her sitting next to me on the bed. "Hey," I rubbed my eyes as I sat up. "I think maybe I can eat something."

"How about stand? Let's try that first." Ashley offered me her hand.

"How do you feel about Nate going on the mission?" I asked.

"I can't stop him even if I wanted, but I don't want to. We're part of this now. I love this place, these people. I'm proud of him for wanting to save Zak." Ashley had tears in her eyes.

"Oh, Ash, who'd ever think two girls with high school crushes on these guys would end up here." I squeezed her hand. "You're the best friend anyone could ever have."

"And you are, too."

Nate and Lucas were already sitting at the table as we came into the kitchen.

"What time are you guys leaving?" I stared at Nate and Lucas with eyes that threatened them to tell the truth.

"Five a.m.," Lucas answered. "We want to come in under the cover of the night, reaching the complex at dawn." He poured me a glass of water. "Drink up."

As I sipped the water, I thought back to the conversation with Rik. "I'm glad Rik explained my brother's obsession about world peace and all, but has he ever thought of the flip side? The STF has power over everyone, even the United States. Won't it make Doug the most powerful man in the world? He can threaten the world with nuclear power, but no one can threaten back."

"Wow, Allie, I never thought of it like that." Ashley placed our food on the table. "Do you think Doug wants to be more than the STF commander?"

"Once he has the power, he could force the Niners out of hiding to work for him," Nate said.

"They'd give in to the threat to keep the peace," I whispered. Right now, I was really terrified of my brother. I looked at Lucas as fear gripped me again. "And now he has the last thing he needs, our son."

* * * *

Ashley and I slept in the master bedroom. The guys didn't want to disturb us when they left. Ashley insisted Nate rest before they left. He planned to grab a few hours in the guest room. I set my alarm for four-thirty a.m. and climbed into bed. *Just try leaving without me, Lucas Montgomery.*

When the alarm went off, I bolted out of bed. Ashley heard it, too, and slipped out of bed as if she knew. We dressed in silence. The boys had left, but Bee sat in the drive, doors ajar, just like I ordered. Ashley followed me without saying a word. Bee flew us into the third level of Headquarters.

"Allie, what are you doing here?" Lucas looked shocked when I stepped out of the car.

"You didn't really think you'd leave without me, did you??" I walked up to him and stared into his eyes.

"I thought we went over this. I don't want you to go. It's safer here."

"My baby needs me. I know how to handle Doug. I'm going, no matter what you say." I placed my hands on my hips and pressed my lips together.

Lucas stared at me. "Fine!" He threw his hand in the air. "Joseph, you'll have to stay behind. Allie's going with me."

I didn't say a word, thinking I'd have to put up more of a fight. Sean directed me to the weapons and gear area and handed me a dark gray suit.

"Pull this on over your clothes. It will stretch to the size you need. It's bullet and fire-proof. Helmets are over there. Pick one that fits."

"Thanks, Sean." I stepped into the one-piece suit and headed for the wall of helmets. Ashley helped me pick one to try on. "Stay at command center with Joseph and John, okay?" I took her hand. "I'll need a friend there."

"Don't worry. I'm not going anywhere." We hugged goodbye, and she ran to Nate's van for one last kiss.

Each pair got in a van, stocked with weaponry, to start their engines. I waved to Ash one more time as Lucas guided our transport behind the caravan of black vans. Each one shifted to jet mode as it took off from the landing pad into the moonless night sky. The Niners could see clearly in the dark, one of their advantages. I couldn't even see the van in front of us.

I kept checking the time, wanting to ask if the van could go any faster. I knew we'd be there in ten minutes, but it seemed to take forever. I tried to remain calm, but the tension in the van filled the air. Lucas hadn't said much during the flight. My nerves were raw. I was afraid to ask questions in case he turned around and took me back. I dug my nails into the arms of the seat, willing the van to get us there as fast as it could.

My stomach flipped over as we began the descent. The van changed to a hovercraft as we came closer to the ground. I could tell Lucas was concentrating on the flight, giving commands in his head and didn't want to interfere. I held my breath until we came to rest in the designated field. Lucas didn't budge. He sat straight, staring out the window.

"Can everyone hear me?" Rik's voice came over the intercom. "Everyone can listen in while I touch base with my connection."

I held my breath, waiting.

Then Rik spoke. "Randolph? I've arrived."

"Cap will be glad to hear. You brought the new recruit?"

"Yes. He's here with me."

"Anyone I know?"

"I think not. His name's Sean McLeod."

"Any Niner is welcome, whether I know him or not. I'll let them know at the gate that you're here."

I prayed we'd make it in. Nate and Julian would remain in the clearing as back-up. Lucas stared at me with a face so serious it gave me chills.

"Strap this pistol to the outside of your lower leg." He handed me the sleek, lightweight weapon and waited for me to comply.

"When you're ready to use it, grab it from the holster and aim at your target. You, and only you, will see a blue dot with a circle around it. That's where the laser will hit. Just think 'Fire' and it will shoot the spot, even if you move the gun away."

"Really?"

"Yes, just trust me. I can't explain the dynamics now."

"What if I change my mind? Or someone grabs my gun?"

"Your weapon is programmed for your use only. No one else can shoot it. If you have it taken away the gun becomes useless. It recognizes you, Allie, like it's part of your DNA. If not in your possession, the weapon automatically shuts down." He stared into my eyes. "One more thing. You only need to think the word 'Fire' and the gun will go off, so be careful. And if you change your mind, think 'cancel'."

"So no bullets will fly?" I pictured those action adventure movies—mercenaries bursting into a building, guns blazing.

"No, bullets. These weapons have powerful lasers that can stun, incapacitate or kill, depending where you mark your intended target."

"So how do I know which one I'm using?" Lucas hadn't explained very well or maybe it was me. "You have to remember I know nothing about these weapons. I've shot a gun at a shooting range. That's all. Please, help me."

"Hopefully, you won't have to use it."

"Not the right answer. If I have to use it, I will."

"Okay, let me start over. If you want to stun someone, think stun as you aim and place your mark. The next step is wound or kill. When you're ready, think 'fire' and the weapon will release the beam."

"Let me practice aloud. I see Doug and want to stop him, but not hurt or kill him. In my head, I say stun as I grab my gun and mark the spot with the blue light. Nothing will happen until I think 'fire', and my gun will shoot the exact spot whether I'm still aiming at it or not."

"Yes, that's right. Makes for quite the element of surprise, don't you think?"

"If I stun him, he will be shocked, but not hurt. But what if I accidently aim for the heart or head when I just want to stun him?"

"Then they're in trouble. Keep that in mind, Allie. The pistol is just like weapons you handled. If you aim for the arm, a person is wounded. Heart, head, vital organs are another matter. You either seriously wound them or they're dead." Lucas handed me a long, sleek weapon. "Strap this rifle to your back. Only use it if we need to blast our way into a locked room or cause an explosion for a getaway. Works the same way only makes a much bigger hole." Lucas grimaced. "Never thought I'd really use these weapons."

I touched his arm. "Let's hope we don't have to."

Levi knocked on Lucas' side of the van. "We're good to go."

"Allie, leave the helmet in the van and pull up the hood of the suit. The helmet was just for crash protection," Lucas released the doors.

I hopped out and struggled with the carrier for the rifle. After much finagling, I got the rifle into place across my back. Sean and Rik led the way through a forest of trees and shrubs. I gave a quick glance back at Nate standing next to his craft. He lifted his hand in acknowledgment.

I worried about Sean. He would play the part of the new Niner recruit and could get separated from us. Lucas, Levi, Jared and I would have an invisible shield force around us. The shield protected us for five minutes then dissolved. The technology hadn't been perfected yet and could only be used once an hour. The Niners had discovered body heat made the force dissolve quickly and hadn't figured out how to eliminate the problem. My suit contained many buttons on the inside wrist, one of which would activate the shield program. I didn't get a crash course on all the choices, so I planned to avoid the other ones unless told to use them.

"When I say green, push the button and the shield will go up," Lucas interrupted my thoughts. "You'll still be able to see us and everything else in the base. I don't know what's going to happen once we get inside, so stay behind me."

He'd get no argument from me. I fell in behind Lucas, Levi and Joseph. We emerged from the woods and walked to the main gate as it began to rise.

"Now! Green button," Lucas whispered.

We followed Rik and Sean into the base and stood in a large, open-air courtyard. Military style vans, jeeps and tanks were parked along the mountain side. A two-story L-shaped complex lay straight ahead.

"Cap's glad you came back to the fold." An STF guard grasped Rik's hand. "And you're bringing a new recruit. Congratulations." He reached over and shook Sean's hand. "I was told to bring you to the office as soon as you arrived."

We marched toward the building that had floor-to-ceiling smoked glass doors. They opened automatically, exposing a room filled with computers, maps, and large screen televisions. A few men worked at stations, but the place didn't look fully operational. I counted four soldiers, making a mental note.

The guard continued up a flight of stairs and into an oversized office. I gazed around at its sparse contents. A huge black leather chair behind a massive mahogany desk was the focal point of the room. Flags of the U.S. and California stood in either corner behind the desk with a framed map of the United States on the wall. The desk had a small laptop, computer pad, intercom and desk set on top. Black leather couches lined the walls, probably for strategy sessions. I spotted one thing so familiar I had to hold my breath to stop the gasp from escaping. A table in one corner held a small framed picture of my parents. We were in Doug's office.

"Please, sit. I'll get Cap and be right back."

The time limit on our shields ticked away. They said I'd get a warm sensation throughout my body when it ended. I panicked as I looked at the others for confirmation. Levi nodded my way. He leaned against the wall on one side of the door with Jared. Lucas and I were on the other. Weapons drawn, we waited. My heart pounded, and blood rushed through my body at a record pace. I practiced the controlled breathing I'd learned in karate to keep steady.

I heard voices then Doug entered the room. A man I'd never seen before followed behind him. The guard who directed us here didn't return.

"Erik, welcome back. Randolph assured me you'd seen the error of your ways." Doug extended his arm toward Rik and turned to Sean. "Welcome, Sean. Welcome to New America."

Nausea gripped me. I choked back the bile coming up my throat. Doug used those exact words with Mom. *New America.* As I recalled, he kept using that name with me during my high school years. New America sounded like a name, some code word. *What does Zak have to do with all this? He's too young to help Doug, and I'm sure he doesn't want to wait for him to grow up.*

My nerves tingled. A shiver shot through my body. I couldn't believe this person was related to me, my own flesh and blood.

Doug gestured to the man standing beside him. "Sean, this is Randolph, one of your Niner brothers and my right-hand man. I don't go anywhere without him."

They had their backs to us when the shields faded. Levi stepped forward and grabbed Randolph around the neck, pointing his gun at the man's temple.

"Whoa, hold on there." Doug raised his hands in the air. "Weapon down." Levi backed off, but still held the gun in Randolph's direction.

Doug turned around and looked directly at me. "Hello, Allison. I've been expecting you." The smirk on his face told me he wasn't the least bit surprised to see me. "Bringing me some *Niners*?"

"No, Doug, I'm here for my son."

"Yes, little Zakary. Such a good baby. He loves his Uncle Doug."

I wanted to spit in his face and lunged forward, but Lucas grabbed my arm.

"Oh, the proud Papa, how touching. Have you even married my sister?" Doug let out a sinister laugh. "And do you know why he won't, Allie? You'll be a shriveled-up old woman by the time he turns thirty-five."

Lucas made a move in his direction. Doug took a step back but kept the sly smile on his face.

"Where is he, Doug?" I stared at him.

"With his mother." Doug's cold blue-gray eyes met mine. He didn't care that he'd stabbed me through the heart with that statement.

I wanted to smack the smile off his face. "I'm his mother."

"For now. He'll forget all about you. Isn't it kind that these smart Niner babies have no memory of their first year? Or should I say four in human years? They get bounced around so much, from family to family or placed in hospitals for tests during those years."

"You son of a bitch!" I screamed. Lucas had me around the waist or I would have scratched Doug's eyes out.

"Oh, wait." Doug walked behind his desk, tapping his fingers together. "He's not a Niner child, is he, Allison? He's even more special. What is it you people call them? Niner-squared? Very unique. Zak's almost one of a kind." He nodded at Lucas. "Congratulations."

As much as I wanted to punch him, I had to let Doug think he had the upper hand. "I want to see him."

"If I may?" Doug nodded toward his desk. Jared walked over and shoved him in the back with the end of his gun. Doug pushed a button on the intercom. "Katrina? Bring the baby to my office." Then he turned and looked only at me. "It doesn't have to be like this, Allison. You and Lucas could have a wonderful life under my protection. Lucas could work with us. You'll be provided with everything you need. The economy isn't what it used to be, and you could live in luxury." He smirked again.

"Never." I glared at him with the most hateful look I could muster, hoping he could feel the loathing.

He took a step toward me, but Lucas came between us. "Don't touch her."

Doug held up his hands. "I just want to reason with my sister."

"Oh, I know what you did to your sister." Lucas glared at him. "Starting when she was a baby. You let her fall and bash her head in for your own selfish reasons."

Doug pressed his lips together. "You don't know the whole story, Niner."

"Then why don't you enlighten me?" I could tell Lucas was stalling for time. The Niners had to be communicating telepathically through their phones, working out a plan.

"There's nothing to tell. Poor Allison fell off a chair and split her head open. Look at her now. She's fine."

"Enough!" I yelled. "Where's Zak?"

"Patience." Doug's attention came back to me. We stared at each other with so much hatred it took over the room. Once I wanted to understand him, find out more about him and why he didn't like me. Now I knew him for what he was. *A psychopath. They lie. They break all the rules. They can be charming and intelligent, fooling those around them. They feel entitled. They aren't close to family members. They anger quickly. They make you afraid and feel unsafe.*

A woman stood in the open doorway holding a baby. As soon as Zak spotted me he reached out his little arms. "Mum-mum," he called. Tears filled my eyes, and I ached to snatch him from her arms.

"Be good for Mommy," she cooed. The tall, slim woman with short, shaggy black hair had a vaguely familiar look about her. I stared daggers at her, wanting to tear her hair out, fistful by fistful.

As I studied her, I felt I knew her. Then it hit me. She looked like Doug's high school girlfriend. I was shocked how much she resembled the girl I'd seen in pictures, although nowhere as beautiful. Her face, more square than round, gave her a harder edge. I couldn't tell if she had blue eyes or not, but Kimmy's shone bright blue in the photos. This woman wore some type of uniform and a vest for protection. *A soldier? Part of Doug's army? Why did she call herself mommy?*

Doug walked away from me and over to his desk, ignoring the woman holding Zak. "You have two choices,

Niner. You can leave quietly, as you came, without Zak, or we take you all prisoners." Doug sat in the big leather chair, hands folded. "I'll have to do something about that name. Zak. Doesn't suit him. His middle name is James if I recall. Dad was so proud when he found out, Allison." He glanced toward the woman in the doorway. "James, that's what we'll call him, Katrina. What do you think?"

Katrina nodded and smiled, knowing her place. I tensed as I watched her shift Zak from one arm to the other. His little eyes latched onto mine, but he stayed silent.

"Dad will never forgive you for taking my baby."

"Oh, he'll be grateful. He was never very fond of Lucas. He always thought the kid acted suspicious—to use his words. I'll say you ran off with him, chose him over the baby."

I gasped. Doug had all the answers, or so he thought. I had to keep acting so I said, "Katrina looks so familiar. Do I know her, Doug?" A flash of pain crossed his face then his expression went blank. "She looks like a girl I saw in pictures back home." He began tapping his fingers together. "Have you talked to Mom and Dad lately? They'd be so proud of you at this moment."

As I continued to talk, I glanced at Lucas hoping he'd picked up on my plan. I didn't have time to connect my phone into their conversation. I raised my weapon and aimed at my brother's head, but I'd already marked Katrina's upper thigh, just above the knee.

"Now, Allison, what do you think you're doing?" Doug gave one nod toward his minion, Randolph. "He can disarm you in a blink of an eye."

"Go ahead, Randolph." I challenged him.

As he took a step forward, I shouted, "Fire."

Chapter Thirteen

I couldn't resist saying the word aloud. I wanted to make Doug jump, but he didn't flinch until he saw Katrina drop to the ground. Lucas was there to catch Zak.

Two guards rushed into the room. Levi and Sean stunned them, leaving them to squirm on the floor. Sean turned to Randolph, overpowered him and gave him a jolt with the gun. Jared took care of Doug, already having a pistol on his back. We ran into the corridor and down the stairs. An alarm sounded, and I knew the four men on the first floor would be waiting. Lucas handed Zak off to me. The men went ahead while I stayed out of sight. I slid along the wall making my way to the exit doors. When I reached them, they wouldn't open.

"Stand back!" I heard Sean call to me, and he pulled the rifle from his back holster.

Lucas threw his body on us. "Stay down!" he yelled over the alarm that wouldn't quit.

The blast caused the doors to implode. We filed through after the explosion, one behind the other, staying low to the ground. I took in the fresh air, relieved to be out of the building. The morning sky had no sun, just gray threatening clouds. We ran through the lot toward the main gates as they began to descend.

"Drop and roll!" Lucas yelled.

The gate was now barely three feet from the ground. Lucas grabbed Zak from my arms. I followed instructions and propelled my body under the moving metal. When I reached the other side, Lucas handed me the baby and followed. Sean continued to fire the rifle, making huge holes in the courtyard. All the men were through, except him.

"Sean! Come on!" Lucas called to him.

Sean skidded toward the gate like a baseball player sliding into base then rolled onto his stomach. He pulled his body under the gate on his elbows, but something went wrong. Part of his uniform snagged the lowering bars.

Spikes shot up from the ground as I yelled encouraging words, then I looked on in horror. One point caught his leg, piercing straight through the flesh. Blood spurted up and out splattering the ground.

"Lucas!" I pointed to Sean as he continued to pull his body to our side of the fence. "Help him!"

Lucas whipped out a knife and cut Sean's suit away. "This is going to hurt, Sean." He yanked the leg from the trap then wrapped the torn suit around the wound just above the knee as Sean rolled to safety.

Lucas threw Sean's arm around his shoulder and dragged him toward the woods. The rest of us sprinted for the vans through the field of trees. Explosions could be heard, but they weren't directed at us. *The field! They're bombing the vans so we can't get away.*

As we raced to the rendezvous point, smoke rose from the area. The STF bombs had zeroed in on our meeting place. Emerging from the forest, a demolished van greeted us. Filmy clouds billowed in the air making it hard to breath. *Nate!*

I scanned the wreckage and surrounding area, searching for him. Julian stepped out of the brush and waved his arms over his head.

"Nate?" I yelled. "Where is he?"

I looked down at my baby and realized he hadn't made a sound during the ordeal. I wondered if he'd gone into shock or was just relieved to be with his mother again. He needed my immediate attention. Our van looked intact so I rushed toward it. Lucas popped the doors open. Hands trembling, I strapped Zak in his car seat. Luckily, Katrina had kept a bottle tucked inside the blanket. His eyes fluttered as he drank, then he nodded off to sleep. I jumped from the van and ran back to the edge of the woods.

"Where's Nate?" I screamed.

Julian motioned for me to follow. My best friend sat leaning against a tree, barely conscious. One side of his face had been horribly burned making me want to look away. An open oozing gash ran down his cheek as Lucas tried to stop the bleeding. I forged ahead and squatted next to him. "Hey, buddy. Can you hear me?"

The burned cheek soaked with blood made him look like some terrible monster. His reddish-blonde hair, matted and soaked with blood, now only covered half his head.

"I've tried to stop the bleeding," Julian said. "I picked up on the incoming missile too late. Never heard it. We got out of the van just in time. The force of the blast threw Nate in the air, and he hit his head against the van. Shrapnel caught him right in this side of his face." He pointed to the grotesque wound. "It all happened so fast. I had no time to detect the bomb. It was like something I never saw before."

"They have Niner technology, too, Julian." I tried to make him feel better. The stress I felt earlier changed to determination to get us all out of there. "I'm afraid my brother will use that knowledge to advance his cause any way he can." I took Nate's hand. "Will he be okay?"

"We need to get him back to the Niner hospital. We have lasers that will start healing the burns and take away the pain. He's lost a lot of blood and needs a transfusion. We need to check for brain damage and finally close up that cut on his face."

I studied the gash. The open wound extended from the top of his ear to the bottom of his nose. It broke my heart to see him that way. One side of his face was pretty much destroyed. *All because of me.* My heart fell to the pit of my stomach. "You're going to be fine, Nate. Hang in there. We'll have you home soon."

"Z … ak?" His looked up at me, eyes filled with concern.

Tears welled in my eyes. "We got him." Part of a smile covered the good side of his face then he passed out.

"Nate!" I screamed. "Nate!" I couldn't lose him, my best friend and confidante, the boy who would do anything to protect me.

"Nate, don't you dare die on me!" I turned to Lucas and yelled, "Let's get him out of here!"

Sean and Rik carried Nate to their van, and Julian hopped aboard. I ran to our van, and Lucas took off into the air as another bomb hit the ground. How could Doug be so heartless?

Ashley needed to know what had happened, and I had to prepare her for what was to come. I turned on the video feed in the van. Her anxious face appeared. "Do you have the baby?"

"Yes, we do." Cheers rang out in the background. "Ash, wait, there's more. We're not in the clear yet."

"What did Doug do now?"

"They found the spot where we landed. Julian and Nate stayed behind as back-up in case we didn't get out. They were Plan B, prepared to come in, if needed."

"But they didn't have to, right?"

"Right, but the STF bombed the site before we got there."

Ashley covered her mouth. "Please tell me they're okay."

"Julian's fine but Nate … isn't. Have the medical team ready and someone waiting on the third floor. We'll be there in ten."

"What happened, Allie?" Ashley lifted her brows as her eyes overflowed with tears. "Is he going to die?"

"I don't know. I'm sorry."

"Don't be. He would never have stayed behind."

I switched off the video screen and began to cry. "Lucas, this is my fault."

Lucas looked at me with tears in his eyes. "No, it's not. Don't start that 'I'm the enemy' crap again. We went through that in high school and where did it get us? A year apart and miserable. It's no one's fault, Allie. It's just the way it is. We'll fix this, the best we can."

"If I'd stayed away, if I didn't give in to you when you showed up at my door at school—"

"If you're going to say 'if Zak wasn't born' I'm going to eject you from this van which, by the way, is in the air right now." Lucas wiped at a tear running down my cheek. "We have to agree not to live our lives with blame or thinking we're not good for each other. We've come too far. Didn't we promise to never let anything come between us again?"

"Yes." I knew he was right, but I couldn't help myself. The guilt was overwhelming. Who could blame me for saying I was the enemy? I'd brought Doug right into the middle of their lives again.

We flew straight into the third floor when we reached Napa. Ashley stood next to a hospital bed, and a team of doctors huddled in the corner.

"Lucas, you're in charge of Zak." I rushed from the vehicle to where Nate was being placed on the bed.

Ashley cried and gasped at the same time. Nothing I could say would comfort her.

Ash and I rushed to Bee on the second floor and followed them to the hospital. When we arrived, Serena, who had come with Julian, told us to go home and get some rest. No one would be able to see Nate until tomorrow. He needed tests, brain scans and a blood transfusion. Treatment would start immediately for the burns. He'd be stitched up today, and tomorrow they'd begin cosmetic work on the scar. Updates would be sent to us on our phones. Nate was listed as critical, but they were known for saving trauma patients and repairing cosmetic damage.

"You haven't spent any time with Zak," Ashley said as we climbed back into Bee.

"This is more important."

"Nate would want you to be with your baby."

I took one look at Ashley, my face crumpled, and I began to sob. She joined me, and we cried the whole way to Spanish Village. As we sat in the car in front of the house, we couldn't move. I sent a text to Lucas to help us.

Sean appeared in the doorway and limped toward the car with Lucas right behind him. They carried us inside, placing us on either end of the couch. Lucas put a sleeping Zak in my arms. I breathed a sigh of relief.

"We have to pray for your Uncle Nate." I told him. "Mean Uncle Doug went too far this time." I glanced around at my friends. "We can't let Doug win. We have to find a way to stop him." Solemnly, we all nodded in agreement.

* * * *

When I woke the next morning, I stared at the ceiling for what seemed like hours. My mind played yesterday's events over and over again. We'd all been too naïve. Doug knew much more than we thought. He didn't ask how we'd found the base or even appear concerned. Looking back, the rescue seemed too easy.

I jumped out of bed and ran to the kitchen where I found Lucas feeding Zak. After kissing them both, I pulled a bottle of water from the fridge and headed for the family room. Sean leaned against the corner of the sofa, phone in hand, working. I curled up next to this big, burly man and put my head on his shoulder. He had been our rock throughout the ordeal. "How's your leg?"

"I'll be fine. They've treated what they could for now." Sean kissed the top of my head. "We're leaving today, Allie. After Nate gets his last treatment, we're all piling in a van and flying to Montana."

Lucas carried Zak into the family room. "Pack what you need. We'll leave as soon as possible. I'd like to get as far from this place as I can."

I looked up at him. "Does Ashley know?"

"Yes, I wake her with every update. She's been asleep for several hours."

"What is the latest update?"

"Burns are lasered and now just need to heal. The skin will be a bright pink for a while. Nate has a concussion, a pretty bad one, and may need a week or two to recover. He's scheduled later this morning for scar correction. After it's done, he should look as good as new. Serena can do all the follow-up treatments back in Montana. She came for you, Allie. We never knew she'd end up helping Nate."

I was relieved Nate would have no permanent damage. Hard to believe the Niners had that kind of technology. The damage to his face had been extensive.

I reached out for Zak, and Lucas placed him between Sean and me. Lucas had changed and bathed him. He even wore a new outfit.

"When will Zak start sleeping less?" I played with his little tuft of dark hair. He slept like a normal baby. He never did a twelve-hour shift but would sleep at least ten straight hours besides short naps.

"He'll give up naps around the age of two," Sean said. "Or in Zak's case, four human years. From then on, seven or eight hours of sleep are the norm. When he reaches puberty our Niner cycle kicks in. Guess we have to give our parents a break until then." He laughed, tickling Zak under the chin.

"But we're not sure about Zak, right?" I wrinkled my brow as I looked up at Lucas.

"Hence, the journal." Lucas held out his hands.

I giggled. "Thus and now hence, old man." I shook my head.

"Give me a break!" Lucas shrugged as he smiled at me.

I hated to change the subject but needed to address a certain topic. "Were any of you surprised by Doug's reaction yesterday? He didn't yell at his men or panic. It's like he expected us."

"Now that you mention it, you're right." Lucas paced through the room. "We didn't have to make any real threats to get Zak out of there."

"Exactly, it's almost like he was prepared for our arrival." Rik's name popped in my head, but I held my tongue. Then something else crossed my mind. Rik never helped subdue the men in the room when we escaped. I played the scene back in my head to check. I saw Jared take out my brother. Sean and Levi subdued the two guards that came into the room, and Sean stunned

Randolph. Somehow Rik managed to get to the vans, and I tried to recall how. *I'm right about Rik, but I'll wait till we get to Montana to discuss it. I want to get as far from him as I can.*

Sean sat up and handed me the baby. "I'll get the van ready and wait on the first floor of Headquarters for you. Send any packages, boxes, luggage my way with Bee. We'll leave as soon as Nate's cleared to go." He tousled Zak's hair and patted my shoulder. "Love you, guys. You're like a little sister, Allie. Don't ever feel bad or think you caused anything to happen." He wrapped his muscular arms around me, and I felt safe.

A lump grew in my throat. "Love you, too, Sean. You know you're walking me down the aisle and giving me away to this one, right?" I pointed at Lucas.

Sean rose from the sofa, and they exchanged air punches. "See you later." He saluted as he left the room.

I smiled at Lucas. "Thanks for having Zak's room ready. You even remembered the other pattern we picked out."

"That wasn't me, Allie. It was all Sean. It was his idea."

"Aww! He's so sweet," Ashley said as she walked into the room rubbing her eyes. She slipped in next to me on the couch and reached for Zak. He began cooing and laughing.

"Tee-tee," he said.

"Did you hear that? He called me Auntie!" Ashley giggled.

"Well, he got part of it, at least." Lucas looked crestfallen.

"He'll say daddy next, I'm sure," I said. "Hey, if we're going to leave, let's get going. Lucas, you did a great job getting your son ready, and I need to catch up."

I headed for the bedroom, looking for items to pack. Zak's room was next. I grabbed the elephant comforter for the ride home. Back in my room, I showered, threw on jeans, t-shirt and sneakers, then pulled my hair back in a casual ponytail. Hard to believe I'd stood in a secret military base rescuing my son less than twenty-four hours ago.

"I'm loading Bee and sending her to the main facility. Last call!" I yelled as I headed for the front door.

Ashley handed me Nate's duffle bag and her small carry-on as I went by. She had ordered her own car so she could get to the hospital before us. The vehicle silently approached and zoomed into the drive. The hatch opened, and I threw their belongings in the back of the car.

Bee popped her rear compartment. "Take this to Sean and come back for us in two hours, Bee."

Ashley flew out of the house. She had a smile from ear to ear. "Nate can have company until his final procedure in two hours. They said it should take an hour and a half. He can travel as soon as they're done. We just have to be a little careful because of the concussion."

"I'm so happy he'll be back to normal soon!" I hugged her tightly.

"His face is still pink and swollen, but that will go away with time. He's calling them his battle scars."

"Tell him he won't be adding to them if I have anything to say about it." I called after her as she headed outside. I watched until her car disappeared down the street and went back into the house.

Lucas and I closed the house, checking for anything we missed while trying to keep Zak entertained. We still had time before Bee returned so we did an extra sweep of the house. I was checking the fridge when I heard a knock at the door.

Puzzled, I glanced at Lucas as he came out of the bedroom to answer the door. I expected to see Sean or Levi on the porch but never Rik. Lucas invited him in, so I joined them in the living room.

"This is unexpected, Rik. You know we're leaving today." Out of the corner of my eye, I watched Lucas slip his phone from his pocket. He slid it under his leg as he sat on the sofa.

"Just came to say goodbye and state my case one more time."

"What case?" I leaned against a wall, close to the baby seat. I didn't trust him. My heart pounded, and my mouth went dry.

"The STF cause. To join Doug and the others."

"What?" Lucas looked shocked, but I wasn't.

I bent down and took Zak from the carrier. "You never defected," I stated.

"No, I never did and plan to return today. I'd like to bring you with me as a family unit. Doug has plans to build a base with houses for families, similar to what we have here in Napa. You can design your home, live in luxury, all at no cost. If Doug could see the Niner facilities in Pennsylvania, Montana—"

"What? Niners never reveal our locations!" Lucas shot up from the sofa, fuming.

"Don't worry. I never gave Doug locations or coordinates. I'm loyal to the Niners, Lucas. You can trust me and the others. I'd love for you to welcome Doug into the Niner fold. Let him see what we have here. He wants to be a part of this."

Oh, I bet he does. Mr. Born One Minute Too Soon to be a Niner.

"Until that time," Rik said. "Everyone is safe in the compounds. You're a smart guy, Lucas. Part of the western region elite. You're quick to come up with ideas and plans. We'd love to have you on board. I'm sure your son will be twice the genius." Rik smiled, but it felt cold, almost sinister. A chill went through my body. I wrapped my arms tighter around Zak.

Lucas stood and took a few steps toward Rik. "You told Doug that Allie was pregnant, and the baby could be born on the twenty-ninth."

"Yes, it was too good to be true. Zak could be the turning point in finalizing the nuclear antidote. By the time he's ten, he'll be challenging us Niners to mental duels." Rik chuckled as if Lucas would join in. Instead, Lucas clenched his fists, and his face turned red.

I began to back away toward the door. I could tell from Lucas' eyes, he agreed. I needed to escape and get help. Zak needed to be as far away from Rik as possible.

"I wouldn't do that, Allison." Rik seemed to know I'd moved, even though his back was turned. "Your boyfriend's marked."

I glanced at Lucas, realizing I couldn't see the blue circle. I had to take his word. Rik just had to think 'fire' to end it all.

"Don't listen to him, Allie. It's alright if you leave."

I shook my head and took a few steps back toward them. My teeth chattered, and my head pounded. Only Rik could cancel the shot. "Doug knew we were coming to the base. *You* told him, Rik." I fought to keep my composure.

"Yes, he hoped you'd do anything to save your baby. He wanted to convince you to stay. You outsmarted us, Allison. Shooting out Katrina's legs was a nice touch. You left her wounded and bleeding. Too bad though, she always defended you. She hoped your family would move to the base, and the boys could grow up together."

"Boys?"

"You didn't know Doug and Katrina have a four-year-old son?" He smirked as he turned my way.

Doug has a four-year-old? Didn't my mom say she wanted to see her first grandchild when I told her about Zak? Blindsided again by my brother, I needed to focus. "Doug's married?" *To Katrina?*

"No, but they've been together for at least a decade."

Ten years? Doug and Katrina had been together since he came back to the states. I was just a little girl. "Katrina volunteered to raise my baby even though Doug kidnapped him?"

"Yes, for the cause. She loves Doug very much."

"I bet he doesn't feel the same," I said as I pictured the girl from his high school years.

"Cap is dedicated to the STF. Everyone knows that, even Katrina."

Were all these people brainwashed by Doug? I'd never follow him anywhere. I'd love to see the side of him that convinced people to be so loyal. Rik seemed to be in a sharing mood, so I decided to keep asking. "What's his plan?"

"Doug has it all mapped out," Rik answered. We're in the process of getting it up and run—"

The front door flew back as Levi stormed in. "You're under arrest, Erik! Stand down!"

My eyes flicked to Lucas, afraid he'd been shot. Instead he rushed over and stood in front of us.

Levi took Rik's weapons, now useless. I realized Levi had disconnected him from the Niner computer system.

"Come quietly." Levi told him. "You're done here."

We followed and stood in the doorway to watch.

"Shouldn't he be handcuffed?" I looked up at Lucas.

"Don't worry. That car's equipped with a passenger seat that will contain him." Lucas sighed as he watched his Niner brothers walk down the drive.

Rik turned in the driveway and called to us, "We're not done here. We'll have the baby back in our possession by nightfall! We can find him anywhere."

Levi dragged Rik the rest of the way to the car, and I slammed our front door shut.

"What just happened?" I cried as I sank to the floor holding my baby. "You could've died! Rik was going to take the baby, wasn't he?"

"Yes, I believe it was his last attempt before he left." Lucas slid down the wall next to me. "Levi disabled Rik's gun before he came through the door. He heard the whole conversation. I knew he was on his way. Thanks for keeping Rik talking so long."

"I saw you slip your phone out."

"Yeah. Levi knew I was marked and revoked Rik's privileges at the command center before he came in. Rik's gun wouldn't have fired."

Lucas grew quiet. Sensing something wasn't right, I asked. "What is it? I know there's still something wrong."

"I was thinking about what Rik said. The STF will have Zak before nightfall, they will find him." He got to his feet. "Quick! Give him to me."

My hands trembled as I handed Zak to him. "What is it? You changed Zak and put fresh clothes on him. Did you find anything unusual? What could they have done?"

My heart pounded as Lucas checked every part of Zak's body then peeled something off from behind his ear. He held up a very tiny clear patch similar to a listening device we'd put on my mom's phone long ago.

"A tracking device. How could I be so stupid? They know where we are. I need to alert Levi."

He ran to the half bath by the kitchen and flushed the patch down the toilet. "We leave now," he yelled when he reappeared.

I grabbed the few things I had ready from the bedroom as Lucas came in behind me. "I just talked to Levi. He agrees it was a tracker. It gave our coordinates away. It will be just a matter of time before the STF shows up. Levi issued a shut-down of Spanish Village. Everyone's instructed to leave their homes immediately. We'll evacuate the Napa facility and be gone by afternoon."

Panic and fright set in. "How?"

"Don't worry. We've done drills before. The residents know what to do."

"I told Bee to come for us in two hours." I checked my phone. "Only fifteen more minutes. I'll tell her to come now."

"It's still too long to wait. We'll have to walk."

I ran to the front of the house and watched out the front window. Families walked calmly down the middle of the street. They pulled luggage and carts, wore backpacks and shoulder bags. Vehicles were lined up in a queue waiting for the people who'd ordered them. "People have done this before?"

"Yes, we practice all the time. I had to do it for real in Montana, remember? Everyone stays calm so we can get out safely."

"No secret escape routes? Bomb shelters?"

"Not with our technology. We can fly out of here in the vans. Two can be put together to make a large passenger jet. We don't want people to be trapped in the village. There's an emergency bomb shelter under the main building, but we'd only use it in extreme circumstances."

"Rik said he would never tell our location, but he lied."

"Niners made the technology but kept their promise. Think. They didn't give our location away ... Zak did."

"Still defending them?"

"No, damn it, I'm not. It's just hard to wrap my head around the fact that my brothers would be traitors."

"Doug will come," I said.

"And when he does, we'll be gone. The place will be shut down, stripped of all its technology—a shell of its former self. We can never come back. It will be the first time we had to sacrifice an entire community." Lucas hung his head, and my heart broke for him.

"Doug wanted Zak, not Spanish Village's location."

"You're right. This was his Plan B, Allie, and a good one. Doug had every intention of keeping him if he could get away with it. I think he wanted Zak more than the location. Either way it's a win-win."

During our conversation I continued to pack and take things to the front door. "We're ready, Lucas."

Zak sat in his front pouch carrier so I could be hands free. The car seat would be left at the house. I opened the front door. A few families still rushed down the streets.

"Lucas? We're the last ones."

"As it should be. I'm in line to become a leader one day. I have to be last." He joined me at the front door. "Most have made it to Main Street or are at Headquarters.

"Nate and Ashley!" Nate would miss out on the cosmetic surgery or be unable to complete it.

"I'm sure they're at Headquarters by now. We'll see them soon. I let Sean know we're still at the house and will meet him as soon as I do a quick sweep of the neighborhood and make sure everyone's out."

The steady stream of people drew to a trickle. Lucas scanned each street by phone.

"All clear. The last of the families are on Main." He looked out at the drive. "Strange, Bee should be here. I used up fifteen minutes with my final check. We still have to walk. Let's go."

As we stepped outside to begin our journey to Headquarters, the town felt eerily quiet. No cars. No people. I glanced around and saw no one. We crossed the street and began the walk to Main Street.

Without warning, no sound to be heard, a bomb hit our home. A thunderous explosion leveled the house to the ground. I screamed out and covered Zak's head with my hand. Lucas pulled us to the ground and covered us with his body. Thick black smoke enveloped us as the winds picked up and raced around us. Dust joined the smoke as it rose from the ground. I coughed and choked on the polluted air.

The noise grew deafening as bomb after bomb went off, exploding more houses in the neighborhood. The thin blanket I'd wrapped Zak in was all I had to cover his face. After what seemed like hours, silence fell over the street. We pulled our bodies up from the sidewalk and faced each other with the kind of fright in our eyes I'd never seen before. When I found the courage to look down the street, nothing was left.

Chapter Fourteen

Lucas and I didn't say a word. We just looked at each other and nodded. My feet hit the pavement full force propelling me away from the destruction. As I ran, I clutched the baby to my chest. The bombs had been silent until they'd hit the intended target. I had no idea which house would be next. When one exploded, we crouched down to wait it out. Every time I prayed it'd be the last.

"Give him to me." Lucas motioned to Zak. "I can run faster. He's slowing you down."

I reluctantly gave up the carrier, and we slipped the straps over Lucas' head. Zak had remained silent throughout the ordeal, but his dark little eyes were wide with fright. He took everything in, looking around without a whimper. I worried about the smoke and dust filling his lungs and adjusted the blanket across his nose.

Lucas surveyed the area. "Most of the side streets are demolished." He nodded straight ahead. "Main is a few houses away." He looked down at his phone. "From what I can see, most of it is gone."

We reached the intersection as the square exploded. I bit my lip to keep control. The smell of smoke and burning debris overwhelmed me. I glanced to my right. A few people still rushed toward Headquarters, dropping their possessions as they ran. Lucas and I were targets in the open space, but the road was our only way out.

"Lucas," I gasped. "Have you noticed when the homes explode there is no shrapnel or pieces of debris? We haven't been hit by anything."

"The houses are imploding," Lucas stated as if he'd already analyzed the attack. "I'm sure those bombs were created by Niners. The land is not destroyed, just the building."

"I hope there are no people under those piles." I gestured to one yard and shuddered.

He pulled his phone from his pocket and studied the screen. "One casualty. Other than that, everyone is accounted for."

"Who?" I trembled.

"Don't know." Lucas shrugged. "That's odd, because we're all connected to the mainframe."

"Thank goodness for scanning. At least we know most everyone made it."

As we neared the final crossroad, something caught my eye in the front yard of the last house on the street. "Bee!" I raced toward her. She lay crushed on the grass, a mangled pile of familiar shiny silver and blue.

I studied the area and saw she had collided with another vehicle, now wedged underneath her. "Lucas, can you do something? Can you move Bee off this pile?"

Lucas handed Zak to me and began to push. "There's another car under her."

"I know. Please help her."

He gave Bee a final shove. "Don't look," he said.

I couldn't help it. I had to look. Rik slumped in the driver's seat of the other car, blood streaming down his face and from his ears, his body torn open from the blast. He was the causality. The cars must have somehow collided when the house exploded. The driver's side of Rik's car was gone.

"Oh!" My hand flew to my mouth. Levi sat in the passenger seat of Rik's car, blood trickling from his right ear. Unable to reach him, Lucas smashed the front window and pulled him out.

"Rik said no one would be hurt," Levi whispered, then grimaced as Lucas tugged him through the opening. "The bombs only destroy buildings, not people. Missiles can sense the warmth of humans and avoid those places. Did everyone get out?" His face contorted into a look of pain and heartbreak.

Lucas held Levi in his arms, tears rolling down his face. "Yes, we're the last of them."

Levi's wounds were extensive and difficult to look at. Lucas gently lowered him to the ground.

Levi struggled to open his eyes. "Get Rik to Headquarters, Lucas," he grunted. "Get the chip in his head."

"I will," Lucas answered.

Levi had no idea Rik was dead. I tried not to look inside the car at the mangled body. Then Levi grabbed Lucas' shirt. "Is Sean alright?"

"Sean? He's supposed to be at the facility waiting for us." I panicked, scanning the grounds for him.

"Go, look for him. Leave me." Levi pushed Lucas away.

"No!" I screamed.

"He knows he's not going to make it, Allie." Lucas stared up at me.

"Yes, you will, Levi. Don't you dare leave us. Hang on! We'll look for Sean and come back for you." I turned to Lucas. "We can't just leave him here."

"We won't."

Levi lifted his hand and motioned back toward the village. "Rik … overpowered me … Sean in van … find him." He slumped back on the wreckage. "Allie," he said in a gravelly voice, "Rik had a message from Doug. He said to tell you he'll see you again. You can't hide forever. Don't worry. We'll make sure—" He gasped for a breath.

"Don't try to talk," Lucas told him.

What did that mean? We'd have to be fugitives for the rest of our lives? "Levi, we have to get you help. We'll look for

Sean and be back soon." I took his hand. "Where should we look?"

"The square." Levi groaned and looked up at me. "Allie? Tell Suzanne I love her." His head fell back, and his eyes closed.

"Levi!" My brain scrambled trying to make sense of this day—the senseless bombings, people running for their lives, this accident. I looked around the smoking village, each home in a jumbled heap of debris. Tears stung my eyes.

I walked slowly back through the village, right down Main to the village square. I scanned every inch as I shuffled along looking for a black van and my dear friend. Small fires dotted the way as I headed down the street, clutching Zak close to my body. I didn't want him affected by the dust that hung thick in the air. Black smoke billowed above us, filling my nostrils with the acrid smell. "Sean!"

I walked past the fountain in the middle of the square, untouched by the bombs. Amidst all the destruction, water still sprung from its center, flowing down to the pool filled with black soot and dust. I sat on the edge, head in hands, staring at the ground. Against the edge of the fountain I spotted a black mirror, one that looked like it belonged on the side of a van. *He must be close by.* I felt it.

"You went too far, Allie. Cars can't drive into the square." Lucas said as he caught up to me.

I reached for the mirror. "But he's here, somewhere. I know it."

We walked back along the sidewalk where stores should have been, examining every inch. The buildings had crumbled to nothingness, just steaming piles of stucco and adobe. We crossed the street and stood in front of the first house from the square.

"Look." Lucas pointed at the shell of a house. "That's odd. Part of the house is still standing when the rest are piles of rubble. Stay back while I take a look." I followed him up the drive, disobeying the order. I spotted a shiny black door peeking through the mound of shattered stucco and red tiles.

"Sean?" Lucas called to him.

"Here, Lucas, behind the van. My leg's pinned. I'm holding up the wall of the house. If I let go, it will fall on me."

The same leg that was injured during Zak's rescue? I didn't know if Sean had the strength to hold the wall much longer.

"Hang on, I'm coming in." Lucas crawled up the pile and slid down between the standing wall of the house and the mountain of debris. Sean needed someone to move the van. He couldn't hold up the wall and push the car at the same time. My heart pounded as the pile began to move toward me. "Keep holding the wall!" I heard Lucas yell. "I almost have it."

Sean screamed out in pain, startling Zak. He began to cry for the first time today. I tried to rock him the best I could and moved farther down the drive. Lucas shouted, "Now!"

The wall of the house crumbled to the ground. I screamed as I watched the wall turn into a pile of rocks. "Lucas!" Could I lose both of them? My heart couldn't take it.

Then through the dust, I saw Lucas dragging Sean away from the debris. He placed Sean on the front lawn and turned to go back.

"Lucas! No!"

"I need to get the van out. There's no way Sean can walk. I can carry him but when we reach Levi I won't be able to carry them both. Stay back!"

I ran to where Sean lay and prayed for the best. He grimaced in pain but reached out to hold my hand and comfort me. Zak stopped crying as soon as he saw Sean. Sean petted his little head, talking in a low voice. We watched as the van broke free of its prison, a little battered and bruised, but working. Lucas jogged over, lifted Sean to his feet and helped him into the van. He whispered something to him as I climbed in the passenger side.

"You okay back there, Sean?" I called over my shoulder.

"Yeah, but I'll feel much better once we get to Headquarters." As we drove down Main, Sean told us the rest of the horrendous story. "I heard about the mandatory evacuation, and I thought I'd come and get you in the van. I was driving down Main when I spotted Levi's car parked by the square. I assumed he was doing a sweep of the stores to make sure everyone had left. I thought he could use some help so I drove down there and parked next to his car. That's when I turned stupid."

"You're not stupid, Sean," I said. "We're all not thinking clearly today."

"Thanks, Allie, but I blame myself. Rik was in the passenger seat of Levi's car. Levi ran toward me, waving his arms. I thought he was flagging me down for help. I opened the door to talk to Rik. He told me the car's computer system had a meltdown during one of the explosions. After Levi was done, they planned to walk back to Headquarters. He thanked me for coming to the rescue. I never got the message about Rik being a traitor. I thought he was doing rounds with Levi." Sean paused for a breath.

"Sean, you can tell us later. You're wounded." I turned again to check on him.

"No." He grimaced as he shifted his body. "I'm okay. I *want* to tell you. Besides, you need a distraction, Allie. You look like you're in shock." He leaned forward and rubbed my arm.

"Maybe I am," I whispered. It felt as if the life had been drained out of me. "Do you think there will be more bombs?"

Sean shook his head. "There's nothing left to destroy. Spanish Village is gone."

I shut my eyes and leaned my head back against the seat. "It seems like the last two days have been a dream. Make that a nightmare." I sighed. "Go on, Sean. Rik tricked you into thinking he was helping Levi?"

"Yes. Levi had him deactivated and on lock-down while he checked out the square. He was coming back to the car when he saw me. He tried to stop me from releasing Rik."

"Sean, you really should rest." I searched the van for a bottle of water and handed one to him.

"No, you need to know. I told Rik I had something in the van that would fix the car. As I dug around in the back of the van, it began to move toward me at a very fast pace. It was all I could do to grab on or I'd have been underneath it. Rik had rammed the front of the van with the car and pushed me into that driveway. I slammed against the house with the van in front of me. My leg got wedged under the back bumper. I almost passed out but fought to stay conscious. I'd just started to push the van off me when a bomb hit the house. I held the wall steady until it ended. If you didn't find me, I don't think I would have gotten out alive. I couldn't let go of the wall to push the van."

I grasped Lucas' arm. "I thought Levi said the bombs could sense life forms in the area."

"If it was seconds, the missile may not have had time to compensate."

Right. I didn't believe anything Rik said. "And what about Levi? If Rik had control of the car, how did Levi end up back in the car with him?"

"We may never know." Lucas shook his head.

"Once Levi regains consciousness, he'll tell us," I said.

Lucas came to a stop in front of the car accident. "Stay in the car, Allie. I'll help Levi in."

Sean released the back doors. They talked so quietly I couldn't hear them as Lucas put Levi in the back.

"I'll cover him, Lucas," Sean told him. "Start driving."

Headquarters had never looked so good as we pulled into the third level to park. Most of the vans were gone. Families had been assigned places to go—other compounds or safe houses.

"Why is Headquarters still standing?" I looked at Lucas before I got out.

"Takes a lot to bring it down. It has extra shields." Lucas jumped from the van.

Waiting medical workers placed Sean on a stretcher and wheeled him to another van. Levi's covered body still lay in the back of the van. Lucas came to the passenger side and helped me out as Zak continued to sleep.

"What about Levi?" I gestured toward his motionless body. "He's in desperate need of help."

"He didn't make it, Allie. I'm sorry." Lucas hung his head. "He's dead."

I couldn't find any tears. Instead I took huge, gulping breaths and held onto Lucas' arm for support. "How are you going to tell Suzanne? The boys?" I pictured Levi's family, three handsome sons and a gorgeous wife, all believing he would outlive them. Now we had to tell them Levi was gone. His words rang in my head. *Tell Suzanne I love her.*

"They're at the winery. We'll see them soon. I sent a message to Jared to meet us at the barn."

Two familiar faces came toward us, Ashley and Nate. Nate's hair had been neatly shaved off the good side of his head. His bright pink face bore a prominent scar across his cheek. He never looked better to me. I flew into his arms. "Nate, oh, Nate! I'm so happy you're okay." I leaned back and pointed to his cheek.

"Not enough time to fix it before the evacuation," he answered. "I'll have to wait until we get to Montana. I may be Scarface forever."

"Don't say that! We'll get you straight to the hospital when we land."

"The burns were the most important, Allie," Nate said. "The cut was deep and needed immediate medical attention. It may be too late to completely erase it when we get to Montana. We'll have to see what the doctors say. Serena and Julian left for the compound before the bombs hit. Serena wanted to consult with the doctors there." He took Zak's carrier from me. "You need a break. I'll take him. Stay here with Ashley."

Ash took my hand and stared into my eyes. "You look like someone beat you up and threw you in a mud pit."

"Levi's dead."

Ashley nodded. "We were here when the call came in."

"Call? No one told me!"

"Shhhh." Ashley wrapped her arms around me. "I think Lucas tried to protect you, driving with a dead body and all."

A dead body? Levi died before Lucas joined me at the square. He wanted to spare me. I pulled back and looked at her. "Rik's dead, too, good riddance. This was all his fault."

"Yeah, I'm not sorry, I have to say. He caused a lot of trouble for the Niners."

"They're too trusting of their own."

"You have to love them for that, but I do wish they'd be more careful. Maybe now they will be." Ashley took me by the arm. "Come on, looks like the van's ready."

When I climbed inside, I saw Sean lying on a hospital bed bolted to the floor of the van. Zak slept in a car seat next to him, holding onto Sean's pinkie. Nate loaded weapons into the back. Lucas talked to a group of men and walked over to the van when he spotted me.

"That's the evacuation team. They'll be the last to leave. Once everyone's out, Headquarters will be an empty shell. I should stay and be part of the final sweep, but I know you'd never leave without me."

"I'm glad you know me so well." I crossed my arms. "If you stay, I stay."

"One day it *will* be part of my job when I'm in charge of a compound. But for now, I'm going with you." Lucas kissed my cheek after he boarded. "Let's go! Head out!"

Nate drove us out of the garage and down the road to the winery. When we reached the wall protecting the compound, Lucas gave silent instructions. The structure crumbled to the ground. Miles and miles of concrete crashed to the earth, as if someone had started a domino rally. I couldn't take my eyes off the magnificent feat unfolding before me. When it was over, a stony path took its place.

"Why?" I looked at Lucas as if that was the craziest thing he'd ever done.

"We leave nothing behind for the STF to find. The team will destroy Headquarters as they prepare to evacuate."

We continued to drive for miles before the barn came into sight. The wall opened on command, and the concrete barrier crumpled to the ground, leaving a stony path along the back of the barn. We drove straight into the building, stopping in the middle of the structure. Jared jumped from the driver's side of a truck bearing the Bella Winery logo. Lucas joined him as we waited in the van. It seemed Jared already knew about his father from the look on his face.

We followed the truck to the winery parking lot, left Sean in the van while the rest of us disembarked. People strolled from their cars to the winery like it was an ordinary day.

"Didn't they hear the bombs? Aren't people afraid to be here?" I whispered to Lucas.

"They didn't hear the bombs, Allie. They were silent until they hit. Our shields contained any noise that was made."

Still it seemed odd to see people sit on the deck and sip their wine, enjoying the view, a stark contrast to what we had just witnessed. Dust and soot clung to my skin. My clothes were streaked with dirt. I longed for a change of clothes and to wash my face. Lucas looked the same, but no one appeared to notice.

Jared took us into the winery through a back room. Suzanne sat at a table, head down, sobbing. John and Joseph were trying their best to comfort her.

"Suzanne," Lucas called to her. She looked up and ran into his arms. "We're all so sorry. Levi was a good man," he whispered as he hugged her then guided her toward the office.

"Lucas!" I called after him. "Tell her what Levi said."

They disappeared into the room, and all we could do was wait. I wondered where Levi's body was but afraid to ask.

Ashley must have read my mind. She placed her hand on Joseph's arm. "What happens now?"

"The team prepared dad for his journey to Montana. They'll bring him on the last flight out of Napa. He'll be buried next to Abe in the cemetery behind the church."

"And the winery? Will you sell it?" Ashley asked.

"No, we'll live here and run it. My father wanted it that way. He wanted Mom to own the winery. It's in her name."

John looked at Nate, examining his wounds. "You really took a beating."

"Anything for the cause."

"We have a cause now?" I couldn't believe he said that.

"Yes, Allie, we do. We have to prevent this from ever happening again and make sure we're never infiltrated by an outsider again."

"So … it's war?" I stared him down.

"In a way, yes. We won't go on the offense, but we will defend our people."

Nate sounded like a Niner, not like someone who'd be heading back to UCLA to fulfill his dream of becoming a director. The tone of his voice had changed. He sounded nothing like my sarcastic, fun-loving friend. "So, you're a Niner now?"

"Yes."

"Never going back?" I asked.

"We chose our house in the village." Ashley said. "I liked the dark green house, but the yellow had more bedrooms."

Nate's face brightened, and he chuckled. "Five to be exact. Still trying to figure out why you need all those rooms, Ash."

Lucas returned but continued to talk to Suzanne over his shoulder. "We'll do as you wish. You're always welcome." He turned to the brothers. "J-men, I'll see you in a day or so. Your mother chose to drive to Montana and not use any of our vehicles. I asked her to drive Nate's car and, if you wouldn't mind, one of you drive mine. We'll fly you back on a commercial flight after the service. Your life is here. Take care of your mother and do as she says. She wants to break all contact with the Niners after the funeral but will let you make your own decisions in the future." He embraced each son then turned to face us. "Ready?"

Zak had been fed and changed while we waited so we were ready. My stomach grumbled. We hadn't eaten since breakfast, but I wanted to keep moving. Sean was still waiting for us out in the van. I felt bad he'd been out there alone, so I grabbed a bottle of wine for him on my way out.

We made our way back to the parking lot and drove to the barn. In less than a minute, the car transformed into a sleek, black jet. I'd seen toys do it, but never in reality. The wonder of these men and this life still overwhelmed me at times.

Lucas gave the command to take off. We rolled to the edge of the barn. The doors slid back to give enough room for lift-off. We rose silently into the air and flew unseen into the clouds under a protective shield.

Lucas grasped my hand. "Don't worry, Allie. We fly low enough that we don't interfere with air traffic. We're never picked up on anyone's radar due to the shields."

At that point, I didn't care. I just wanted to go home. The closer we came to the Montana compound, the calmer I became.

On our final descent, the jet converted to a hovercraft and gently landed in the third floor of Montana Headquarters with barely a bump. Lucas ushered us out of the van and to the elevator. "Fourth floor, everyone. We're not going home yet."

A team waited to rush Sean to the hospital, and we headed for the elevator. When the doors opened, Julian stood outside them looking so serious, it scared me.

"You made it!" He grabbed Lucas by the shoulders, checking him over. "The evacuation team is on its way. They planted the surveillance camera in the mountains. We've been monitoring the area since they left. Come, see for yourself."

The Napa compound, or what was left of it, was displayed on a large white screen. Military jeeps and vans emblazoned with 3-2-9 pulled up to the destroyed headquarters and parked. Doug, wearing camouflage, jumped out of the first jeep, gun drawn. They circled the remnants of the building and picked through the rubble.

It gave me chills to watch my brother. He headed back to his vehicle, leading a procession to Spanish Village. They traveled up and down every street. I hoped they'd find Rik, but they drove right past the car accident. I gave Lucas a questioning look.

"He's not there. The team buried him in the mountains out of respect."

Lucas had Zak in a portable carrier, his little head gray with dust and ash. Guilt poured over me. "We should get him home, Lucas."

"I'm sorry I kept you," Julian said. "I wanted you to see this. You've all had a long, horrific day. I'm making it longer. But I do want to say, I'm sorry I wasn't there to help. Serena wanted to get back here as quickly as possible after Nate's surgery." He shook his head. "Please go home. I'll see you tomorrow." He turned to Nate. "Serena wants to see you at the hospital. Are you up to stopping by before you go home?" Nate nodded as Julian handed him keys. "For your new home."

We shuffled to the elevator, barely able to pick up our feet. Beetle waited for us along with a car for Ash and Nate.

"Let me know what happens, Ash," I said. "Sorry, I must smell like a burn barrel." I hugged them both and joined Lucas for the ride home. "Was it just a few days ago we were living in our tiny California apartment, happy and planning our future?"

"That future has changed now, Allie," Lucas said. "We can't live that life anymore or live on the outside ever again."

"Because we're at war?"

"Because we're at war."

Being at war was what my brother wanted. Doug took everything by force. We had to be smarter than that. We needed to find another way to win.

Chapter Fifteen

Today was Levi's funeral. The sun shone brightly upon the day. Not a cloud in the beautiful, blue summer sky, contradicting the sadness in the Niner community.

Nate kept postponing his treatments, using the funeral and security issues as excuses. Serena encouraged him to start before it became too late. I had a strange feeling he wanted a reminder of this past week, a scar on his face. Ashley kept silent on the subject. When I brought it up; she wouldn't discuss it.

Sean's leg had to be put back together after being smashed to pieces by the van. His knee would have to be replaced after the two injuries, and he might walk with a cane and a limp for the rest of his days. For him, that could be a long time.

The Zimmer family had arrived yesterday and made all the arrangements for the funeral. First, we'd go to the church for a short service where speeches would be made then walk to the cemetery after the ceremony. Some of the nurses at the hospital volunteered to watch the babies and any children not going to the funeral. We planned to drop Zak there on our way to the church.

Lucas looked so dashing in his dark suit and tie I almost forgot we were headed to a funeral. I wore a simple black, short-sleeve dress and heels, hair pulled back at the nape of my neck with a large black bow.

Lucas came up from behind and kissed my shoulder. "You look beautiful." I turned and embraced him, never wanting to let go. "I have some news," he said. "I hope you'll like it."

"I can't imagine what it could be." I looked up at him.

"I'm taking over the Montana compound, becoming its next commander. Julian's taking Levi's place as regional commander for the western states. He'll oversee the building of a new compound somewhere in California. We're still working out logistics, buying land, and another cover like the winery. He'll come and go from here, but eventually will move to the new community."

I gasped. "Serena? And the girls?"

"Sorry to say they'll be gone, too. It won't be for a few years. Serena's looking forward to designing her own hospital. Julian said she's very excited."

I sat on the bed. "Well, I'm not."

"Are you happy for me?"

"If that's what you want, of course I'm happy."

"You'll have Ashley living down the street."

"They're staying forever, aren't they?"

"Yes, I believe they are."

I was happy about that news but unsettled that they had to give up so much. Their families would never know where they lived or be able to visit. I let out a breath of air. Nate once had dreamed of becoming a famous director. Ashley would never get her degree.

I finished getting Zak ready, and we summoned Beetle. Lucas carried Zak to the car. I hated to drop him off so soon after the kidnapping. *Please be there when we get back.*

As we drove to the hospital, I thought of the trauma we'd just gone through. "Lucas, how's Julian holding up? He's been so calm. Didn't he say Levi was like a brother? He was one of the Niners who rescued Julian from the plantation."

"His first duty is to the community. He's holding it together because he knows he has a job to do, but I agree.

He needs to show some emotion. Maybe today will help him grieve."

"I think we all might need some help."

Lucas reached over and squeezed my hand. "I think that's a good idea. I know someone you can talk to."

Beetle stopped at the hospital, and Lucas ran in with Zak. We drove to the church where several people were milling about the grounds. Ashley and Nate waited for us by the entrance. We went into the foyer of the church together.

Suzanne and the boys greeted guests. She looked drained but composed. They planned to head back to California tonight, and we'd probably never see them again.

"I'm so sorry, Suzanne." I took the hand she extended.

Her face froze, and she gave me a cynical gaze. "Are you now?"

I felt like she'd slapped me. "Yes, of course I am. I wish I could've done more for Levi."

"Maybe he'd still be alive if *you* hadn't come to California."

I gasped and took a step back. Lucas stepped between us. "You don't mean that, Suzanne, I'm sure."

She turned her cold eyes my way. "Oh, I'm sure."

"I'm sorry for your loss." He rubbed her arm and took my hand, leading me down the aisle of the church. "You know that's just the grief talking," he whispered.

I swallowed hard and nodded. Suzanne was right. All of this was my fault. I'd led Doug right to us.

We reached the front pews and slipped in a row behind Julian and Serena. Organ music began to play, and Levi's family came down the aisle. They sat in the front row on the opposite side. Men from the California compound spoke, followed by each of Levi's sons. When the speeches ended, Julian stepped out into the aisle. He gazed in the air then around at the crowd.

"Born a Niner. Die a Niner." His voice boomed through the church. "I was taught that message at a very young age by a loyal, loving brother. Levi protected me, encouraged me and was always there for me. Now he's gone. He left me to fend for myself on this earth. I want him to know I can go on because of what he taught me, the love he gave me. The day he rescued me he made that little baby a promise. He promised I'd know my mother, father and sisters one day. He promised to care for me and watch over me. He promised a better life for me, even better than the one he'd lived, and encouraged me to strive harder, learn more and excel at everything. He lived up to those promises … and more. To honor his memory, I pledge to continue doing what he taught me and encourage others to do the same. The hole in my heart will never fill and will always be a reminder of my brother." He bowed his head and a tear trickled down his cheek. I barely heard his last words. "Born a Niner. Die a Niner."

Complete silence took over the church. Then slowly, one by one, each Niner boy or man stood. Lucas joined in and after they all seemed to be on their feet, Nate stood. It was a powerful statement that needed no words.

We streamed out of the church, following Suzanne and her family to the cemetery. Her sons carried their father's ashes, passing them from one brother to another as they walked. We gathered around Levi's resting place. His ashes would be placed in a small plot with an engraved stone bearing just his name. If these cemeteries were ever discovered there would be no dates or information found.

I looked around at everyone with a heavy heart. Suzanne cried uncontrollably, and the boys openly wept. Sean used a cane to walk, and Nate looked fresh off the battlefield. All these people were wounded in one way or another because of me, because I came into their lives. Suddenly it hit me how similar this was to the situation I'd found myself in a few years ago.

Back then I had stood in a diner looking at all the people I loved. I couldn't go with them. I realized I was the enemy. And now? I was still the enemy to all these wonderful people. My connection to Doug made them bigger targets than they already were. My baby put them at an even bigger risk. Doug would never stop looking for Zak. I had to put a stop to this or it would never end.

As we walked back to the church, I encouraged Nate to come to the hospital with us and have his scar examined. "At least let them look at it," I said in exasperation. The burns were healing nicely, but the wound on his face still needed cosmetic treatment.

"Today's not a good day for that, Allie. Maybe tomorrow." Nate shook his head and headed for his car.

"Allie." Ashley grabbed my arm. "I need to tell you something. "Do you remember the Gilchrists from last Fourth of July? They had a son, Ryan. His father died last month, and his mother's very ill. She's been in and out of the hospital. We're thinking of letting him live with us."

"Oh? Is that why you wanted all those bedrooms?" I smiled at her generosity and the maturity she showed.

"Yes. He's fifteen so he'll just need us for, oh, twenty years or so?" She laughed.

"Levi would be proud. You're paying it forward." I patted her shoulder and headed for Beetle. "I'll talk to you later, Ash. I want to know more."

After picking up Zak, I felt restless. I wandered the house as Lucas did some work from home. I made my way to the great room. "Lucas, I'm going to take Zak for a walk in his stroller. It might clear my mind."

"When you get back, I might not be here," he answered. "I'm going to see the J-men before they leave."

"That's fine, don't worry about me." I gave him a kiss and placed Zak in the stroller, heading out the front door.

As I walked toward Main, fear welled up inside me. It grew stronger and stronger as I walked, and I pushed the stroller faster with each step. I thought back to my life before Lucas. I was sixteen, and the world was a simple place. I had an escape plan mapped out. I didn't want to live in a small town my whole life and planned to live in a big city one day. Lucas caught my eye sophomore year, always appearing to be alone in the hallways. I named him the mysterious loner. When he showed up in my AP English class junior year, I couldn't believe my luck. My prayers had been answered. He became a needed distraction until I left for college.

Then all hell broke loose after I turned seventeen. I didn't plan to fall head over heels in love with him. I had no idea I'd become part of this unknown world of Niner men and want to protect them at any cost. But most of all, I didn't know my psychopath brother lived a secret life— STF commander and longed to be a leader of something he called New America.

I need to leave this place with the baby and never come back. I need to keep everyone I love safe. I came to a halt. "Zak, Mommy has come up with a plan. Please forgive me."

I turned the stroller towards home. "The first thing we're going to do is de-scan us so Daddy can't track us. If he could, he'd find us in minutes." I had transportation. My Jeep had been returned and parked on the first floor.

Sean and I had a recent conversation about tracking. He told me the ins and outs of scanning and how to de-scan yourself. The only way to break the bond was to notify the main computer. An alert went out instantly to every person connected to you so they'd know they couldn't track you. It was like saying to someone, "don't call me anymore" or de-friending someone on social media. Or like me, leaving this life forever.

I had to get into Headquarters, go to the third floor and use the main computer. Zak and I needed to be removed from the system. According to Sean, everyone had a choice. Inside, people who lived in the compounds had to be tied to the computer to use all the amenities of the village but not when they left.

While there I'd ask the computer to de-scan us from everyone's phones at once—Sean, Nate, Ash, anyone who would track Zak and me. A message would be sent out to all parties. I hoped it would take a few minutes. If I understood what Sean had told me, multiple requests could take a minute or two. That was all I needed.

My step quickened as the house came into view. *Beetle, come to the house.* Lucas didn't track my every move in Victorian Village, so he'd have no idea what I was planning.

"Please, Lucas, please! I hope you've left already," I said as I crossed the street. Beetle sat in the drive, and I patted her side. "I'll be right back."

"Lucas?" The house was quiet.

I rushed upstairs, throwing clothes and items I needed into the largest luggage I could find. Tears welled in my eyes as I placed the engagement ring on the dresser. I bit my lip, fighting back the pain. No time to grieve my loss. I ran up and down the steps loading the car. As I did, I told Beetle how great her sister, Bee, was and how gallantly she died for the cause. I didn't know if the car understood me, but I thought she sighed. Finally, I ran back inside one more time to bring Zak and his baby seat out to the car.

Headquarters, Beetle. First floor. She seemed to shiver as if to say, "Don't do this."

"I'm sorry. I have to find a way to live under the radar, never to be discovered by Doug. I'm going to change our names, live incognito in a big city," I explained to her. "Please try to understand. I love these people that much."

After I packed the Jeep I turned to Beetle one last time. *Go to your parking space.* She appeared reluctant to leave. *Go. I love you.* She tipped her front as if to bow and left for the second floor.

Zak and I headed to the third floor. People had been given the day off for Levi's funeral so no one manned this floor. The main computer had been mounted on the wall, no bigger than a laptop, easy to take along or destroy. I stood in awe, thinking of all it could do. It held the Niner lives in its hands.

I stared at the flat box willing it to help me. I took a deep breath as tears pricked the corners of my eyes. *Descan Allison Sanders, Code five-zero-seven, from the Montana compound computer.*

I stood perfectly still, expecting to feel something, a zap or a tingle. A light flickered on and went out. "That's it?" I yelled at the computer. "Alright then. Here's the next one." I took another breath. "Delete my tracking list and people who track me."

I watched as another light went on then flicked off.

"Zak, It's your turn." *De-scan Zakary Montgomery per his mother's request, code five-zero-six, and his tracking list.* I held my breath, waiting for the light. The computer seemed to be mulling over the command. *Come on! I don't have all day.*

A voice startled me causing me to jump back. "Reason for de-scan."

"I'm leaving the compound to visit my family," I answered.

"Allison Sanders and Zakary Montgomery are de-scanned. No tracking will occur in the outside world. Your codes and information will be kept in our files. All privileges are still in force inside the compound. Once off campus, you'll be deactivated. When you return, you will be automatically scanned upon reentry."

"Oh." I looked at Zak. "The computer talked to mommy. I guess it's okay to leave."

As I rushed to the elevator, I heard something that made my heart race. "Notifications to all parties will begin in sixty seconds."

"No!" That wasn't enough time. I needed to get out of the compound, through the maze and blend in with general traffic. I ran back to the computer. "I need a half hour."

Tears ran down my cheeks as I waited. "Please do not notify for thirty minutes." Zak patted my face and looked at me with questioning eyes. "Please! For him." I buried my head in Zak's chest.

"Thirty minutes," the computer answered. "Notifications will begin in thirty minutes."

"Thank you," I breathed a sigh of relief. I deleted my life here and severed ties with friends. No time to mourn, I had to keep moving. "Come on!" I pounded the elevators doors. "First floor!"

The elevator ride from hell seemed to take hours. I ran to the Jeep and opened the back door. Zak stared at me as I placed him in his car seat with trembling hands. I sped out of the garage and glanced back one last time in the rearview mirror. "I'm sorry, Lucas. This is the only way I can keep you all safe."

The steel doors that blocked the entrance to the compound were my last obstacle. I commanded them to open; grateful my privileges weren't revoked until I reached the outside world. "Goodbye, Victorian Village," I said as I drove through, commanding them to close behind me. The very last Niner order I'd ever give.

My heart ached as I drove away. Tears kept filling my eyes even as I swiped them away. I'd called this place home for almost a year. Now, through the gate, I was free. I drove for about a mile and pulled over. The Niner phone lay on the seat next to me. I picked it up, turning it over and over in my hands. *The cell's equipped with a blocking device so it's safe.*

I dialed the number Mom had given me, hoping it was the wrong one. I cringed when I heard his voice. "Doug, you son of a bitch, it's Allie."

"Well, hello, dear sister. Finally coming in?"

"Never! I'm calling to tell you I'm leaving Lucas and the Niners. I have the baby, and you'll never find us. Leave them alone and try to find me. If I have to be on the run the rest of my life, I'll do it to protect them."

"My, aren't you loyal?"

"Like you, Doug? You have a son you never told us about! Mom and Dad don't even know about him or Katrina."

"They will, soon enough."

"Doug, I don't know what gene pool you came from, but I'm glad I didn't get any of that DNA. You are cold, a killer, and a poor, lousy-ass son and brother. I hate you beyond hate. Oh, and by the way, I'm not done with you. You think *I* should be looking over my shoulder? Well, let me tell you, you better be looking over yours. I've learned to be one badass chick, thanks to you."

I hung up before he had a chance to talk. With all my might, I threw the phone out the window. It shattered into pieces on the pavement, but I made sure by driving over it a few times.

I punched the gas, speeding through the Montana forest. The final exit from the compound came into view. The opening in the brush was much easier to find on this side. Phoneless, I checked my watch as my heart pumped erratically. "Twenty minutes. I can do it."

The Jeep was my bulldozer, busting through the branches to the other side. I doubted that any Niner security watched. They were at a vigil for Levi. Regardless, I had a head start.

The maze seemed easy from this direction, but I felt like I drove forever. Finally, the main highway came into view. I wouldn't stop until I was far from here. Far from the place I considered home, far from the people I loved more than anything. Far from the man I loved with all my heart. I would protect them with my life forever.

* * * *

I drove straight through the night and into the next morning, only stopping to buy a prepaid phone and a highly powered caffeinated beverage. I had no idea where I was going or what I'd do next, but adrenaline kept me going.

Without realizing it, I'd traveled straight to California, LA to be exact. Not the best place to hide. I couldn't go to the apartment. Lucas wasn't stupid; he'd look for us there first. I drove aimlessly up and down the streets until

I stopped in front of a group of townhouses, surrounding a grassy parkway. Parking in the first space I found, I took Zak from his seat and walked up to the farthest home from the street. I knocked on the door, not knowing what to expect, hoping I'd made the right decision. The door flew open.

"Allie!" Will raised his brows in surprised. "Come in. What brings you here?"

A strange, horrible feeling washed over me. I'd made a terrible mistake. Will could be living with someone or have a steady girlfriend. "I just need a place to stay tonight. Then I'll be out of your life forever." *You're expecting a lot from him. Brace yourself for what's to come.*

"Come in. Sit down." Will held the door back. "You need to start from the beginning. First, does the baby need anything?"

Will was so kind, tears spilled from my eyes. "No, he's fine." I placed Zak next to me on the sofa as I wiped my cheeks. "I hope I'm not interrupting anything."

"No, it's just me here. My roommate moved back home at the end of the quarter. I have two empty bedrooms. Want to rent one?" He laughed, but I considered it. No one would look for me here.

"Seriously? I can pay you." I made sure I'd taken enough cash until my new identity kicked in, and I could get a job.

"Did you and your mystery man get married?" Will leaned back in his chair, waiting. Funny he called Lucas a mystery, because I had once thought that, too.

"No, we didn't."

"He left you?" Will now sat on the edge of the chair.

"I left him. It's hard to explain."

"I've got all day."

"Well, let's just say I need to protect myself and the baby. It has nothing to do with him. Remember my brother, Doug?"

"Yeah, he didn't sound like the greatest guy."

"He constantly tried to break us up and wanted to take my baby away, raise Zak himself." *Always tell a version of the truth. One Will would be able to believe.*

"So you left, even though you didn't want to."

I nodded. "It's for the best. I had to protect my son. No way would I let Doug take him."

"Don't you think that's rather harsh? Just pick up and leave?"

"I didn't know what else to do," I whispered.

"I'm not judging, Allie." Will got up and came over to the couch and sat next to me. "If I was your man, I'd hunt you down until I found you. I'd never let you go."

"Please don't make me feel any more guilt than I already feel." I put my head on his shoulder and began to cry. I fell apart and became a complete mess. He guided me to one of the bedrooms, shut the door behind him on the way out, and left me alone. The bed was calling out to my fatigue, so I flopped back onto the mattress.

The next thing I knew, I woke to a man's voice and a baby laughing. *Lucas is playing with Zak.* I smiled as I heard the voice again. I sat up with a start. This time I knew it wasn't Lucas as I took in my surroundings. *I'm in Will's apartment.* I slid out of bed, opened the door and walked out to the living area.

"Hey, Allie, how are you feeling? It's almost dinnertime. I found some diapers and bottles in the baby bag. Zak's all set. Aren't you, Zak?"

Zak laughed. I could tell he liked Will. He was a good guy, so I wasn't really surprised.

"So what are your plans, Ms. Sanders?" Will looked up from feeding Zak. His blue eyes connected with mine, and I felt safe. I knew I could trust him.

"I need to change my name and Zak's. It can't be done legally. Doug would find me within a day." I didn't want to say Doug *and* Lucas would find me.

"Wow, straight to the point. So we need to get new names and social security numbers for you. I think I got a guy."

"You do?" My eyes widened.

Will pulled out his phone. He talked to someone, hung up and dialed again. After asking a few questions, he waited and finally said, "How much?" He looked at me and held up his hand, spreading his fingers. "Five thousand." I nodded then he made sure I understood. "Each."

I wouldn't have much left, but it was manageable. The sooner I got the name and social security number, the sooner I could get a job, credit card and apartment. Will wrote down the information and hung up. "Are you sure this is what you want?"

"Yes," I whispered. I sat down next to him on the sofa. "Is it okay if we stay here until I take care of things? If you have a girlfriend, I totally understand."

Will chuckled and shook his head. "Oh, Allie, you were always a wonder. I've dated a few girls, nothing serious. No one will show up here, if that's what you think. Come on, I have dinner almost ready."

We sat at Will's dinette table like old times. I had Zak in his portable seat, and he seemed perfectly willing to listen to our conversation. He performed, too, saying 'mum-mum' and 'tee-tee' for us. We clapped and told him how smart he was. He grew smarter by the day, standing up, playing with toys for long periods of time, putting them in order and mixing them up and putting them back in the same order. I watched him group things by size and color and look at me with pride. On his first birthday he should be like a six-month-old, but his skills seemed far beyond that.

"What should our new names be?" I took a sip of wine and finally relaxed.

"I don't know if you get to pick or not. We'll have to see. You know what we should do tomorrow? Take Zak to the gardens on campus. I think he'd like it." After seeing the look on my face, Will said, "Not a good idea, right? I have a feeling we're staying in."

"I'd give anything to go there, but it's too dangerous. Staying here too long is also a bad idea. I should leave as soon as I get the identities."

"Then I'm coming with you. There's no way I'm letting a mother and child fend for themselves."

"That's so sweet, Will, but not necessary. I'm pretty good at taking care of myself."

"No one will be looking for a family, Allie."

He was right, but I couldn't accept the offer. "I can't be a family with you, Will. I don't want to hurt you ever again."

"I'm volunteering this time. I don't expect anything. I just want to make sure you're safe. Let me help you get settled then I'll leave. Deal?"

I couldn't pass up the generous offer. "Only until school starts," I said. "Promise you'll return here?"

"I promise."

After dinner, we set Zak's portable crib up in one of the bedrooms. My room was directly across from his. I didn't sleep as well this time around, tossing and turning, the sound of bombs going off in my head. I must've screamed out because Will rushed in.

"What is it? What's wrong?"

I sat up in a cold sweat. "The bombs? Did you hear them? Oh, that's right, you can't. They're silent." I began shaking violently. Will wrapped his arms around me until I stopped. Gently he laid me back in the bed and slipped in next to me. Finally I slept.

* * * *

Will and I fell into an easy routine around the apartment. I insisted on cleaning, and he made the meals. We went for walks to get fresh air each day but never left the property. Will taught Zak to catch and throw a ball as he sat in his stroller.

As I watched them play, I realized how much Zak needed a father. I wrestled with Will's idea of pretending to be a family. Will would make a great dad, but I didn't want to hurt him more than I already had. He said I made a drastic decision, and he was right. I had to stick to the plan.

Doug probably had seized the school records and gone through every "Will" who attended UCLA. Will could become a liability in the future. For now, he was a safe place, and I could use his help in the next few months.

His phone distracted my thoughts. He motioned for me to go in the house as he spoke into the phone. "We'll be right there. Yeah, twenty minutes." Will rushed into the house. "It's time, get half the money." He disappeared and came back with his car keys. "All set?"

We drove to an old business district in a seedy part of town. Will pulled up in front of a nondescript brick building with peeling white paint. He honked the horn, three quick times then one long. A rusty metal door swung back, and a man wearing a baseball cap and sunglasses strolled out, a toothpick dangled from his mouth. He sauntered over to the passenger side and handed me a card.

"Pick a name, darlin', and be quick about it." He looked me, spending a little too long on my chest. "Weight? Height? Write 'em down. Here." He handed me a pad and pencil. "You want a driver's license, don't you?"

I nodded and scanned the card to find a name I liked. *Carli Nelson.* I pointed to it. "The kid?" He shoved another card at me. My finger went up and down the rows. I felt sick to my stomach, not wanting to rename my child. "Hurry up!" My finger stopped at Austin. "Austin, it is." He smiled and switched the toothpick to the other side then made his way around the car to Will.

I gasped. "What are you doing?"

"I can't go on the run with my own name, can I?" He smiled at me and looked over the card.

"You two want the same last name, like you're married or something? Might have to charge more." The guy with the toothpick gave Will a sly smile.

Will stared him down.

"Just kidding. You got the money?"

Will handed him a roll of bills and said, "Wyatt. Make my name Wyatt Nelson. Call us when they're ready."

"Write that down, sweetie, on the pad," he said as he pointed with the toothpick. "All the names, heights, weights."

My hand shook as I wrote. Will gave me his numbers. I wrote mine and handed the paper to Will to pass to Mr. Wonderful.

"One more thing." The guy leaned into the driver's side window and gestured at me. "Dye your hair. Blonde would be nice. You're quite a looker. But as a blonde?" He whistled. "I'd let you share my bed anytime."

Chapter Sixteen

The driver's side car door flew open, and the man was slammed against the building. Will jumped out so fast I didn't have time to register what happened. He had the man by the shirt pushed up against the wall.

The guy held his hands in the air. "Can't you take a joke, man?" The sly smile came back. "Seriously, she needs to dye her hair. Don't you agree?"

Will released him, stepped back, and glanced in my direction. I nodded to let him know I'd do it. "Make her license say she's blonde." He placed his finger under the guy's nose. "No more comments about my girl."

My heart raced. "Will! It's okay. Come on."

He hopped back in and floored the gas pedal as soon as the car was in gear. We zoomed down the gravel drive and out to a main street.

"I feel like we're two outlaws or gangsters!" Wanting to lighten the mood, I laughed as the wind from the open window whipped through my hair. Then it hit me. Will had just spent five thousand dollars to help me. "I'll pay you back."

"Don't even think about it. Now we have to decide where you want live. We'll make plans to move there and find you a job."

"I was thinking New York City, big enough to get lost in and lots of museums. Only I don't have proof of my art history background anymore. I wanted a job in one of them."

"I'm sure you could charm your way in." Will grabbed my hand as he drove, and I didn't pull away. He changed his name for me. Maybe we could be together.

"Watch out!" I screamed as a truck pulled in front of us. Bee's crumpled body flashed before my eyes.

"He's a safe distance away, Allie. Boy, you're jumpy. Is there something more you need to tell me?"

"No," I shook my head. Will could never learn my secrets. I had to get a hold of myself and hide them better.

"Well, think about it. This isn't the first time you've cried out."

When we returned to the townhouse, I sat Zak on his elephant blanket in the living room. "From now on, your name's going to be Austin. Do you like that name?"

Zak looked at me with a wide smile and a little drool came out of his mouth. He started cutting his first tooth at four months, and Lucas wouldn't be entering that milestone in his journal. I grabbed a notebook from a pile of Will's books and wrote the date and information. Maybe one day I could figure out a way to get all the data to him.

"Da-da." Zak pointed to Will as he entered the room. I gasped as he said the word for the first time. Zak thought Will was his father, and it broke my heart. The sooner I got out on my own, the better.

"Whoa, Zak, I'm not your dad." Will glanced at me for confirmation.

I hung my head and whispered, "We have to let him say it. You have to be his father if you're coming with us." *I'm sorry, Lucas, please forgive me.*

* * * *

A few days passed and no word from our forger. I lay in bed, staring at the ceiling, hoping he'd call soon. Will went to the drugstore and bought a box of hair dye after we returned home. My hair was a medium brown, and it didn't turn as light as on the package. I thought I still looked too much like myself so I had Will drive me to one of those quick haircut places. I ran inside while he waited in the car with Zak. When I came out I no longer had long hair. Parted to one side, I had long bangs that fell over one eye with the rest of the hair reaching just below my chin. It was layered shorter in the back, longer in the front.

"Drug store," I ordered.

Will left the car running while I went in to buy another box of hair dye. I picked one of the lightest colors possible. "That should do it."

Behind the check-out a digital sign displayed the day and time. Today was June thirtieth, the day I'd picked for my wedding. Now it was just another day. Tears welled in my eyes as I dug for money to pay the bill.

"Are you okay, miss?" The teenage clerk wrinkled his nose as he studied me.

"I'm fine. It's just that—" God, what could I say! "I got my hair cut. It was really long and now I feel like I've made a mistake."

"Well, if you don't mind me saying," he said as he handed me my change. "You look hot. And if you're going to dye your hair that color, you'll look even hotter."

"Thanks. I think." I grabbed the bag and headed for the car.

"I'll put Zak down for a nap then dye my hair." I told Will as I got in the car.

"Sounds like a plan." He winked at me and drove away from the store.

I glanced around. *Goodbye, LA. I'll miss you.*

* * * *

I sat on my bed, watching the clock. Ten minutes before I could wash the gooey mess out of my hair. The chemical smell started to overwhelm me. Each breath made me a little more nauseous. Or was I sick because today should have been my wedding day?

I pictured Lucas in my head, wearing a tux, standing under a trellis covered in summer flowers, waiting for me to come down the aisle and marry him. He waited and waited, and I never came. *I marry you, Lucas. Right now, I consider myself married to you. I will be faithful and love you till death do us part.*

Zak had been sleeping for quite some time, and I strained to hear my baby. Panic overtook me. It seemed too quiet in the apartment.

Flying from my bedroom, I rushed to Zak's room to find his crib empty. "Zak!" I screamed and ran to the living room.

"Hey! He's right here, Allie, with me." Will held him up.

"Oh, thank God. I was so afraid Doug had somehow found us and taken him." I was almost out of breath as I tried to explain.

"Allie, sit down. You have some serious issues going on. You need to talk to someone. If not me, then call your mom or find someone you can talk to."

"No, no, I'm sorry. I'm just overprotective." I studied my child in Will's arms. His hair had begun to fill in making him look more like Lucas each day.

"That look is back in your eyes, Allie, the dark place no one can reach. The only time I saw you without it was the day you broke up with me. After you left the park, I wished you'd get to stay like that for the rest of your life. Call him, Allie. End this now."

"I can't."

"Okay, then there's something you can do. Go wash that stuff out of your hair."

When I returned, washed, blown dried, and very blonde, Will's phone rang. He glanced at the screen and stared up at me. "It's him."

"Take the call."

"Yeah, we can come now. Sure, give us a few."

I waited for him to finish the call. "Will, I have one more favor to ask. Although I hate to part with it, I need to get rid of the Jeep. When we get there, can you ask the forger if he knows someone?"

"Sure."

"Thanks." We didn't talk again until we reached the business district. "Today was supposed to be my wedding day." *Why did I just say that?*

Will nodded, not saying a word. He blew the horn, hands tense on the wheel. I prayed we wouldn't have another confrontation. The guy in the cap appeared, handing Will the documents to examine. Money exchanged hands through the open window.

"Anyone interested in a Jeep, about six years old, not stolen. Just want to get rid of it without going through the paperwork."

"Bring it back later today. I'll give you three thousand for it."

Will looked at me as if I should decline, and I said, "I just want to get rid of the car."

"Fine, we'll be back later."

The guy made a gun shape with his hand, pointing it toward me. "You got a hot one there. I was right about the blonde hair, wasn't I? Bet you can't keep your hands off her."

"Will, go. Drive," I commanded.

As we peeled away, I looked back at my smiling baby. "Austin, Wyatt and I are taking you to a new city to live. You're going to like it there." I turned to Will. "You still don't have to do this."

"Allie, or should I get used to calling you Carli? I told you before I want to do it."

"If you live with us, I'll feel obligated." To me the word 'obligated' meant a lot of things—marriage, sex, partnership.

Will threw his head back and laughed. "Don't you know I'm aware of that? I don't expect any wifely duties from you. Let's see how things go." He took my hand, and I grabbed on tightly.

Time to change the subject. "I researched apartments in New York City," I said, "and found a rent-controlled building close to Central Park and the museums. It's a two bedroom and affordable for the city. I have more than enough for the deposit and two months' rent. If I could make all the arrangements from here, I could ship stuff to the address."

"You've been doing your homework, haven't you?" Will still had a smile on his face. "I guess we could find a second-hand store for some furniture when we get there and buy a cheap bed."

One bed? I cringed. "I plan on sleeping in the same room with Zak."

"Yeah, yeah, right, slip of the tongue. I guess I was in husband mode."

* * * *

"Ready?" Will hoisted the baby bag on his shoulder and handed Zak to me. "Welcome to New York."

After maneuvering through the airport, we took a taxi to the apartment, heading straight to the management office. I signed some papers and got our keys. The manager called us Mr. and Mrs. Nelson. It sounded odd, but I had to get used to it. As I pushed back the apartment door, we were met with the boxes we had sent, stacked against a wall.

"We have our work cut out for us." Will shifted through them and found the portable crib. "Pick your room."

We walked down a hall and I peered into both bedrooms. "Sorry, but I have to take the bigger one."

"You're not really sorry." Will poked me in the side, and I giggled.

He put his arms around my waist and pulled me close. "Welcome home." He planted a sweet kiss on my lips then went to work setting up the crib.

When he finished, I kissed his cheek. "Thanks."

He dug in his pocket and showed me his phone. "Let's hit these stores I bookmarked before we left. Maybe we can get some things delivered today or we'll be sleeping on the floor."

"Groceries, too," I added. *We sound like an old married couple.*

I settled Zak into the mobile baby carrier and attached him to Will's back. Now that he was bigger, we had started carrying him on our backs instead of the front. He sat up tall and proud.

As we headed out of the apartment door, Will looked up and down the street. "This way." He pointed to a subway station. "Not too far."

We disappeared down the stairs into the station. Each step I took carried me farther from my old life. I hoped I could stay in New York for a while. But somehow I knew I would be looking over my shoulder for the rest of my life.

Chapter Seventeen

Two weeks flew by, but I still didn't have a job. Zak started to crawl and kept us busy. I secretly noted his progress in the notebook. The only thing I did off-schedule was call my mother.

"Allie, where are you?" She cried when she heard my voice.

"Mom, please don't cry. I'm so sorry, but I had to leave, but I'm fine, really."

"I don't understand what you're doing. Lucas has called over and over, asking if I know where you are or if I've heard from you. Where are you?"

"The next time he calls, please tell him I'll always love him."

"That's it? That's all you have to say?" I could hear her sobs subside into sniffles as she calmed down. "Doug said you should come home and live with us. At least you'll be with family."

"I can't, Mom."

"Why not?"

I hesitated. I didn't want to tell her the truth and risk breaking her heart but made my decision on the spot. "Doug kidnapped Zak, Mom. He tried to take him away from me. He didn't bring him home the day you let him take Zak for a walk." I waited for her reaction. "Mom? Are you there?"

"Doug would never do something like that. There must be a reasonable explanation. I'll talk to him."

"Please, Mom, don't believe anything he says. You can't trust him!" But I knew my words were falling on deaf ears. I finally ended the conversation, not making any promises. "I'll try to call again when I can. I love you."

As I hung up I heard her calling my name, but I couldn't talk anymore. Doug was her son. I should have known I'd never get her to believe me. She'd never see the evil in him.

Smashing the phone against the outside of the apartment building, I picked it up and threw it in the trash. I was getting good at destroying prepaid phones and tossing them away like I'd bought them at a dollar store.

I tried to wipe the phone call from my mind as Will and I left the apartment building, looking like the typical married couple with our baby in a stroller. Museums surrounded Central Park. I planned to go into each and every one to ask if they had any openings. I decided face-to-face might work better than checking on-line for jobs. Will and Zak would hang out in the park and wait for me. We decided to make it a fun day and have a picnic.

After two "No, sorry, we're not hiring at this time" responses, I began to feel defeated. Will pointed to another museum and said, "I think that one's calling your name."

I laughed. "I'll try after lunch."

We spread out the blanket and ate, watching Zak fall asleep after he was done.

"Go," Will said. "I got this. We'll be right here when you return." He seemed quite sure of himself. I soaked in his quiet strength and hoped it would help me on my quest.

I took long strides through the park, quickly reaching the white round building that spiraled into the sky. A deep breath calmed me as I entered the museum. I walked straight to a help desk and asked for the employment office.

"I don't think we're hiring. Did you check on-line?" The older lady pushed her glasses up her nose.

"Please?" I must have looked desperate because she picked up the phone. Her eyes widened. "I'll send her up."

My heart soared. I had a chance. The woman sent me off with directions.

"You came at the right time, Mrs. Nelson," the thin, balding man behind the desk said when I arrived. Looking frazzled, he gestured for me to come in. "We just had someone who worked in the gift shop quit today. We'd like to fill the position as soon as possible. Can you start tomorrow?"

"I have the job?"

"Yes, if you want it. You seemed qualified."

"I didn't give my qualifications."

"Dear, I can just tell. Do want the job or not?"

"Yes! Yes, I'll take it."

"Then be here nine a.m. sharp. Come to the office when you get here, and we'll fill out the paperwork. Follow me. I'll introduce you to our two *loyal* employees."

Still in shock, I followed the man to the gift shop. I wanted to sing out how happy I was to be there. A gift shop job in a museum would be as close to the arts as I could get considering my situation.

"Parker? Abby? Could you both come here?"

A tall, slim man with red hair who looked a few years older than me nodded as he walked toward us. Abby, a short, stocky woman, appearing to be in her thirties, shuffled over.

"This is Carli Nelson. She'll work part-time for the rest of the month until she learns the ropes, then we'll schedule her fulltime."

Parker stuck out his hand and smiled. "Welcome to the shop." He pushed his black framed glasses back into position. I took his hand and smiled.

"Yeah, hi, I'm Abby." She also shook hands and gave me a wide grin.

"It's nice to meet you both. I guess I'll see you tomorrow." I couldn't believe I'd landed a job and wanted to run to Central Park to share the news. "Anything I should know?"

"Be on time and dress nicely." Abby whispered like she was telling a secret even though everyone heard.

I nodded and thanked them as I headed for the door. Almost skipping like a little girl, I felt the best I had in a month. The dreams had lessened since being in the city. I didn't think bombs were going to explode everywhere I went. I caught my reflection in a storefront window. A slim, blonde girl bounced merrily along. "Wow. I need to gain some weight." A real wake-up call. I hadn't taken care of myself in weeks

Will sat on the blanket right where I had left him. I waved and ran to him. He put his finger to his lips, Zak must still be asleep.

"I got a job," I whispered.

He rose from the ground, and I rushed into his arms. Instinctively we kissed. Not a passionate Lucas kiss, but I liked it. I felt my feet lift off the ground. Will twirled around then placed me gently on the ground. I gazed into his beautiful blue eyes, realizing what I'd just done. Will leaned down and kissed me again. I felt so safe, I kissed him back. The sad fact? I only felt safe ... and nothing else.

* * * *

Up bright and early the next day, I rushed to get ready for work. Will would be a stay-at-home dad.

For the rest of July, I'd work part time, but when August arrived, I'd go fulltime and need look into childcare. My head spun with a to-do list. I loved keeping my brain occupied with regular, everyday activities, no time for dwelling on the past.

I never learned the name of the man who hired me, so I checked out his nameplate on the wall before entering the office. The frazzled man behind the desk still looked like he was on his last nerve. "Mr. Marvin? Hi, I'm here to fill out my paperwork."

"Yes, let's get it done right. Ms. Head of Operations is breathing down my neck. The dragon lady wants everything done yesterday, to perfection. It's my turn to be evaluated today. She comes around once a month to personally rake us over the coals ..." He put his hand over his mouth. "I said too much. Please forgive me."

"It's perfectly fine. Who am I going to tell?" I shrugged, making light of it, and Mr. Marvin relaxed.

"You're a sweet girl, Carli. Welcome to the team. Now go on downstairs. Abby's waiting for you."

I pulled the door to the gift shop open to see Abby, being on the shorter side, standing on a small stool. Her arm stretched high above her as she tried to place an item on a top shelf.

"Here, let me get that for you." I took the box from her hand and slid it into position.

"Thanks, I see you're right on time. I'll show you how to run the register then we'll go over the inventory. After that we'll do a store walk-through." Abby paused. "Am I going too fast for you?"

I smiled. She reminded me of someone I missed very much, my best friend, Ashley. "No, you're fine. Keep going."

For most of the morning, in between customers, Abby continued to train me. She was kind and funny and got a little carried away about things just like Ash. "So, you're married?" she asked.

"Yes, my husband and I just moved here with our son."

"Oh! You have a child. What's his name? How old? You look awfully young to have a baby ... ooh, sorry, didn't mean it to sound like that!"

Tears filled my eyes, and I had to turn away. She better stop acting like Ashley or I'd be hugging her soon.

"No, it's fine. My son, Austin, is almost five months old. Wyatt is home with him." *Is that right? What did his new birth certificate say?*

"Wyatt. I like that. Sounds sexy." Abby winked.

"Yes, he's okay."

"Got a picture?" Luckily, I had many pictures of "the family" on an old unregistered phone. I pulled it out and opened a picture of the three of us.

Abby placed her hands on her hips. "He's okay? Girl, he's gorgeous. He could be a model." She studied the picture a little longer, making me nervous. "Now who does he look like?" She pointed to Zak.

My heart skipped a beat. "We decided a long-lost ancestor." I tried to laugh. *Hope she thinks it's funny.*

My shift was almost over when Parker arrived. "So, did you survive Abby? She's probably showed you the whole store, the inventory in back and told you her dress size if I know her."

Abby came up behind us. "Parker, if you weren't my best friend, I'd give away all your secrets!"

I gathered my things, ready to go home. "Abby, you were so helpful. Thank you. I'll see you tomorrow."

"Love to see that husband in person!" she called as I went out the door.

My mind cleared during the walk home. I enjoyed staring in windows and people watching. In no time I opened the apartment door. To my surprise, Will and Zak greeted me, holding flowers.

"He insisted." Will pointed to Zak. "Didn't you, buddy?" He gave me a gorgeous model grin, white teeth and all. "How'd the first day go? Come. Sit and tell us."

An iced tea waited on the table, and as I sipped, I told the two men in my life about my day. "Now that you've done something nice for me, let me reciprocate. How about if I give you a guy's night out? You hit the town and have some fun." Silence filled the room. "Will? I want to do something for you. You've done so much."

"Then marry me and be a real family." He looked away.

"Will—"

"I know. It will never happen. I love this kid. I love you. Isn't that enough for now? You heard the old saying. You'll grow to love me?" He took my hand and stared into my eyes. "You're not going back to him. Be with me."

"Not fair to you." I looked at his handsome face, really looked and saw a wonderful man who deserved more than I could give him. I was being selfish. "Maybe you should go back to California sooner. I'll step up the nanny search."

"No. Don't. I promised I'd stay. Besides, I'd just worry if I was back in LA and call you every five minutes."

"Are you sure?"

"Yes, I'll even help with the nanny search."

* * * *

Parker and Abby had been in a state of panic for a week. We had cleaned and straightened nonstop. Now the day had finally arrived. The Director of Operations was coming to the shop to do her monthly inspection. I learned her name was Ms. Baker—very dedicated to her profession, never married. Parker said she was married to her work with an exaggerated eye roll added in. I'd come in early to find Abby and Parker huddled together.

"Hey, you two look so nervous!" I couldn't believe the looks on their faces, two scared rabbits stared back at me. "She can't be that bad!" I giggled.

"Just wait." Abby lifted her eyebrows. "One little thing out of place ... bam!" She slapped her hands together. Parker gave her a nudge and motioned toward the door.

A tall, statuesque, auburn-haired beauty stepped into the shop, not a hair out of place. Her suit appeared to be the latest fashion, probably bought somewhere along Fifth Avenue. Her hair was stylish, swept up, pinned in back with feathery bangs and a few tendrils framed her face. Her make-up looked flawless. I guessed she was in her mid-thirties.

Ms. Baker walked directly up to Abby. "I heard there's a new girl. I'd like to speak to her." Abby stood, mouth open and pointed in my direction.

"Hi, I'm Carli Nelson." I stuck out my hand, and she took it. A slim, gold nametag pinned to her suit said, *Carol Baker, Head of Operations*. "Nice to meet you, Ms. Baker."

"I've heard good things about you from visitors. They say you're quite knowledgeable and helpful."

"Thank you."

"Any experience? Education in the arts?"

"Three years of art history, but I was unable to finish and get my degree."

"She had a baby." Abby said then covered her mouth.

Ms. Baker gave her a steely gaze with brown eyes that reminded me of Lucas', and Abby backed away. "So, you *do* have some experience?" She turned back to me.

"Yes, my dream was to find work in a museum, much like this."

"Well, would you be interested in working behind the scenes? Cataloging, setting up new exhibits, just getting your feet wet? It may mean a few more hours of work each week."

My heart dropped. I just started fulltime and more hours seemed impossible. "I… would love to … but I—"

"Have a child. I know. Not married?"

"Yes, I do … am ... married. Wyatt's home with the baby, but travels." Thankfully, an excuse had spilled out of my mouth. "We still haven't found a nanny or any childcare for Austin."

"Well, you work on that. I'll stop back in a day or so for your answer." Ms. Baker gave me a smile that didn't reach her eyes then stared down Parker and Abby. "Everything looks fine here. You two are to be commended." She started for the door but turned back. "I'll let Mr. Marvin know he did quite well with the new hire."

Abby clapped her hands in excitement as Ms. Baker walked out into the museum. "A promotion! After a month! Hope you'll come back and visit us."

"Of course, I will." I couldn't believe my good fortune. "I just need someone to watch Austin so I can take the job. Wyatt will leave soon."

"Leaving?" Abby covered her heart with her hand, feigning an attack.

"For work, silly," I said. "Didn't you hear me? He travels for work. He'll be gone a lot and can't be a reliable sitter." I put the story into motion, preparing everyone to think I was on my own and couldn't depend on Will. The promotion was the best news I'd had since being hired. I couldn't wait to tell him. I knew I should stop depending on him for support. *Just one more time.*

Will would leave the end of August and not return until after Christmas. I insisted he not come back until then. He put up a good fight, but I won. He needed to be with his family on the holidays, not with me.

When I stepped into the apartment after work, I found Will cooking, and Zak sitting in his highchair. Zak held a spoon and banged on the tray. Every time he hit the tray, Will put a tiny bit of applesauce on the spoon. Zak fed himself, getting most of it on his cheeks. Watching him was bittersweet, I was missing out on these moments. I took a deep breath, reminding myself I couldn't be a stay-at-home mom as I'd planned and sat down at the table.

"You two are quite a team!" I laughed and took over for Will, putting the applesauce on the spoon. Zak appeared happy to have a new playmate. While I played with him, I told Will about my visit with Carol Baker.

"You're going to take the job, right?" He brought a plate from the stove and put it in front of me. "Eat."

I dug into the delicious hot and spicy stir fry. "I want to take the job but haven't found childcare."

"Take the job. We'll worry about that later." Will joined me at the table. "You know I was thinking I could move here after I graduate. I'm sure I could find a job."

"I'm sure you could." I wanted to say "and also find your own place" but didn't have the heart. Deep inside, I knew I could convince myself to marry Will and live happily ever after. Another part of me cringed at the idea of cheating on Lucas. Then there was Zak. How would I explain to Will that Zak would turn six months old on his first birthday and wouldn't be one until the next? Easy now, but difficult was still to come.

"You know," Will said as he reached out to touch the bottom of my hair. "I'm getting used to this." His hand made its way to the back of my neck as tingles ran down my spine.

"Will." I gestured at Zak.

"Is busy playing." He moved his chair closer. His knees touched the side of my thigh. His hand brushed against the hairs on my arm causing me to lean toward him.

I squirmed in my seat. *Oh my God, I want him.* I cleared my throat. "Will."

"You already said that, Allie. God, you're so beautiful. You don't even know it, do you?" His hand rose to my cheek, stroking my lips with his thumb. "Brown hair or blonde, it doesn't matter."

I couldn't believe I let him get this close. Too late, I was all in. I didn't want him to stop. His hands traveled to my sides, running slowly, sensually up and down my body. The kiss would come. I sensed it as I felt the breath on my shoulder move up my neck and over to my lips. He teased. I waited.

My lips searched for his, hungering for a kiss. I wanted his mouth on mine, his hands on my body. Oh, it had been too long. Will finally stopped the torture, and his warm lips melted into mine. He pulled me onto his lap as he kissed me. I could feel he wanted me badly. My arms went around his neck. *All he needs to do is pick me up—*

"Mum-mum. No. No."

Back to reality.

* * * *

On the walk to work the next day, I decided to accept the job. Millions of women did what I was doing every day. Maybe I could be Head of Operations one day, climb the ladder of success. Amused by my change of heart, I lightened my step as I reached my destination.

Abby appeared out of nowhere, startling me. "Good news, Carli! I found you a sitter." My heart pounded at the thought of leaving Zak with a stranger. "My sister! She's staying home with her baby for a year and could use extra cash. We meet her after work if you'd like."

I threw my arms around her. "You're a life saver!" I sent Will a text, and he quickly returned, *Go for it.*

"Now the bad news." Abby frowned. "She lives a few blocks away from you in the other direction from the museum, a little out of your way."

"I'll make it work, don't worry!" I'd have time to visit with Abby's sister and get to know her before Zak started going there. "Abby? What's your sister's name?"

"Oh, sorry! It's Mia. You'll love her and her baby, Zoe, is two months old and adorable."

Abby was right. Both Mia and Zoe were adorable. Mia looked just like Abby with dark red hair instead of black. I didn't know if Abby had dyed her hair dark or Mia had gone red. They both had sparkling hazel eyes with golden flecks and friendly smiles. Zak would love going to Mia's home.

"You need to take all the hours you can get in this economy. You're lucky to have a job. I was nervous taking a year off." Mia shook my hand while she talked.

"Yeah, you're right." Had I missed something? I'd been so preoccupied with my life, I hadn't paid attention to the news in a long time. That was the second time I'd heard about the poor economy. I'd better wake up and pay attention.

I returned to the apartment filled with excitement. Zak needed to like his new home and the people. He hadn't been around any children since I'd taken him away from the Montana compound. It was time for him to start a new life, too.

* * * *

Will's last day in New York came too quickly. We made plans to meet at the museum and go out for lunch. I'd been working on a large project the past week and hoped I could slip away. Carol Baker was very hands on and checked in daily for updates. People described her as cold and business-like, but I found her to be just the opposite. We had friendly chats during the weeks I worked for her.

"Ms. Baker, I hope you don't mind if I leave a few minutes early today. I'm going to lunch with my family. Wyatt leaves on his business trip tomorrow."

"Carli, it's about time you started calling me Carol. Don't you think?"

Actually, it had never crossed my mind. "Okay, Carol it is. Would you like to meet Wyatt?"

"I'm heading down to the lobby so I'll walk with you." She wore a gray, custom cut suit, trimmed in black. No matter how she dressed, it was hard to hide the fact she was quite buxom.

Will sat on a bench with Zak in the stroller, looking like the perfect family man—or on a photo shoot for a magazine.

"You didn't tell me your husband was a model," Carol said so matter-of-factly I almost believed he was.

"No, no, he isn't." I shook my head.

"I could get him a job anywhere in the city if he'd like." She raised her eyebrows at me. "How could you let *that* get away?"

"He loves his job, even if he travels a lot." I scrambled for an answer.

Will stood and took Carol's hand. "I've heard so much about you. Nice to meet you."

Carol held his hand for a little longer than the usual handshake. If I *was* Will's wife, I'd be jealous.

"I guess we should go." I moved behind Zak's stroller and started to push. "I'll be back soon ... Carol."

She nodded as she headed off in another direction.

"Wow," Will looked over at me. "She's hot." His eyes widened. "Oh, sorry, but you know what I mean."

I laughed. "Yes, I do. Now we better go visit Abby and Parker or they'll never forgive me!"

Chapter Eighteen

Will had been gone for two months. Autumn had arrived in New York City along with cooler air. Fall foliage covered the trees in Central Park. Zak and I took long walks there when I wasn't at work. He was doing well at Mia's, and I'd managed to carve out a life for us here.

At times, I looked over my shoulder thinking Doug followed me and wondered how long it would take for him to find me. I expected him to pop out as I rounded every corner.

My latest resolution was to not think about Lucas. If I did, I became depressed. I thought of the life I should be leading. It made me panic to the point I couldn't breathe so I erased it from my memory. The fact that I was keeping everyone safe kept me going—the Niners, Lucas and Zak. I'd brought the wrath of Doug upon them and now, hopefully, I'd removed it.

I was cataloging and storing a huge exhibit at work which kept my mind busy and off the fact that today was my birthday. Carli Nelson had hers in September, not November fourth. According to her records, Carli turned twenty-two, not my real age of twenty-one.

I hummed "Happy Birthday" as I worked. My phone buzzed. I never took personal calls, except from Mia. Today was the exception.

"Hey, birthday girl, how's it going?"

"Will! Hi! Everything's fine. Are you studying and focusing on classes?"

"Yes, but what about you? No problems? Anything you need me for?"

"No, but thanks for asking." He'd fly out here in a second if I asked. Zak was a healthy Niner baby. I'd never taken him to a doctor. The only doctor he'd ever seen was Serena. She said he'd get shots on his first birthday, and I didn't know if she'd meant this year or next. I was grateful Zak wouldn't get the typical baby illnesses or colds. When Mia asked who my pediatrician was or when his next appointment was I had to lie. I shivered as I realized lies had become a part of me. Lies, lies and more lies.

I pinched myself because Will was still talking, and I hadn't heard a word. "It was nice of you to call on my birthday. But as you know—"

"Your fake one's in September," he said.

"Yeah. Will, I've got to go."

"I'll call you later, when you're home."

"Sure, bye." I noticed Carol heading my way, relieved I ended the call in time. Although we got along well, she was my boss, make that everyone's boss.

"Carli!" She called as she came nearer. "I need a drink, a large one, after work. You in?" She slapped her hand on the table in front of me.

"I … um …"

"Oh, yeah, I forgot. The kid. Call the husband and tell him you have a business dinner with me tonight."

"He's not home," I said as I looked up at her. "Traveling."

"Is that man ever home? It seems he's always traveling. Not my business though." Carol held up her hand. "You have a sitter, right?"

"Yes, Abby's sister."

"Call and tell her there's a large bonus coming her way if she watches the kid a few more hours."

I couldn't tell my boss no, so I did as she asked. Mia agreed and wanted me to tell her the details later. She probably called Abby in the gift shop as soon as we hung up to gossip. "All set." I told Carol.

"Great, come to my office at five. I'm knocking off early tonight."

My day got a little brighter. I'd celebrate my twenty-first birthday in the city. I finished up the major tasks that needed to be done then cleaned my area. I touched up my make-up and brushed out my blonde locks that now skimmed my shoulders.

I pulled on a pink cardigan over my black dress. Not the latest fashion, but it had to do. I headed for Carol's office. She was putting lipstick on when I arrived and gave me a Cheshire cat type smile.

"My, don't you look … sweet. Lose the sweater." She smiled again, but it didn't reach her eyes. "I do hope you're old enough to drink."

"Yes, I'm twenty-two, just turned twenty-two." I stammered. This would be the first time I'd be out drinking in public.

"You *do* drink?"

"Oh, yes … wine."

"Well, let me introduce you to the world of martinis." Carol came around her desk and put her arm around me. "The closest martini bar is just a cab ride away." She deftly hailed a cab when we walked out of the museum. Before I knew it, I was seated across from her in the bar/restaurant.

"Carol, may I ask you something?"

"Sure." She stared around the room looking for a waiter.

"Why me?"

"Meaning?' She asked without giving me a glance as she waved a server to our table.

"Why ask *me* out for drinks? I'm sure there are lots of people at the museum who'd love to go out with you."

Carol threw her head back and let out a hearty laugh. "You sound like my mother. You think I should have friends my own age?" She winked.

So, Carol was aware of the age difference. "Well, it's just that I'm married, have a baby—"

"And seem so innocent to the ways of the world and the city. Yes. I guess I trust you, Carli. If I get too drunk or spill too many secrets, I don't think you'll tell."

I nodded. "I try to be a good friend." Inside, I cringed. I'd hardly been a good friend to the people who meant the most to me.

"Plus, who am I supposed to have drinks with, Max Marvin?"

"Oh. My. God. Is that really his name? He sounds like a superhero or his alter ego!" I couldn't help laughing, and Carol joined in.

"Yes, that's really his name. Now, thanks to you, I'll never be able to look at him again without seeing a red cape!" Carol held up her glass in a salute.

"And wearing nothing but his boxers!" I couldn't believe I said that, but we both cracked up. Carol and I sipped dirty martinis and chatted about the day. After the second drink, the talk turned serious.

"Your son. Austin? He doesn't look like you or that drop-dead gorgeous husband," Carol said, one eye closed as she studied me with the other. "Spill."

My heart raced. Carol was a smart woman, and if I made up a lie, she'd see through it. I had to give her a version of the truth. "Austin's not Wyatt's son." I hung my head.

Carol covered my hand with hers. "Does Wyatt know?'

"Yes, we dated in college. An old boyfriend showed up. I broke up with Wyatt, spent a few months with the ex and ended up pregnant."

"Does the ex-boyfriend know?"

"Yes."

"And the bastard left you."

"In a way, I left him. I knew it wouldn't work. Wyatt took me back and never talked about it again. He treats Austin like his own." I got teary-eyed. "Wyatt's a wonderful man."

"But you love the ex."

A tear trickled down my cheek, and I wiped it away. "Always," I whispered.

"Young love." Carol raised her glass at the waiter. "We're ready for a dinner menu."

Relief swept through me. I didn't think I could handle another martini or I might be tempted to tell her everything. We shared a bottle of wine during the meal and kept the conversation flowing.

"You dated a rock star? You're not going to tell me who it is, are you?" I baited her, hoping she would.

"Not fair to him. He wanted to marry me, have me follow him around the world. Yuk, not for me." Carol sipped her wine and smiled. "He was sweet and caring ... after he came off the stage." Her eyes drifted off to another place then she snapped back. "I had my chance to get married and never took it, probably still could get married if I wanted. I'm dating a banker. He's pretty serious about the relationship."

"Are you?"

"I don't really know. That's why you and I are out tonight instead of me and the banker."

"Oh."

"Enough about me. Tell me more about you. Where are you from? What made you interested in the arts?"

Stay as close to the truth as possible. I told her I came from Montana and went to school in California. I didn't want to talk about brothers or sisters so I said I was an only child. That seemed to satisfy Carol's curiosity. Our talk turned to art and continued straight through dessert.

"I'll ride with you to the nanny's house." Carol hailed another cab outside the restaurant. My head spun from the martinis and wine, but I also felt a little carefree. It was a great way to spend my twenty-first birthday—at a martini bar in New York City.

As we pulled up in front of Mia's apartment building, Carol handed me some money. "Oh, no, I couldn't take that." I pushed her hand away.

"It's not for you, it's for the sitter. I said there was a bonus for her, didn't I? One for each hour."

I took the money, gazing down at four hundred-dollar bills. "Carol, that's very generous of you. I should be the one paying her."

"On your salary?" She laughed heartily. "Honey, I know what you make. If it makes you feel better, give her your hourly rate, too."

"Thanks for everything. It's been a great birth—"

"Birthday? Is it your birthday today? You should have said something!"

"No, no, sorry, it was in September. What I meant was … well … you'll think I'm silly. I never got to celebrate my twenty-first out on the town. I was just thinking about that now." *Good save.*

"You were pregnant."

"Yes." The truth popped up again.

"Well, then I'm glad I made your night."

I slipped out of the cab and waved goodbye, turning to go into the apartment. A weight seemed to lift off me. I didn't feel so alone in the city. I'd made friends, and if Carol liked me, I could have a long career at the museum. It was hard to believe everyone was afraid of her. Smiling, I opened the door to the building and rang the buzzer. As I waited, I sang a quick little verse of "Happy Birthday".

* * * *

I hadn't talked to Mom on my birthday, so I bought a prepaid phone on the way to work the next day and called.

"Allie!" I melted at the sound her voice, full of love, sadness and surprise rolled into one. "Happy birthday, honey."

"Thanks, Mom. I wanted to hear your voice."

"It's so good to hear yours. I love you, sweetie."

"I love you, too."

"And you called at the perfect time!"

What the hell does that mean?

"Hello, Allison." I nearly dropped the phone at the sound of his voice. "We're close to finding you. It's just a matter of time."

"Doug." I spit out his name.

"You're on the east coast. I checked with Dean."

He's trying to bait you. I never talked to Dean.

"He said you might show up at his place on Duck, but I thought you were too smart to do that."

"Really? But I bet you went there anyway."

"First place we looked." He paused. "Mom, I'd love some tea? Could you make me a cup?"

He's getting her out of the room. Here it comes.

"So…where were we?" he hissed.

"You're trying to figure out where I am."

"Tracing your phone as we speak."

"Good luck."

"Niner technology is a thing of beauty, Allison. They make advancements every day. Soon they won't need phones or connections to computers to find people."

I bit my lip to keep from saying anything.

"Allison, are you there?"

"Yes, jackass, I am."

"Now there's the sister I know and love." I could picture his face. Blue gray steely eyes, his strong jaw clenched and his mouth twitching into a sinister smile. I could almost smell his cologne in my nostrils.

"Are you done?" My hand trembled as I got ready to smash the phone. Part of me believed he could track me down.

"We will find you, bitch, and your Niner bastard," he growled. "It's only a matter of time. Enjoy your life on the run, for now. One day, that kid will be mine."

I raised my hand in the air and brought it down hard against a brick building. "Son of a bitch!" I kicked at the wall. "Jackass! Jerk!" I ran my hand through my hair. My stomach clenched into a tight ball. I pulled a water bottle from my bag and drank, putting out the fire inside. I had to go in the museum and act natural. *Get it together. He could be bluffing. If Lucas hasn't found you, how could Doug?*

* * * *

Holiday season at the museum was a busy time. People came from every corner of the globe to visit "the city that didn't sleep" to see what it had to offer. Parker and Abby had the gift shop tastefully decorated with seasonal items from around the world. I helped them finish decorating after closing one night. We all converged on Mia afterward. Her husband worked late most nights, and she enjoyed the adult company.

Mia had been keeping a record whenever Zak had done something new. It would be a wonderful keepsake for him when he was older, and also a great reference for the journal I kept. The cover of the book said "Austin", and my heart sank each time I looked at it. Still, I loved the book and checked it daily.

"Look, here," Mia said as we arrived. "Today I swear he tried to say Zoe, and I wrote it down. It was so adorable. He'll be walking soon, Carli. He pulled himself straight up today, let go and just stood there beaming. He's so strong and healthy, you're lucky." I didn't know how to thank her for all the love she gave to Zak and put into the book.

The day before Christmas Eve Mia looked at me, brows crossed, when I came to pick up Zak.

"Is Wyatt coming home for the holidays? Seems he's away more and more."

"Yes, he should be home later tonight." I lied. Will would fly in the day after Christmas and stay the week. We'd celebrate New Year's before he flew home on the second. I would spend Christmas day alone with my baby.

* * * *

The day after Christmas the door flew open. Will stood in the entryway, his blue eyes sparkling with anticipation. He wore a leather jacket with a scarf tied around his neck, looking very sexy. A light snow had begun to fall, and a few flakes stuck in his dark blonde hair. Loaded down with presents and a duffle bag, I helped him in.

"Da-da." Zak pointed at him from his highchair.

"He remembers me!" Will smiled from ear to ear.

"Of course, he does." My heart ached when I heard "da-da" come from my son's mouth for another man.

Will had risen to the challenge of that job, and now I needed to accept the consequences.

"Come on, sit, dinner's ready." I helped him off with his coat, and he grasped my arm, pulling me toward him.

"Merry Christmas, Mrs. Nelson." He gave me a long, lingering kiss. I felt my stomach flip in a good way. I placed his coat over a chair to dry and hurried to fill our plates to keep busy, focusing on the task at hand rather than the kiss. I could almost give in and admit that I could be with Will. It felt so good to have a man touch me, kiss me again. *Wrong man*, I scolded myself.

After dinner, we headed to the living room and sat around the small tree I'd bought. We ate cookies and tore open presents, letting Zak play with the wrap and boxes that he found more intriguing than the actual gifts. Playing to exhaustion, he fell asleep in Will's arms.

We put him down and tiptoed back to the kitchen. Will took me by the hand. "I brought something for us. Since I didn't get to celebrate your birthday," he said as he pulled two bottles of champagne from the fridge. "One for each celebration, your birthday and Christmas." He pointed to a gift hidden behind the tree. "Open that."

I found two beautiful fluted silver-rimmed champagne glasses in the box. "They're gorgeous!" I bounced up from the floor and rinsed them as Will popped open the first bottle.

We went into the living area, plopped on the floor, and leaned against the sofa.

"One more to go." Will placed a beautifully wrapped package in my lap.

A soft lavender blanket was nested inside the box. "Will, I love it."

"I remembered how you said you're always cold this time of year." He stroked my cheek with his finger. I wrapped the beautiful blanket around me as I held up my flute for a refill. Will emptied the contents of the first bottle into my glass.

"You know everyone says you look like a model, Will. Carol said she could get you a job in the city anytime." I'd never meant to tell him that, but he looked so damn good coming in that door.

"Really? I'll take that as a compliment. But all I care about is what you think." He tapped his glass against mine. I leaned in for a kiss. "A champagne kiss," I said after it ended, realizing the drink had gone to my head.

Will hopped up. "Time to open the second bottle. I'll be right back."

The champagne made the night carefree and festive. No dark places for me tonight, no bombs, no kidnappings or death, just bubbles floating in my head. Another glass was placed in my hand, and I accepted it willingly.

Will slipped back into his spot, adjusting the blanket around me. I snuggled closer. He unbuttoned his shirt about halfway and rolled up the sleeves. I really wanted to kiss him again. The champagne urged me on, and before I knew it, I felt his lips on mine, not knowing who began the kiss.

We slid to the floor, wrapped in the blanket. I felt my sweater slip over my head and my jeans pulled off, unaware if I did the removing or Will. Panties were all that remained. Will was on top of me, bare-chested. He made sure the blanket stayed securely around me and continued to kiss and caress me. I felt like I was floating above us, watching someone else.

His kisses became more intense, but gentle at the same time. He traveled down my cheek to my neck leaving a trail of kisses as he went. His hands found my breasts, and I arched my back at his touch.

"I love you, Allie," he whispered in my ear, followed by a trail of kisses to my shoulder. He lifted his head to look into my eyes. "I never asked. Does the bird on your shoulder have special meaning?"

"Don't talk." I grabbed him around his neck and pulled him down to my chest. I wanted him so badly, I didn't have time to make up a story. I ran my hands up and down his muscled arms feeling his strength.

The heat grew between us. I wrapped my arms and legs around him, bringing him so close we were almost one. I needed him to love me. As I ran my hands up to his shoulders, the phoenix tattooed on mine flashed through my head. *No!* I didn't want to be reminded of my old life. I had gotten the phoenix to remind myself I could go on no matter what life handed me. Now it made me think of Lucas.

Lucas. The name echoed through my head. I had married Lucas. How could I be so careless, so stupid? I knew I'd created the marriage in my mind, but I married him, pledged my faith and loyalty to him. I said I wouldn't hurt Will again and went back on that promise. My floating body merged with the real. We wore no clothing, skin touched skin. If we went ahead, it would only fill a physical urge I craved.

"Will?"

"Don't worry, I have protection."

"I … can't," I said with a sad, sorry voice. His body went limp against mine. "I'm sorry."

Will bolted up and headed for his bedroom, slamming the door. I threw my clothes on. I ran down the hall, turned the knob to his room, but he'd locked it. I tapped against the wood. "Will? Please, talk to me."

"Not tonight."

I slumped against the door but decided he was right and walked slowly back to my room.

The next morning as I lay in bed, I tried to compose a speech to smooth over the rough edges of last night. Although the night had been a fire of emotions, I couldn't let it happen again. I wanted to tell Will we had to remain friends. I didn't want to hurt him, but was that entirely true? I already had. I was torn between two worlds, confused, how could I make any decisions? I'd have to give him a version of that.

Showered and dressed, I got Zak ready for the day. I saw Will's duffle bag at the apartment door as I headed for the kitchen.

"Will?"

He emerged from his room. "Just finishing up here. I'll be gone and out of your life soon."

"I don't want you out of my life."

"It's apparent you do."

I slumped in a kitchen chair, looking at him with sad eyes. He was right. I'd used him, and it needed to stop. "You don't know how sorry I am."

"You don't have to keep saying you're sorry. I've heard it enough times. I thought if I gave you some time, we'd have a chance. I love you, Allie, you know that. I offered to marry you and become a family, but it falls on deaf ears. I can't keep doing this. I guess I'm the one who's sorry. I hate to leave you alone here, but you seem to be getting on just fine without me. I'll call and check in once in a while … as a friend. Have a nice life." He threw on his jacket and grabbed the duffle bag. Then he stopped, turned to look at us with tears in his eyes. "Little guy, gonna miss you." The door opened, and he stepped through, gone from my life forever.

I dropped my head into my arms that rested on the table and wept. I'd made such a mess of things I didn't know where to start to fix anything. If only I could tell Will the truth, maybe he'd leave without hating me. I could go home to live with my parents. My mother would be happy. I could stop looking over my shoulder. but not really. Doug would have what he wanted at last.

The one thing I couldn't do, the thing I wanted most in the world, was to go back to Lucas. Crying harder, I longed to see his face, hear his voice and be with him again. I felt a spoon bounce off my arm and gazed up into my son's eyes, Lucas' eyes. I smiled through my tears. My baby needed me. I wiped my face and got breakfast ready for the two of us. The way it had to be.

* * * *

Winter had been brutally cold, snowy and lots of ice. It made walking to work a nightmare. I finally gave in and took the subway.

As the winter days began to wane, so did the weather. By the end of February, I was able to walk to work again. The snow melted, giving way to warmer days, unusually spring-like. I took a few days off for Zak's birthday. I couldn't decide if I should celebrate on the twenty-eighth of February or March first, so I decided to do both.

Austin's birth certificate listed his birthday at the end of March, so I'd have a party with our new friends on that day. My time off would be a special celebration between mother and son. A year ago I'd been terrified Zak would be born on the twenty-ninth and viewed it as a curse. Now he was here, I don't know why I'd been so worried. He was such a blessing. I'd do it all over again, exactly the same way.

Memories flooded back from those special months in Los Angeles when we were a happy family of three. Doug changed everything when he took Zak away. He used my mother and did unspeakable things to my family. Speaking of family, I laughed when I recalled a conversation with my mom. She told me Doug got married on New Year's Eve to a wonderful girl named Katrina, and they had a son who was almost five. When I asked if she was shocked, she replied Doug had kept it quiet because of his work. He needed to protect his son and wanted the family to forgive him. He could do no wrong in her eyes. Mom and Dad had been excited to meet their grandson, Colton.

I planned to take Zak to Central Park for Birthday-part two. But as I placed him in the stroller, a stab of pain went through my heart, and I made a quick decision.

"Zak, I'm going to stop and buy a prepaid phone on the way to the park. It will just take a minute," I said as I zipped into the store.

When we reached the park, I found a secluded bench and dialed Lucas' number. My hand shook as I punched each key. I hesitated and almost threw the phone away, but one look at Zak's cherub face helped me touch the last number.

"Hello?" Lucas' voice sucked the breath from me. "Is anyone there?"

Chapter Nineteen

"Lucas?" I barely could say his name.

"Allie? For God's sake, Allie, is that you?"

"Yes."

Where are you? I'll come and get you."

"I'm only calling because it's Zak's birthday. I'm not coming home." When I heard Lucas' voice, everything I missed came rushing back.

"So you're going to call me once a year on Zak's birthday?" Lucas sounded angry, something I'd never encountered before.

"Yes … no … I mean …"

"What? What do you mean? No, better, yet, tell me why you did this to us?" he screamed.

"To protect you, Zak … everyone. It's my fault. I brought Doug into your lives."

Lucas' voice grew calmer. "Allie, it's not your fault. How many times do I have to tell you that? The STF was already looking for us before I met you."

"And I helped their cause."

"Not really. How can I convince you to stop blaming yourself?"

"You can't. We're all safe now. That's what matters. Would you like to talk to your son?" I held the phone close to Zak, and he grabbed it. The phone had a speaker so I could hear, too. "Talk to him, Lucas."

"Zak, this is Lucas, your father." He sounded so formal. "I hope you're being a good boy for your mother. She's very special, smart, beautiful, strong. When you get older, I want you to take care of her for me. I love you."

Tears filled my eyes, and I searched for a tissue in the baby bag.

"Da-da." Zak pounded the phone on the stroller, and I gently took it away.

"Lucas? Are you still there?"

"Yeah," he whispered. "He finally said it. He knows me, remembers my voice." I didn't have the heart to tell him Zak called a lot of men that—the grocer, the phone salesman and, of course, Will.

"Allie, we don't know a lot about Niner-squared babies, but I want to pass this along. Zak may have memories sooner than the usual Niner baby. We said one year for Niners after four years of real living. It could be much sooner for Zak, just thought you should know."

"Thanks." I thought of Mia's baby book and my journal. I wanted to share so much with Lucas but held back. "We have to go now. I'm relieved to hear you've had no more issues with the STF."

"There hasn't been any. The last one was a stroke of luck for them. They bugged Zak. Remember?"

"Because of me. Please let's not end the conversation like this."

"Fine. I love you and won't stop looking for you."

"I love you more than you know." I knew I should hang up but resisted. "Lucas? How are Ash and Nate?"

"Furious with you, missing you like crazy, looking for you every waking minute. Shall I go on? You've been gone eight months! Don't you see how much you're hurting us? You think you're protecting us, but it's just the opposite." His voice sounded angry again. "This wasn't the way, Allie."

"I'm so sorry, I love you all. I hope you know that," I whispered.

"Lub! Lub!" Zak shouted.

"Oh, Lucas, that's the first time he's said that." I cried into the phone. "I have to go, really, I'm sorry." I needed to stop saying sorry, so I hung up.

"Da-da lub mum-mum." Zak's first sentence.

"Yes, sweetie, Daddy does love Mommy, and Mommy loves your daddy, too." I smashed the phone against the park bench, dropping it in the nearest waste receptacle. I took some deep breaths and got myself together. Zak looked expectantly at me.

"Let's go play." I told him. We stayed in the park for another hour then headed for home. It had been good to hear Lucas' voice, but now I couldn't stop thinking about him. I daydreamed he found us in the park, and we finished the day together as a family. When Zak was in bed for the night, I curled up on the couch and had a good cry. I never wanted my baby to see me sad or cry about the situation I chose for us. He needed a happy life, one I planned on giving him.

* * * *

"Thanks for doing this, Carli. I'll only be gone an hour or two." Abby called me from the gift shop. She had an emergency dentist appointment and asked Carol if I could fill in for her. We should have asked Max Marvin for permission, but since Carol was my friend, we went over his head to avoid the hassle.

"Carol said it's fine as long as you're back at your job for the afternoon shift, Abby. She really needs me on the crew. A new shipment of art is coming in. Did I tell you she wants to train me as her assistant?"

"Really? Go for it, girl!"

"It means more hours. I told her to ask me again in a few years, when Zak's bigger and I feel more comfortable at the museum."

"Think carefully about that, Allie. Do you really want to pass up this opportunity? Mia might take another year off. You need to talk to her. It will work out. Carol's a good friend to have at the museum. Don't throw it away. I'll see you soon."

Carol and I went out a few times a month. I saw her as a big sister rather than my boss. We just didn't go drinking, she took me shopping and on short excursions around the city. She even found a hairdresser that toned down my bleached blonde hair, to a more subtle golden color. Carol looked out for me and didn't like the fact that Will was gone so much. She had no idea he left for good.

I met Carol's much younger banker boyfriend. He hung on her every word and appeared to be head over heels in love. She, on the other hand, didn't seem that taken with him. Carol always managed to find something wrong with every man she dated. I started to wonder if she compared them to a long-lost love as I might do one day.

I headed for Carol's office when I arrived at the museum. "Hey, Carol! How are you? Just checking in. I'll be at the gift shop, then lunch and back up in time for the shipment."

"Great, woman of many hats. What would I do without you?" Carol worked on her laptop without looking up. "Bring me a salad when you go for lunch. Do you mind?" She opened her desk drawer and pulled out a fifty, still without eye contact. "Get something for yourself, too."

I'd stopped arguing about money long ago. "The usual?"

"Yes, dear, thanks. I have a date with the banker tonight." She finally looked at me.

"Are you ever going to call him by his name, Carol?" I smiled.

"No, I think not." She returned my smile. "I'm afraid he's going to ask me to marry him tonight."

"What?" My eyes widened. "You only started dating him in October."

"My thoughts exactly. See we *are* in the same sisterhood." Carol winked.

"Why tonight? In the middle of the week?"

"It's his birthday, I think. Let me check. She grabbed her phone and quickly touched the screen. "Yep, here it is. March fifteenth—Banker's BD."

"Well, good luck. What are you going to say?"

"Yes."

I stopped in my tracks as I had turned to leave and spun around.

Carol laughed hysterically. "No, silly, I would say no. Let's pray he doesn't ask."

If Carol wasn't in my life, things would be pretty boring. She kept me on my toes. I resisted her attempts at a makeover, except for the hair, but one day she'd get her way. Smiling, I took the stairs to the gift shop. Abby was working behind the counter, straightening merchandise. "I'm reporting for shop duty, ma'am." I saluted her.

Abby ran around the counter and gave me a quick peck on the cheek. "Thanks so much. You're an angel. Parker will be here in about an hour. I hope you don't mind being on your own till then."

"No, it's fine. Get going."

The shop wasn't busy. I strolled around admiring the new items they'd ordered. I heard the door's bell, signaling we had a customer, and rushed to greet them. A tall, handsome man with a cane walked through the door. My eyes widened. My jaw dropped. I stared dumbfounded and almost fell over in shock. *How did he find me?* "Oh my God. Sean!" I didn't know what to do, run or hug him.

"Well, I finally found you." He gave me a broad smile like he found the final piece to a jigsaw puzzle. I couldn't resist and hugged him tightly. He felt a little less broad, like he'd lost a few pounds.

"You're looking well." I admired his clean-shaven look and blazer jacket over his polo and khakis. He'd let his hair grow, making him look less fierce.

"I've lost a few pounds for the knee surgery. Might even get rid of this cane eventually." He held it in the air. "As for the clothes, I had to look the part while I visited every museum on the Northeast coast."

"You've been museum hopping?"

Sean chuckled. "Not on my top ten list, but yes, I have. When you called we only got a fast read on the area you were in. I said I'd look for you and would let everyone know if I found you. I've been in every big city and their museums from Boston to Philadelphia."

My phone call had tipped them off to my location. I scolded myself for not thinking things through beforehand.

"Busted. Niner technology. I should've realized." But secretly I was beginning to wonder if I'd wanted to get caught.

"You free for lunch? I can meet you back here when you get a break." Sean asked.

"Sure, I'd love to talk. Please don't let anyone know you found me."

"As you wish." He nodded once.

"You probably scanned me so there's no use running." I joked.

"No, I haven't. It's totally your choice if you wish to have lunch with me or see any of us again. Just hear me out."

I nodded. "Come back in an hour."

My head pounded. Hundreds of questions ran through my head during the hour. First and foremost, I wanted to know how everyone was. I wanted a rundown on each person. Maybe I should let Sean begin the conversation and see what he said. My mind spun out of control.

Parker arrived right on time. He air-kissed me and shooed me out the door. "Have lunch in the park. It's another beautiful day!" He called after me.

I left through the museum's main entrance to find Sean standing by the side of the building. Seeing his familiar face again brought me to tears. I bit my lip to gain composure. I couldn't let him break me down.

"Where's Zak? You have a sitter?" he asked as he joined me.

That's the first thing he wants to know? Well, I guess he's concerned and wants the information to pass on to Lucas.

"He's with a competent babysitter." I looked directly at him. "I know you could follow me without me knowing."

Sean smiled and put his arm around me. "Where's a good place to get some take-out?"

I headed to a little deli I liked and ordered Carol's salad to pick up later. They knew just how she liked it. Sean ordered, and we headed to the park, finding an open bench. We sat in silence as we ate. I was getting annoyed. After all this time, didn't he have questions? Was he angry?

"Sean! Say something."

"What do you want me to say, little one? That I miss you? We all miss you? We don't understand why you left? We've spent countless nights debating the reasons? That the lights are completely out in Lucas' eyes? What? You tell me."

"Lucas?" I whispered.

"He just goes through the motions since you left and took his son. Ashley has so much to tell you, confide in you, she's bursting at the seams. The twins wonder when they're going to be flower girls in a wedding that will never happen. Do you want me to go on?"

"No." I shook my head. "I never thought of it like that. I'm just trying to save—"

"Well, stop trying. No one can save the world. Come home and work with us, not against us. We're spending more time trying to find you than developing new programs and equipment to stay ahead of our enemy."

"Enemy?"

"Yes, we never had an organized group trying to track us down before the STF. We consider them the enemy."

"Doug's up to something, isn't he?" Sean remained silent. "It's bigger than wanting the Niners to join him. This is just stage one. Am I right?"

"His numbers are growing, now that his army is privatized. I heard the pay is good. Doug's in total command. They're starting to leak headlines to the papers, blogs, and on-line news sources that the economy is failing. That's all I know."

"You've learned all that since I left?" He didn't answer. "Sean!"

"We've known before that."

"Will you please stop talking in riddles? Tell me what's going on."

Sean took out his phone and brought up a headline dated last year. *A Better Way* it screamed in bold type. Below, the subtitle said, *Time for America to wake up and smell the coffee. Economic recovery is all in the mind.*

"Do you want to explain?" I wrinkled my nose.

"Subtle scare tactics. What do people worry about most? Money. The economy. The article talks about how the country's been in recovery for decades and nothing's happened. There has to be a better way."

"Doug's way," I said.

I watched the people in the park go by in a haze. Some walked dogs, others jogged or rollerbladed. Couples sat on blankets in the grass enjoying an afternoon meal. None of them had any idea a war went on right in their homeland, their own country. A secret military operation was trying to infiltrate and take over a group of men whose only crime was being different. That difference made them valuable, a commodity to be obtained at any cost.

Imperialism. The word that haunted me came to mind. Doug was the head of a group planning to take over the Niners and make them comply with the STF ways. After that, he had an even bigger plan, one the Niners had just started to figure out. Doug was capable of taking over the country. I shivered at the thought as I stared at the clueless people in the park.

Sean was right. I couldn't save the world. Lucas was right. My only priority should be the Niners. I stood in the way of their safety, keeping them from their true calling, inventing and designing things that would help the world. I needed to go back. I needed to lend a hand. I'd been immature in my thinking. At the time I thought I'd ensured their safety by leaving so I ran away. All I'd caused was heartache for everyone.

"Come back, Allie, we can fight them together." Sean interrupted my thoughts. "We worked on a double shield to protect the compounds. Julian decided to stay in Montana and expand there. With technology today, it's harder to acquire land without anyone's knowledge. He decided to lay low, improve on what we have."

I continued to stare, lost in my thoughts.

"I'll walk you back, Allie." Sean stood. "As I said before, I won't tell anyone I found you, but you're not getting rid of me. I'll stay here forever if need be. I'll protect you and Zak with my life, for whatever's left of it."

"You won't have to do that, Sean."

"Try and stop me."

"No, what I mean is you won't have to stay here. I'm going back."

"What?" His brows raised above his sunglasses. "Did I just hear you say you're coming back? Just like that?" He picked me up and swung me around. "Is it okay if I call Lucas and let him know?"

"He's mad at me. Isn't he? I can't blame him."

"Yes, but he'll change his mind as soon as I make the call."

"Would you mind giving me some time? I have to get back to work, pick up Carol's salad on the way and finish logging a shipment that's coming in."

"Sure, I'll walk you." Sean beamed like a proud papa. "Will I finally get to walk my girl down the aisle?"

My head began to spin. I'd left my wedding plans in limbo. Some things had been ordered and others needed final decisions. Not able to remember what I wanted or how I'd planned the day was the least of my worries. I pictured the most important thing, Lucas under the flowered trellis, as I imagined him the day I married him in my mind. "Yes, I hope you will if Lucas still wants me," I whispered.

We strolled back to the street and waited to cross. A yellow cab zipped by leaving behind a trail of fumes. The city had its own charms—smells and all. I'd miss it. "Sean, I want to thank you. I never really got to tell you how much I appreciate everything you've done for me throughout the years."

"Just doing my job."

"It's more than that. I love you like a—"

"Father? I'm probably old enough to be your great-great grandfather!" He chuckled.

"No, silly, I was going to say like a big brother."

"Well, if we're being truthful, I love you, too, like a little sister. You and Lucas are the nearest I've got to family."

"We *are* your family, Sean. Don't ever forget that." Sean stood outside as I entered the deli to pick up the salad. As we headed back to the museum, I couldn't help notice how natural it felt to be walking the streets of New York with him.

"Sean, thanks for finding me, for not giving up, despite my efforts to keep you all away. I've been an idiot."

"No, you haven't. You're young. You thought with your heart instead of your head."

"How old are you really? So much wisdom and patience oozing from you!" I laughed and patted his arm.

"Thirty-two, do the math." He teased. We stopped in front of the museum. "I'll be here to pick you up later. We can continue the conversation."

I gave him a quick hug as I did the math. He looked quite good for a 128-year-old man.

A huge burden had been lifted from me. I noticed the blue skies and the sun shining brightly for the first time today. I guess I'd taken it all for granted before or just didn't notice. "Yes, meet me after work. We have a lot to talk about."

* * * *

Sean stood patiently waiting outside Mia's apartment. I planted a seed that there was a possibility of Wyatt and I moving back to California. She appeared genuinely upset but agreed to keep it to herself. As I left the building, Zak in arms, he pointed at Sean. "Da-da!"

Sean extended his arms, and Zak went to him immediately. "Hey, little guy, I missed you."

"Awn." Zak played with Sean's buttons on his shirt.

"He knows me, Allie." His eyes welled with tears.

My jaw dropped. I took a minute to compose myself and said, "Lucas said he might retain his memories a little sooner than normal Niner babies. But I didn't expect this!"

Zak let Sean carry him all the way to the apartment, chatting with him in baby talk, probably telling him about his day. I unlocked the door. "Here we are." I held out my hand to invite him in.

"Just put him in the high chair, Sean. He's happy there and can see what's going on. I'll fix his dinner then make something for us." I moved deftly around the kitchen and fed Zak in no time. "Where are you staying, Sean? I have two bedrooms. You're welcome to stay here." I'd recently moved into Will's old bedroom to train Zak to be on his own at night.

"I'm fine where I'm at, don't worry."

"Well, the offer stands."

"Thanks." Sean glanced around the apartment as he paced in the living room.

"Something else?" I asked. "What's bothering you?"

"I need to tell you something, Allie. Sit down."

My heart started to pound. "Lucas? Is he okay?"

"Yes, he's fine. It has nothing to do with him. It's about the day the California compound was bombed." I nodded, urging him on. We all had to deal with that day in our own way. "Remember I told you Rik was in a car parked by the square?"

"Yes, you said you opened the door to talk to him because you thought he needed help. Levi ran toward you, too far away to stop you."

"That's right. Rik said the car was disabled and it had locked him inside. I released him. When I went to the van, he started up the car and rammed the van. When Levi saw what happened he jumped in the passenger side of the car to try to stop him. I'm sure they fought and Rik overpowered Levi. That's why Levi was in that seat at the crash scene, because of me. Rik was heading back to Headquarters with Levi as a hostage."

The memories were clearly etched in my mind. The scene flashed before me—Bee, a pile of discarded metal, Levi mumbling his last words, Rik's body torn open. I broke out in a cold sweat, my hands clenched at my sides.

"Well," Sean said. "That was my fault. I caused Levi's death. I know you blame yourself, but it was me."

"No, Sean, it wasn't your fault. All the circumstances leading up to that moment were caused by ..." I wanted to say me. *You're a victim like everyone else.*

"But you see, Allie, it was my fault. All of us working security at command central have the same powers, the same control. We're considered equals. Levi locked Rik down in the vehicle, and I unlocked it, releasing Rik from Levi's restraints. I unleashed Rik on all of us. Levi was killed because of my stupidity." Sean hung his head. "I never checked my messages, never saw Rik was a traitor."

"Oh, Sean, I'm so sorry. I didn't know."

"You left before Lucas got back from the evaluation meeting. He would've told you then."

"Are you sorry you taught me how to de-scan myself?"

"No, everyone deserves that right. I did it before I left, too. No one knows where I am."

"They will soon, I'm sure. If you found me in two weeks, the rest are not far behind."

"I asked them to let me do this alone."

We sat quietly for a while. Zak took everything in, eyes focused on us. I wondered if he understood. "Sean, do you think Zak remembers?"

"The bombing?" He glanced over at him. "Ask him."

My hands began to tremble. "I can't."

"Do you want me to ask?" Sean stood and walked to the highchair. "Zak, do you remember going to Spanish Village?"

He nodded his little head until I wanted to run over and hold it still. Tears filled my eyes.

"And do you remember the bombs? I asked.

Zak's head bobbed up and down as I screamed.

"Allie," Sean grabbed me by the shoulders, "calm down. You're scaring him."

Zak joined in the crying as I rushed to take him from his chair. "I'm so sorry, Zakkie. Mommy didn't mean to make you cry. It's okay. We'll be okay. Sean's here."

He stopped crying as soon as I said that and threw his arms out at Sean. Sean took him from me and brought him close to his chest.

"That's right, little man. Uncle Sean will never let anyone hurt you." He kissed the top of the baby's head, rocking him back and forth. "He needs his father." Sean looked straight into my eyes.

"Not yet. Please," I begged. "I need to get my bearings. So much has happened in such a short time. I will return to Victorian Village, but I have to let Carol know I'm leaving. Give my notice." I took a breath. "Sean, would you mind keeping Zak with you while I make dinner?" I rubbed Zak's little back. "Okay?"

Zak gave me a smile and took Sean's face in his chubby hands. "Awn, Mommy."

"Oh!" Another first. "He just called me Mommy, Sean. It's been mum-mum till now."

"That's great." Sean sat in a kitchen chair bouncing Zak on his lap. "The kid's a genius. Must run in the family." He grinned at me.

"I can still argue it's my fault for bringing Rik to the Niners." I called over my shoulder as I headed for the stove. "I overheard a conversation when Doug kidnapped me in high school about the Niners being kept in the dark. Lucas sent a message to Julian. That's when Julian contacted them."

"I can dispute it!" Sean argued. "We now know it was part of the STF plan to send a double agent back to the fold, long before you met Lucas."

"Oh."

"See everything doesn't lead back to you, Allie."

"Ka-li." Zak smiled up at him.

"What did he just say?"

"He's correcting you. He thinks my name is ... was Carli."

"You changed your name? Of course, that makes sense. What's Zak's?"

"Austin."

"Aus-ty, no-no." Zak shook his head.

"He doesn't seem to like that name." Sean chuckled and held Zak in the air. "You don't have to be Austin anymore, little guy. You're going home."

"I asked for time, Sean."

"And you'll have it. Just let me know when."

* * * *

The next few days I walked around as if in a dream, nothing seemed real. I couldn't believe Sean had found me, and Zak and I would be going home to Montana. My schedule at work remained the same. I went in daily without telling anyone my plans.

Sean came in the mornings to care for Zak. I called Mia and told her Wyatt came home early from a business trip. I apologized for the abrupt ending and said we didn't need her services any longer because we planned to move back to California.

"Could you stop by one day after work so I can say goodbye and give you the baby book?"

"Sure, I'll stop by tonight."

One of the most difficult things to do was say goodbye to Mia and Zoe. They loved Zak and treated him like family. I would cherish the baby book for the rest of my life. I dragged my feet as I came closer to their apartment. There was no kind way to say I'd never see them again, so I'd have to lie.

"When are you giving your notice at work? I have to bite my tongue every time I talk to Abby so I don't tell her." Mia placed the Austin book in my hands.

"Friday's not the best day to do something like that so I'll wait till Monday. I'll miss everyone so much." I hugged her with all my might. *Goodbye, my friend.*

"We'll stay in touch, won't we?" Mia said it like she knew the opposite was true.

"Sure." I hugged her again and quickly made my exit. I promised Sean I'd bring New York style pizza home and stopped on the way to pick it up. Funny how Sean and Nate felt more like brothers than the ones I actually had. If Nate had been here tonight, it would have completed the family.

"Hey, Sean, I'm home," I called as I stepped into the apartment.

He came out of the bathroom with soaking wet towels over his shoulder. A sly grin came over his face. "You warned me!" We both laughed as I realized Zak had his nightly bath. "I wanted you to come home to a clean baby. I'll feed him while you get the pizza ready."

"Sean, you're spoiling me!" I grabbed a bottle of wine from the fridge and popped the cork. Balancing the bottle and two glasses, I carried everything into the living room. I kicked off my shoes and plopped on the couch. "I love work, but I'm glad the week is over."

We talked late into the night until I could hardly hold my eyes open. Sean checked in on Zak then headed home. He really hadn't said where he was staying.

A knock on the door startled me, but my first thought was that Sean had forgotten something. I threw open the door. "What'd you forget?"

I almost fainted at the sight of him. Lucas stood in the doorway, handsome as ever, leaning against one side holding a red rose. *Déjà vu.*

Chapter Twenty

We didn't speak as I fell into his arms. I felt his lips on mine as he lifted me into his arms. I pointed the way to my bedroom, and we fell onto the mattress. I tore at his clothes as he pulled mine from my body. I couldn't get enough of him, the taste of him and held him so close I never wanted to let go.

After making love, I rolled over, grabbed his shirt and threw it on, reminding me of our first weekend together. I tiptoed to the kitchen and grabbed the unfinished bottle of wine and two more glasses to bring back to the bedroom. As I turned, I jumped, almost dropping the glasses. Lucas stood behind me.

"I'm coming back," I said as my eyes traveled up to meet his. His dark eyes had lost their spark, he needed a shave and his dark brown hair had grown out to the point he looked like he did in high school.

"Are you?" His eyes turned cloudy. "Let's talk, in here." He nodded toward the sofa.

"Okay." I followed after him. "You have every right to doubt me."

He spun to face me. The wounded look on his face said it all. I set the wine and glasses on the table and slid his shirt down my shoulders, letting it drop to the floor. Lucas' eyes widened, and his face softened. I wrapped my body around his as he lowered me to the sofa.

"Allie," he said softly into my hair. "My God, I missed you." He kissed every part of my body.

I pulled his face up to meet mine. "I love you. It was always you."

He melted into my body and kissed my lips over and over. He deserved an explanation, but it could wait.

After our love making ended, Lucas sat up and poured two glasses of wine. He handed me one and said, "I guess you're finally legal. You probably bought this bottle yourself."

I smiled shyly. "Yep." I leaned against him as we sipped our wine. "I have so much to tell you I don't know where to start. I'm giving two weeks' notice at work on Monday. I was going to pack my stuff and come back to Montana with Sean." I sighed. "Well, that was the plan. Now that you're here I want you to stay. We'll go back with you, although Sean wasn't supposed to tell you where I was."

"He didn't." Lucas shifted to face me. "He moved into one of our apartments a few days ago under an alias, another Niner's name. We figured it was him." Lucas gave me a slight smile. "I followed him to your apartment."

"I'm sorry, Lucas, for leaving. I never should have done that to you. Looking back, it seems a little drastic."

Lucas' body tensed. "If I didn't know Zak was sleeping in the next room, I'd be shouting this, Allie, so maybe it's a good thing he is. You took my son from me. I thought I'd never see him again. Worse than that, you broke my heart. I couldn't believe you left right after the funeral."

"I wasn't thinking straight. I was just so mad at Doug, confused by all that happened and blamed myself. Can you understand that?"

"Yes, but I wish you turned *to* me rather than away. How can I trust you? How can I be certain this won't happen again?"

"You can be certain. I was with you every day in my heart. On our wedding day, I married you."

"You what?"

"I married you, in my mind. I promised to love you, be faithful and loyal only to you."

The stern look on Lucas' face vanished and was replaced with a look of longing and sadness. "I did the same."

"You did?" I slid closer to him, kissing him over and over. "Very romantic, but I always said you were. Please forgive me, please?"

Lucas kissed me for a long time. My lips tingled when we parted. He ran his thumb over them. "How could I not? There's nothing to forgive. We'll work this out at home."

"Home. Sounds good."

We dozed on the couch, and the sun woke me in the morning. Lucas was up and in the kitchen with his coffee.

"Zak's a sound sleeper." He brought me a cup.

"He'll be calling me soon." And like magic I heard, "Mum! Mommy!" I raced to his room and brought him out to the kitchen.

"Da!" Zak pointed his chubby finger at Lucas.

I was shocked. "Lucas, he's never called anyone that. He usually says da-da."

Tears filled his eyes as he took the baby from me. "My, he's grown!"

"He's taken a few steps when I hold his hand. I'm sure he'll be running all over the place soon."

"I'm amazed at the progress he's made. A Niner baby would be like a six-month-old at this stage. Wow, he can stand up on his own!" Lucas had placed Zak on the floor, and the baby walked toward him.

"He's walking, Lucas! He's walking for the first time!" I laughed and cried all at once, thrilled he got to share the moment. This could be the breakthrough we needed and hoped it would help us heal.

* * * *

Monday morning I waited until Carol was alone to give my notice. My heart ached at the thought. She'd been in and out of the back rooms all morning, and I finally grabbed her to ask her to lunch. "My treat," I told her.

Carol raised her eyebrows. "Something you need to tell me? You look like a girl that had sex all weekend. Is the husband home?"

Carol had a habit of coming straight to the point, so I just nodded to keep her from asking more questions. "Come and get me whenever you're ready."

As she walked away, I realized I'd never asked her about dinner with her banker, the night she thought he might propose. I forgot to check her hand. Now I felt like a fool for being so selfish and only worrying about myself. I'd remedy that at lunch.

Carol shoved me in a taxi when lunchtime arrived. We took off to an unknown destination.

"I'll need a drink, won't I?" She raised an eyebrow as she stared at me. The car pulled up in front of a very exclusive restaurant, I knew I couldn't afford this and slipped my phone out of my handbag to call Lucas.

"New phone? Never saw that style before." Carol admired it from a distance.

I nodded and put it away without using it. "Just checking on Austin."

The maître de showed us to a back table. Carol ordered a bottle of wine and pushed aside the menu. "Spill." Our eyes locked.

"First, you spill. What happened with the banker?"

"We broke up. Now you go."

Shocked by the news, I said, "Do you want to talk—?"

"Nope, now what's up with you? You look different somehow. Happy."

"Well, first I have to give you my two weeks' notice. I'm leaving. We're heading back to California. Wyatt got a promotion and—"

"Cut the crap, Carli. This has nothing to do with Wyatt, does it?"

"Carol! Do you have a crystal ball or something?" She could be so exasperating at times. I couldn't lie to her.

"You never looked like this when you talked about Wyatt or say you had sex with him. What's up with that relationship? Do you even love the guy?"

"No … well, yes," I stammered. "You see, Wyatt and I aren't married. He just came with me to New York to help me settle in and went back to school in California. We're just friends."

"All the sex you had this weekend …" Carol sat back and slapped the table. "The old flame is back!"

Suddenly shy, I looked down at my hands. "Yes, and Za … Austin and I are going home with him."

"Carli, you were about to call your son a different name. Did you change your name to hide from the ex? Oh, I'm loving this. Here I thought you were this sweet little thing from Montana, and I have Mata Hari sitting across from me!" She took a long drink from her glass and banged the empty goblet on the table. "That's my girl!"

I had to laugh at her antics. "It's not as dramatic as that." If only she knew, but I doubted she'd believe me. But, knowing Carol, she just might.

"So, what's your real name?"

"Allie … Allison."

"And Wyatt?"

"Will, Will Hollins."

"You wouldn't mind if I looked him up?" A smile spread across her face.

"Carol!"

"I'm just asking. You can say no."

Mulling it over, I decided it didn't bother me. "Go for it. He's at UCLA. I'll give you his address and number later. He'd probably love to quit school. He's been there six years. And he did tell me he thought you were hot." I winked.

Carol rubbed her hands together. "Just what I need, a distraction."

We finally ordered lunch, and when we finished, Carol picked up the tab amidst my protests. "After a girlfriend confides in the other, it's the least I can do. I hate to see you go, Allie. You had a future at the museum. But I don't blame you for wanting to follow your heart. Grab the bull by the horns and don't let go." She gestured with both hands.

Then it struck me. Carol had let her true love go.

"Who was he, Carol?" I looked directly at her.

"Oh, it was so long ago." She played with her glass. "Just a high school romance, the typical cheerleader and football quarterback. I thought it seemed too cliché and wanted more out of life. Nothing was going to stop me from my dreams, not even love."

"Where's the quarterback today?"

"Happily married after a long career in the NFL." Carol patted my hand. "Time to get back."

"Have you seen him since high school?"

"Yes, many times, high school reunions, on the television doing interviews."

"You don't have to pretend with me, Carol. I can see you still love him." I took her hand. "Maybe one day—"

"Yes, maybe, but for now, Wyatt, or should I say Will, will do nicely." Carol laughed. "I'll miss you. You're like the little sister I never had. I saw something in you from the very start, and I'm never wrong. Whatever you do in life, you'll do well. Never forget that... or me."

"How could I ever forget you? We'll stay in touch, I promise." My eyes filled with tears when Carol gave me one of her looks saying she knew better. "You're like a sister, too. I'll miss you the most."

Returning to work a little late, no one questioned where I'd been. I slipped down to the shop, knowing I had to tell my two friends goodbye. Parker was waiting on a customer, but Abby was free. I walked slowly over to her. "Can we talk?"

Abby froze in place. "Mia warned me something was coming. This is it, isn't it?"

"I'm leaving. I just gave Carol my two weeks' notice."

Abby appeared stunned. "I thought you were here for good. You were so settled—apartment, husband, baby. Darn! I want you to stay." She threw her arms around me.

Parker finished up and joined the hug. "Why are we hugging?"

"Carli's leaving us!" Abby wailed. I wanted to cover her mouth, but instead I began to laugh.

"Boy, I'll miss you two!" I hugged them tighter.

Returning home after work, I found Lucas sitting on the couch, arms folded across his chest. "Hmm, that looks like an angry pose." I teased.

Lucas held up the deactivated phone I used to show pictures of Will, Zak and me. "You never told me he was here," he said in a calm voice as Zak played in the corner of the room.

"I didn't want to make you angrier or upset. Will hasn't been here in months."

"Months? When was the last time?"

"Christmas. He left because he knew I'd never be with him." I saw Lucas relax, and his arms unfolded. "I didn't know where to go when I left Montana. I found myself driving straight to California. As I drove by the apartment, I realized that would be the first place you or Doug would look. So, I went to Will's."

Lucas hit his head. "I never thought you'd go there and never checked. Boy, was I stupid."

I rubbed his arm. "You're not." I sighed. "He said we could stay the night. He helped us get new identities and got one for himself. He said if we traveled as a married couple it'd raise less suspicion."

"I bet he did."

"Let me finish. We flew to New York in July, settled in here. Will returned to California for fall quarter. He came for a few days over the holidays, and that's the last time I saw him. Please don't be mad. He helped me and was great with Zak. I don't know how I would've done it without him." *That sounds bad. Quit now while you can.* "You know what I mean. We never ..." Guilt crept over me. "We kissed a few times. One night it went a little too far, but I stopped him. That's why he left."

"That was the end of it?"

"Yes."

Lucas tugged on my arm and pulled me down next to him.

"How can I ever make it up to you?" I asked.

"I can think of many ways." He took my face in his hands and kissed my lips. "The first is to get married." He dug in his pocket and produced my engagement ring. "It killed me to find this on our dresser." He slipped it back on my finger. "But this makes up for it."

I kissed him again, knowing I would never leave his side again. "I promise to never leave you and will even put it in our vows."

Lucas threw his head back and laughed, a happy laugh. "I'll take you up on it." He laid me back on the couch and cuddled up next to me as we watched our son play. I couldn't wait to get back to Montana—to my life, my friends, my home.

Chapter Twenty One

When we stepped off the private plane in Billings, Montana, I finally felt at peace. Maybe I'd made mistakes, but I'd also learned from them. I ached to see Ashley and Nate. The ride to the village seemed to take forever.

I left behind the two wine glasses on the empty floor of the apartment. Lucas and I placed them there together, and I hoped it would bring closure to that life. As hard as it was to leave the city, excitement built as we grew closer to the mountains.

As we turned onto the dirt road and headed into the pine tree forest, I relaxed. The van burst through the shrubs, and we came out on the other side to finish the drive to the compound. Lucas pointed out things to Zak as we drove along.

"Just think it in your head, Zak," he said. "We have you programmed into the main computer." The van stopped at the compound's entrance. "Tell the door to open." To my amazement the huge door unlocked. "See, you did it! High-five, little man."

Zak called Lucas, Da, since the day he first saw him in New York. Men were da-da, but Lucas was Da. He knew his father. As we traveled along, Zak pointed and said, "Da". Lucas patiently explained whatever it was.

Allison Sanders, rescanned. All privileges restored. Welcome back. "What did you say?" I turned to Lucas.

"Nothing."

"I swore you did. I heard I was rescanned."

"Oh! That's the computer. You're linked to it through your DNA now."

I crossed my brows and stared at him. "New updates?"

"We have to keep up. The main computer is gone, replaced with a small chip embedded in a wall on the fourth floor. It can't be found easily and is set to self-destruct if anyone invades."

"I take it there's back-up?"

"Of course, only the security team knows where. For now, just think of you and the computer as one. Anything you want, just think it in your head."

"Didn't we already do that?" I felt confused.

"For some things, yes. I'll give you a short lesson now and tell you more later." Lucas leaned back, propping Zak up on his legs. "Both of you listen closely. You won't need a phone anymore, unless you really want one. You'll be given a chip. It's your link to the computer. Zak will carry his in an armband. Adults can have it embedded under their skin." He tapped below his hand. "Right here, at the top of the wrist. You won't lose it that way."

"True." I shivered. "But in most movies having something put under your skin never ends well."

Lucas chuckled. "Maybe we can dispel that image. This will be used for good."

Made sense, but I still had a bad feeling. "Can I deactivate if I'm captured by Doug?"

"Good question. You know we tried to think of all the angles before recommending it for the general Niner population. You're in total control of your chip. You can shut it down, and even make it disintegrate." Lucas looked at me. "Safe for the body to absorb, don't worry. Once it's in, you won't know it's there."

"Okay, so how does it work?"

"You bring up your own personal screen like this."

A floating screen appeared in front of Lucas. Zak giggled and clapped as one materialized before him.

"I need one, too!" I stuck out my lower lip. "But I don't have a chip."

"You do, Allie. I had it installed in your phone. We had to come up with a way to carry it around for now. The old guys insisted." Lucas smiled. "Go ahead. Give it a try."

Do I have any text messages? A virtual screen floated in front of me. "Oh!" I covered my mouth. "I have over twenty messages! Do you see that?" I glanced at Lucas.

"Only if you let me. You have to give permission."

"You can't see my screen?"

Lucas shook his head.

"I saw yours!"

"That's because I told it you could."

"This is so awesome, Lucas. Will it work in the real world, too?"

"Yes, but we know better than to try it out there. You never know who's watching and wondering what we're doing. I have one more surprise when we get home."

The van entered Headquarters parking garage and followed the ramp to the third floor. Banners and balloons filled the space with twenty or so people waiting in a corner. As we emerged from the van, I was greeted by "welcome home" and "we missed you" instead of the scolding I deserved.

Ashley separated from the crowd and rushed toward me. "Allie, don't ever do that again!" Her arms flew around me. She held on as if she'd never let go. "I missed you so much." Her eyes widened. "And you're a blonde!"

Lucas stepped out of the van with Zak in his arms, and her attention turned to them. "Zakkie!" She held out her arms. He wiggled away from Lucas to go to her.

People surrounded me. Julian and Serena. Both twins talked at once. A few neighbors and people I'd met at the hospital greeted me. A boy I thought looked familiar stood off from the crowd. *I know him. Oh yeah, Ryan Gilchrist, the boy I met last summer. His father died, and his mother was ill. So nice of him to come.*

"Ryan." Ashley motioned him over. "Allie, do you remember Ryan?" I nodded. "Remember he came to live with Nate and me? He's our son now." She smiled brightly as if to say don't ask any questions.

"Ryan! It's good to see you again." *His mom must have died.*

"Welcome home … Mrs. … Ms …"

"Call me, Allie." I gave him a hug.

Nate hung back from the others, and I couldn't read him. His reddish-blonde hair had grown back, but he kept it shorter. He had a faint U-shaped scar on his face traveling from the corner of his nose to above his ear.

"Nate?" We embraced, and I cried uncontrollably. I'd missed him so much.

"Don't ever do that again, little one," he whispered in my ear.

Lucas took Zak from Ashley and motioned for me to join him. "Thank you, everyone." He told the crowd. "It's been a long day so if you don't mind, we'll head home."

A quick goodbye to all the well-wishers and suddenly we were in the elevator, going down to the second level. Beetle waited by the door with two other vehicles. As we climbed in, Sean, Nate, Ashley and Ryan emerged from the elevator and hopped in the other two.

"They're coming over, right?" I checked Lucas for confirmation.

"How could I stop them?" He laughed and touched my cheek.

"Da lubs Mommy." Zak kicked his legs in the car seat.

"Yes, he does, and don't you forget it." Lucas turned and tickled his foot.

"Do you think he can walk me down the aisle?" I joked.

"He'll have to fight Sean for the privilege."

Beetle turned into our drive, and I gasped. The house looked so inviting. I'd forgotten how much I loved it.

"Dinner first, then strategy meeting. We have a lot to tell you," Lucas said as if nothing had changed. He waved to the other two cars coming up the drive. "But first, this." He planted a luscious kiss on my mouth. He dropped back and stared at me. "I never said anything about your hair and neither did you."

"Do you like it?" I grew anxious. I had gotten used to it, but still wasn't sure of the color.

"Yes and no. You have to decide." He shrugged.

"I've been growing it out." I laughed. "And I'll change back the color."

Sean jumped out of the first car and helped Lucas with the luggage. Nate and Ashley parked behind him, but Ryan stayed in the car and drove away.

"Ash, he's more than welcome!" I called to her.

"Teenagers! Bee will get Ryan home safely." She waved her hand at the disappearing car. "Just wait, Allie." She pointed at Zak.

"Bee?"

"Oh, sorry, I knew I should've checked with you but you—"

"Weren't here?"

Ash nodded and said, "I hope you don't mind. I wanted a name for our car. I named it in honor of her."

"She would love it." I linked arms with my friend as we headed into the house.

We gathered around the dining room table to eat. After dinner, Zak fell asleep in his highchair from exhaustion. "He's had a big day." I lifted him out and took him upstairs.

Tears pricked the corners of my eyes as I stepped into the room we'd decorated for Zak before he was born. It was neat and clean, everything in its place. I pulled back the navy and white striped comforter trimmed in white eyelet and placed him in his crib, his rightful home.

"Sorry, baby," I whispered. "I didn't mean to keep you from this. I was scared for all of us." I turned on the baby lamp and joined the others assembled in the great room. I sat next to Ashley and took her hand. "Forgive me?"

"Allie, I understand your fears. We debated them over and over. I always took your side."

Of course my best friend had defended me. I would have done the same for her. "Tell me about Ryan."

"His mother passed away in January. He pretty much lived with us anyway, so the transition was easy. The emotional side was tough. His counselor said he must get used to death because he'll live so long. Still, they were his parents. We're giving him time. He's just fifteen and won't be sixteen until—"

"Zak turns two."

"Right! Always need to do the math," Ash said as we laughed. "And now add in Niner-squared math."

"Allie, Ashley. Are you ready for our discussion?" Lucas sounded so formal it took me by surprise.

"He takes his new duties as Head of Security very seriously," Ashley whispered. We started to giggle as he stared us down.

I suppressed my laugh, proud of Lucas for stepping up and wanting to take charge of the Montana compound. Since Julian had stayed, he'd trained under him. Regardless of how ready he thought he was, I knew he had much to learn.

"Rik was a double agent, trained and sent to recruit Niners from the inside. The extra prize for them was unexpected." Lucas turned to me. "Zak."

"Rik was prepared to come back as a plant, no matter what?" I asked.

"Yes. We've learned more. The bombs, designed by the STF Niners, were meant to destroy our homes, not us. They wanted to flush us out, have nowhere to go. They planned to bomb a compound as soon as Rik fed them the coordinates, but he never revealed any of our locations before his death. In a strange way, Rik was still loyal to the Niners. I think once he got back here, he couldn't do it. Doug realized that so he planted the tracking device on Zak." Lucas took a deep breath and paced back and forth in front of us.

"As we said before, Doug let us leave the STF complex too easily. It was a red flag, one we missed. Once Doug knew he couldn't get us to stay or convince you, Allie, to join him, he had a back-up plan ready. He had his girlfriend come in with Zak knowing we'd take him by force if we had to. Doug let us get away."

"And I have news for you," I said. "Doug married Katrina."

"How'd you find that out?" Ashley asked.

"I call my mom once a month. She told me about the wonderful New Year's Eve wedding ceremony and wasn't even hurt she was kept from her four-year-old grandson."

"What? How does he get away with it?" Ashley looked at everyone. "We hate Doug. Although," she said as she faced me, "loathe is a better word now."

"I agree." I nodded. "He used the secret operation as his excuse, and my parents bought it."

"I wonder," Nate chimed in, "if Doug has ulterior motives for getting married. Why after all this time?"

"Interesting thought," Lucas said. "We'll never take anything for granted again. We're at war."

I cringed. The Niners were the best of humanity. They just wanted to live in peace and help the world. Now they were forced into a situation they had been able to avoid for centuries. I placed my head on Lucas' shoulder, feeling the weight of the world come down on everyone in the room. We were at war with my psychopath brother who used people to get what he wanted. "Sometimes there has to be war before there is peace."

"What did you say?" Ashley pressed her lips together.

"Something Doug told me long ago. I never told anyone. It's his mantra." I breathed out slowly. "We may have to embrace that thinking, too."

Lucas wrapped his arm around my waist. "I didn't know you carried that around with you. I'm sorry, Allie."

"What's the plan?" I asked.

"We're working diligently on a beam to destroy any incoming bombs, like the one we dealt with in California. Rik disengaged our tracking devices and shield some time before those bombs arrived. We were distracted. Nate was wounded then Levi's funeral. We'll never leave Headquarters manned by one person again. Men wanted to attend the funeral, and we thought for a short time, it'd be okay." He ran his hand over his face in frustration.

"Rik volunteered to go on the rescue mission which made us trust him. He had the authority to go anywhere and not be questioned. Looking back, we shouldn't have been so gullible. And now Levi's dead because of our stupidity." Lucas put his head in his hands, and I rubbed his back.

A soft tone sounded in my ear. I had a call on my virtual phone and excused myself. "Serena?"

"Allie, I hate to call so late, but I really need you to bring Zak in for a check-up tomorrow. He needs those shots." I cringed and realized Serena meant he needed those shots on his very first birthday.

"We'll be there. Tell me when."

"Ten in the morning? Is that good?" Serena sounded too business-like.

"Yes, it's fine. And Serena, I'm sorry. I missed you, and I'm glad you're not moving away."

Her voice softened. "I missed you, too."

"Lucas." I waved at him to come to the kitchen while the others talked. "I know you have new duties now, but can you break away to meet Zak and me at the hospital tomorrow? Serena wants to see him."

"Of course, I'll stay home until it's time to go." He kissed my forehead. "Thanks for telling me."

I grabbed his arm as he was about to leave. "I know I have to gain your trust again. I won't keep anything from you ever again, I promise." I pulled him to my level and kissed him.

"I just need time." Lucas went back to the great room. I followed behind realizing I still needed to make amends. Lucas had been deeply hurt and wouldn't recover any time soon, and the rest probably felt the same way.

"Everyone?" I waited for all eyes to be on me. "I want to apologize one more time. I'm sorry I hurt you by running away. Sean said it was because I was young and thought with my heart, but I want to say it was because I was stupid. I acted first before thinking things through."

"Allie," Ashley said. "We forgive you. I might have done the same thing."

"Really?"

Everyone nodded in agreement.

But something else still bothered me. "I have to ask one more thing about Rik. You said he was still with the STF when he came back to Montana, but he must have changed his mind at the last minute. Was he protecting the Niners or loyal to Doug?"

"That's a good question. I'll guess we'll never know." Lucas shook his head.

"The Niners have been sequestered for a long time," I said. "You're too trusting of your own, Lucas. Think! Rik was willing to help Doug instead of protecting the compound. You're still making excuses for him." I wanted to scream from frustration. "The Niners need to wake up and realize the old ways don't work anymore."

Nate sat forward. "I have to agree with her, Lucas. Rik knew if he cut power the STF would find their way here. We didn't find out until later that he shut down all our security measures."

Lucas took it all in but said nothing.

"I think we should wrap it up for tonight." Nate stood and stretched. "I need my beauty sleep to keep up with these Niners."

"He tried to do a three-hour sleep thing but became a walking zombie." Ashley laughed as she rose to join him.

"Nate?" I called out to him as they headed for the front door. I pointed to my cheek. "The scar?"

"They did a good job, didn't they?" He smiled.

"I thought they'd fix it with plastic surgery?"

"Allie, he could have been completely disfigured if it wasn't for the Niners' technology. We'll take the scar." Ashley gave me the look I recognized for "we'll talk later".

"Yes, I'm thankful for that, too." I nodded. Sean hugged me goodbye and followed them out, leaving Lucas and me alone.

"Wine? Is it still available from Bella?" I glanced over at Lucas.

"Yeah, a new transporter was installed in the back of the winery. Jared keeps me supplied. What would you like?" Lucas went to the wine fridge.

"Anything red." I curled up on the couch as I was handed a glass. "Lucas? Do you have dreams? Nightmares about that day?"

"Mostly when I'm awake." He slid in next to me. He took my chin in his hand and looked deep into my eyes. "The sparkle has been missing from your eyes. Is that what it is? Nightmares? Memories of the bombing and Zak's kidnapping?"

"Yes." I nodded as tears streamed down my cheeks. "They were bad in California and a little better in New York. Now that you said the bombs weren't meant to kill people, it helps. I thought my brother was a cold-blooded killer for months, hating him every waking moment."

"Allie!" Lucas pulled me close. "Now it's my turn to ask for your forgiveness. I can't imagine what you went through. Dealing with this all on your own because you thought you had to. I promise you, right here and now, you'll never have to go through anything like that again. You have a whole community to support you, not just me."

I lay back in Lucas' arms, feeling safe and protected. Maybe tonight the bombs wouldn't be dropping into my dreams.

Chapter Twenty Two

The next day I searched for my wedding plans. I found the picture of the dress buried in an old file on my laptop and printed it. Flying down the steps, I held it in the air. "I'm ordering this today."

Lucas looked up from feeding Zak. "You're positive that's the one? You could shop on the wall with Ashley to make sure."

"I will, but not for the dress. I'm sure this is the one." I kissed my two men and grabbed a bottle of water.

"I have a favor, Allie." Lucas locked eyes. "I'd like to change the wedding date."

"Why? I had my heart set on June thirtieth."

"Karma. I just want to change it."

"Okay, what day?"

"May fourteenth, my dad's birthday," he said.

"I think that's a wonderful idea!" I threw my arms around his neck. "I'll only have four weeks to get ready though."

"Not a problem in the Niner world." Lucas smiled so wide his eyes got those little crinkles in the corner. He looked good today, handsome and sexy in a black t-shirt and jeans. His arms rippled with muscle.

"I love the Niner world!" I returned his smile then grew serious. "I have one more problem." I looked at Lucas with sad eyes. "I hope Serena's not mad at me."

"She's not."

"How do you know?"

"I talked to Julian this morning. I told him about your PTSD. He suggested we talk to Serena. She can recommend someone for you to talk to."

"PTSD?"

"Post-Traumatic Stress Disorder."

"I know what it is. You think I have it?"

"Yeah, ever since we got back from California. You're showing a lot of the signs even now—nightmares, flashbacks, feeling emotionally cut off from others, having difficulty sleeping, thinking you're in danger. Should I go on?"

"Maybe you're right. I should talk to someone."

"Talk to Ashley about Rosanne. She's a great counselor and psychiatrist."

"Is that the counselor Ryan went to after he lost his parents?" I asked.

"Yeah. She lives on our street. She's married to Oliver, the head of our bio lab."

"Rosanne and Oliver, sounds like a couple out of *Wuthering Heights*."

"You're not going to start comparing me to Heathcliff again, are you?" Lucas joked, remembering back to our high school days.

"No, I won't torture you with any comparisons. How old is Oliver?"

"Late thirties, maybe thirty-eight. You know Niners don't keep track of everyone's age." He winked.

"Okay, I'll see Rosanne after the baby gets his shots. Will you bring Zak home? I'll text Ash and ask her to meet me here to start planning the wedding. I'm not waiting another minute."

"Sounds good." Lucas lifted Zak from his chair. "You seem more like yourself today. I'm glad." He kissed the side of my head as I followed him out the front door. Beetle waited in the drive and her doors popped open when she spotted us.

Zak pointed and said, "Bee!" He'd adjusted to all the changes in the past few weeks very well.

"Lucas, do you think he remembers back this far? He was only here for a month of his life."

"Yeah, I'm afraid so. He has memories of everything."

"How can you tell?"

"He's too familiar with things. He nods like he already knows when I try to explain."

I placed my hand on my throat. "Everything? He knows it all?" Mother's guilt washed over me as I remembered his little head nodding up and down when asked about California.

"Allie, don't beat yourself up. You didn't know."

We pulled up in front of the hospital and headed to Serena's office. I was nervous about the shots, hoping Zak wouldn't cry. Serena's voice could be heard in the hall, and I raced to greet her.

"Allie, you're looking much better today." She hugged me. "Let's get you started on some vitamin supplements for a while."

"Am I forgiven?" I nervously twisted my fingers together, waiting for her answer.

"Yes. I was never mad, just disappointed you didn't come to me." She rubbed my arms. "Now let's take care of that baby, then you."

What Serena considered a shot was nothing more than an eye dropper placed against Zak's skin. "Some babies cry but there's no real reason," she said. "This doesn't hurt. There, Zak, all done." She smiled at him.

"I'll see you at home," Lucas said as he took Zak from the table.

"Send Beetle back for me." I patted Lucas' arm.

Serena motioned for me to follow her. "I talked to Rosanne. She had an opening this morning. Come on, I'll take you over."

A petite woman with curly blonde hair sat behind a large, mahogany desk. She rose when she spotted us and leaned over her desk to shake my hand. "Allie, nice to meet you. Please, sit down."

I glanced around and noticed Serena had disappeared.

"So where would you like to start?" she asked as she reached for her coffee mug.

"High school?" I tried to laugh, but realized I was serious.

"Okay, let's start with high school. That's when you met Lucas?" She looked at me, waiting for the answer. Her golden-brown eyes said I could trust her.

"Yes, but it doesn't have anything to do with him. My problem is with my brother, Doug. I want to kill him." I didn't expect that to come out of my mouth.

"Understandable after what he put you through. I've been given some of your history," she clarified.

Relieved that someone understood and already had knowledge of my situation, I sank back into the chair. As everything tumbled out. I told Rosanne how Doug put tracking devices on me without my knowledge, kidnapped me and used my mom against me during my junior year of high school. "He pushed me around when he held me captive."

"Pushed you?" Rosanne's eyebrows raised.

"Well," I said as I hung my head. "He threw me up against a wall. He slapped me across the face."

"That sounds violent."

"He didn't care. He just wanted information about the Niners. That's his whole life. His family? We mean nothing to him."

"Sounds like he's quite the psychopath."

I lifted my head, eyes filled with tears of relief. "Yes, I agree. You're the first person to say it aloud and confirm my suspicions."

"So you've felt that way about him for some time?"

"I researched personalities, trying to figure him out when I was younger. When I read the traits of a psychopath, I thought it described him well."

"You know you can't change him." Rosanne studied my face, waiting.

"I wanted to," I whispered. "I couldn't believe I was related to someone like him."

"You have to let that go. You're not Doug."

"I found out he caused this scar on the back of my head." I touched it instinctively. "I was just a baby when it happened. Since moving to California, he's kidnapped my baby and bombed Spanish Village. To top it off, he never told my parents he had a four-year-old son. Now that they know, they're not even mad." I squeezed the water bottle I held so tightly it caved in on one side.

"You're mad at your parents. It's okay. You have lots of pent-up anger inside and need to get it out."

"Yes, it feels good." I felt better telling someone, knowing I wouldn't be judged. "No matter how hard I try to make my mom understand Doug's evil, she doesn't hear me."

"No one wants to believe that about their child, Allie. You have to come to a place in your mind where you can accept it. We can work on that first, if you like. We'll break down each problem and tackle them one by one."

Rosanne was right. I felt frustration and anger over something I could never change. If someone told me Zak was evil, I'd never believe it. "That's probably a good place to start." I nodded. "I'm a little better now that I know the bombs weren't meant to kill anyone. I thought Doug tried to annihilate Spanish Village and its people."

"Does it help to know Doug isn't all bad?"

"Yes, it does." A slight smile crossed my face. "You live down the street from us, I hear."

"Yes, we'll have to get together outside of business hours."

"I'd like that. I need a few more friends."

"Then we'll see what we can do about that. Come back next week. We'll talk again. Same time?"

"Sure." I nodded and got up, realizing the session was over. "It helped, Rosanne. It really did."

Leaving the office, it dawned on me I'd been holding back feelings buried deep inside from high school. I tried to be strong after I sent Lucas away, but at UCLA I'd been a walking zombie and again in New York City. I never sorted out my feelings. Counseling might be the first step to be free of the past.

When I arrived home, Ashley was playing with Zak in the great room. Lucas sat at the kitchen table working on his virtual screen. "I'm home!"

"My, aren't we perky?" Ashley laughed. "Don't you love Rosanne?"

"Yes, and if she helped you and Ryan, I hope she can do the same for me."

"Get over here, and let's get started. New season for weddings, you might want to make some changes."

"It won't hurt to look." A screen, the same size as the white wall, floated in front of it. Floral designs—bouquets, table décor and garland—filled the screen. "I can finally decorate that wall. Hang some family pictures."

"Great idea," Ashley said. "I'll help."

"Nate's here." Lucas raised his hand as he headed for the door. "You two have fun."

"Hey! We're not even married yet and no kiss goodbye?" I stuck out my lower lip.

"Sorry." Lucas rushed over, gave me a quick kiss and tousled Zak's hair.

"Tell Nate he has to make sure Bee picks up Ryan after school. I might be busy." Ashley held out her arms, pretending she wanted a kiss, too.

"Got it." Lucas surprised her and gave her a kiss.

After he left, I sat on the couch and pulled Ashley with me. "Tell me about Nate. What happened after I left?"

"He was so distraught you left, he went looking for you. He started the cosmetic procedure but didn't finish the treatments. That's why he has the faint scar. I'm not supposed to tell you because he thinks you'll go on the run again if you find out. He doesn't want you to blame yourself for the scar. It was his choice."

"Oh." I breathed in deeply, trying *not* to blame myself. "If he'd stayed here, the scar would be gone?"

"Yes."

"I'm trying."

"Don't go there. Allie, it's time you focused on you and your wedding, not the past. Be selfish for once. Let's buy the most expensive flowers and dress we can find!" We laughed. "Spending money always helps."

"I noticed Nate and Lucas have grown even closer. I like that. I'm focusing on the good now. How's that?"

Ashley fell silent for a moment. "There's one more thing you need to know about Nate."

My heart raced. "Go on, don't make me wait."

"He's seeing Rosanne, too. I think he has PTSD but won't admit it. At least he goes to see her. They've become close. She's like a second mother to him."

"Mother? She looks about thirty."

"Oh, no, Rosanne's in her mid-fifties." Ash paused. "Her husband, Oliver, works at the Innovation Center. He's head of the Bio Department. We think he's working on a 'fountain of youth' serum. It's just a rumor, but we think Rosanne's the test subject."

I swallowed hard and felt my jaw drop. "Fountain of youth?"

"Think about it. The Niners live a long time. Their wives and children die before them. It's a hard life at times even though it sounds glamorous. Oliver and Rosanne don't have children. It's just the two of them. They're very much in love. I don't know all the details of the drug, just the gossip I've heard."

"Wow! Does Lucas know?"

"Yes, but he's not saying a word. He has private meetings with Oliver. Maybe you can find out something." Ashley looked at me out of the corner of her eye.

"Okay, I'll see what I can do." It seemed like we'd just transported back in time as two best friends plotting away in my bedroom. Then it hit me. Nate and Ashley couldn't go home either. "Ash, I'm being so selfish. I didn't ask how you're holding up after the bombing. Do you have any contact with your family? Will you ever go home?"

Ash laughed. "Now you sound like me with all the questions. Nate and I were at the hospital when the bombings happened. We weren't in the village, like you. We didn't experience it firsthand. I wasn't too affected, mostly worried for the people. I wanted everyone to get out safely. I think it pushed Nate over the edge, though. The village bombing happened right after the bombing at the STF complex. He was still fragile, his burns were being treated, and we had to evacuate. When you went missing, he blamed himself. He said he wasn't a good enough brother to you and was determined to find you." She took a breath. "To answer your second question, yes, I have contact with the family, but they're busy and hardly miss me. One less mouth to feed."

"Ashley! Don't say that."

"Sorry, it's middle child syndrome. The parents thought I was at school all year. What does that tell you? Now I've told them we're staying in California for the summer. Nate's following his dream and all. Little do they know it's to be a Niner and not a director." She giggled. "Their phones show our old numbers on their caller ID. We're in the same boat as you, Allie. Doug's looking for us, too. I don't know if any of us can go home again. Nate feels bad for his parents but doesn't *want* to go home. Rosanne's helping him with that, too."

"Do you think we can ever go back?"

Ash shrugged. "Maybe some day. It's too dangerous right now. Nate's working on an app that will resemble a video chat application for our families. He'll upload it to their phones and computers when it's ready. Our parents are so behind the times they'll buy whatever we tell them. We can talk to them face to face without worry."

"My parents already know how to video chat."

"Well, tell them it's an upgrade or something. A new icon will show up on their screen. Easy, right?"

"Yeah, I guess they'll like that. Now let's get back to this fountain of youth. What bothers me the most is—"

"If Doug finds out." Ashley read my mind.

"Yes, can you imagine what he'd do if he knew?"

"Well, he never will. Now let's get back to wedding plans. I hate to tell you this, but Lucas sent everything back after you left. We have to start over from square one."

Chapter Twenty Three

Lucas had worked hard updating command central. He felt there was no need for the stations, individual screens and equipment. The chip held all the information of the compound. The office could be a virtual environment if the old timers agreed.

I received a message to come to Headquarters as soon as I was ready for the day. Sean would come to the house to watch Zak.

"Very mysterious, don't you think?" I asked my child as I sensed he was choosing his food for breakfast.

The transporter signaled a delivery. I found oatmeal loaded with fruit and another bowl with just fruit. I closed one eye and stared at him. "Is that for me?" I pointed to the fruit bowl.

He nodded and banged his tray. "Mommy, eat!" He gestured toward the fridge. "Milk and water."

"Okay, bossy. Hold on." I laughed as I set the bowl with oatmeal and fruit in front of him.

A knock on the door interrupted us. Sean called as he stepped inside, "Babysitter's here!"

Zak banged away on his tray. "Awn!"

"Thanks, Sean." I grabbed the water and headed out.

"Mommy!" Zak gave me a stern look.

"Okay." I turned back and took the bowl of fruit.

"Beetle's out there, Allie, ready and waiting." Sean kissed my cheek as I passed by.

"You two stay out of trouble." I pointed their way as I rushed out the door, wondering why Lucas needed me.

When I arrived, Ashley waited at the elevator. "Were you invited, too?"

"Yep." The doors opened, and we stepped inside together.

"Do you know what this is about?" I asked.

"No clue. He just said to come to the fourth floor."

The doors parted to expose Lucas, a big smile on his face. Instead of us getting out, he joined us inside. We took the elevator to the first floor.

"The visitor's parking garage?" I looked at him with questioning eyes.

"Just wait." Lucas held up a finger and motioned for us to follow. He walked to the spot where I had parked the old Jeep. In its place was a dark gray newer model. "For you." He dropped the keys in my hand. "I knew you had to sell the old one."

"Oh." I touched his arm. "Does that mean you trust me?"

"Yes, Allie. I want you to know I'm with you one hundred percent. If you ever feel the need to flee, I want you to have that option."

"Aww, that's so romantic." Ashley rolled her eyes.

"Thank you, Lucas." I threw my arms around him. "But I won't ever run away again." I looked at Ashley. "Ash, I love you, don't take this wrong. But why is she here?"

"In case you tried to escape." Ashley giggled. "I would ride shotgun."

Lucas grimaced as if I caught him. "Working on the trust issues." He held up his hands.

"I'm going now, Lucas. Ash and I have stuff to do." I winked at him, hoping to keep the mood light. I grasped her hand and tugged her toward the elevator.

"Where are you headed?" he called after me.

"Home," I shouted over my shoulder. "Trust issues." I shook my head as we stepped inside.

"He needs time, Allie. The car was a big step." Ashley squeezed my hand.

Nate leaned against Bee as we pulled in the drive. He reluctantly agreed to help with guy stuff for the wedding.

"Girls," he said as we got out of the car. "I forgot I promised Ryan we'd go to the square and look for new baseball equipment. I guess I better learn how to catch a ball." He'd never been good at sports, but since Ryan had a keen interest, he was willing to give it a try

"Sure, go ahead, baby." Ash kissed Nate on the scar. "We can handle it. No complaining on the day of the wedding though."

"I won't. Promise." He kissed her back.

As we climbed the steps to the porch, I paused. "Has he asked you to marry him?"

"Allie!"

"Don't act all shocked. It's a good question. You two plan on living here forever. So the natural step is marriage."

"One wedding to plan is enough." Ash smiled, but I knew better. "I always dreamed of getting married in that little park back home, you know the one with the gazebo. Can't see that happening now."

"I'm sorry," I frowned.

"Don't be. We've made different choices in our lives. That's all."

"There's a gazebo in our park, Ash."

"Maybe one day ..." Ash looked away. "Hey, I almost forgot. I have something to show you."

We dashed into the house, and Ashley brought up some type of entertainment magazine on our large screen.

"You still like those, don't you?" I giggled, remembering the stacks of gossip and entertainment magazines in her old bedroom back in Virginia.

"Yeah, look at this."

Staring back at me, large as life, were Will and Carol. Ash showed me a montage of pictures from a fundraiser in New York City for the museum. Under their picture it said, *Carol Baker, Head of Operations, with her boy toy, model, Will Hollins.*

"Oh. My. God!" I turned to Ashley wide-eyed. "She found him, turned him into a model and is dating him. Good for her! Wouldn't she love to get her hands on the fountain of youth?"

"I thought you might be upset." Ashley touched my arm.

"Not at all. I wish I could call Carol and congratulate her, but it was better to cut ties altogether." I stared at the picture. Carol looked radiant, and Will appeared happy, too. It was so good to see them. "Do you know where Will's modeling? That happened awfully fast."

"He's done some print ads. His agency is based in New York City."

"Are you holding out on me, Ash? You have a lot of information on Will and his new career."

"Well, you're busy with the wedding. I didn't want to bring up old memories."

"I'm glad you did now. I wondered what they were up to these days. Let's try to find some pictures of him."

"Try? Don't need to do that." Ash turned to the screen, and a catalog for men's apparel appeared. Will modeled designer suits in the picture. Page after page, showed him in all types of attire.

"Da-da!" Zak pointed excitedly at the screen.

"Yes, Zak, that's Will. He was your friend in New York. You remember him, don't you?" I almost forgot he was playing at our feet after I shooed Sean out the door. I picked him up. Zak nodded and took my face in his little hands, pulling me toward him.

"Kiss? Is that what you want?" I asked, rubbing noses with him.

"Allie, he's so smart I can't get over it. I've seen a lot of Niner babies. They're bright and healthy but still seem like babies. Zak's already surpassed them—walking, talking, giving commands in his head. And boy, is he strong."

I held him close, thinking of what we'd gone through together. He had memories of it, I was sure now.

Lucas walked into the house, and Ashley's screen shut down. I looked at her questioningly, but she shook her head. I hadn't done it either. We both looked at Zak and realized he'd turned it off, not wanting his father to see a life-size Will in our living room.

"There's my family!" Lucas looked relieved I was still here.

"Lucas, you have to stop worrying if I'm going to be here or not." I kissed him and handed him the baby. "Ashley and I need to finish up. Do you mind?"

"Mind? Never." He disappeared out the back door with Zak. Lucas had built a small playground for him to crawl around in.

"Now that's a smart baby!" Ashley let out a huge sigh as I joined her. We laughed and fanned ourselves with our hands for added drama.

We brought up another screen and wrapped up the last of the wedding details, except flowers, and double-checked our lists.

"Lucas is going to have Nate and Joe, his great-nephew, as his groomsmen. You and Serena are my bridesmaids. Well, you're my maid of honor, Ash." I rubbed her arm. "Sophie and Kristina are flower girls. We hope Zak will walk down the aisle with them. We're set with dresses and suits."

"I'm glad you started over with new colors and a different wedding dress, Allie. It was a smart thing to do."

"I'm thrilled I found out about the hydroponics center here. They're doing my flowers." I hugged Ashley. "Thanks for all your help. Couldn't have done it without you, bestie."

I studied her. Strong and brave. Beautiful and smart. Her green eyes could back a person down in a second. She'd become a woman while I'd been away. Her silky brown hair had grown longer, almost halfway down her back. Her curves had filled in, and she had the stance of a warrior princess. I hoped to be Ashley one day.

She started for home, right down the street from me. Watching as she crossed the street and turned the corner, I envied her. She accepted the Niner life so willingly when I found excuses to fight it. As Rosanne said, I was a work in progress.

I headed for the backyard to join Lucas and Zak. "I think we should tire him out and put him to bed early, don't you think?" I placed my hand on Lucas' shoulder.

"He's having fun, Allie. Let him stay up." Then he glanced my way and saw a bottle of wine in my hand. "Oh, yeah, we can call it quits for the day. I could use some grown-up time."

"It can be grown-up time all night long if you wish." I ran back toward the house with the two of them chasing me, laughing the whole way. "Zak, you're such a big boy. Daddy doesn't even have to carry you." I put him in a booster seat at the table and ordered his favorite dinner. "No high chair for you either!"

I placed the plate in front of him, and he ate without help. Lucas poured wine and grabbed cheese and grapes from the fridge. He then ordered a fresh loaf of bread. As we waited, I decided to ask him about the fountain of youth.

"Lucas, why does Rosanne look so young? I heard she's fifty-four or five." I batted my eyes, trying to look innocent.

"Yeah, she looks great for her age."

I put my hands on my hips, channeling some of my inner-Carol. "Her husband's in charge of the Bio Department. Now, spill."

"If I do, you can't tell anyone yet. Rosanne's brave for trying this out. Oliver doesn't know the long-term effects. She's his human guinea pig."

I remained silent and nodded, wanting him to finish.

"It's a fountain of youth serum. Oliver thinks it can be used once, maybe twice. The best age to begin treatments is late thirties to mid-fifties. It restores twenty years of your life and continues to work for fifty years. Then you'll start to age again. She could live for one hundred and fifty years or longer. If Rosanne was fifty-two at the time of the first dose, she's thirty-two now. She'll stay that age for fifty years then begin to age again."

"Wow! So she's done the treatment."

"Yes, two years ago. Oliver monitors her daily. No negative side-effects so far. It could be offered to the people of the village in another decade." Lucas smiled at me and tilted his head.

"Oh, no," I said as I held up my hands. "I don't know if I could do it."

"You have plenty of time to decide."

The bread arrived. Lucas took it to the living room, spreading a blanket. "Paris?"

"Anywhere you want to go," I answered. We wouldn't be there for long if I had my way. "Zak's done eating!"

I handed the baby off to Lucas. He had the touch for putting him to sleep. Less than five minutes later he returned. Wine was poured, and the toast readied.

"To our wedding," I said. "May the day be one of new beginnings. And I promise not to be a runaway bride ever again."

We tapped our glasses and downed the wine while looking into each other's eyes. Setting the glasses on the floor, Lucas scooped me into his arms and headed for our bedroom. Our night together had just begun.

* * * *

"Are you awake?" I could feel Lucas' breath on my cheek.

"I am now." I rubbed my eyes. "What time is it?"

"Early, six a.m."

"Something happen?" As I tried to focus, I smelled coffee and reached for the mug. "Coffee?"

"Would you prefer water?"

"No, I have a feeling I'll need this." I'd been able to sip black coffee in the morning even since Zak was born.

"Come down to the great room when you're ready." Lucas left the bedroom.

I threw on some clothes and followed him downstairs. "What's up?" I sat on the sofa and tucked my legs beneath me.

"First, let me start off by saying, this is not your fault."

I choked on my next sip and tried not to spray coffee on the carpet. "Doug?"

"More like the STF."

"What's the special task force up to now? Are they looking for me? Zak?" I could tell by his face this was serious. "Lucas!"

"They found the Pennsylvania compound."

My hand began to shake. He took the cup from me, setting it on the table.

"You're positive."

He nodded. "We may call for an evacuation to be on the safe side. Julian's on his way to P.A."

"Is that safe?"

"He's commander of the western half of the country. Rupert is his eastern counterpart and lives in Patriot Village."

"Patriot Village, the first compound Abe set up in the states." I sighed, and sadness overtook me. "I thought you set up double shields at all the compounds."

"Not yet. Rupert and Julian made the decision as to which one would be first. Our compound was given the green light, especially after what happened in California. We should be done in a day or so. Then we move on to the next one."

"You never told me how many compounds there are in the U.S."

"Four. We're down to two if P.A. goes." Lucas settled in next to me.

"Could this be a false alarm? It's happened before."

"I don't know." Lucas shrugged. "I wish it was."

"Where's the other compound?"

"It might be better if you didn't know."

"Lucas! I'd never tell." Then I realized, I may not have a choice. I could be drugged or threatened. I wouldn't care if my life was threatened but wouldn't risk Zak's. "I understand. Don't tell me."

I lowered my eyes and stared at the floor. Doug had ruined another wonderful moment in my life. I was home, happy and planning my wedding. Now, I could only think of the Niners and the families in Pennsylvania, not flowers and dresses.

"I know what you're thinking." Lucas lifted my chin. "We're still getting married. This town needs something to celebrate. Promise you won't cancel on me." Lucas wrapped his arms around me, and I nestled against his chest. I heard his heart beating, felt his chest move up and down with every breath. Together, with him, I felt whole.

"I won't cancel. We'll marry." I whispered then sat up and stared at him. "I want in."

"On?"

"Everything. Promise you won't leave me out of any plans. Let me be part of this."

"If it means you stay and we fight this together, I promise." Lucas touched his ear. "It's Julian."

"I want to hear. Put him on speaker."

"Julian, Allie and I are both here."

"I don't have much time, Lucas. We have the last of the families in the vans. We're working on a sweep of the village. Since this was the original U.S. compound all the STF Niners are aware of its location. Rupert feels one of Doug's Niners gave away the coordinates. Thank goodness we're one step ahead of them. They have no idea we've developed software to detect their bombs."

"Do you have the beam in position?"

"Yes, we won't know if it works until the first bomb arrives, which should be any minute now."

"Are you still at Headquarters?" Lucas sounded concerned. "Get in the bomb shelter and conduct everything from there."

"On my way. Rupert's setting up there with his security team. Regardless what happens, we have to clear out and shut the place down. They know where it is." His voice sounded sad.

"Keep us informed … and good luck."

We sat in shock trying to absorb what Julian had told us. Anger and sadness filled my body. I wanted to punch something. "That was Julian's original home," I sobbed. "Most of the older Niners grew up there." I covered my face with my hands. "What is he trying to do, Lucas?"

"Doug? He's trying to flush us out. He needs us, Allie. We don't really know why."

"Once he has you, then what?" I raised my tear-stained face to look at him and remembered back to the day I had sat in Central Park with Sean. "Never mind. I know. He'll have the power to take over the country."

Chapter Twenty Four

I stared at the blue skies and bright sunshine from my bedroom window and felt blessed. My dress lay on the bed, pressed and ready. The flowers would be delivered shortly by Ramona, the head of the hydroponics staff. She was knowledgeable and helpful when I visited the facility. Right then and there, I'd given her the job of wedding planner.

The doorbell signaled that the wedding party had arrived. I ran down in my robe and opened the door to a large group of people, my wedding planner front and center. "Ramona!"

I hugged her, and the people filing in behind her— Julian and his family, Ashley, Nate and Ryan. Julian would whisk Lucas away until we met later in the village square for the ceremony.

"Lucas! Julian's here!" I called up the stairs.

Julian had returned safely from Pennsylvania. I wanted to hug and squeeze him, relieved he'd made it home. The Niner technology had worked like a charm. The beam sought out and locked on to the bombs in the air. The missiles got through the shield of Patriot Village, just like in California, but the Niners destroyed the bombs before they hit their targets. But the sad fact? Patriot Village was now a ghost town.

We made a pact when Julian got home. The day of the wedding would be about happiness and love. No future plans, no talk of war or strategy on this day.

Baby in arms, Lucas came down the stairs ready to go. Zak took one look at the twins and screamed to stay. He loved Sophie and Kristina so much. He fought to be released from his father's arms as they headed for the door.

"I can watch him, Mr. Montgomery." Kristina held out her arms. Zak tried to wiggle away from Lucas.

Lucas glanced my way, and I nodded. He let Zak slip into Kristina's arms. "Be good, little man," he said as he followed Julian out the door.

Serena and Ashley followed me up the stairs to dress for the wedding. The twins would get ready last. Ramona stayed downstairs with the kids and worked on the bouquets and floral head pieces. I'd chosen the Virginia bluebell as my flower along with white roses. Ramona had babied and coaxed them along at the center. She'd woven the bluebell into wreaths for the girls and into the headband of my veil. Serena and Ashley would wear decorated combs in their hair.

My dress was a modern taffeta ball gown--strapless fitted bodice with the skirt feathering out into a sweeping train in the back. A simple pale blue satin ribbon traveled around my waist. I gently touched my Phoenix tattoo, reminding myself I had risen from the ashes again, but this would be the last time I'd start my life over. This is the life I wanted.

The flower girls would wear white with blue sashes. Zak's outfit consisted of a one-piece pale blue short-sleeve suit and white knee-high socks and shoes. Our rings had been attached to his collar on white velvet ribbon.

"Well?" Ashley came out of my bathroom and spun in place. The strapless tea-length dress was perfect. The blue satin gown matched the ribbon on my dress. It had its own slim belt in blue around the natural waist. The dress flared out into a full skirt. Serena came into the room next. I looked lovingly at my two bridesmaids.

"This is it, girls." We gathered into a group hug.

"I'll get the twins." Serena disappeared, leaving Ashley and me alone.

"I was an idiot," I said with a sigh.

"Don't say that, you went through a lot." Ashley sat on the edge of the bed and pulled me next to her. "No one blames you. You need to get that through your thick head, Ms. Allison Sanders. I thought Rosanne was working on it."

"She is. I guess I'm just checking." I cleared my throat. "I feel you guys don't completely trust me. I ruined that for all of us."

"We do trust you. It's just that ..." Ashley paused. "The three of us trust each other more. Do you know what I mean?"

"Yeah, I do. I'm working to change that."

"We love you and want you in our lives. We don't want to look away and when we look back—"

"I'm gone." I pressed my lips together. "I understand and pledge to fix that. I'll become the most trusted, beloved woman in the village." I grabbed Ash's hand. "You always had my back. I tried to have yours but maybe didn't do such a great job. Now, it's my turn. You can lean on me forever."

"And you can lean on me." Ashley squeezed my hand. "Now let's get you married!"

When we reached the first floor, Sean stood at the door, ready to take us to the square. He brought the van so we could fit in one car. Ramona had left for the park to check on the final touches to the gazebo and seating. She even decorated Zak's stroller if he grew tired of standing and placed a few hidden toys in it, too.

The twins jumped up and down when they saw me, ooh-ing and ahh-ing about the bride that appeared out of nowhere. They were so precious in their gowns I could have eaten them up.

"Let's go!" Sean rounded everyone up and out the door. He drove us to the back entrance of the restaurant where we'd hold our reception. We waited inside until the signal was given. The band had assembled next to the gazebo. When they started to play, we'd walk out of the restaurant and follow the path to the center of the square.

Ramona rushed in, flapping her arms up and down like she was about to take flight. I giggled thinking that was the signal. "They're playing! Let's go, girls."

She handed everyone their flowers. I brought the bouquet to my nose, taking in the scent of roses. Ramona guided the kids outside. She placed Zak in the middle, and he clung to Sophie and Kristina's hands. They stood outside the doorway, watching for Ramona's consent to step on the white runner that led to the gazebo. She gave the nod, and they walked down the aisle. My heart melted at the sight. Serena went next, then Ashley. Finally, Sean and I made our appearance.

I heard the strands of "Canon in D" as we grew closer to the carpet. I held my head high. Lucas seemed far off in the distance, but our eyes met. We locked on to each other. I saw no one else. I would become Allison Montgomery today, and no one could stop me.

Zak made it to the front with the girls and was now in Lucas' arms as I arrived at the gazebo. We kissed and, as a group of three, we were married.

It was a wonderful day. I focused on the good things that happened throughout the day. I tried not to think about my parents missing my wedding, planning to remedy it later.

I tried not to think about Doug, his plan for world domination and his thirst for kidnapping my son. I tried not to think about the day everything was destroyed in California, ending a way of life many had known for decades. The Pennsylvania compound had been saved, but people had been scattered across the country. But for now, Montana was safe. I looked into the sky, focusing on my life, my child, my husband. And I was happy.

The End

Preview – Twenty Nine Degrees
Chapter One

My heart pounded as I dug through the dresser drawers. *Not there!* Tempted to throw my clothes on the floor, I realized it wasn't a good idea. The room needed to stay neat and tidy.

Where is it? The false identification was my only way out of the Montana compound. Lucas said it was well done so I hid it away, deep in a back corner of a drawer for safe keeping. I might need it one day, and that day was now.

The fake ID had been a necessity when I had to run away from my life with Lucas. I'd taken our baby, changing his name from Zakary to Austin, and I'd become Carli Nelson. Those were troubling times, but I had to protect Lucas and the Niners.

I dyed my hair blonde and got a job in New York City, working in an art museum for months. Could my natural brunette locks hold up to a dye job again? I smiled as I thought of the picture on the license, blonde twenty-one-year-old Carli Nelson with short, chopped-off hair. She didn't look so bad. In fact, I was told I looked hot by the creepy guy who sold me the license. I dug my teeth into my top lip to keep from laughing.

Lucas Montgomery would always be the love of my life, even if I never saw him again. I labeled myself the enemy a long time ago. I was toxic to him and to his fellow brothers, the Twenty-Niners or Niners for short. My psychopathic brother, Doug, was head of a special task force, the STF, looking for these men so he could create some type of super army. I hated thinking of Doug.

It made my stomach churn, not in a good way. Even though I was his baby sister, I meant nothing to him. I was just a means to an end. He wanted my child and my husband. I had become a bargaining chip, and that was the reason I'd left Montana the first time.

I sighed as I thought back to the days of running from Doug, running from Lucas and the life I dearly loved. I knew I had to stop blaming myself for everything that had gone wrong, but it wouldn't happen overnight.

"Looking for this, Mrs. Montgomery?"

My heart flew to my throat as a tingling sensation swept through my body. I turned toward the bedroom door

"Lucas, you scared me." I placed my hand on my neck, feeling the pulse beat rapidly against my finger.

He leaned against the doorframe with my license between two fingers, looking handsome and sexy as ever. He had let his hair grow out since we'd lived in California as college students and some of the dark strands fell over one eye. Those deep pools of chocolate brown stared right through me, making me want to melt right into them.

"Yes, I was looking for that." I walked toward him, arm outstretched to take the identification.

He lifted his arm over his head. "Not so fast."

"Lucas," I said as I placed my hands on my hips. "You still don't trust me? Did you think I'd go on the run without you?"

"Maybe." He wrinkled his nose.

In his other arm, he held our son, Zakary James. Zak was born on February twenty-ninth during a Leap Year, like his father. Since his dad was already a Niner, he became a Niner-squared, inheriting super genes—unique, even to the Niner community.

No living Niners had sons born on that day. None that we knew of to date, and there were no handbooks to consult. Some knowledge had been passed down by word of mouth. We knew Zak would age twice as fast as a regular Niner, and his skills would be doubled. On Zak's first Leap Year birthday he'd turn two, instead of one like regular Niners who aged every four years.

My little super baby. I took him from Lucas, breathing in his clean fresh scent. He should look like an eight-month-old, but Zak already resembled a toddler.

"I've got my ID right here." Lucas dug in his pocket and held up the card. "Luke Nelson. Wherever you got yours, it was carefully done. I stuck with the same last name." He put his arm around me. "Are you ready for this? Do you think you can leave the compound? I know you feel safe here. I'm sorry we have to go to all this trouble, but Sean insisted. He takes his responsibilities as Head of Security seriously."

"I wouldn't want it any other way. Rosanne said I should be fine. Anyway, she's coming with us, right?"

"Why shouldn't our resident counselor come on our honeymoon?" Lucas smiled.

"It helps to know she'll be there if I need her. While on the run, you know I had horrible nightmares about bombings and thought someone was going to kidnap Zak daily."

"It's not surprising after what we went through in California. And from what you told me when you finally came home, I knew you had PTSD," Lucas said.

"Post-traumatic stress disorder." I shook my head. "I thought only soldiers suffered from it."

"Anyone can, from any traumatic experience. What we went through in California was eerily similar to war. The STF leveled the California compound with their silent bombs. The place ceases to exist because of ..." Lucas put his hand to his brow. "I shouldn't talk about this in front of Zak."

I leaned my head against his arm. "We decided it's okay, remember? He has to be part of the discussions, good and bad. We have to say it. If it weren't for me and my brother Doug—"

"No, no, Mommy," Zak said, as he covered my mouth with one of his chubby hands. He had retained memories from almost the time he was born. He knew I'd say it was my fault, that I led Doug to Lucas and the Niners.

"See," Lucas said. "Even he knows you're not to blame. This would have happened no matter what. As I keep telling you, technology took off in the new century. We have a tough time staying ahead in that department."

"That's not true. You Niners, with your IQs and talents, will always win out when it comes to technology. You were forced into this situation, but now you need to go on the offense. The Niners are a peace-loving group. It's not in your DNA to fight or hurt people."

Men, born on February twenty-ninth, were light-years ahead of us in thinking and inventions. Their humanity made me love them all the more. Doug saw them as fighting machines. They could see in the dark, needed little sleep, had acute hearing and possessed the strength of five men. The everyday world had no idea they existed.

Lucas chuckled. "We realize we've been sequestered from society for centuries and needed an outside opinion. You opened our eyes. Now where were we?"

"You told me Rosanne's coming on the trip."

"And Oliver."

"Of course, I'd expect her husband to tag along."

Lucas laughed, and I spun Zak around as we joined in the laughter. What a difference a few months had made. In March I'd been in New York City, working at an art museum and celebrating Zak's birthday alone. Although it wasn't a leap year, I planned to have a birthday party each year. I'd called Lucas from Central Park, unable to resist. The Niners tried to track my call, but somehow I outsmarted them by using a prepaid phone. Sean, our dear friend and protector, ended up finding me after searching the east coast, going in one museum after another until he found me. After talking with him, I was convinced I needed to come home.

I set Zak on the bed, letting him bounce on the mattress. I gazed up at Lucas. "Do you think this is a good idea? Leaving the compound?"

"We deserve a honeymoon. Don't you agree?" He winked.

"No one takes an entourage with them. Usually it's just two people—the bride and the groom."

"Well, that's how we roll." Lucas sat on the edge of the bed next to me. "Thank you for marrying me, Allison Sanders."

"Don't you mean Allison Montgomery?" I teased.

"Yes, I do." He kissed my cheek. "Our wedding helped heal the wounds of the community. We were never attacked before. No one knew we existed until the military became curious."

"And Doug was assigned to lead the task force." I shivered. "And now that he's in complete control, it scares me. I never thought a private company would take over and fund his work."

"Yeah, he's not part of the country's armed forces anymore. He doesn't answer to them."

"That's what scares me, Lucas." I looked over at Zak who had stopped rolling on the bed. His dark eyes, so like his father's, stared at me. He sat upright, cocking his head to the side. His dark brown hair, tousled from rolling, stuck out in every direction. "We're doing it again." I gestured at the baby.

"You know what, Zak?" Lucas reached for him. "We're taking you to see two of your favorite people, Kristina and Sophie. The twins can't wait to see you. They'll take good care of you while we're gone."

"Don't you mean Uncle Julian and Aunt Serena?" I asked. Julian was commander of Victorian Village with Lucas being promoted to second in command from head of security.

"I'm trying to soften the blow," Lucas whispered. "He loves the girls. We have to bribe him."

"Why are you whispering?" I giggled. "He can hear you."

"Da!" Zak raised his hands in the air. "Zak go with you."

"Sorry, kid," Lucas stood and lifted him into his arms. "Zak stays."

* * * *

Beetle, our Niner transportation, zoomed into Julian's driveway. I always loved the drive through Victorian Village. The town felt cozy and quaint with houses painted different colors from that era. Ours was barn red while others were yellow, blue or dark green.

"Allie?" Lucas touched my arm, and I shivered at his touch. I wanted to fall into his arms and shut the world out, but we needed to deliver Zak to our friends, Julian and Serena Howard. "We're here. Are you okay?"

"I'm fine, just thinking." I watched Lucas take Zak from his car seat. "I'll miss him while we're gone."

"He's safer here. Besides you can see him daily from your chip." Lucas kissed the top of Zak's head. "Little man, you're going to visit your favorite family. Be a good boy while Mommy and Da are gone."

I touched the top of my wrist, where the chip had been implanted. It took the place of our cell phones, which were really so much more. I now only had to think a command, and it happened. I could bring up a virtual screen instead of looking at a real one. I made phone calls through a command then heard the voice as if I held a cell phone to my ear.

"Kissy! Soffie!" Zak's baby voice rang out when he spotted the twins running from the house. Eight-year-old Kristina and Sophie loved him and thought he was the smartest baby in the world. Their parents followed behind them.

Julian had the strong, confident look of the Niner men and the irresistibly handsome gene. He had lived for over two hundred years. I still had trouble thinking of Lucas as an eighty-four-year-old man, and here was a man who'd lived for centuries. In Niner years, Lucas was twenty-one and Julian in his forties.

Julian had been born on a Southern plantation in a little cabin. The Niners somehow found out about the baby that didn't grow—the first clue he was a Niner. They traveled south and snuck onto the plantation property to rescue him. Eventually, Julian's whole family was brought to the Pennsylvania compound to live a free life.

"There's our little man!" Julian reached for Zak, but he clung to Lucas.

"He wants to go with us," Lucas said.

"Kid's got a mind of his own, doesn't he?" Julian winked at us. "Hey, Zak, did you hear that?" He put his hand to his ear. "Beetle's calling you. She wants to know if you'll take her for a drive." He tickled Zak's belly, making him giggle.

Our personal car at the compound was a futuristic-looking Beetle car that I'd named long ago. She responded to mental commands and needed no driving assistance. Suddenly her doors flipped open, and she moved closer.

"Zak!" I called to him, knowing he gave the command. "Julian's teasing."

"No, I'm not." Julian winked at me as Zak flung his little body into Julian's waiting arms. "I'll take him for a spin. We'll be right back."

I grabbed Zak's bag from Beetle's backseat. "Okay, but not for long."

"I just heard from Nate. They'll meet us at the airport." Lucas slipped his arm around me. "Happy?"

Tears welled in my eyes. Could I truly be happy? Since my return in March, I'd tried hard to forgive myself, but a little piece of me carried a huge weight of guilt. I'd taken took my son from his father. I'd left my friends wondering if I'd ever return.

"I love you, Lucas. More than you'll ever know."

"You proved that twice, by sending me away in high school, then running away last year. I understand why you did it, but I don't want you to ever do that again. Now it's my turn to protect you. Trust me?"

I nodded, unable to speak. My throat closed, and I would choke on any words.

"You don't have to worry, Allie. We double-checked security. We'll never fly commercial again and only use our private jets. We're using aliases, and I created some for Nate and Ash."

"I know all this, Lucas." I finally found my voice.

"Just going over it one more time." He smiled at me and squeezed my hand.

"Let me take that," Serena said as she reached for the bag. "Zak will be fine, Allie. Go to Hawaii and enjoy yourself."

Hawaii. Just hearing the word made me feel serene and peaceful. It was the safest place the Niners said we could go for our honeymoon. It wouldn't be a typical one. My best friends, Nathan Kalas and Ashley Donovan were also coming with their adopted fifteen-year-old Niner son, Ryan.

"Allie, you heard Serena. Everything will be fine. Let's go." Lucas placed his hand on my back and guided me toward the Howard's car.

"But Beetle isn't back. Our things are in there."

"Julian transferred them to his car when you were talking with Serena. We'll use theirs to get to Headquarters."

"Oh, I get it. He's distracting the baby so we can leave." A pain went through my heart, not getting to say goodbye, but Julian had a great idea, and I shouldn't ruin the plan. I climbed into the car, without saying another word. I knew I'd burst into tears, and that wasn't the way to start a honeymoon.

We transferred to a black van once we reached the parking garage at Headquarters, the Niner's all-purpose vehicle. Then we drove to the giant concrete wall separating us from the rest of the world and continued through the forest to the secret passage. We burst through bushes and shrubs to wind our way down a confusing maze of roads in a pine forest, dodging well-placed boulders and fir trees. We were soon on the highway traveling to our destination.

"Lucas," I said with a sigh. "We discussed this trip so many times, always with a positive outcome. I hope it works out as well in real life."

"What could go wrong?" Lucas lifted one side of his mouth. "We have twelve people, twelve different personalities coming together in Hawaii." He winked. "Let's hope the sea breeze and warm sun does its magic."

What could go wrong? My head hurt as scenes swept through it. We'd invited Nate's parents. His mother would be heartbroken if she didn't see him soon as he was her only child. Then she'd meet Rosanne and see the bond she had with Nate. And even though Ashley thought her parents hardly missed her, I knew the opposite to be true. She suffered from middle child syndrome. We planned to surprise her and not tell her they were coming. Would she be pleased? My parents caused the greatest difficulty. We had to think of a way to get them to Hawaii without telling Doug, and Nate had come up with the plan. But what if it didn't work? Doug was my biggest fear and always would be.

"My parents should be thrilled by the surprise trip," I said. "Since it's a free vacation and they're flying on a private jet. What's not to like?"

"Nate said Ashley's parents will be picked up first. The limo will go from his house to yours. He's a great friend, Allie."

"Yours or mine?" I closed one eye as I stared at Lucas, teasing.

"Both." He laughed. "Thanks for sharing your best friend with me. He's my first non-Niner friend, and I'm glad he decided to live at the Village."

"He and Ashley gave up a lot." I leaned my head back and gazed up at the van's ceiling. "Ash took to this life faster than I did. She picked out a house, became a mom to Ryan ..." I bit my bottom lip.

"Hey," Lucas said as he brushed my face with his hand. "You're doing it again. Being too hard on yourself."

"Lucas," I said. "Ash loves Nate as much as I love you. Only we did things differently. She proves her love over and over. I run away."

"You wanted to protect me. I get it." Lucas took my chin and turned me to face him. "We are not discussing this again. It's over. We're starting a new chapter in our lives."

I leaned over to kiss him as the van pulled up to the airline terminal. "We're here," I whispered. "Just when it started getting good."

As we boarded the plane, Nate greeted me. His reddish-blonde hair that used to stick out in all directions had been neatly cropped close to his head. His golden brown eyes met mine and I saw the love and trust he sent my way.

"Hey, how are you doing?" He gave me a bear hug. "Just want you to know I disabled all the parents' phones. Yours won't be able to call Doug on the way to the airport."

All of our parents had special phones, gifts from us, which could be controlled and monitored by the Niners. I felt a little guilty that I had once suspected my mother was Doug's spy, but the phones were a necessary evil.

I touched Nate's face. He still bore the faint scar from the explosion at the STF complex, the day we'd rescued Zak from Doug. "You're the strongest, bravest person I know," I whispered.

"Don't let your husband hear you say that." He chuckled as he gave me a wink.

Rosanne joined our little group and put her hand on my back. "Are you going to be okay, Allie?"

"Yes, I'm grateful you're coming with us." I always had to take a second look when I saw her. Rosanne was Oliver's guinea pig for a youth serum. The recipient gained back twenty years in age and would remain that way for fifty years. Then, the aging process would begin again. Rosanne was in her fifties but looked thirty. Oliver told Lucas he was positive it could only be used once. Trying again might kill a person, and that was a chance he'd never take. It was a great invention for the Niner community. The serum would keep their loved ones alive longer.

Rosanne and Oliver were very much in love, his motivation for the project. They'd tried to have children, but even with Niner technology, they hadn't been able to conceive. So Rosanne decided to get her degree in counseling to help the community.

The bond between Rosanne and Nate was strong. He'd seen her for his PTSD after returning to Montana from California. The explosion had burned half his face and shrapnel from the van had created a large gash on the same side. But Niner technology had made him whole again, except for the scar that traveled from the bottom of his ear to under his nose. He saw Rosanne as a mother figure, and she treated him like a son. I hoped his mom wouldn't see the connection as clearly as I did.

"Hey, let's get the party started!" Sean boarded the plane, cane in hand. He, too, had been injured during those days in California. First, his leg was caught under a metal fence at the STF complex, then crushed a few days later when he was pinned between a van and a house in Spanish village during the bombing.

"Sean!" I waved him into the cabin. "Join us."

His limp seemed less pronounced as he walked toward me. The Niners had replaced most of the leg with synthetic parts, and he was determined to throw the cane away one day. He had lost weight during the ordeal but still had a strong, muscled body. He'd let some of his black hair grow in but kept the unshaved look. He winked at me and there was a twinkle in his brilliant green eyes.

I searched the cabin for Ashley. We made eye contact, and she lifted her hand. She'd cut her long brown hair to shoulder-length, layered in front, after the wedding. My heart skipped a beat as I held her gaze. We had been through so much together, and here she was still with me on this incredible journey. She patted the spot next to her on the leather sofa.

"Excuse me," I said to the group and joined her. "I feel better you're here." I sighed as I sank down beside her.

"And I love that we're all going to Hawaii! I can't wait." Ashley squeezed my hand.

Nate came down the aisle and sat next to Ash. I leaned over her and asked, "Are you ready to explain the new people in your life to your parents?"

"Yes … and no. I don't want to hurt my parents, but on the other hand I can't wait for everyone to meet."

Ashley turned to him. "Nate, you've discussed this with Rosanne, but you need to practice. Tell Allie what you plan to say."

"Really?" He wrinkled his nose.

Ash kept staring at him until he raised his hands in defeat. "Okay!" He looked at me. "Mom, Dad, this is Rosanne and Oliver. I met them at UCLA, and we've remained close. They're philanthropists, patrons of the Arts at the college. I applied for a grant to make a student film, and they funded my first attempt at a movie." He chuckled. "We clicked, and they took me in as their second son."

"Second?" I lifted my brows.

"Ryan's playing the part of their son this weekend." Ashley said. "We didn't know how else to introduce him."

"Yeah, that makes sense." I nodded. "You can't say this is Ryan Gilchrist. He's fifteen but really sixty. His parents just passed away and we adopted him."

"Shhh, here he comes." Ashley gave me an elbow to the ribs. "Hey, Ryan! Sit here with us."

"Don't you mean go sit with your fake parents?" He ran his hand through his dark blonde hair, his blue eyes filled with pain, as he slumped in a chair across from us.

"We discussed this, Ryan," Nate said. "Let's see how things go. Ash and I have been a couple since high school, but we're barely twenty-two."

"Sorry," Ryan said with a shrug. "I'll be good."

"You better be," Ashley said in her best mom voice.

Nate looked at me. "So do you think my mom is going to pick up on all of this? Be jealous?"

Yes! "Maybe you shouldn't say the second son thing." I cringed.

"I have to tell her something close to the truth. I'll try to spoil her this weekend and be the best son possible. I talk to my parents whenever I get the chance."

Now he made me feel guilty. I'd neglected my parents for long periods of time. I hadn't seen my dad since the summer I was pregnant with Zak, and it had been a year for my mom. She'd flown to California to see Zak when he was a baby and led Doug right to us. He'd kidnapped my son while visiting Mom at my apartment., telling her he'd take the baby for a walk and never returned. I tensed, trying not to show my fear.

"Allie," Nate leaned over Ashley and patted my knee. "Are you okay?"

"Just thinking, that's all. It's nothing." I touched his hand. "You're a good son."

"And I don't blame you for not being a good daughter." His expression showed he meant it. "Your dad did some unspeakable things when he let Doug drag you off to that old motel when we were in high school. I know he feels guilty now and so does your mom. She's blames herself for Zak's kidnapping and yours. They're not as clueless as you like to believe."

"Doug's still in their lives." I wanted to scream, but it barely escaped my mouth.

"He's their son. I know it's hard to accept, but it's a fact. They need all their kids. Aren't they almost social security age?"

I laughed at his joke, which in reality was true. They *were* social security age. Nate was always able to get through to me in the darkest moments. "Yes." I nodded.

"See, we're all good." He leaned back in his seat and looked at Ashley. "Now get me to Hawaii so I can make this beautiful woman my wife."

"What?" Ashley looked as if her eyes could pop from her head.

Nate lifted his shoulders and held out his hands. "Surprise?"

Don't miss what happens next! Read:
Book 3 Twenty Nine Degrees

BEFORE YOU GO.

Join Nancy's Mailing List and never miss a release!

http://nancypennick.com/

Continue reading the series:
29 (Twenty-Nine)
29² (Twenty-Nine Squared)
29° (Twenty-Nine Degrees)
29∞ (Twenty-Nine Forever)

THANK YOU FOR READING

Did you enjoy this book?
I invite you to leave a review at your favorite book site, such as
Goodreads, Amazon, Barnes & Noble, etc.

DID YOU KNOW LEAVING A REVIEW...

Helps other readers find books they may enjoy.
Gives you a chance to let your voice be heard.
Gives authors recognition for their hard work.
Doesn't have to be long. A sentence or two about why you liked the book will do.

OTHER BOOKS BY NANCY PENNICK

Waiting for Dusk Series
(Young Adult)

Waiting for Dusk (Book 1)

Call of The Canyon (Book 2)

Stealing Time (Book 3)

Second Chances (Book 4)

Taking Chances (Short Story)

Broken Dreams (Prequel)

The Clan MacLaren Series
(Historical Romance)

My Highlander Husband (Book 1)

Donnach's Daughter (Book 2)

The Heart of the Emerald (Book 3)

Now and Forever (Book 4)

MacLaren Strong (Book 5)

Homecoming (Book 6)

The $ecret Billionaire $ociety
(Contemporary Romantic Suspense)

Chase (Book 1)

Nash (Book 2)

Finn (Book 3)

Beau (Book 4)

Gabe (Book 5)

Kade (Book 6)

The Elusive Mr. Smith (Book 7)

ACKNOWLEDGMENTS

Leap Year and February 29th are now quite special to me. Because of that day, I created the Niners, men with high IQs and super abilities. They are kind and want to help the world. But as in the real world, nothing is that simple. Someone always wants what they can't have. I wrote Doug Sanders in a way that you may never like him, but hopefully can understand where he's coming from. And as Allie says at the beginning of the book, "Is life that black and white?" Maybe not.

I can't begin to thank the people who helped with my series. My son designed the most awesome covers ever. His talents are many and as I like to call him, a "jack-of-all-trades". He tells me to get writing when I slack off, pushes me to improve the blurbs and taglines until I want to scream. Yet in the end, it all pays off, and I love the finished product.

The next member of my wonderful team is Beth Housing. She is the most amazing editor, and I couldn't have done this without her. I can't say enough about the time and effort she's given this project.

Then, of course, is my beta reader and sister, Sue. She never says no and always say yes when my book is ready to be seen by someone other than me. She is a fan, because she wants to be, and I'll always appreciate that.

My husband, Ron, is always in my corner and I thank him for that. But that's not all he does. He listens and reads and edits. What more could an author ask for in a husband?

ABOUT THE AUTHOR

Nancy Pennick, author of the Waiting for Dusk series, has been writing nonstop since retiring from teaching. She credits her series, *29*, to the originator of Leap Day, basing her story on that distinctive day. Born and raised in Northeast Ohio, she resides in Mentor, OH. Nancy is married and has one son.

www.ingramcontent.com/pod-product-compliance
Lightning Source LLC
Chambersburg PA
CBHW031149120726
47905CB00006B/1869